The Do-Over

Home is not merely a place, but also a *time*.

Love calls neither *master*.

Kimberly Ann "Kiki" Kinsler is a twenty-one year-old college student excited to be returning home to Portland, Oregon for summer break and eager to see her family.

Instead of the happy homecoming that she anticipates, Kiki's world is upended by an unimaginable tragedy. Her parents and younger sister are dead, victims of Little Mo Biggs, a tragically accidental monster, himself a victim of profound parental neglect and abuse.

Kiki is also attacked and hospitalized but survives.

In the hospital, when all appears lost, she is given an opportunity to wipe away the nightmare, to un-do it, and *correct* the senseless tragedy.

A second chance, a wonderful, improbable, and miraculous gift, that doesn't come easily.

To reclaim her future, Kiki must first correct the injustices of Little Mo's *past*, which only can be corrected *at the root*.

In doing so, she learns that home is more than a place, it is also a *time*, and must confront the parallel challenges of life and love, past and present, in a love story with a foot in each world, 2012 and 1981.

The Do-Over is a novel of hope, love and second chances.

We all dream of a second chance.

The question is how far would you go for yours?

Also by Andrew Hessel

Rush to Dawn

The Old Dog's New Trick

Imperfect Resolution

Author's Note

If you've come looking for a *Cups Drayton* crime thriller, this isn't one of them, but stay with me a minute. I think *The Do-Over* is a novel that will touch you; the pages will turn and you'll be glad you read it.

I'm the author, and I guarantee it. Why?

I love this book, and for more than the obvious reasons.

For example, I can't point to any one genre and say it's *one of those*. There are elements of different genres, so you may as well call it a thriller-love story with a dash of fantasy and a sci-fi twist, and while that's not quite right it's not all wrong, either.

So how did this happen and why did I write it?

The truth is I didn't plan on it.

But stories like to take on lives of their own; this one surely did. The characters revealed it, as they like to do; crazy as it sounds, that's how it is for me, and I grew to love them.

Late last summer, Lynne and I were having a drink on the patio one Saturday night. *Imperfect Resolution* was just wrapping up, and she asked, *what are you writing next?*

More Cups stories to tell, I said. I had ideas for three novels I was playing with.

She smiled, and then asked innocently, *what do you think people want?*

Now, that's trickier, I thought, and then said, *what we want – and what we need – is a little hope. The world seems so dark at times a little piercing-of-the-gloom couldn't hurt.*

Then, she asked the really big one: *Ever thought about writing a novel of ... hope?*

Not exactly, but I am now, I said, and knew I wanted to live with that amazing idea a while, and let it simmer and stew.

For me to take a detour from the *Cups* series, it had to be some story.

Stepping away from *Cups* wasn't easy. I miss him, and the other characters of the series, too, and intend on reconnecting with them again soon.

But, the idea that came to me thrilled me, and even better it *moved* me, and the writing of *The Do-Over* was nothing less than the most fun I've ever had.

And get this, what's coming from a crime fiction junkie of the first order.

Beyond everything else in the novel, I couldn't be more surprised by the love story or more delighted with it.

I hope you enjoy *The Do-Over* and will be happy that you read it. A writer can't ask for more than that.

Please visit my website, read my blog, Friend me, Like me, shoot me an email, enjoy life and otherwise be well and happy.

All the best to all of you and all of yours and, as always, thanks for reading!

May the pages turn and deprive you of sleep.

Andrew Hessel
PORTLAND, OREGON

April 2012

The Do-Over

A novel of hope, love and second chances.

Andrew Hessel

Copyright 2012

ISBN: 978-1475102673
Andrew Hessel
Old Dog Publishing
Portland, Oregon
USA

www.PleaseReadMyBookBeforeIDie.com

andrew@PleaseReadMyBookBeforeIDie.com

This novel is dedicated to my nephew, PJ.

Life in a random universe is inexplicably unfair.
Those who find the strength, courage and grace
to transcend it are the real heroes.

*"Parting is all we know of heaven
and all we need to know of hell."*
EMILY DICKINSON *"Parting"*

*"I love her and that's the beginning
and end of everything."*
F. SCOTT FITZGERALD

Chapter One

KIMBERLY ANN KINSLER **had been called "Kiki"**
since her baby sister butchered Kimberly, and
authored the nickname. Kiki had stuck and
suited her perfectly.

Her first two years of college had raced by in a blur. A chaotic,
frenzied, happy and wonderful blur, she had to admit, but where
did the time go? Just like that, her college career was already half
over. A reminder time wasn't unlimited and tempering her exuber-
ance for summer break.

She remembered Mom and Dad driving her down her freshman year.

Her father huffing and sweating lugging box after box into the
dorm, while her mother expertly organized the cramped room getting her settled. This was followed a few hours later by the tearful
goodbyes and mixed emotions she felt watching as her mom and
dad drove away, home to Portland, while Kiki stepped out, living
on her own for the very first time.

She remembered feeling excited, a little nervous, ready, but a
bit scared, too.

"Like it was yesterday, but simultaneously ancient history," she'd
thought lately.

Now, before driving home and spending the summer with her
family, she was packing up personal items from her first apartment, and loading what she was taking home for the summer into
her Subaru Outback. She'd already learned going home wasn't easy
and straightforward.

1

It wasn't as if, just like that, she could turn back the calendar and slide seamlessly into the dutiful-daughter-at-home mode, pretending nothing had changed, when in fact everything had changed. Kiki knew she wasn't a totally independent adult, not quite, but the migration from childhood was nearing completion, and she'd never again look at things through a child's eyes.

On this side of the change there was simply no going back.

The apartment in Eugene had been a huge step, more for her parents than Kiki.

Her mother was strongly in favor of a second year in the dorm.

Her daughter protested vehemently on two grounds. She couldn't survive another year of dorm food, that, given a choice, no one would actually voluntarily *want or choose* to eat. Plus, the thought of repeating the dorm experience struck her as freshman *déjà vu:* totally pointless, unnecessary and embarrassing. Kiki appealed to her father for his help in dragging Mom into the modern world.

"I know you understand this, Daddy," she pleaded, "So can't you *please* talk sense into Mom?"

Bill Kinsler hadn't yet discovered the secret of saying 'No' to either of his daughters, and doubted this was the right time to try again. In the end, he didn't. After lengthy discussion, her mother acquiesced, but not without a great deal of negotiation and imposing a condition or two.

"We trust you, Kiki," her mother said, "but the world is far more dangerous today, and the penalties for mistakes – even innocent ones – can be severe. The consequences are not always fair. You've already had a glimpse of that. You know I only want to protect you."

This wasn't the obligatory warning tendered by clueless or overprotective parents.

That mother, father and daughter loved each other was a given.

The Kinsler family was a strong and tightly knit bunch, clearly devoted to each other. Not to say they hadn't had their fair share of rough patches along the way, every family's path is replete with them.

There was the usual yelling and moodiness of outraged teenagers who know what their parents can't. The periodic epic fights with her younger sister Janie, for no reason other than she was the younger sister, and only one of them could be the center of the universe. Kiki was once meted-out a three-day suspension for skipping school after providing a bogus note from home her freshman year. And, on one unfortunate night early in her junior year, she had found herself in the wrong place at the wrong time with some pot. That led to a brush with the Oregon judicial system that was scary, expensive, and resulted in six months of court ordered "treatment and urinalysis," which she performed dutifully and without complaint.

And from it all, Kiki Kinsler had learned invaluable life lessons.

Fortunately, there were no life challenges that the Kinsler family hadn't been able to overcome. The inevitable testing that come of raising daughters, rather than undermining the family, strengthened their bonds and brought them even closer together.

After graduating with solid grades, and far more bright spots than blemishes considering the whole of her record, her youthful indiscretions didn't hinder or slow her down. She was clearly a really good kid, and a solid, young woman. At worst, Kiki was guilty of no more than being a kid, and more than worthy of admittance to the University of Oregon Honors College.

In persuading Tricia, her father put it this way: "Let's not focus on a bump or two. That would be unfair, and a mistake when the rest of the time she's shown such good judgment, honey," he told his wife, "And let's not forget that she'll be living with Jenna. We've known her since elementary school and Kiki couldn't have chosen a better roommate in her first apartment."

Kiki's mother couldn't argue, didn't really want to, and gave in.

Her father advised Kiki that managing her time would make everything possible. She could have fun, *and* do everything she was there to do.

"It's not like we expect you to study day and night and not have fun, not at all. But some kids see every opportunity to party as a can't-miss," he told her, "and that's not how it is. Such a short-sighted approach to college, to life, leads to trouble. Have a blast," her dad said, and meant it. "Just be smart. With good habits you can have it both ways," he added gently.

Her mother's counsel, delivered on an entirely different subject, was highly directed.

"Relationships take time, and a lot of work, Kiki," she began. "Sometimes, there is nothing harder than learning what's really inside another person. Moving too fast can lead to painful disappointments that can be very difficult to get over. Be patient, don't force it, and guard yourself until you do."

Armed with good advice, and heeding most of it, she returned to the U of O.

Kiki and Jenna found a great apartment in an old three-story house just off campus.

The Kinslers had been right to trust their daughter.

She was human, not perfect, and had had a terrific sophomore year.

At Kiki and Jenna's apartment on University Avenue there was a little drinking and a little pot, but no more than is part of college life the world over, in dorms or apartments. The girls were sensible, responsible, managed to have a great time, and do well in school.

To no one's surprise, they got along as they always had.

Together on the road to young adulthood, their friendship only deepened.

The two old friends were good influences on each other and were always there for each other. Kiki was a year older, a broken leg delaying kindergarten a year when she was six. For all of their newfound freedom, they kept things in good balance, went to classes, and did their work.

In Kiki's case, however, there was also the boy. Justin Monroe, a senior from L.A.

They'd met in Spanish class. Swept off her feet, things got serious in a hurry.

She'd fallen hard and fast, losing her head and succumbing to a whirlwind combination of his surfer good looks, what she initially took for worldly sophistication of his experience in ways she was not, and his clear sense of his direction and future. Justin was confidently on the way to Med School at USC. For a time, she thought he might be the one, but when the newness of her first serious relationship dimmed, and the sexual heat cooled, she knew he wasn't.

He expected everything from her but gave little or nothing back. She now believed that he didn't respect her for who she was, but how could he? He didn't know her, and getting to know her, or anyone for that matter, wasn't really his way. More and more, she saw him as self-centered, at times unkind, and if she were honest about it, not really a nice person. Shocked to have fallen for someone she really no longer enjoyed being around, she saw he'd fallen into bad habits, too. She was no prude, but Justin was getting loaded too much and not handling it well. Now the end had come and she couldn't get away fast enough.

Choosing to end it was something she couldn't have conceived of a few months ago.

Falling out of love is easier than to extricate yourself from a relationship, she discovered, but as Justin's graduation neared, a perfect path presented itself. He wanted her to transfer to USC or UCLA so they could be together while he was in med school. Kiki nearly choked on that gloomy vision of sacrificing her life by dedicating herself to *his*.

"I'll miss you, Kiki," Justin said, incredulous that *she* was dumping *him*. Then he asked, "Won't you miss me?" He was shocked, his face flushed, and in it she saw more anger than hurt. Justin's reaction reinforced her resolve, glad that she'd come to her senses just in time.

"Of course, I'll miss you," she said kindly, finding it was easier to lie. "You need to focus on med school, and I need to finish what I've begun here. We have all the time in the world, let's see what happens," she said with an air of finality, and pecked him on the forehead.

After he'd left, the significance of what had occurred hit hard.

That her mother's words of advice echoed shouldn't have come as such a surprise.

"Mom's usually right, and was this time," she told herself. "Thank God I listened!"

Kiki was anxious to discuss it with her mother once she got home. When the time was right, just the two of them. She imagined them having coffee, sitting outside on a lovely Oregon summer morning, sharing a little pastry somewhere. Good friends talking about things that mattered, and the truth of it hit her suddenly, sweetly punctuating its meaning with a stunning emotional clarity.

Her mother, she realized, was her best friend.

Equally powerful was what she'd learned about herself.

A little ashamed of how she'd treated people at times, it stung deservedly. In the mirror of Justin's imperfections, Kiki saw the reflections of her own childlike shortcomings, and the truth of it was unpleasant. She was guilty of many of the very things that she had found so distasteful in Justin, and a wave of embarrassment washed over her. Childhood might explain self-centered thoughtlessness, she knew, but couldn't excuse it. Still, despite the awkwardness of seeing herself truthfully and honestly revealed, she was grateful for it. Part of her knew she was lucky for the lesson, and that the knowledge taken from it was priceless and empowering.

She resolved to change on the spot, and take steps to make up for it where she could. Not to be insipid or syrupy, but to be a kinder, more thoughtful friend, and daughter ... and sister.

These thoughts of home and family brought happy tears to her eyes.

But due to an unexpected development yesterday, she'd be leaving later than planned.

Kiki and Jenna had decided to continue living together next year, which meant driving down later in the summer to hunt for a new apartment. Inconvenient, because they liked their current place well enough and would have happily stayed, but that's not how the landlord-student housing world spins in a college town. How little you get for how much you pay often borders on larcenous. When the property management company jacked-up the rent and fees excessively, they said *no thanks*.

"We can do better," Kiki said.

"Even in Eugene," Jenna seconded.

Good news arrived unexpectedly and changed everything, thanks to simply being around when, unannounced, the owner of the property dropped by just days before their lease expired. They'd met him only once before, right after moving in before classes started the previous fall.

Chester Owens was in his seventies, but hardly looked his age.

Active and fit, his eyes were friendly and bright.

He had an easy manner, and asked them to call him "Chet". In worn khakis and a faded denim work shirt, he looked simultaneously stylish and down to earth. In spite of his age, he looked youthful with a smile that lit-up his face and brought one to yours. Chet Owens might have been the poster boy for how everyone would like to look in their Golden Years.

He'd owned the house for fifty years, and rented it for the past twenty.

Kiki and Jenna were the apartment's third renters since turning the management of the property over after deciding he'd no longer do it himself. They were nice girls, and there had never been a problem. The kind of tenants he appreciated and wanted to keep.

"I hate to see you go," he told them, after they explained why they were leaving. "Would you give me a day to look into it?" He asked, scratching his chin.

The next morning, Chet stopped by to hand-deliver a new lease.

"The property management company came to their senses," he said with a wink. "You'll notice the rent is $100 less than the old lease, and I won't require security deposits this time."

The girls were speechless, and thrilled.

"I'm unhappy with the way they handled this, and not only because you're good tenants. Told 'em if they wanted the business for my properties, they'd eat the difference, treat people more fairly, and talk to *me* before changing things, *anything*," he said sternly, a twinkle in his eyes. "I'm sorry about this, but hope you'll change your minds and decide to rent the place for the next school year. And if you do, if any problems aren't resolved properly, call *me*."

They accepted Chet's generous offer on the spot, signed the lease, and hugged him.

After he'd gone, the two friends huddled and made a list of what, given the sudden change of plans, had to be done to unwind what was no longer necessary. They spent the rest of the day working on it.

First order of business for the girls was to cancel a U-Haul reservation they'd made, as well as the self-storage unit they'd rented for their furniture and boxes. After reinstating utility accounts they'd just closed, they unpacked boxes of bathroom, kitchen and pantry items, and reconsidered what to take back to Portland, and what to leave behind in the apartment for next school year.

Chet had made things a lot simpler for them. They were thrilled having a place and spared the hassle of finding a new one. Moving-out and going home had become infinitely easier. Their cars, no longer over-stuffed, instead had little more than their summer clothes, laptops, CDs, DVDs and their essential personal items.

Kiki couldn't wait to get home and anxious to get going, it was already late afternoon.

In her car, Kiki sent her parents a quick text message.

On my way –can't wait to see you!

She'd be home in time for dinner.

Chapter Two

THROUGH A DINGY DORMER window in the attic, the man watched the home across the street. His massive, hardened body, thickly muscled from decades of punishing physical labor, filled the tiny space, leaving him little room to move around. He held a pair of toy binoculars to his eyes, his most precious possession. He'd taken a beating from his father after discovering them in a box of old toys in the garage, forgotten and covered with years of cobwebs.

The big man didn't remember his mother's joy, watching her young son unwrap them on their last Christmas morning together before she died. He had no memories of his childhood.

Studying a home and its occupants can be mind numbing, yet it was the one thing in his life that gave him pleasure. Ironically, Morris Biggs Jr. "Little Mo" was ideally suited for it.

Little Mo knew others saw what he did as bad things, but he didn't understand why.

That part of his brain, in fact most of his brain, simply didn't work properly.

His intellectual capacity, cruelly limited by a brain fried from an untreated fever as a six-year old child, was overmatched by most things in life. He had a vague sense he was different from everyone else, without the context to understand why that was. Even as a child, people saw him as big, dumb and impaired. His inability to speak and communicate reinforced that view.

People who didn't know him found him scary, as did most of those who did.

When he was finally brought to the ER, it was already too late. After weeks of treatment and tests, doctors pronounced him irreparably damaged, a now tragically defective little boy. From that starting point, parental neglect doomed him. His splintered and fragmented brain functioned in a disconnected vacuum; Little Mo's world was a limited and disassociated jumble.

"Cognitively," the lead specialist had related to the boy's father, "we might have had a chance if the fever hadn't raged for so long before treatment," stopping just short of adding, *you negligent irresponsible moron.* "Too much damage was done. Sadly, while he has some function, it is disjointed, and ... he has a certain base competency, but only in specific, narrow ways, and in unrelated bands at the lowest and most marginal levels. He may never be able to live on his own yet, with your help, a full chronological life and modest improvement may be a real possibility. I wish I had better news. I'm very sorry," *for the child*, he thought to himself.

Ignoring that, Morris Biggs Sr., with no sign of emotion, asked in a tone more a statement of fact than a question, "So, he's fuckin' useless, like some kind of a functional veg?"

The doctor, stunned, again, by the father's brutish insensitivity, nodded slowly before he continued. "Remarkably, his physical recovery is complete, despite the significant brain damage. Reasoning and processing, to evaluate and make decisions, appears to be the primary loss. This also impacts his ability to distinguish between right and wrong or understand good and evil. The net effect is not unlike the most severe retardation, as anything complex is beyond his capacity."

"Uh, huh," Morris Biggs Sr. said, looking impatient and almost bored but not devastated.

The doctor was incredulous that this big, scary dude could be this dumb and uncaring.

"The next year, more likely two, are critical. Unless he gets what he needs, now, his prognosis is bleak. Proper intellectual stimulation may enable him to learn, or at least use what he'd learned prior to falling ill. There are many unknowns, starting with the fact that brain rebooting after trauma like this is as inexact as science can be. We honestly don't know how much progress, if any, is possible, or not. That's up to *you*," he said pointedly, and getting no reaction, wanted to strangle the man. "You see, Mr. Biggs," the doctor said, softening his tone, "I believe that for Little Mo, abstracts, concepts, the big picture – legal or moral – are things he may never understand." The doctor saw the boy's fate all too clearly and the child's dismal prospects saddened him terribly.

Any fragile chance the boy might have had died with his mother. Left to this pitiful excuse for a father, Little Mo was better orphaned. Morris Biggs Sr. was himself the product of a stern, negligent and unthinking father who had cared little for children, none less than his own.

Under any circumstances, "Big Mo" would have continued that tradition.

Their year together before Little Mo fell ill left no doubt about that. Big Mo couldn't have been less interested, or less capable, of caring for even a healthy child. Little Mo's fever, and the subsequent lack of treatment, combined to serve as the fatal catalyst for a run of even more tragic childhood luck for the young boy.

In the hospital, Big Mo had barely listened to the doctor's diagnosis and prognosis. Understanding little, disinterested in learning more, he got what he thought mattered: The boy was a lost cause and he was stuck with him. He should walk away and never look back – and still might. Big Mo cursed his rotten luck.

"At least I'll get free labor from him out of the deal," he muttered to himself.

The care and nurturing his son needed for any real chance in life, he'd never get.

Even his nickname, Little Mo, reflected his father's disdain, not affection.

A damaged six-year old boy was sentenced to the worst that life might offer.

People get lost in all kinds of ways. We lose our way, our faith and our bearings. We lose confidence and perspective. We lose love and support. When guidance and kindness aren't in play, a diminished universe of possibilities dwindles to nothingness. Lost souls fall through the cracks of life's indifference until all hope is … lost.

Big Mo made certain that the world gave up on his son as he had. He believed there was little chance understanding the boy's thoughts, and really didn't care to, so he never talked with him.

Instead, their communication came in grunts, commands and blows.

He was raised more like a pet than a child.

"Most puppies and kittens in bad homes got more from their owners than this unfortunate child received from his own father," observed a horrified Social Worker in the hospital.

Most days, Big Mo left food and water out for the boy, along with a limited selection of worn and discarded clothes that were rarely washed. The boy slept on an old, stained mattress in the drafty, unheated garage. The two never ate meals together, and other than work – Little Mo provided what amounted to slave labor for his father's hauling and yard work business – and other than the regular beatings his father took great pleasure in administering once or twice a week, there was no interaction between the two. The son never questioned or appeared to have any thoughts about his treatment.

He didn't appear to think at all.

But we never really know what goes on inside a man's head or heart.

If doctors and scientists view the brain as an organic mystery, even less is known of its most private inner workings. Any perceptions or opinions of what might be are just guesses, educated guesses perhaps, but little more.

What Little Mo thought, or felt – if he hoped or dreamed – all that was imprisoned and locked deep inside him. If left to his father, it would remain forever unknown. Big Mo did his best to make sure of it.

Morris Biggs Jr. never attended school, so what constituted his formal education came courtesy of Sesame Street. The entirety of his social education came by witnessing Big Mo ordering laborers around, ogling women and then stroking himself for effect. Other than work, his exposure to the outside world was limited to a black and white television in the garage and a VCR where he watched Big Mo's old porn tapes after his father migrated to DVDs on his new 56" plasma flat screen in the house.

With his ignorant, ill-mannered father serving as his default role model, Little Mo's massive body matured normally, and six days a week of hard manual labor developed him into a powerfully strong man. Reaching maturity, he felt physical urges he didn't understand. Without guidance or training, he never would. A stunted mind housed in a formidable physical shell living in a sadly small universe.

Morris Biggs Jr. never had a chance.

Whatever the world thought it saw in Little Mo it couldn't *know* him; instead, typing him, branding him, passing judgment, writing him off and moving on without him. Leaving him a discarded creature forced to fend for himself, oblivious to ethics and morals and incapable of critical thinking. But cunning enough to get by, and against all odds, the damaged boy evolved.

Little Mo was a good worker.

A strong, tireless and unquestioning slave laborer, there were specific tasks he performed extraordinarily well. Big Mo viewed it merely as fair payment for the trouble and burden he'd been saddled with.

Like a mistreated cur, he returned his father's cruelty with a sadly unreciprocated loyalty and blind obedience. Over time, he developed the wary distrust of a dog unsure of his owner's intentions, and learning from experience to avoid inviting more than his father's usual wrath.

The boy was paid a pittance.

"Too dumb to know better," his father joked.

A healthy body and feral survival instincts helped him to adapt well enough to have a few secrets. Little Mo carefully hoarded his dollar bills and change in a shoebox hidden in the garage.

To his father's surprise, he showed up one day riding an ancient Schwinn. The bike had squeaky wheels, a rusted-out frame, and what remained of a seat, but allowed him to move freely about the city. Big Mo didn't care, and never monitored where the boy disappeared to on his own time.

He was interested only in his son showing up for work six days a week.

Little Mo had received no follow-up to the initial medical evaluation more than twenty years before. Harsh circumstances had compounded his personal tragedy, but the human spirit, even a severely damaged and chronically disadvantaged one, isn't so easily denied.

Over time, Little Mo learned how to passably communicate his muddled thoughts in select situations like a small market. His size and unkempt appearance frightened people, but he picked his spots, and in his limited way, interacted with the world where he could manage it.

Minor victories he celebrated alone.

Unable to speak intelligibly, he grunted and pointed, realizing limited success. He was clever with hand signals that at times seemed to be understood. People who did understand him warmed to him, as if cheering any small achievement for the sadly disabled man.

In tribute to the resilience of a fractured spirit, something growing inside the damaged young man was more than most would have ever suspected. Credit the fundamental longing of the race for companionship, affection and human contact trumping his lack of understanding and social estrangement. He couldn't express or explain his feelings, but Little Mo reached out, however ineptly. Instinctively, seeking a connection to a world oblivious and indifferent to his existence, he was drawn to the occasional kind families he encountered through work. He'd watch safely from a distance at first, before making his ill-fated attempt to approach them.

It never went well.

Doomed to fail despite benign intentions, his separation from society grew more acutely severe. Unable to communicate what he himself didn't understand, these sad attempts yielded only disaster and his father's wrath at again having to clean up after my dummy son's messes.

Little Mo Biggs frightened people, and their reactions frightened him. They saw a huge, wild-looking man suddenly appearing uninvited. Fearing the worst they reacted accordingly. Incapable of expressing himself, the predictable, inevitable end result was trouble.

Trouble was one thing Little Mo did understand.

He was all too familiar with what came of it, and did all he could to avoid it.

A year ago, his father's landscaping company had worked for the Kinslers' next door neighbor until dissatisfaction with Big Mo converted them to *former customers*. Ironically, the Kinslers had encountered Little Mo a time or two and smiled kindly at him. Ever hopeful, he'd misinterpreted their kindness, mistaking it for more than it was, and in his way, looking for more.

The vacant bungalow across the street provided an agreeable venue to watch, and by his pitiful standards was luxurious. Amenities like hot and cold running water, protection from the elements, and a relative degree of comfort were far beyond anything that he was accustomed to. These days, no one paid much attention to a home, which blended into the neighborhood to the point of being invisible.

Even the blanched *For Sale* sign anchored to the mailbox looked tired.

The recent additions of *Bank Owned* and *Price Reduced* mini-signs signaling urgency to expedite a sale, hadn't increased interest or traffic. A glutted housing market, tighter than ever credit requirements and sinking appraisals killed most deals.

The home sat unoccupied and largely forgotten.

So, in a feeble attempt to mitigate its losses, the bank had shifted into *cut-off-its-nose-to-spite-its-face mode*. Now the lawn was mowed every other week, and the once lovingly kept beds in the front yard were ignored. A once cute cottage no longer was.

Looking less and less desirable, it became more and more forgettable.

If the bank couldn't get it off their books, they could at least strike it from top of mind. Banished properties like this one that fall between the cracks are easy pickings for a man needing nothing other than an anonymous safe harbor. There was no longer a functioning security system, so getting past the flimsy lock on the back door was easy.

Unseen and unnoticed, getting past it went unreported.

No one cared.

Little Mo watched the family, the Kinslers.

He had tried many times to pronounce their name but couldn't manage it.

In his late-fifties, Bill Kinsler was almost handsome – a nice looking man but no George Clooney – and a great guy. He was not a big or powerful man, being of average height and weight, with thinning blonde hair and a winning smile. He'd married a woman who was probably the best looking babe he'd ever gotten a shot at, jumping at the chance and never regretting it.

Earnest, solid and good-natured, William Kinsler was a hard-working pediatrician who loved his work. A kind man and a loving father, he was reliable, steady, and devoted to his wife and kids. His habits seemed ingrained and didn't vary. Each morning at 7:20 a.m. the garage door opened when he left the house for work. It remained open until he returned home by 6:30 each evening, even if his wife left the house during the day.

Gaining entry into the home couldn't have been easier for Little Mo.

The mother, Tricia, also in her mid to late-fifties, was one of the lucky ones whose sensuality and beauty had thus far defied time. A brunette with a classic porcelain complexion, she was always well dressed, but rarely provocatively, despite a traffic-stopping figure.

Little Mo liked them all, but it was the daughter that fascinated him.

He'd learned her name was Janie.

One night while he watched, he'd risked crossing the street to listen to them and get a closer look. Janie's older sister was away at college, but he wasn't sure what college was. Overhearing that Janie was going away in a year saddened him, though he didn't understand what a year was. For now she was here and this made him glad.

In his way, Little Mo was smitten with a classic teenage blonde bombshell.

A conflicted and confused emotional cycle Little Mo couldn't understand created within him a tension that overmatched and paralyzed him. Starting always with a low humming in his head, at first it was barely audible, but before long it built to a screaming whine agitating and blinding him with pain that wouldn't stop. Frightened and alone he instinctively and feebly reached out.

The Kinslers had once been kind to him. Alone, at night, he thought of Janie.

Chapter Three

EUGENE IS JUST over a hundred miles south of Portland, less than two hours straight down Interstate 5. Kiki's excitement about returning home increased with each mile she drove north. She was getting older, knew there might not be many summers left with her family, and she treasured this one, intending to make the most of it.

Just south of the city limits she exited onto OR 217 and headed to the southwest suburbs. Every year seemed to bring more development and with it more traffic, but it felt great to be back in the city. The familiar sights and landmarks of her hometown were everywhere and she smiled at the sight of them.

The old neighborhood looked much as it always had. The trees seemed a little taller, perhaps, and she noticed new cars in a couple of the driveways of their closest neighbors, but in the ways that mattered, it was mostly as she remembered, and brought a wave of happiness.

The drive had taken longer than normal. The sun was setting and it was already getting dark. Her arrival had been delayed due to temporary rerouting through construction. Then the poor decision of a tractor-trailer long hauler, who should have known better, brought traffic to a virtual halt south of Wilsonville for half an hour.

Kiki pulled into the driveway; surprised to find the garage was closed.

She was expected and her parents should have left it open. She checked her phone. There was no reply to her text, and she dropped the phone on the passenger seat. She'd get it later when she came back for her things. Maybe her father had come home early, she thought, he would have done so for her. He was always there to help, bringing her things in through the garage because it was much closer to her bedroom. But he would have left the garage door up. Puzzled, she entered the four-digit code on the keypad, and waited as the door creaked and groaned as it opened.

The unlit garage was deep in shadows.

Stepping inside, her eyes took a minute to adjust.

The light in the garage door opener should have come on, but maybe it had burned out. She made her way to the back of the garage, fumbling for the light switch in the dark. Turning it on, nothing she might have seen could have come as a greater shock. She screamed, and it became an involuntary keening catching in her throat. Tears rolled down her cheeks, a cold sweat chilled her despite the warm early evening temperature, and she felt her heart seizing up in her chest.

"Daddy? What? Oh, God, no, please, no, no, no."

In front of his Acura coupe, her father's still form lay at an odd angle on the concrete floor with his face looking up. Sightless eyes didn't respond to her. A pool of dark blood surrounded his head like a crimson halo.

Kiki didn't know what to do and soon realized there was nothing she could do.

Her first thought was that he'd had a heart attack. She knelt down and fearing the worst, felt his carotid artery, praying for a pulse. There was none. Nothing could have prepared her for the shock of discovering her father this way. She knew her father was dead.

The blood rushing in her head was a deafening roar; she couldn't hear, she couldn't think. She rubbed her eyes, hoping to make the horrific images go away. It couldn't be real, it must be a dream, a horrible dream, but it was no dream. Now she saw that her father had taken a blow to the head, his left ear looked mangled and the early signs of bruising had begun to show. There was no blood on his face so she suspected he'd cracked his head when he'd fallen.

Attacked? The thought made her shiver, a fresh wave of panic rose within her.

"Mom? Janie?" She called out, but there was no answer. *"Mom? Janie?"*

Kiki sprinted through the door leading to the kitchen. Terrified at what she might find.

~~~~~

Little Mo Biggs was at the end of the hallway leading to the bedrooms at the back of the house when he heard a woman's cry and a door slam. Then footsteps, someone was coming. He returned to Janie's bedroom, where she lay motionless on the floor, her windpipe crushed by his powerful hands.

It had all gone wrong.

He didn't understand exactly why but knew it was bad.

Tears of frustration running down his face shone, collecting where his thick beard began. The sticky sweat of sheer panic, nothing at all like the honest sweat of hard labor, had matted and dampened his long hair, hanging to his shoulders where it had escaped the ponytail in a brittle rubber band. Little Mo's fragile psyche had been wrenched by the clumsy failure of his effort, disastrously propelling him into a hyper-agitated state. He had to get away, run and hide, but knew only one way out and someone was coming. Trouble was coming. Trouble scared him.

The loneliest of fatally stricken minds couldn't process further, and offered no help.

Functioning in the most narrowly linear of ways, he could react instinctively but not cognitively. Driven by a need that overwhelmed him more and more, his feeble attempt to reach out had netted disaster. Frightened people fearing him, he had to quiet them, to stop them, to avoid the trouble that would surely come if he didn't. More than anything, he feared trouble, because trouble led to beatings. Doing as his father, or others told him, avoided some but not all of them. His father loved the beatings too much. They were part of him, and his lifestyle.

Unconsciously he traced a scar low on his scalp that had always been there and always hurt. If he didn't get away, if others came, there would be big trouble and more beatings.

19

Little Mo could mimic, and by watching his father or the other men in convenience stores, do what they did to get things as they did. The recent successes with the odd, if kindly, store clerks, only intensified his desire to find a place, but came without context or perspective of his own. They were no less put off or frightened by his freakish persona, his sadly garbled grunts and pointing, but were paid to find a way to work with any creature that was breathing and had cash.

The past thirty years had clearly defined the anomalies of his existence.

He was an island of a man lost in a sea of humanity.

Unable to connect, but consumed by the need of it, sentenced to abject loneliness but unable to tolerate or understand it. The bad things he did were never premeditated, rather utterly primal and without either forethought or remorse. He was capable of neither.

The hand dealt him by a random universe had created a tragically accidental monster.

~~~~~

The only home she'd ever known was at once foreign and familiar.

A surreal schism in a new order of things not yet completely unveiled to her.

She felt dazed and confused. None of it was real, but all of it horrifyingly real.

The walls and furniture in every room seemed to have been recast in a filtered light, as if she were seeing them for the first time. In shock, terrified and dreading each step taking her deeper into the hallway, she couldn't stop herself and pushed on, barely aware of her body moving. The sounds of the house, the appliances cycling, the walls creaking, branches pushed by the wind dragging against the windows, were absurdly loud and she wished she could turn down the volume.

Her breathing was uneven. Ragged gulps of air followed by moments when she unknowingly held her breath, only to gasp, gulp again, and after just tentatively catching her breath, manically repeating the cycle she couldn't break.

Someone was here; someone still in the house and had left muddy tracks in the hallway.

She shivered, terrified with fear.

The invasive violation, a rape of her private and protected space, tainted the reassuring security she'd always felt here. Standing in the hallway outside her parent's master suite, the door, emblazoned with a bloody handprint, was closed. The only sound now was her labored breathing. She hesitated before turning the handle to open the door and look inside.

Kiki was torn between her urgent need to know and a rampaging fear of what she'd find. Once she knew, everything would be changed forever. There would be no going back, and no escape from whatever was inside. This would be the fateful next step on a journey descending into despair, a journey she was wholly unprepared for. The question emerging was one for which she had no answer:

"How will I survive, can I survive, the new reality of my suddenly shattered life?"

Fresh tears blurred her vision.

Kiki made no effort to wipe them away, but blinked reflexively until she could see.

Those tears were a last living link to what had been but she sensed no longer was.

She placed her hand around the doorknob, which felt cold but oddly charged, as if a current were running through it. More thoughts were screaming for attention, pummeling her from all directions at a time when she was helplessly vulnerable to their ominous onslaught. Her heart and mind were overrun by dread and hopelessness, fear tying her stomach in knots. Too much, too fast, nothing made sense and there was no time to process it.

Feeling more alone than at any time in her life, the young woman opened the door.

Butted up against the far wall, the headboard of her parents' bed faced the door.

Her mother was sitting up in bed, but had slumped awkwardly to the right. Bruising was evident where powerful hands had crushed the air from her throat. Eyes vacant, staring off into space, but seeing nothing, Kiki had no doubt that she was gone, and closed her mother's eyes, and then briefly closed her own, wanting, wishing, praying, to will away the sight, but knowing she couldn't. Opening her eyes, she couldn't bear to look, but couldn't look away.

"Mommy," she said in a cracked voice. "I love you so much, Mom."

Another wave of tears came but the young woman knew she had to stay alert.

Her eyes kept moving, looking around the bedroom for signs of … what? She was living a nightmare and anything was possible. Her most naked childhood terrors beckoned. Would the boogey-man leap out from the closet or spring up from under the bed? The monster that had done this could still be here and at this moment danger and fear trumped her horror and pain.

At her mother's side, she tenderly touched her cheek, still warm, and kissed her lightly on the lips. The faint scent of the perfume she favored triggered another painfully sad memory and Kiki wondered when, if ever, those would stop coming. The mind plays cruel tricks in that way, demanding inordinate time and attention before reluctantly relinquishing its hold.

She backed out of her parents' room, almost respectfully, peering out into the hallway before stepping out. Seeing no one didn't make her feel safer, the uncertainty added to her sense of exposure and vulnerability to an unseen threat. Kiki had no idea what to do next, but feared that whatever she did might be fatally wrong. In slow motion she closed the door behind her, willing the lock not to click, but remain silent. She chastised herself for failing to look for a weapon in the garage, or stopping in the kitchen for a knife, or calling 9-1-1

She felt for her pocket for her phone, but remembered leaving it in the car and cursed.

My phone! I should always have it with me; I always do – except now when I need it.

The fact that she was unarmed was unnerving, but the idea of brandishing a weapon couldn't have been more out of character. She couldn't remember ever hitting anyone – other than her sister during one of those absurd fights they had as young children. Those times when they senselessly pounded each other to no ill effect, neither of them ever actually landing a blow, but never

22

failing to anger their parents. She and Janie had always laughed about them later.

A bittersweet memory of one of those moments came to her that she forced away. For now she could only absorb the shock, and prepare, as best she could, to weather the next one, summoning her dwindling reserves and steeling herself against what she feared was ahead.

Her thoughts were now fixed on Janie. Maybe she wasn't home – please let her be out!

Kiki began moving down the hallway to her sister's bedroom.

On the way she took a quick look into her own bedroom, but couldn't bring herself to enter. The room was empty, looking as it always had, and today, incongruously normal.

I may never again know normal.

Anticipating her return, her mother had recently dusted, vacuumed and changed the linens on the bed. Fresh flowers from the yard filled a small face on her bureau. Despite Kiki's protests that it was unnecessary, her mom never failed to do this.

"It's my pleasure." Mom would always insist.

Kiki could hear her mother saying those words, knowing she'd never hear her again.

Shell-shocked and in a fog, she stood outside the door to Janie's room without moving. Listening, she heard nothing. The faint lingering of her mother's delicate floral fragrance was gone, replaced by something totally different and unfamiliar. The air was filled by a thick scent that was out of place and alarming, hinting of the earth, dirty and stale, sour and cloying, all that mixing with rank body odor and unwashed clothing.

There was someone in Janie's room!

She retraced her steps, fumbling her way to the kitchen and found a large carving knife.

The one her father used to carve the Thanksgiving turkey.

She choked back a sob.

Just what will you do with it?

As she began to leave the kitchen and return to the bedrooms, she glanced at the hanging dry erase board the family used for phone messages and other news. The large board had been recently wiped clean. A single message was now filling the space.

She'd always admired her mother's hand, the attractive but efficient cursive Kiki envied but had never been able to emulate, and not for lack of trying. Uncharacteristically, this time her mother had printed in bold block letters, like lettering on a sign. Each letter was thick and black, but outlined in a different color. Her mom had penned a message.

WELCOME HOME, KIKI!!!!!
WE LOVE YOU!!!!!

Choking back another sob, clutching the knife in her right hand, she left the kitchen.

Outside her sister's room Kiki's heart was pounding, a thumping filling her ears only she could hear. She turned the doorknob slowly and gasped.

A huge, wild looking man was standing next to the bed.

He was leaning down over Janie who lay unmoving on top of the comforter. She was fully clothed and staring blankly into space with the same unseeing look Kiki had seen in her mother and father's eyes.

At that critical moment Kiki did the worst possible thing.

"Get away from her!" She shrieked in a voice she didn't recognize as her own.

The man whirled around. Only a few feet apart they stood transfixed by each other.

The man was big, 6' 4", possibly even taller, thickly muscled, and appeared to be in his thirties, early or late, she couldn't tell. He was strong with the look of years of hard physical labor and filthy. What she could see of his face was caked with dirt, as were his clothes. Long, matted black hair had come loose from being tied back and fell nearly to his shoulders. His massive beard reminded her of ZZ Top. His eyes were wild and unfocused, and while clearly agitated, he didn't seem afraid, rather, somehow detached in an odd way and confused.

To her surprise, she saw he'd been crying.

Then he said something unintelligible, more a grunt. Words too garbled for her to even guess what he might mean. After he repeated it, the same incomprehensible grunt delivered in some manner of an urgent entreaty, pleading, desperately pointing and waving his arms. When she again failed to respond, he took a step towards her

A scream erupted from deep within her and shattered the quiet of the room.

I should have called 9-1-1. What was I thinking? I wasn't. Move on, get away.

The man's presence was simply terrifying.

Kiki had never felt fear like this. She had to get away, but her mind and body were at odds with each other, working furiously but at cross purposes. As her blood turned brittle and cold and she shivered before breaking into a fevered sweat. Everything was wrong, nothing made sense, unnerved and believing she was coming unglued, Kiki turned to flee, but as in a dream her legs were heavy, leaden and felt disconnected from her body, refusing instructions.

Get away, to safety, to find help, to survive.

The carving knife clattered on the floor as it slipped from her hands.

Acting quickly, the big man pounced like a big cat and was upon her with a single step, tackling her from behind, bringing her to the ground. She was stunned by his the speed and the effortless grace of reactions, how quickly a man his size had moved, and his great strength.

The man was on top of her.

The odor she'd noticed was stronger now, filling her senses. A sour bile rose in her throat. She was tasting fear for the first time in her life and had never felt so helpless and lost.

Although she was powerless to stop him, she squirmed and twisted, using every bit of her strength to try and break away, but couldn't move, pinned totally by his great weight. On her back, she looked up and saw that his tears had made fresh tracks down the sides of his dirty face.

She screamed again and picking up her head he bashed it against the floor.

Kiki felt the power of his strong hands tightening around her throat.

There was no way to resist him and the world began to go dark.

Chapter Four

DRIFTING IN AND OUT of a dreamlike state there was no sense of time, or of anything else. Given Kiki's condition this was a blessing.

She had no idea where she was, or *if* she was at all.

The mind's defense mechanism had bartered abject horror for confusion, a fair exchange affording her medical and emotional sanctuary to lick her soul-piercing wounds and find the will and the strength to survive them. Grave physical injuries after nearly being strangled to death had landed her just shy of Death's doors and inside ICU, and it took all that to shield her from the carnage of her homecoming. Dealing with the aftermath of the tragedy would come much later.

Kiki's life was changed forever.

Her old life was gone.

At twenty-one, the notion of life spinning such a curveball is unfathomable, and the dose of real life she'd been force-fed was the equal of any cinematic horror. Her mom, dad and sister had always been there for her, she counted on it. Kiki knew they always would be, but in an instant, no longer. They were all gone and she was alone. Without warning and for no earthly reason, the anchors and emotional lynchpins of her life had been savagely rendered to memory.

When, *if*, she recovered, her new reality would be one she never could have imagined.

The blessing of fighting for her life in Intensive Care was it spared her from thinking.

ICU's job is to save your life today, to give you a later to
contemplate what it means if you're so inclined. Kiki had been
discovered clinging to life by the Portland Police, summoned by a
suspicious neighbor six hours after the attack. She had yet to regain
consciousness. The injuries were serious, and initially feared to be
life-threatening, but now, days later, that danger appeared to have
passed. She was steadily improving and the doctors now hoped she
might soon regain consciousness, possibly in the next forty-eight
hours.

Kiki had sustained severe damage to the larynx, and while she
was expected to speak again, her voice box had been bruised. Only
time would tell. The perpetrator had nearly choked her to death,
but inexplicably stopping just short of it, perhaps thinking he had,
the detectives speculated.

EMTs treated her while still sprawled upon the floor, barely
breathing and unconscious. Her vital signs had been alarming,
weak and erratic. For an unspecified period of time she had suffered a diminished and inadequate supply of oxygen to the brain.
Doctors were still unsure of the extent of the damage, and cautioned that it could likely be some time before they knew more.

After all, so often with modern medicine, it's as much as
guesswork as science.

The neurologists suspected that she was floating in a nether-
world reality of blurred consciousness. Until she awoke and spoke
with her they couldn't know, and until mind and body functioned
normally and in harmony again, there was little they could do for
her. It was assumed that it would be some time before Kiki could
begin to process the extraordinary events, but they were wrong
about that.

She was coming around and already coming to terms with
much of it.

Her eyes remained closed and while unable – or too weak
– to open them, was aware of voices and the presence of people,
moving in and out of her consciousness. Doctors and nurses, 'm
alive and in the hospital. She felt no desire or urgency to determine
precisely who they were or what they were doing. There was no
urgency and fatigue weighed heavily, so she gave in to dreamless
sleep, wrapped in the protective safety of a soothing and peaceful
calm.

The next time she awoke her consciousness and mental clarity were returning.

The temperature in this place was neither warm nor cool. Oddly, she had little perception of her body but a heightened awareness of bright lights, electronic sounds and the bustling of people as they poked, prodded and spoke to her in words that she began to recognize.

Kiki still hadn't opened her eyes, but could have, she was quite ready.

That she was in a hospital was both a scary and comforting thought.

Feeling calmer and safe, she fell back into a deep sleep.

"Kiki," a voice spoke to her gently.

Upon first hearing the voice, Kiki wondered if it was her imagination or part of a dream. But hearing wasn't quite right, it was different than hearing. More like she'd felt it … or sensed it. Or, maybe, the thought occurred to her, she was losing her mind and was delusional and imagining it.

Given the cataclysmic events she'd begun to remember, who could blame her?

She'd opened her eyes the last time she awakened.

No doctors or nurses had observed it, but she had returned to the world of the conscious and the living. She'd been welcomed back by shattering memories, and vivid, heartbreaking images of events more shocking than she could bear. She would have given anything to make them go away, but couldn't. They were permanently etched in memory, like emotional baggage she'd carry with her always, and Kiki couldn't conceive of how she would ever escape them.

Then the voice, deep but soothing, it sounded … kind, spoke again.

"You'll be alright, child, everything will be alright."

Puzzled, she asked, "Who are you? Are you …?"

"Think of me as you like, we're called many things."

"This has to be a dream."

"This is no dream."

"Why are you here? Have you come to help me? Can you make everything right? Can you bring my family back?" She pressed.

"No, I can't do that ... if only I could undo all that needs to be undone, and redone, in the world."

"Then, why are you here and what is it you want from me ... what can you do?"

"We can offer you hope. And I've come to give you that chance."

"I ... I don't understand. Things like this just don't happen, at least to me. I must be dreaming."

"No, while you aren't fully awake, this is no dream. You were seriously injured and are in the hospital being well cared for. You will recover, but that's not why I've come to you. I need you to listen to me, now, child. All is not lost. I have a gift for you, but if you are to use The Gift successfully, you must follow my instructions completely and do exactly as I say."

"This makes no sense, it can't be happening. I must be delirious or something." Bubbling frustration was compounding her confusion, and it had become hard to breathe. She felt like she was drowning. This was insane, or she was.

"You haven't lost your mind and you are not crazy," the voice continued, as if reading her thoughts. "You can relax about that, you're just understandably weakened and confused."

"That's a small comfort, I suppose, but it tells me nothing ... Whoever you are, why can't you just fix things, aren't you ... in charge?"

"Sadly, no, we're not."

"Forgive me, but that only makes this harder to believe. You must be in charge!"

"The record of man in the world clearly suggests that isn't the case, don't you agree?" The voice sounded almost resigned and regretful, but continued. "In our defense, asking that we define a universe still growing and evolving is beyond even our capacity. The universe is more organic, and complex, than you imagine, and your role in it is larger than you understand."

She detected a faint note of amusement in his words.

Apparently, whoever it was had a sense of humor.

"But, you're supposed to be in charge, someone has to be!" Kiki insisted again.

"Man has flourished, if not thrived. The sheer numbers exceeded the plan's expectations, and his poor stewardship and the less admirable qualities of human nature have exacerbated our dilemma."

Hearing those words only supported her belief that this had to be a dream.

"No way I'm in a hospital bed discussing epistemology with ...
who?

Him?

Him who?"

Kiki had always been conflicted about religion, resigning herself to be a non-believing believer, skeptical of everything including her own doubts. Still, dream, delusion or whatever, she had to see what it was she could do. Could it really be as he said?

"So, what are you telling me? That there is no God, but we have friends in 'High Places' and that every now and then you reveal yourselves and help a few of us? Is this my chance to appeal to the Highest Court? And if we're such a great disappointment, why not just wipe the slate clean and start over? Why even bother with us?"

"I'm afraid you vastly overestimate our ... scope at this level."

Kiki didn't comment at that, but listened intently.

"The world is man's responsibility, not ours. Understand that none of this is intended as a moral indictment, Kiki, but the systemic requirements necessitate perpetuation, and the human race is our best and only chance. The world was created of inanimate and organic things, given to sentient creatures with the capacity to freely make decisions, good and bad."

"So, if we're on own, what exactly is it you do?"

"We can assist in small ways and hope such threads of grace multiply."

"And I'll have a chance, for my parents and my sister?"

"With the tool, The Gift I mentioned, yes."

"Tell me, then, tell me!"

"Around your wrist is a remarkable band. Do you see it?"

She looked at her wrist, puzzled the band was so hard to see, and then touched it gently. It was there. "Yes, I do. It's hard to see. I've never felt anything like it, cool to the touch, and smooth like glass."

"To most people it is invisible."

"I don't understand ..."

"Touch it, a digital display appears, like a watch face with unusual options. The date, month and year are shown. Do you see it? You can re-set the date, and re-live it. Go to sleep and awaken, after making The Journey, in that time, with a second chance."

"But that would be nothing less than a miracle," Kiki said, incredulous but hopeful that when she awakened this wouldn't have been simply a bizarre dream.

"Miracles ... many call them that. We think of them as ... corrections."

"There must be more to this," Kiki said, skeptical but wanting to believe. "Why me?"

"We can't change the world, but we can assist a few people of good heart who have suffered greatly. Our belief is that they will do good works for themselves and for others."

"Works? Does this mean more than a one-time thing?" Kiki asked.

"I don't mean to avoid the question, but the answer isn't clear. It is different for each of you; possibly as many as a dozen times in a lifetime, never less than half that. Sadly, you see, there is a pronounced physical toll ... you must be judicious in your ... selections."

"Is that it?"

"No, there is more you will learn, but for now one thing is most important of all."

"What's that?"

"If the change is to be made permanent, you must do more than simply re-live the day."

"I don't understand, how can ..."

"Listen to me, child. You must go back farther, much farther, all the way to the root of the events which you desire to re-do."

"I still don't understand ... going back, where? Or why?"

"Destiny has a way of refusing to be denied. Without correcting at the root, destiny will reassert and ultimately realize its original effect."

"But, that's impossible! How could I possibly know what to do?"

"With my help you'll come to understand. We'll talk again. For now, before I go ... let me tell you about Morris Biggs Jr., known as "Little Mo.""

Chapter Five

KIKI HAD NO MEMORIES of being admitted to the hospital. The leaving she'd never forget. Today her emotions ranged from anguish and despair to a faintly rekindled hope.

Discharge from the medical facility meant giving up its protective umbrella, the comfort and security, trading it for a new life thrust upon her she couldn't have imagined. That new life would include embarking on an impossible adventure that, while it defied all logic and reason, was the single most important thing she'd ever do.

After first determining, if she could, whether this was real or she was living a delusion.

In body, she was sufficiently recovered. The doctors found no reason she wouldn't enjoy the good health and vitality of a normal twenty-one year old woman at her physical peak.

But in spirit, in her heart, she felt hollowed out.

Her soul had been numbed by sadness so deep and cold it left her with a deadening ache she feared she might never be able to overcome.

Back in the world with a mostly firm grip, but totally unprepared for the gruesome aftermath of profound loss, or to embrace the fantastic new possibilities of her life.

The hospital stay afforded her only time enough to begin coming to terms with it. Kiki doubted she'd ever feel whole again. Her physical strength was returning, but would forever be paired with a sorrowful emptiness that she feared would be her constant companion.

How do people ever get beyond loss like this?

What if, in spirit, there are some things for which there can be no healing?

Whatever the answer, for now it didn't' matter, her life had assumed a single purpose.

If only she *believed*. She had to, but how could she?

She leaned both ways, but believer or not, was on board now. She had to be.

The truth was she wanted to believe, and wished she did, but it was simply too fantastic. Every day tested both her skepticism *and* her faith. Neither prevailed, neither conceded, they battled to their daily draw and would soon return, vigorous and refreshed and have at it again, each side devising a new tactic and donning a fresh facade in a battle neither tired of. Weary of it, but unable to escape it, Kiki accepted it.

"Whatever it takes to reclaim my family and my life," she said it aloud, her resolve complete.

There had to be some logical explanation for the band around her wrist, she knew, but it was The Gift, and the possibilities it represented, that kept her going. Whatever it was; the band, the bracelet, the watch, the chance, the Do-Over, offered to her by … who?

She had to call him *something*.

What she was being offered was straight out of the Guardian Angel's playbook.

So she settled on thinking of him as The Guardian.

It was a perfect fit.

There was so much to do, too much, she felt overwhelmed, feared it was too much for her, for anyone, she wasn't up to it. Could anyone be up to it? She had no idea what to do, or where to start. Then it came to her so quickly and clearly it startled her.

Prepare for departing the here and now – for a here and then.

By staying busy, she'd consume herself in getting ready.

For how long she couldn't know, for now, just get ready.

And as she prepared new questions arose. Some diverting, others daunting, such as …

Was time travel like space travel?

Assuming she was successful, and actually did journey back in time, upon returning from so many years in the past, how much time would have elapsed *during* her absence? Would it be like fictional astronauts returning from a long voyage to a world so thoroughly changed that they no longer recognized it? Their world, the one they'd known, and all those they'd loved, long dead and turned to dust upon their return. Would her journey be a sadly odd twist on Einstein's relativity theory? For a brief moment she was tempted to run it by her physics professor but feared he'd recoil, boot her out of his office or have her committed. She wouldn't have blamed him for doing so. It was crazy.

Wasn't it?

Logically, if logic mattered, questions like these were better asked of The Guardian. Regrettably, nonplussed and out of it the first time, there were many questions she hadn't thought to ask when she'd had the chance, regretting more and more that she hadn't.

Surprisingly, her logical mind rose to The Guardian's defense. A second chance couldn't mean returning to an unrecognizable world. If that were the case, why bother? More likely was she'd return to the *now* she'd left, rejoining the present after the merest blink of passing time. Nightmare over, the slate wiped clean of senseless tragedy. Or so she hoped.

But she couldn't quite believe it was real, and was soon reviving the ongoing debate.

She constructed a litany of reasons why none of this could be possible, starting with the simple fact that the assault explained a fragile mental state playing the predictable tricks. Left to sort out an inexplicable life experience with shattered defenses and diminished capacity, she was desperate to return to trusting her judgment and instincts. Given the circumstances, the inability to do so now was easy to understand and certainly not uncommon in a hospital. Or maybe, along with everything else, she had temporarily lost her mind. However long it might take, the sooner she dismissed all this nonsense, the sooner she'd be on the road to whatever recovery might be.

Except she couldn't quite believe it *wasn't* real, either.

The battle between faith and doubt continued, tilting first one way, then the other.

She'd been wide awake and clear-headed for The Guardian's second visit.

This time there were no doubts, none.

Late during her last night in the hospital, The Guardian returned and had spoken again. And this time Kiki knew it was no dream. Afterwards, strengthened and comforted by a proof more convincing than even the invisible band around her wrist.

The accepting, the believing, the knowing; she'd been given hope if she dared believe.

After the Second Visitation, she believed with all her heart. She had to.

"Hello, Kiki," the voice said. "You're much better today, and going home soon, I see."

Kiki looked around her hospital room, seeing no one, but knowing she wasn't alone.

"I am better," she replied, "and, yes, I'll be going home tomorrow."

"You wondered if you'd hear from me, again, if it had been a dream, but you no longer doubt." The Guardian wasn't asking a question, but instead was making a statement he knew to be true.

Kiki didn't answer, unconsciously fingering the band, as he continued.

"You have ... questions, I know," he said evenly and waited patiently.

She had many.

Taking a deep breath, she asked, "You told me the number of times I can use The Gift, or whatever, is limited because there is a physical effect."

"Yes."

"That can't be all of it. Please tell me more. I know you said that I must make judicious choices, but all of that is in the future. Long after I've done what I have to for my family. I'm asking what else I need to know – now!"

"You're young and strong, but when you return you may feel quite weak for a time. It seems to be more pronounced the farther back in time you go, and with each Journey."

"*What do you mean by 'Each Journey'? I'm struggling seeing beyond the first one. And how exactly do I use what you've given me? When I look at the band, it's plain, translucent and nearly invisible. Sometimes I forget I have it on. But when I touch it, it comes alive and changes into ... I don't know, some kind of a weird digital time-piece Steve Jobs might have dreamt up with a little more time.*"

"*I understand why you'd say that, but you'd be surprised how old it is.*"

Kiki was tempted to ask, but didn't.

"*The band is what you make of it, and its appearance is ... is customized by each owner's perception. It functions universally, as it always has, but people see it in their own way and in their own context, as something that is comfortable and familiar to them. Think of it as a rather unique timepiece with a touchscreen and features you'll recognize, but with a few surprises. Essentially, when you're ready, you'll choose a destination in time; the day, month and year. Adjust the settings, go to sleep, and when you awaken, you'll be there.*"

"*So that's The Journey you mentioned before,*" *she said, momentarily lost in the implications.* "*And my life, now coming straight out of a sci-fi novel, comes equipped with a wrist band that controls a time travel device?*"

"*Call it that, if you like.*"

"*Whoa. I don't get this. With all your powers, why don't you just fix things? Why me? And why leave it up to me and require me to go to such extreme measures?*"

"*Because your future is rooted in the past, and what you make of it is up to you alone.*"

"*Will you be guiding me or at least watching over me? Can you help me when I'm ... back there?*"

"*I'll be watching, but cannot help in a direct way. Whatever will be is not because of us, it can't work that way. Your future is in your hands. Whatever will be is up to you.*"

"*You're missing my point; maybe I'm not making myself clear. Just what exactly am I supposed to do? What can I do? How do I do what I have to do? You can't blame me for believing I need more than moral support,*" *she said,* "*It seems so unfair!*" *She added, growing angry, unable to hide her frustration, and not sure she cared. Shocked by her tone of voice, she stopped. Taking a deep breath, then another, she soon felt calmer and began again.*

"It's not like I'm heading to the beach for a weekend. You can at least help me prepare, can't you? I can prepare, can't I?" Kiki felt better, stronger, standing up for herself.

When The Guardian didn't answer, she continued.

"Don't you see?" She was almost pleading for his understanding. "How else do I ensure my chance isn't wasted?" Her tone had grown exasperated. "And exactly what did you mean, before, about going back to the root?"

"I can help you with that."

"Please do." Kiki said, thinking he finally sounded like a Guardian Angel should.

"First, the root is nothing mysterious, rather the logical place to begin anew"

"It's not so logical to me!"

"Before making your journey to the past, you must learn more about Little Mo Biggs, and determine what the pivotal events were in his life that determined his future. I've already told you a little about him, you must learn more. You're going to find that history isn't as whimsical as the poets and philosophers would have us believe. Research the life of Morris Biggs, Jr. and you'll find the root. Return to that time and make a difference for the boy. When you do, you could change his future as well as your own."

"So, his chance is my chance?" Kiki asked.

"Yes, his chance is your chance."

"Okay, I guess I can do that, but what about my life, my life in the here and now? Do I just leave, disappear without a trace and assume everything will be hunky dory when I return? That seems unlikely. The truth is it's all more than a little scary."

"There's nothing to fear."

"Easy for you to say, but that's no comfort at all for me. From my perspective, things look quite different. I'm leaving the world that I know, for one that I don't. I'm depending on some kind of device that can't possibly exist and going back in time to correct an injustice that I had nothing to do with, but is at the root of my personal tragedy many years later. And as for making things better, apparently everything rests on my shoulders because you claim that it's beyond you. Oh, really? You know what I think? I think that I should not only be scared to death but questioning everything, starting with my sanity for believing any of this."

"We wouldn't have chosen you without having confidence in your strength and goodness."

Kiki sighed, clearly frustrated by answers that seemed like non-answers. "Oh really, like that should make it all better … okay, what else can you tell me? There must be more."

"You'll need someone to mind your affairs in your absence. A trusted friend … although, you must understand that if you're successful, the world you'll return to may not be exactly the one you're leaving. It will have been … corrected."

"And that's supposed to be comforting, I suppose. Let's see if I've got it right. You're saying if things go as I hope, my friend and I we'll still be friends, as we are, now, right? But all may not be as it was, because I will have corrected it?"

Kiki thought she heard The Guardian chuckle softly, hoping he was laughing with her and not at her.

"Your friend will be your friend … save the odd chance that Little Mo Biggs crossed your friend's life, but that is unlikely. Is there someone you have someone in mind?" The Guardian asked her this patiently. "I'm sure there must be someone you can entrust with this favor."

"Yes, but I'm afraid that explaining all of this may scare her off."

"I'm sure you'll find a way to… present it. The truth, as foreign and unlikely as it may seem, is always the wisest course."

"I'm sorry, but I still don't get why you don't fix this, since you seem to know so much," Kiki said.

"We can only provide the tools. The rest is up to you. I'm afraid you have no choice other than accept that for what it is."

Kiki sighed, resigned to accept because what else could she do? "Is there anything else I should know?"

"When you set the date, a display will appear, much larger than the band itself."

"What sort of display?"

"You'll see a three-dimensional window of your … destination."

"Do you mean like a map, or a hologram?" Kiki asked.

"Not quite, it's more a window."

"What kind of window?" She pressed.

"Why it's a window to the past."

Chapter Six

MORRIS BIGGS JR. PEDALED his Schwinn back across town to his father's dilapidated tract house. He walked the old bike into the garage, parking it close to the mattress serving as both his bed and sofa. This space had been his living quarters for the past thirty-one years as Little Mo would be thirty-seven years-old tomorrow, but he had no awareness of that. He'd never had a birthday party, never attended one, and had no idea what a birthday or birthday party was. He felt safe in the garage, if safe was a word that applied to a discarded, solitary life.

Abandoning the garage as he had his son, his father seldom came here.

The exceptions, thankfully, were few, and came when the old man was angry – or mean-drunk – or both, and itching to take it out on his very own defenseless victim who never fought back. Big Mo kept his business separate, working out of what he called *The Barn*, a rickety steel pole building at the back of the property that stored his landscaping equipment and supplies.

A line of shallow, grime-caked windows ran midway up the garage's back wall, allowing Little Mo a clear line-of-sight between the house and pole building. He could observe all foot traffic between the house and the barn, other than the garage, the two most important places in his life. That each trip his father made between them was so significant was a piteous reflection of the life Big Mo had bestowed on the son he didn't love or want.

The distance from the house to The Barn wasn't great, as the lot was less than an acre. The walls of the garage were paper thin and without insulation, so Little Mo heard the voices and sounds of living from within the house. Over the course of his lifetime he had been conditioned to every life sound emanating from the house. The openings and closings of every door, every creak, every voice, and the subliminal emotional reactions the sounds within elicited from him.

Each time his father disappeared into the Barn brought a slight smile.

Each time he ignored the garage and returned to the house promised a small relief.

Each time his father chose the garage door Little Mo prepared for a beating.

The pain had ceased bothering him years ago.

He barely felt the blows any more, and made no effort to defend himself.

His father was a much older man now, no longer as strong, but cruel as ever, or more than ever. Little Mo's work-hardened body had become impervious to physical pain, but his intellectual deficiency couldn't spare him totally. Although he'd never understand why, on even the basest level, the beatings reinforced a primal sadness that he felt, as if melancholy had been grafted to his DNA.

Sometimes involuntary tears filled his eyes and he'd hear a woman's soft, tender voice.

It might have been his mother's voice, but Little Mo couldn't know.

He didn't remember his mother.

But the gentle, caring words he couldn't understand stirred something within him, a fragment recalled from long ago without any context. The vaguest and disjointed of associations with a tenderness and affection never been part of his life experience. As much as anything could, it was this inexplicable yearning that explained his determination for the human connection he'd never had, yet ineptly and feebly reached out for.

Little Mo heard a phlegmy cough, followed by a crunching of heavy boots over the loose gravel which served as a grass substitute in what otherwise would have been the home's back yard. These familiar sounds triggered an immediate reaction. His father was coming. He would have sought cover if any was available to him, but there was nowhere to go, nowhere to hide.

Training his eyes through the window, his breath caught as he saw his father making his way from The Barn, this time veering toward the garage. The old man's graying, thinning hair was wild, his clothes dirty and worn. His lurching gait, bloodshot eyes and the presaging scowl on his face announced his state of mind without saying a word: Mean drunk and mad at the world again, seeking out his usual target for no earthly reason other than the brief moments of twisted pleasure it offered him, tormenting and abusing a helpless target that never fought back.

Big Mo kicked the door open; this was his preferred mode of entry.

Entered that way so many times the lock no longer latched securely and the door needed reframing, adding to cold, damp drafts his son had no choice but to endure. Little Mo shrank back, wishing he could sink into the mattress, disappear into the shadows, but there was nowhere to hide, and he was unable to do anything but wait. And, like always, take what came.

His father stood over him, breathing unevenly, with wheezy gasps.

"The fuck you lookin' at, you dumb piece of shit?" Big Mo spat on the floor for added emphasis, and then asked, "And where the hell you been?"

Little Mo didn't speak, he couldn't.

He couldn't organize his thoughts or understand his feelings, and didn't know the words and couldn't speak them. He didn't hate his father, hate requires a series of judgments Little Mo couldn't make. He did fear him, however, as fear requires little more than the desire to survive. He hated him on a visceral, if non-cognitive level. Little Mo survived by avoiding him when he could, submitting and obeying him when he couldn't. And of course, taking whatever the ugly old man dished out, because taking it meant less trouble, and ended it.

Until the next time.

This was Morris Biggs Sr., the sole human constant in his son's life.

"Come over here, closer to your old man, dummy," his father said, "and lemme get a closer look at you."

Little Mo didn't move and his father repeated his demand.

"Move it, boy! You don't wanna rile your pop. Don't make me come for ya, it's only worse when I hafta," he slurred, pointing his finger to a spot closer to him.

Little Mo slowly edged his large body over to the edge of the mattress, closer to his father towering over him. Without another word Big Mo back-handed him across the face, drawing blood at the corner of his mouth.

Morris Biggs Sr.'s chest was already heaving from the exertion, as he looked down upon his son through bleary eyes, shaking his head in disgust. Blood was dripping from his son's mouth, running freely down one side of his chin, and falling as drops on to the mattress. This part of the mattress was home to a congregation of many such drops gathered over the years, most of them no longer red, but dried and almost black.

These were the bloody mementoes of countless beatings.

Big Mo's eyes were gleaming with a kind of drunken blood-lust, and out of habit his hands went to the big, tarnished silver buckle of his wide leather belt. After pulling it out from the loops of his jeans, he first held it by the tongue, and began what had become his perverse parental ritual. Next, clenching the tongue in his right fist, wrapping it a few times around his wrist, until the buckle was dangling loosely just above the ground.

The belt had been transformed into something he could work with. The buckle a weapon he could easily control and could cut deep. When he tired of that, he liked doubling-up the leather, resorting to administering dozens of lashes across his son's back. Drawing blood after whipping his son through his flannel shirt was a personal challenge Big Mo Biggs never tired of.

~~~~~

Jenna Woodson sat next to her best friend Kiki Kinsler in the rear seat of the black hearse making its slow crawl out of the cemetery gates. They were the only passengers and sat quietly. Since Kiki's family had been lowered side-by-side into the ground, neither girl had said a word. This was nothing at all like their usual non-stop conversation when they were together.

The small service was subdued and almost private.

Neither side of the family had living relatives.

Her Mom and Dad, both only children, had often joked that their marriage was a union of orphans. Kiki hadn't placed a notice in the newspapers and had made no calls. She'd been too weak in the hospital recovering from the attack, and after being released was too emotionally spent. Besides, she reasoned, what does it matter? *Soon I'll be off to un-do all that has happened, if The Guardian was to be believed.*

A few family friends and neighbors, Jenna's family, and a few of her dad's colleagues had appeared. No one was more welcomed than Clark Bannion, her father's best friend and attorney, ably assisting without intruding, remaining in the background, kindly and without pressure.

Bannion tried to be strong while making no attempt to hide how grievously wounded he was by the shocking and senseless loss of his oldest and dearest friend, and a family so close he felt part of it. Since childhood, Kiki had grown to love him as a favorite uncle, trusting his judgment implicitly and knowing he loved her uncon-ditionally. Jenna's parents were there for her, too, another adult lifeline for a young woman now on her own.

Jenna's eyes never left her childhood pal's face, searched intently for a clue as to what she was thinking. During the service, other than occasionally dabbing at her eyes with a handkerchief, Kiki had shown virtually no emotion.

From Jenna's perspective, this was beyond bearing the burden stoically. She was puzzled – and troubled – by it. Kiki had always been an emotional person, so responding in this manner couldn't have been more out of character. At the same time, Jenna also knew that after all her friend had experienced, Kiki couldn't have much left; she had to be physically exhausted and emotionally drained. It was heartbreaking to watch, and she wanted to do any-thing she could to help, but didn't know how.

Jenna reached her hand out, placing it gently on Kiki's shoul-der, while twirling strands of her own black tresses around an index finger with an almost manic determination. As the hearse accelerated down the arterial and turned onto the ramp to OR 217, she ended her silence.

"I can't remember you ever this quiet, Kiki," Jenna began. "There has to be a lot bottled-up inside. If you can't talk now, if it's not the time, I understand ... I just want you to know I'm here for you whenever you're ready, and always will be. Okay?"

"I know," she told Jenna, "and thanks. Everything ... everything has happened so fast, as if life shifted into fast-forward and won't return to normal speed. Sounds pretty crazy, huh? I'm sorry, Jenna, I can't believe any of this is my life. I'm just beginning to feel like I may make it."

"You're entitled to do whatever you need to do. I just want to help, however I can, whenever you need me."

Kiki nodded. "They told me you were at the hospital every day. I never thanked you. That couldn't have been easy for you. I want you to know how much that means to me."

"You'd have been there for me. We used to joke about how close we've always been, like sisters from different mothers, but no joke, we've been friends always. What friends do, right?"

Kiki nodded again, and then asked, "I feel like there's something else you want to say. So, go ahead. I don't think we have to worry about interruptions in the back of a hearse."

Jenna seized the opportunity she'd been offered and jumped right in.

"Through everything, you've *always* told me what you're feeling, but now – after this – *nothing*. I can't know what you're feeling, I get that. But keeping everything locked inside does you no good, it can't. So, yeah – I want us to talk, about how you're feeling. Don't bury it, or hide from it. And more than anything, Kiki, I want to help you and want you to let me help you."

Kiki sat quietly, and then a broad smile appeared.

"Can I take your smile for a 'Yes'?" Jenna asked.

"You have no idea how badly I want to talk and how desperately I need your help," Kiki said. "But, I have to warn you – this is one of those times to be careful about what you ask for."

"I'll take my chances. Let's have it," Jenna answered.

Kiki saw that the hearse had made great time. Just now entering her neighborhood, they would be home in minutes.

"We're almost at the house. We'll talk out everything there. Care to join me in a toast to Mom, Dad and Janie?" She asked with a wry smile.

"I'd be honored, and I'm more than happy to do anything that loosens your tongue and helps you to open up and talk to me."

This time, Kiki's grin led to a giggle she couldn't suppress.

"You think that's funny, huh?" Jenna asked.

"I know you're thinking a drink or two will help me open up and talk. Ordinarily, there might be some truth to that, but ..."

"But what?"

"When you hear what I need to tell you, you'll be glad to have a drink in *your* hand."

Chapter Seven

KIKI HANDED JENNA her drink and sat opposite her on one of the two facing couches. Everything, it seemed, evoked painful, bittersweet memories that tore at her heart.

Jenna sensed this, wanting to help. She could only wait for her friend to begin.

"You could never call my Mom and Dad big drinkers, but as long I can remember, they'd sit like this, just the two of them, on Saturday nights before going out to dinner. They called it their time, it became a family tradition. They'd sit listening to music, catching up, happy just being together without Janie and me for a couple of hours. I …." Kiki's voice cracked, and she stopped.

Overcome by memories flooding back, she closed her eyes, hanging her head.

"I remember," Jenna said, eyeing tears glistening on her face. "You dad like to brag about making your mom the perfect vodka martini, and always had a bottle of Svedka in the freezer for the occasion. He used to brag it was unbeatable for the money."

"Dad loved a good buy, didn't he?" Kiki asked, as she sighed, and looked up. "He had the vodka right, it's really good and a great buy." Kiki took a deep breath, let it out slowly and continued, "Jenna, we've talked about this before from time to time, and it's changing the subject big time, but do you believe in God? "

Jenna thought a moment, and then answered. "I want to, and I do, most of the time, so, yeah, I believe. I know you've always had … issues with faith, doubts. We all do, faith has its blind spots. I think they're unavoidable, but part of faith is having faith. Why do you ask now? Other than the fact that we've just returned from your family's funeral, I mean."

"You can relax about that. I didn't suddenly *get religion* and have no plans of running off to hide in a convent, it's nothing like that. The truth is, I'd like to believe, and there are times when I do, but my rational side has always challenged my faith. For me, logic, science and the evidence of what I *see* in the world aren't so easily dismissed. But I'll believe in *anything* if it means there's a chance I can change what happened. I guess that's what makes this, what I'm about to tell you, so … difficult."

"Now you're losing me," Jenna said, "What *this* are we talking about? And tell me what it is that makes this, whatever it is, so difficult, Kiki?"

"Okay, but it's going to sound so crazy I wouldn't blame you for running out of here."

"Well, that's not going to happen, so try me."

Kiki took a deep breath before answering,

"In the hospital, I had an experience, an epiphany or something I guess you could say."

Jenna sat up straighter, put her glass down on the coffee table. "Like *what*?"

"I don't know what to think about it, much less what to call it."

"Well, you were seriously hurt, head trauma, unconscious for a long time and I know the doctors debated calling it a coma and treating it that way. On top of that, they pumped you full of heavy duty drugs that could cause people in hospitals to have wild dreams, or whatever."

Kiki nodded. "I know, that's what I told myself after – The Guardian – that's what I call him – spoke to me. You know me, I never stop doubting. I'm the original cynic, it's my nature, always has been, and I'll always look for a second opinion if I dislike the first."

"Oh, yeah," Jenna agreed.

"I tried hard to convince myself of what was obvious and logical, that *none* of this, none of this could possibly be happening. After going through this nightmare it's not surprising at all for something utterly weird and crazy to jump out of my brain. I was in a drug-enhanced deep sleep and my body was a mess. My mind, among other things, was trying to cope with a tragedy I may *never* recover from. Fair to call that fertile ground for practically anything, I'd say."

"But something happened to change your thinking, what was it?" Jenna asked, reaching for her friend's hand, giving it a quick squeeze signaling both her affection and solidarity.

Kiki looked at her, eyes pleading to believe her incredible story. "There was a second visit. The Guardian came to me again, the night before I was discharged. This time there would be no doubt. I had recovered, in mind and body, well enough to be sent home at least. I was awake and clear-headed. It was no dream and I'm absolutely convinced it was not a delusion. What I'm trying to say, and part of me can't believe I'm saying it, it was *real*, Jenna."

"Wait." At a total loss for words, Jenna's mind was spinning. There could only be only two possibilities. Kiki had lost her mind, but after spending hours with her she didn't believe that, or she'd actually had an epiphany just as she claimed. Finally, she asked, "Was it God?"

"Funny you ask. I did. A higher power, certainly, but what exactly I couldn't say, and get this, he wouldn't, either. Would you believe me if I tell you that, whoever or whatever it is, when it came to that, *he* was evasive. It didn't seem to matter much. Maybe because having the conversation was all the proof I needed, to believe what I needed to believe."

"That makes sense, I guess."

"What he did say is *they* are called lots of things, and what we call them, well, that's up to us. It turns out lots of things are up to us."

Jenna's jaw had literally dropped. Realizing that, she self-consciously closed her mouth.

"It gets even wilder," Kiki continued. "He – they – can't – or won't – just wave a magic wand and make things better. A few people are given a second-chance. How they choose I can't say, but I qualified. But it's not just about me, or my family, there's more to it than that."

"What do you mean?"

"The man who killed them, and attacked me, The Guardian told me *his* story and it's beyond heartbreaking. This is the man who murdered my family, yet it *touched* me. Can you believe that?

But his life redefines child abuse and parental neglect. My tragedy is something I'll find a way to survive. I have the capacity and the support," she said and gave Jenna's hand a squeeze. "Morris Biggs Jr.'s tragedy is infinitely crueler because he's *living it*; he's never had a chance or a choice, he's incapable of helping himself and has never had support, no one, ever."

"Yes, but it's too incredible," Jenna said softly, "What do you mean? What can you do?"

"If prevent his mother's death, maybe he'll have a chance to live a normal life."

"But how can you prevent something that already happened? If you could, somehow, I guess you would have to go way back could do it," Jenna mused.

"They, The Guardian, called it *going back to the root*. Evidently, the changes are only lasting if they are made at the root. Apparently, anything less and destiny likes to reassert itself, and will find a way to repeat the outcome that needs correcting, what *I'm* trying to correct."

"This is just too incredible. Like I said before, I don't know what to say ...I suppose at the root means you have to change things for this, this killer, this ... monster ..."

"I can't think of him that way. He's Little Mo Biggs," Kiki said.

"Whatever, I guess I don't understand why you have to give him a second chance."

"You think I've totally lost it, don't you?" Kiki asked gently. "I can't blame you for that, I know it sounds crazy. How could I actually go back thirty-one years to fix it? But I can."

"*Thirty-one years???* You mean as in *1981*???" Jenna asked, stunned by the math. "Maybe you have lost it ... I'm kidding. If only you had some proof!"

"Actually, I do. No doubts, and when you see it, you'll agree. Guaranteed."

"Now, you're kidding," Jenna scoffed. "You are, aren't you? What kind of proof?"

"Let me show the latest in *timeless fashion*," Kiki said, and held out her left wrist. "Can you see the band? Even I can't see it at times, but give me your hand, you can feel it," Kiki said, and brought her friend's fingers to the band. "Do you feel it?"

"I do feel it, I can barely see anything but it's so smooth, not like metal, more like glass or polished stone," Jenna exclaimed. "I take it this would be the gift from your Guardian friend?"

"Let me take you for a little spin," Kiki said, with the faintest, playful chuckle.

She ran her hands across the band, and a digital metamorphosis took place.

A virtual video screen appeared. Larger, taller and wider than the band it had appeared out of. Time, day, date and year were displayed along the top of the screen, controlled by what looked like buttons for smart phone apps stacked in a column to the left of the display. Kiki pointed to a single oversize button that ran along the right side.

"See the embossed hourglass icon?" Kiki asked Jenna, who nodded that she did. "When I figured out what it did, I thought it was a rather amusing design feature. The Guardian's design team apparently isn't without a sense of humor and style. I'll set the band to thirty-one years ago. Watch what happens when I push the hourglass button."

The band was no longer translucent, becoming a fiery copper, and no longer as cool to the touch. The small display morphed into a three-dimensional image area the size of a large tablet. What appeared was a view of this very house, then the room they were sitting in, thirty-one years in the past; vaguely familiar, yet dissimilar.

Then and now, it appeared, are the *yin* and *yang* of time travel.

"He called this a window to the past, and that's just what it is," Kiki said quietly. "I've learned that the default setting is the current GPS location. We're looking at this house, this room, thirty-one years ago, nearly ten years before I was even born. The location can be adjusted, there's a button for that. I'll change the coordinates to downtown Portland. I've got a date in mind, give me a second."

Kiki input a date and waited until the display reflected it.

"Do you recognize this, Jenna? I'd be shocked if you didn't."

Jenna gasped, and then studied the images closely, fascinated, but staying silent for a few minutes and then smiling broadly.

"I can't believe it, I'm not seeing this, but that's us, with our dates, on our way inside the Art Museum, Prom Night, Junior Year.

God, I loved that dress – more than I could say for my date. There was never any video, but this angle, the perspective is unusual."

"What do you think now?"

If you're crazy, Kiki," she said, "that makes two of us. I have only one question."

"What's that?"

"Other than suggesting that you buy some 1981 Apple stock, how can I help?"

~~~~~

An hour later, Kiki had laid it all out, giving Jenna the unabridged version.

They then began attacking details, feeding off each other's ideas as they worked.

While Kiki was away, Jenna would have POA over her affairs. All the necessary steps and provisions would be made with the assistance of Clark Bannion. Until Kiki returned – or things changed of their own volition because of what she'd done back in 1981.

Kiki was also tapping Jenna's research, computer and people skills.

"I need you to research the Biggs family thirty-one years ago. It may not be easy," Kiki admitted, "but the more we know the better prepared I'll be."

Jenna had surprised Kiki at the end of their freshman year, announcing her shift to a major in criminology. After graduation, she planned on law school and to then applying to the FBI, hoping to work in forensics and investigations, with an emphasis on databases and other analytic tools of evidence. She had an affinity for technology. A computer science professor teased her about minoring in *hacking*. What Kiki needed from her now would test skills she was still developing, but Jenna would more than make up for that with her intuitive gifts.

The task presented formidable obstacles.

There wouldn't be much on Morris Biggs Sr. beyond tax returns, and the official record of Morris Biggs Jr. stopped where it had begun more than three decades ago. It got worse. Today we take complete information for granted. Virtually everything we do, everywhere we go, everything we say, is captured in some way on some level by someone. 1981, on the other hand, was nearing the end of the pre-digital era. Back then it was hard copies or nothing at all.

Storage and access, if the files they needed could be located, were huge unknowns.

While Jenna researched the Biggs family, Kiki planned to immerse herself in the history and culture of 1981. Knowledge of the times might give her an edge. Even without one, her gut told her the journey might be disastrous without learning as much as she could. Her ability to understand and fit in a world where she would always be out of step, out of time, might determine success or failure.

When they finished for the afternoon, a general plan was in place. Kiki talked about what she believed might come after, and the role she hoped Jenna would want to play.

"Looking into the future isn't easy, especially when our focus is going back to the past, but let's think positively," she told Jenna.

"My mother always says attitude makes a difference. I believe it. We should look ahead. What do you have in mind?"

"There's no way to know what the effects on me will be. According to The Guardian, it varies with the individual, but my impression is that I can't underestimate the physical toll. And how many times I can use the device is limited."

"Aren't you frightened? I would be," Jenna said, shuddering slightly.

"A little. My hope is that I can do this in one trip back."

"I hope so, for your sake."

"With luck, the nightmare will be washed away like chalk on the sidewalk in the rain. My family returned to me, and Little Mo given a life."

"And then?"

"With the remaining journeys, however many trips I can make, we'll choose deserving people. I owe The Guardian that, and I'll need you to help me find them, and do what we can."

"Let's get started," Jenna said simply. "We'll be like modern day technology superheroes. How much time *do* I have?"

"As much as you need but hopefully as little as possible," Kiki answered.

Chapter Eight

KIKI HAD KNOWN CLARK BANNION all her life, but had first visited his law offices with her father. The memories of that fateful morning, after the pot fiasco of her freshman year in high school, were vivid and fresh. Meeting "her lawyer" had been nothing at all like she'd expected.

Rather than staid or sobering, Clark's offices offered the rare combination of being both welcoming and professional, inspiring confidence. The attorney was her dad's closest friend, and usually included and in attendance for holidays and special family occasions. That morning, however, she had been introduced to the *other* Clark Bannion.

Meeting him as a client had revealed the man beyond his obvious legal skills. There was none of the condescension often coming from older people. He spoke directly to her as an adult, not a child, without ever sounding judgmental or appearing aloof. In the midst of a crisis that both frightened and embarrassed her, he was comforting and demonstrated a competency that helped her through it. She'd always loved him, but after that morning trusted him totally as her attorney, advisor and friend.

Over the years, a deeper friendship evolved that she valued more and more.

Today, in late afternoon, she sat in an overstuffed leather guest chair opposite his desk. After a fierce hug and a peck on her cheek, Clark sank into a worn leather high-back executive chair she guessed was older than she was, but looked incredibly comfortable.

His personal office was an odd mix of dark, heavy wood, impressive leather furniture, overflowing bookshelves, framed diplomas and photographs, and peppered with University of Oregon Duck memorabilia.

"How are you doing, kiddo?" he asked with a weak smile, settling back into his chair.

"I'm fine," she sighed. "Well, mostly fine, I guess … I still don't believe any of this."

"I don't, either," he said and paused, then leaned forward. His shift to business was seamless and easy. "I got your text, and think I understand what you want to do, but have no idea why you need any of this. Can you tell me your reasons behind it? You know you can tell me anything, and if you ever need anything, you should make me your first call."

Kiki smiled and looked at him, holding his warm and caring eyes, knowing she really could tell him anything.

And what a fortunate thing that is!

Without warning, and ready or not, she'd been thrust into adulthood alone and on her own. The old anchors of their relationship were gone, and she looked at him differently now; no longer through the eyes of a child. Paradoxically, he was also the only remaining link to her parents, to her old life, and to her childhood. She imagined how incredulous he was going to be hearing what she was about to tell him.

As her plan had developed, it quickly became clear how much she would need his help and professional guidance. In some ways, she felt like one of the explorers she'd studied in school. Not really a stretch, she thought, the fact was that she was preparing to venture blindly into the great unknown. The uncertainties of such an unlikely journey inundated her with questions she couldn't answer, and to her surprise, she was mostly okay with that. After all, she had nothing left to lose and that did put many of her concerns to rest.

What she lacked in experience, she countered by tapping her good instincts and an agile yet orderly mind. Kiki was confident and unafraid to think and act creatively. Her parents had always joked about this side of her, he dad claiming that she'd been that way since she was a child, always been willing to *color outside the lines and make her own picture.*

She'd prove it now, preparing by itemizing and prioritizing what needed doing, and then, dividing the tasks between Clark Bannion, Jenna and herself. From a leather portfolio she withdrew a half-sized manila envelope, and handed it to him. Then, from her over-sized purse, she pulled out a metal box, six inches deep and large enough for envelopes like the one Clark was now holding.

His handsome face bore a quizzical look.

"This is your show, Kiki," he said and waited.

She took a deep breath and began speaking in a low, carefully measured voice.

"I guess it is. There are two documents inside the envelope. First, there are instructions regarding my affairs. I'm giving Jenna POA for routine items, and ask you to counsel her – as if you were talking to me. I trust her as I trust you, Clark. The rest of the pages are my attempt to formalize, in a written record, what I'm going to tell you. This is the story of what has happened to me, what *I think* it means, what I'm *doing* as a result, and what I hope is the outcome. Read it later; after I've gone – I'm sure you'll want to – but for now just listen. And lastly, keep the pages in a secure location, like a safe, ideally something you've had since you first began practicing. Do you have anything like that?"

Clark narrowed his eyebrows, considering her words. "As a matter of fact, I do. This humble abode is my first and only office. I bought the building in 1979 and have been here ever since. The old floor safe under my desk has been here almost that long. I had it installed right after I moved in."

"Good."

"Now," he said perfunctorily, "the plot has thickened. What's the deal with the box?"

"I'm taking this with me. I'm just showing it to you now, so you'll recognize it, later," she explained, turning her palms up, as if asking his understanding.

"Okay …" he said slowly and paused briefly, apparently to frame a question that she stymied by raising her hand, a non-verbal signal to bear with her and allow her to finish.

She smiled wryly. "I'm not leaving it, but after I've gone, you'll *have* it. Store the docs in it, and I'll use it to communicate so you know I'm … well."

Clark didn't comment, but Kiki saw doubt flicker across his face that was soon gone. As expected, she'd lost him.

"Is this where Captain Kirk and Scotty beam me up, or something?" he asked with a small chuckle.

Kiki closed her eyes and exhaled the deep breath she'd been holding.

"It is where the story gets a little fantastic, Clark," she admitted, and blushing a little. She smiled, and then leaned forward. "Look at me, look me in my eyes." Her tone had grown hushed, conspiratorial. "You know I'm not crazy, but after you hear me, you may wonder, at least temporarily. Don't worry; I take no offense. In your place, I'd hardly blame you, but I'm asking you to trust me, and hear me out. And after you do, I know we'll both believe that the impossible – fantastic as I know it sounds – is *possible*. And here's the clincher. I can *prove* it."

Without commenting, Clark Bannion had steepled the fingers of his hands together, resting his chin thoughtfully on them, considering her words and considering his response. Kiki liked it, thought it lent him a lawyerly, almost a scholarly look. Until that moment, she had never realized what a handsome, vigorous man he was. She'd never thought about him that way, although she knew everyone wondered why he'd never married. As long as she could remember, he mom had called Clark Bannion *the most eligible bachelor in Portland*. Over the years, many beautiful, intelligent women had been seen on his arm, but only briefly. None of them had shown any staying power. None of them had ever caught and reeled him in.

"I see a lot of your father in you, Kiki," he said softly. "I have no doubt he'd be very proud of you," he added, meaning it.

"Thank you, hearing that means a lot to me."

"Excuse me a moment," he said, and pulled open the bottom drawer of his desk on the right. Reaching in he brought a bottle of very old and very rare The Macallan, and then two cut crystal double old-fashioned glasses, placing them on his desk between them. "A gift from him, years ago, after your *brush with the law*. Ridiculous how much he paid for it. I'm not a Scotch drinker, he knew that, of course, but he said it would make me a believer. And he was right, and that tickled him. He loved being right, especially with me. Since then I've kept it for the most special of special occasions and there have only been two, until now." He sighed, and breathing deeply before continuing, asked, "Would you join me? I've got this feeling what I'm about to hear qualifies."

Relieved that he wasn't dismissing her out of hand, she nodded and relaxed. She'd turned twenty-one last December, and considering the tale she was about to tell, a dose of liquid courage wasn't a bad idea. Using his thumbs, Clark gently eased the top from the bottle with real reverence, smiling all the while. Then he spun around in his chair to a small humidor on a credenza behind his desk and held up a Macanudo Ascot, as if asking her permission. Aficionados might have called it a small smoke, but it was just enough for him.

"If it bothers you, I'll open a window," he told her, not quite apologizing. "I love a good cigar with whisky like this," he confessed.

"No problem," she replied, "just get comfortable."

"OK, Kiki," Clark said, and a short while later with two fingers of great Scotch in their glasses, and with the first series of impressive smoke rings drifting to the open beam rafters of the ceiling above them, settle back in the old chair that seemed molded to his shape, and asked, "Why don't you tell me the story."

~~~~~

For the next thirty minutes, Clark listened intently, without interrupting or asking a single question. His face was impassive, offering no clue as to whether he believed her or not. Kiki had begun by recounting all that she remembered about returning home, and what she'd encountered when she did. Then she moved on to the two visitations from The Guardian and shared her initial doubts as well as the great hopes she harbored for what she planned.

Kiki concluded her monologue with the nuts and bolts of what she intended to do and what she needed from him while she was away doing it. It was after this that Clark Bannion let out a deep breath and asked his first question.

"Let me see if I've got this straight," he said, and sipped his whisky. "You're going back to 1981 and the objective, summarized, is to alter Little Mo Biggs' future. With that accomplished, by ...

rescuing him from his fate, you believe that the tragedy that has befallen your family will be … corrected. Is that right?"

"I'd say that in classic lawyerly fashion, you've distilled it neatly," Kiki answered, "forgive the whisky pun; it was unintentional and just came out that way."

He dismissed that with a wave of his hand.

"Another question, then," he continued. "I assume that the "proof" is the bracelet or whatever?" When she nodded vigorously, he followed with another. "May I see it?"

She was wearing a stylish sweater jacket with long sleeves that covered her wrist. Pushing up the left sleeve, she extended her hand towards him.

"Do you see it?" she asked.

"Maybe, but no, not really," he answered, and looked puzzled.

"Keep watching," she replied casually. "The truth is, until I work it, for lack of a better way to phrase it, I don't always see it, either, most of the time. Even so, I can always *feel* it. When my fingers touch what I call the face, it morphs, turns on, or whatever, and the control panel and buttons appear, like this," and she demonstrated how it worked for him.

This really got his attention and he stood up, wide-eyed and amazed at what he saw.

"Maybe you should be sitting down for this next part," she said seriously.

After setting the date and time on the bracelet to today's date, thirty-one years ago, a three dimensional image was projected from it that appeared to sit atop Clark's desk. The effect was somewhere between holographic image and some kind of cinematic special effect, and came with astounding resolution and clarity.

"My God," he gasped, "I never would have believed it, but I believe it now. It's my office, there's no doubt about that, only it's my office over thirty years ago. I recognize the old furniture and that hideous painting I hung up. And there *I* am. Christ, was I ever so young?"

"I can't believe I'll be meeting *you* – and working with you – back there, and back then," Kiki said. "So, now you know."

"Now, I know."

"Tell me what you think."

"My head is spinning, but for now we'll leave it at we need to meet again, right away. Tomorrow, but this time we should include Jenna. Not only to prepare her for what she'll do while you're back there, but also to prepare all of us in ways you may not have considered. I'll also see what I can come up with on Morris Biggs Jr. and send it to you."

Chapter Nine

THE NEXT MORNING, Kiki, Jenna and Clark Bannion met in his Southwest Portland office, but this time they weren't gathered around his desk. The two young women sat side-by-side on a couch reserved for more casual conferences, with Clark swallowed-up in an overstuffed club chair at a right angle to it. On a coffee table he confessed had belonged to his parents – pointing to initials he'd carved in it when he was seven – was a stainless carafe of coffee on a tray with cream, sugar, Splenda and saccharine he claimed a few old school purist clients insisted upon.

Clark noted that physically, the two young women couldn't have been more different looking. Jenna was petite, no more than five foot two. Kiki was at least half a foot taller. And while Kiki was fair, with light brown hair and blue eyes, Jenna had dark eyes, short jet-black hair and an olive complexion. Kiki had a slim and lithe figure, Jenna was voluptuous and curvy.

Clark had set the agenda for this meeting, building it around the requests Kiki had made in the documents she'd provided the day before.

He spent the first half-hour covering them.

"To summarize," he continued, offering the girls more coffee before refilling his mug, "Jenna managing your affairs is a minor matter. A few items to sign and we're ready for that."

"I'm sensing a "But" coming," Kiki said. "What is it?"

"Insuring you'll be able to function back then. The good news is that government, banking procedures and recordkeeping were far less sophisticated thirty years ago. But that doesn't mean we can't expect issues if you appear without adequate documentation. A plus is that Identity Theft existed but bore little resemblance to today's epidemic and there was no Patriot Act that mandated additional layers of verification."

"What then?" she asked.

"You'll be appearing out of nowhere, with nothing, with zero history. We'll have to somehow create an identity with enough hard copy items to allow you to function as you'll need to. For example, what you'll need to get a Driver's License, open a bank account, apply for a job, or rent an apartment. Obviously, we can't send money back with you, because it looks different today, and we can't wire transfer funds back in time. Fortunately, documents won't be examined as closely as they are today, and the world wasn't yet computerized with everything on-demand. The likelihood is that your documents won't be crosschecked against the issuing agencies, either. I don't remember that they did anything like that in those days. My point is that while your documents don't have to be perfect, they have to be good enough in order to pass a casual bureaucratic look and be rubber stamped."

Jenna hadn't said much thus far, but seized the moment to speak up.

"I think I can help with some of it," she started.

"What are you thinking?" Clark asked.

"I can research how basic docs looked then, and … make Photo Shop do a lot of tricks."

"I'm grateful," Kiki said, "and should apologize."

"For what?" Jenna asked.

"For ensnaring you in my criminal web before you've even graduated college, gone to law school, or applied to the FBI, as I sweetly lure you into participation in illegal enterprises. That goes for Clark, too."

"I wouldn't worry about it," he commented.

"Why is that?" Jenna asked.

"Think about it logically, it's simple, really. *How* would they prosecute an illegal act committed more than thirty years in the future using a technology they couldn't possibly understand by someone who hasn't been born yet?

With that, the three erupted into simultaneous laughter.

"Finally," Kiki said, wiping her eyes.

"Finally … *what*?" Clark asked.

"Finally *something* in all this is logical, that's what."

"By the way, girls, I think the criminal aspects of all this are the last thing we have to worry about."

"Your lawyer is your partner in crime, so you can always sue me for malpractice. If it goes bad, we'll all go to the slammer together!"

They all laughed again and Clark continued.

"Okay, Jenna, do your research and let's see what you come up with. Afterwards, we'll confer about exactly what we'll need. I've got a few ideas on that subject. If there is something you can't find I may be able to help with copies from some of my old files. You may want to consider using an out of state Driver's License for Kiki, like California They're turned in routinely by newcomers to Oregon and in those days there were so many no one thought twice about it. She won't have to take a driving test, either."

Jenna nodded enthusiastically and made some notes on her own legal pad, as Clark turned his attention back to Kiki. "Any thoughts about money?" he asked.

"I think so, an idea I was planning on running by you."

"Go ahead."

"I've got my grandmother's diamond engagement ring and matching earrings Grandpa bought her for her seventy-fifth birth-day. Mom's most prized possessions; she had them for over twenty-five years. They are much more than family heirlooms, Mom had them appraised for insurance purposes and they're worth a for-tune. She vowed to never sell them, but it would be so easy to take them with me. If I sold them back there, I could deposit the money into a bank account. Wouldn't that work?"

"It should," Clark answered thoughtfully, stroking his chin.

"What?"

"Let me think about how and where you should do it."

"Maybe you'll get them back, after everything has been cor-rected," Jenna volunteered cheerfully.

"That's a pleasant thought, but you should slow down, Jenna. We're getting a little ahead of ourselves," Kiki said and gave her friend's hand a quick squeeze.

"Now, what?" she asked, turning to Clark who had again fallen silent, stroking his chin. "I recognize the wheels turning in your head."

"You'll need my help back there."

"How?"

"Will the device, in the past, allow you to show him – me – our time, now? God, hearing that come out of my mouth, it sounded so convoluted I almost confused myself – do you know what I mean, did it make any sense?"

"It does. I'd like to answer your question, but have no idea if the device will work in reverse, but I'll find out soon enough. I *think* it should, I'm assuming it will or I couldn't come back. I do have an idea, though," Kiki said.

"Let's hear it."

"You could write yourself a letter that I'll deliver …to you. God, that sounds weird, too. The letter should include something that only you could know and maybe include a photograph that he'll recognize as legitimate while we blow his – *your* – mind with something you haven't seen … yet. Now I'm sounding like you did," she said unable to suppress a giggle. "And I'm getting a little dizzy trying to keep everything straight in my head. Did all that make sense to you guys?"

"As much as any of this does," Clark replied, and made another note on a yellow legal pad. Having filled up a page he'd started a new one.

Jenna spoke up. "I don't suppose there is any way for a cell phone to work across time," she ventured.

Clark shook his head. "No cell towers, besides, the technology was new; no networks, no products and no users, so it wouldn't matter, because from there you won't be able to send or receive," Clark said.

"That's right, I should have known that."

Clark shrugged it away. "Not really, maybe it's not so obvious. How do we know? How could we know since we've never played this game … hopefully, talking it through builds a safety net of some kind, but I see communication as a one-way street: You'll be able to use the box to contact us but, unless I'm missing something, I see no way for us to reach you."

"At least the box gives some kind of connection. I know I'll be cut-off from everyone and everything. It's scary. I'll leave at that for now. Living back there means I'll be making a lot of adjustments to a world without cell phones, long before computers were commonplace tools, no Internet and a decade before information became such a fundamental part of our consciousness and everyday lives. They had VCRs and microwaves, at least. Okay, what else?"

"This may be a minor issue, but I think it's important for you to look the part and fit in, without drawing attention to yourself. You know, stuff like clothes, shoes, hair styles, those sorts of things," Jenna said. "There are also colloquial idiosyncrasies that would be their own red flag. The things we can identify and prepare you for."

"That's a good point, I'm impressed," Clark agreed, "and presented like an argument from a future attorney. How will you handle that?" he asked Kiki.

"Actually, that's an easy one. We can research what we need to know online. And Jenna and I will do a little shopping at vintage clothing stores. There are some on 23rd Street and over in the Hawthorne District, aren't there, Jenna?"

"I love those stores and if we can't find what we need there, we'll hit the thrift shops."

~~~~~

The next day the two young women spent most of a gorgeous early summer day haunting shops and boutiques for clothing and shoes that would fit into the fashion world of 1981. Punk was wildly popular then, but that wasn't Kiki's style. Thanks to First Lady Nancy Reagan, and more to her taste, the color red had staged a major comeback, along with shoulder pads and bold stripes.

Designer jeans had legitimized dungarees as a staple for nearly everyone, the big brands were Calvin Klein, Gloria Vanderbilt and Sassoon, Jenna informed Kiki, who thought the ones she already had might do. Emerging shoe brands like Nike, Adidas,

Reebok and New Balance were reinventing athletic and casual footwear.

They enlisted a helpful and earnest sales clerk who happened to own the shop.

Her name was Anna Fischer, a refugee from the Garment District in Manhattan. She named her store *Timeless Duds*, and really got into the spirit of their quest with a number of helpful suggestions after Jenna explained that Kiki would be attending a *Retro-Costume Party for the Ages*. Anna told them that while there was an abundance of some items, others were gone forever.

"Some things were never designed to last for long," she said somewhat sheepishly.

"Pre-planned obsolescence isn't a new idea; it's always been in fashion."

Jenna whispered to Kiki they'd either have to get creative or she would have to fill-in the gaps with a little shopping once she arrived in the past.

"You'll have some real fun online, just Google *Eighties Fashion* and you'll find pages and pages of listings," she told them. "There are new ones all the time, and some amazing costume websites you can shop that sell practically anything and everything. I browse them regularly. Many of the items that I stock are things I've found in places I never expected."

"That's the secret weapon when it comes to the Internet," Jenna agreed. "Drill down deeper, you'll never know what you might discover!"

"I just had a thought about shoes," Jenna said. "Converse All-Stars, the canvass shoes, haven't changed, so that might work for starters."

"Great idea," Kiki said. "I've already got a pair of black ones."

With their shopping finished, they stopped for a slice of pizza at *Escape from New York*, a Portland institution with Bay Area roots that for years had offered authentic New York-style wedge slices and pies out of a cramped storefront.

New Yorkers would have approved.

"A good day's work," Kiki said. "I'd say we really accomplished a lot.

"Shopping is never work," Jenna countered, playfully.

"That's true, isn't it? What's next?" Kiki asked. "I know how your mind works, you're always thinking ahead."

"Guilty as charged. I've got a great idea for us when we get all these things back to your house. We'll relax with a glass of wine and then it will be time for me to give you background information and some critical need-to-know education."

"What kind of education?"

"A look back at history, with a heavy emphasis on pop culture," Jenna smiled. "I know you'll find lots of it interesting," she added with a mischievous grin.

Kiki smiled back. "It seems like ancient history. We weren't even born then."

Chapter Ten

BEFORE THEY COULD BEGIN, **Kiki's phone chimed an incoming text message.**
"It's from Clark," she told Jenna, and read it aloud.

Attached is Little Mo's medical record.
FWIW, the only record I could find.
A little odd, but so is all of this, hmm?
Horrific stuff, but it explains a lot.
Still digging into Morris, Sr.
Let's meet tomorrow.
Clark

Clark hadn't undersold the account of six-year old Morris Biggs Jr.'s visit to the ER late in the summer of 1982. Kiki gasped, shaking her head more than once while reading it. Once finished, she handed her phone to Jenna, who grimaced as she read it.

"That poor child, he was so young! Well, now we have a good idea how an innocent little boy was turned into a killer," Jenna said.

"This is heartbreaking. The doctor's comments really condemn the father, don't they? That explains why The Guardian told me I'd have to go back to the root. God knows what Clark may turn-up about him. Okay – let's talk about life in Portland, thirty-one years ago."

"I know you've spent a lot of time looking at 1981, getting a visual feel as we did with Clark in his office, and that's a good thing," Jenna began. "But –"

"It's not enough," Kiki finished for her. "So what do you think, I need to know."

"Obviously, I'm no expert on the subject. I realize these are uncharted waters, but I think you – we – can do this. It should be okay," her friend said, trying to look convinced saying it.

"I'm worried it will be nowhere as easy as we'd like to think," Kiki said. "Are you?"

"Yeah, because it's not your time, maybe that's no big deal, but maybe it's a real big deal. Doesn't it seem reasonable to expect some culture shock? Isn't it possible you won't fit in? People, and the way they lived – everything was different. Even if you aren't a stranger in a strange land, there is the problem of fitting in to do what you're going to do. It's not your time."

"I'll find a way, I have to. Talking as little and listening as much as possible, at first."

"Preparation has to be the key, and approaching history, differently, with a real vested interest, that should matter," Jenna added thoughtfully. "We need to understand how to help you avoid saying or doing something that makes you stand-out in the wrong way to the wrong person at the wrong time. To me, that would seem to be the biggest risk."

"I'm wondering about that, too, another reason to listen and learn and say as little as possible ... starting by listening to your ideas. It can only help me."

Jenna smiled thinly and began. "You're going back to late summer, the end of August 1981, which was an interesting year from a historical standpoint. This was only the beginning of the age of consumer technology and the computer age had not yet begun in earnest. The signs were there, but it was still years away. IBM had just introduced the first PC and Microsoft was just unveiling MS-DOS, so it was before Windows became the user-interface of choice. The primary competitor was the Commodore 64, long forgotten. Compared to what we see as appliances or commodities we take for granted today, most people didn't even *have* computers, and those that did knew them as machines that were enormous in size but low-powered without software and applications to do much. Mostly geeks, not mainstream like it is today."

"I can see how technology could trip me up," Kiki said, "we take so much for granted today, and none of it existed over thirty years ago."

"On that subject, the term, *Internet*, was used for the first time that year. But its origin, as you know, was educational institutions at first, and then extended by the military and scientific communities. Moving on, 1981 was also the year the space shuttle Columbia, the first reusable spacecraft, made its first voyage. The Titanic had been located, and Sandra Day O'Connor became the first woman Supreme Court Justice.

"The Seventies had just ended, the Eighties would be known for *Big Hair*. A lot of forgettable bands, but many of the heavy metal bands endured and many years later had become mainstream. Back then, no one would have imagined Led Zeppelin selling Cadillacs. Many of the big bands from the Sixties and Seventies were still rocking. I envy your chance to see some of them in their relative youth – and prime. Punk was in and spearheaded serious fashion departures from the past. We know about jeans – and designer jeans were the rage, and real spendy. There was a famous ad campaign that featured Brooke Shields who was a teenager at the time: *Nothing comes between me and my Calvin's* was a marketing classic and a huge success."

"I heard about it in freshman marketing class, celebrity spokespeople were hot," Kiki remembered, "and marketers were just beginning to tap their power beyond what it had been. The campaign pushed suggestive limits. Compared to the rest of the world we've always been so parochial."

"We've got to get your shoes right. Athletic shoes, running shoes were fashion must-haves, and becoming the footwear of choice, but other than that, women's shoes sported three-inch block heels, and leg warmers were wildly popular. To find those you might have to do some shopping when you … arrive. We can outfit you in advance with jeans that will pass, but the shoes are another story … although at the *Timeless Duds* shop you mentioned your Converse All-Stars. We see in all kinds of wild colors today, but back then it was only black or white. Didn't you say you have a pair of blacks?"

"I did, I do."

"Nice. Okay, 1981 was a time of high inflation, 10.35%. The country had suffered through a recession and an oil embargo that had just ended. Comparatively, gas was still cheap, $1.25 a gallon, *after* the embargo. Minimum wage was $2.75 an hour. Imagine trying to live on that! Interest rates ranged between 15-20%, derailing Jimmy Carter and bringing in the Ronald Reagan era. He ran on things like "trickle-down economics" and a "new conservatism" but ultimately, in the eight years that followed, did a number of things that current members of his party would revile, like raising the debt ceiling after lowering tax rates and increasing spending,"

"Ironic and fascinating, but nothing I'll talk about," Kiki commented. "I plan on ignoring politics and trying to avoid referring to things I know that haven't happened, yet."

"Exactly, and resist the temptation to make a killing with big sports bets or stocks," Jenna said jokingly.

"Yeah, right ... out of curiosity, where was the Dow back then?" Kiki asked.

"From my research it was hovering around 875, isn't that incredible? These days, if it sinks under 10,000 traders are lining up to jump off the ledge."

"It's all relative, I guess. What else?"

"Lots of other interesting tidbits I hope will give you additional context. Diana had just married Prince Charles. It would be months before Britney Spears was born."

"Wow."

"AIDS had just been identified, but the epidemic was only getting started. American Airlines introduced the first Frequent Flyer program. A 19" color television cost around $399. It's interesting that consumer electronics are the one commodity that over all the years and despite inflation and all that, where we get more today for the same price or even less. 3M invented *Post-it Notes* – by accident. MTV was launched, and along with it came music videos. No CDs yet, and certainly no DVDs. The first VCR for the general public was Sony's Betamax in 1975. The VHS format came shortly after and won the battle. By the end of the Eighties, 70% of homes in America owned a VCR.

"People were watching dramas like Baywatch, Knight Rider, MacGyver and Hill Street Blues on television. The most popular comedies were Cosby – I'm not sure which one, he's had so many

– Cheers and Golden Girls. Monday Night Football had become an institution on ABC, although it's moved to ESPN now. This is an example of the nuances you should be careful with, the little things that could trip you up. ESPN was in its infancy; even industry insiders had their doubts about its viability. Cable television was growing, but the number of choices was a fraction of what we have today. Satellite networks hadn't yet exploded and small dishes for consumers were many years away. Dishes sat on the ground and were ten feet wide back then."

"I need to think less, not more, don't I?" Kiki asked.

Jenna nodded. "And be aware of language, slang, I mean. It's a funny thing about language; some words are still with us, but others are long gone."

"Can you give me some examples?" Kiki asked.

"Sure, awesome is a great one. So are others like stoked, dude, rush. Others that were commonly used then are more dated today, like Mondo, bitchin', righteous, tubular and gnarly. And there are two words you should avoid."

"Which words?"

"Hacker was a term used in the computer industry by insiders, until a Newsweek article in 1983. And Yuppie didn't come along until a year later in '84."

"You've done a great job with this, Jenna," Kiki said, praising her efforts. "I'm grateful."

Her friend shrugged. "There's more for us to do today, we aren't finished."

"What's next?"

"So far we've focused on giving you the right look, historical grounding and cultural context. That was easy, legal, and straight forward … unlike your identity, which isn't. This is trickier."

"I take it I'm about to see the fruits of your first criminal labors," Kiki joked, but neither of them laughed. The fact was there was really nothing funny about it, and if things went wrong because of it, her journey to the past could be difficult in ways she dreaded thinking about.

~~~~~

Next, Jenna showed Kiki what she had been working on.

She reached into a leather satchel on the floor and pulled out a large manila envelope. Opening it, she turned it upside down, and four innocuous looking business-sized envelopes spilled out of it onto the coffee table.

From the first one, she withdrew a California Driver's License. It was laminated with Kiki's picture and looked totally authentic.

From the second came an ordinary looking Social Security card that didn't look brand new, showing years of storage, and a slight curl at one corner.

The third envelope contained a notarized Certificate of Live Birth, also from California, high school and college transcripts, and a resume that looked right and showed her recent employment history.

Jenna pushed the fourth envelope off to the side, where it remained unopened. It was plumper that the others and she explained. "I can't send files on a thumb drive, there's no way for you to read them or print them out. So to be on the safe side, this envelope contains original copies of everything I've created and shown you. Make sure you take good care of it."

All of the items were in the name of Elaine Marie McCann, twenty-four years old.

"Nice to meet you, Elaine Marie," Jenna said playfully, as Kiki looked over the items before her, clearly impressed by the quality.

"You can call me Lainie. Exactly how *did* you manage all this?" she asked.

"Clark and I discussed each item," Jenna began. "He's been amazing, by the way. We assessed the risks, taking into account the degree of sophistication of government, educational and financial systems and procedures of the time."

"I don't see a credit card, that wasn't possible?"

Jenna shook her head. "Too risky – there is no way to provide that now, from here."

"I'm not surprised."

"Clark and I discussed that, too. We have no way to create an active account. On the other hand, we could tap static aspects of the past and create what you'll need to open a bank account and get one. We've given you what we're as confident as possible can be provided safely. Much of it comes from the Internet, of course. I was able to research how items looked back then, that was easy, and then print copies or recreate them if I had to. Thank God we're living in the digital age. Laser printers, Photoshop, and a cheap laminator from Office Depot made it quick and easy.

"I could have hacked into DMV, but we decided it wasn't necessary. I did hack into the high school and college registrar's offices, to create your records. Employers on your resume are out of business. The only risk – and it's a slight one – is you aren't in the high school yearbook, but it's a remote chance that you run into someone who would remember, know or care."

Kiki said, "I'm sure you're right, but there's no way to do this without taking a few chances."

"That's just what Clark said, more than once. We do the best we can, and protect ourselves by limiting the exposure to areas less likely to blow-up on us."

"My dad used to say that success in life requires luck on top of everything else, but I doubt he had anything like this in mind," Kiki said wryly. "But his point is well taken and we're due for a little luck. Have you been able to research Morris Biggs, Sr.? I need to know what happened to Little Mo's mother, how she died, and the impact that had on her son that led to the man I … met."

"No, when I met with Clark the day before yesterday we talked about the best way to handle it. We agreed that it made sense to divvy up the research and for me to concentrate on the background and identity pieces. He volunteered to research the history of the Biggs family, and I'm glad for the help. Besides, his legal entrée may open some doors that I couldn't."

Kiki grunted her agreement, and was about to say something when the brief silence in the room was shattered by Jenna's cell-phone notifying her of a new text message.

Jenna glanced at it, looked up, and said, "Speak of the devil. Clark wants to see us first thing in the morning."

"Did he say anything else?"

"Just that he's found some interesting stuff and is excited to show it to us. He'll provide bagels and coffee. The man thinks of practically everything, and has sure made my job easier. I can see why he and your dad were such great friends and why you love him. He's special."

Chapter Eleven

THE AROMA OF FRESHLY BREWED COFFEE **hit them immediately upon entering Clark's office.**
"It reminds me how hungry I am," Kiki said. "Dad used to have bagels and coffee with Clark once a week, for years, as long I can remember," she added wistfully.

Tracie Running, Clark's trusted assistant for over thirty years, from the very beginning, waved them right in and moments later appeared with a tray of bagels, cream cheese, and a small tub of a white fish spread that she explained had become her boss's latest culinary addiction.

"Clark loves it so much that he no longer sends me out for lox. Okay, we've got onion, poppy seed, sesame seed, or cinnamon-raisin bagels from Kettleman's. They're fresh, I stopped for them on my way in to work, but I can toast them for you if you like," she offered.

Just then Clark swept in, face flushed with energy. His eyes were sparkling, and he was unable to contain his excitement. Despite all this, he gave the girls some unsolicited advice.

"Toast 'em!" he said, shrugging out of his suit jacket and draping it casually over the back of his high leather chair.

"Why? They're soft and fresh, still warm!" Jenna protested.

"That's true. These bagels are the real deal and delicious just like they are, but toasted, and with a little whitefish spread on top of the cream cheese? That's the bagel art, perfected!"

Kiki and Jenna took his advice, and they were soon all munching contentedly.

Wiping his mouth with a paper napkin, Clark broke the silence. "Before showing me the identity docs that Jenna's created, let me tell you what I've learned about the Biggs family. Fair to say they have an interesting history, especially the father, Big Mo."

"I'm curious how you did it," Jenna commented. I spent a couple of hours looking into it before we met the other day and had no luck at all. Little Mo's medical report tells us it's all about his dad. What I don't understand – still, about Little Mo – is how that could be the only record we can find of a man of his age. It seems ... impossible."

"Not really, there are logical reasons for it," Clark replied. "Thirty-one years is a long time, and it predated the digital migration. Thanks to the Internet, most everything that happens today will be captured, somewhere, but not so when we're talking about the past. How far back they digitized is a factor of time, money, and when they made their transition. Most organizations were forced to draw an arbitrary drop-dead date, even law enforcement, government, court records, etc. That meant orphaning all the documents and records before that date to musty basements and dusty storage warehouses. Many were lost, destroyed or shredded long ago."

"Apparently, you found a way around all that," Kiki said, genuinely impressed.

"I'd love you to think I'm Superman, but I'm not. I had lots of help. My old friend, Elliot Rose, is Chief of Detectives for the Portland Police Bureau. *He* has access to nearly everything. Beyond PPB, municipal, county and state records, he's well connected with senior FBI officials and those boys are linked to most every database on earth. Elliot made a couple of phone calls to some senior intelligence analyst pal of his in Miami. He came up with a lot."

"Once again, it's who you know," Kiki said. Your text, yesterday, and the way you flew in this morning, I could see you are with the news. Let's hear it. What did he find out?"

"The Biggs family has lived in Oregon – Portland – since the late Sixties, but originally came here from St. Louis. Milton Biggs, Big Mo's father and Little Mo's grandfather, moved the family to Oregon in the summer of 1969. Big Mo would have been nineteen at the time and, piecing things together, was a rebellious kid, none too happy about the family relocating to the West Coast. In the end, it would appear that it worked out well for him. No fatal legal trouble and he ended up with a business.

"Here's what happened. Milton Biggs had worked for Anheuser-Busch all his life, as a warehouse man and truck driver. Other than his longevity, there was nothing noteworthy about his career, and as far as we can tell, AB was his only employer in Missouri. He apparently worked part-time for the brewery during high school. In all those years, Milton never advanced beyond the laborer ranks, but maybe he never sought more than that. He was content and a solid worker that never caused any trouble."

"Then why did the family move?"

"It seems his son, Morris, was a wild, unmotivated, not overly bright kid growing up during turbulent times. The Sixties were much more than assassinations and Viet Nam. It was a time of challenging everything – pushing hard against the conformity growing out of the Fifties after World War II and the Great Depression. Not just college kids got the headlines, but tough, savvy, working class kids, all rumbled with the system. By the time Morris Biggs Sr. got his driver's license he already had a record. Nothing big, the charges included underage drinking, a citation for disorderly conduct at a high school dance that was dismissed to keep it quiet, and a couple of fights. Then, senior year, at eighteen, he got expelled. A prom night went terribly wrong and his path took a life-changing turn. Staying on his rebellious path, he chose the darker fringes and never turned back."

"By darker, do you mean criminal?" Kiki asked.

"No, not really, a better way to put it might be calling it his vocational lifestyle direction. Later, he did get involved with criminal stuff, but that came *after* the event. There was a big prom night party at the vacation home of one of his classmates. A girl died that night, but the case was murky from the start and maybe bungled. She was apparently a wild one with her own history, so it never developed beyond a high school tragedy of a kid perceived as already on a self-destructive path. There was no doubt she'd been through some rough stuff, but investigators viewed it as a group-grope. They were never able to pin it on anyone, so it went away. Nearly eighty people were at this party, and everyone there was questioned. No one was charged. The juveniles skated through, but older guys like Big Mo who were eighteen at the time, were talked to – officially – and the records of those interrogations made it into the system.

"Maybe Milton Biggs felt guilt about being a shitty dad and responsible for his son turning out to be a fuck-up and only getting worse. Milton was no great brain but did know a change of scene was needed for Morris. He was right about that, but failed to understand what the West Coast was all about in those days. Portland, like the rest of the cities in Western Oregon, was comparatively tolerant. The living was easy and with plenty of drugs, kids into having a good time, and an already thriving sub-culture where urban hippies could find jobs without *copping to The Man*, as they used to call it.

"This was a hugely popular choice, and the hip choice. All across America, but few places more than in Oregon, people on the fringes, if they didn't push it, were left alone and could find a way to get along. In the decades since then, most of them found their way back to the mainstream and have been reintegrated. But to this day, in Oregon and throughout the West, a fair number are still *livin' the dream up-country* or in the shadows and largely off the grid."

"Were there any serious legal problems in Morris's future?" Kiki asked.

"Not much, another DUI and a disorderly conduct. He was running with a wild bunch that grew pot back in the hills and sold it up and down the Willamette Valley. In a couple of cases he was noted as a Person of Interest. Mostly down-played, at least according to one file that called it small-time chump-stuff, with no real volume, so they didn't stay with it long, and those traffickers managed to stay out of jail despite failing to stay off law enforcement's radar. So, in the end, Big Mo's old man changed careers, paying his parental penance by giving his son something to do."

"Do you know why he chose Oregon?"

"Yeah, it was work. When he brought the family to Oregon a job was waiting at the old Blitz-Weinhard Brewery in Portland, driving for them. This was the original Oregon brewery, by the way, and some of the brands are still around, although they've since been swallowed up in consolidation deals. If I recall, they sold first to Pabst in 1979, but now are owned by Miller. Anyway, Milton Biggs wasn't with Blitz long, by '79 he'd been gone for years.

He'd cashed out his retirement in the mid-Seventies and used a big chunk of it to buy a landscaping company," Clark sat back and took a breath.

Kiki spoke up.

"Easy to see why it made sense for them. Big Mo was living on the fringes and earning his living in the underground economy. His father was giving him an option that was best for everyone. Big Mo gets a job without ever having to worry about an application, resume, record, references or any work history whatsoever. His dad gets to pay parental penance and more than keep a close eye on him; rein him in – as much as was possible – and in the process his son gets more of a chance than he ever could have had without it."

"Exactly. Working in the family's landscaping business became his career. In '76, Big Mo married Teddie West, the bookkeeper and office manager. She was six years older, in her early thirties, and he may have knocked her up. Little Mo was born less than five months later."

"Was it a forced marriage?" Kiki asked.

Clark shrugged. "Something like that, I'd say. Regardless, Big Mo avoided serious trouble after that, and apparently learned enough to run the business effectively when his father died of a heart attack on the job in the early eighties. The circumstances, by the way, are more than mildly interesting to me. The cops and the Medical Examiner looked at it because it was work related. A few questions were raised, but despite the old man having no prior history of heart trouble it went nowhere. The funeral was … quick."

'In itself, that might not mean anything," Jenna offered, "there are many religions with traditions that like to get 'em in the ground right away and move on."

"That's true," Clark admitted, "but Morris Biggs isn't what you'd call a spiritual dude. Anyway, I'm not editorializing. I'm just reporting what I've learned without judging it."

"I get that," Kiki replied. "Still, I'm not so sure we should totally dismiss part of the profile of a man who, the more we learn about him, the uglier he is. Breaking the law didn't faze him and there's ample reason for us to believe he had the capacity for violence."

"Which is a perfect segue, thank you," Clark responded. "The next five years – the first five years of Morris Junior's life, are revealing. The landscaping business wasn't exactly highly rated by the Better Business Bureau. There were complaints from a number of angry customers about workmanship, completion, and billing. Many turned into small claims suits. Big Mo won some and lost some, but there's a pattern. There were labor disputes, too. Employees not being paid in a timely fashion, stiffed for overtime, quarterly taxes and reports were lax and late. On a similar front, the business wasn't a favorite with its creditors; there were issues there, as well."

"That surprises me," Jenna commented. "Big Mo had inherited what appears to have been a thriving enterprise, *and* married the bookkeeper – the office manager, right? You'd think Teddie would have had a handle on all that."

"Don't forget it was Big Mo's business and he wasn't what you'd call the prototypical successful business operator. He also may never have been fated for happily wedded bliss, or wanted it, for that matter. He probably dominated her, abused her, forced her to do things and when he ultimately tired of her, or she balked, and he lost control of her, decided it was time to act. Nothing I've found shows even a shred of affection or admiration for the man. He was gruff, crude and disinterested in winning friends or influencing people. And, if he married Teddie because he had to, the marriage may have been doomed from the start."

"Maybe he resented Little Mo," Kiki said softly. "Just how did his mother die?"

"In a fall, a freak accident," Clark answered.

"A fall," Kiki repeated tonelessly. "Do you believe it?"

"More than thirty years later it's hard not to … but it's clear you have doubts."

"Even if we pass on the possibility that Milton Biggs' death wasn't natural causes, we'd have to be blind to miss the pattern that's developing with this man. Teddie's death could have been a convenient end to what might have been a loveless, forced marriage, saddling him with a kid he didn't want. Do we know any more about the marriage? Did you find any record of a domestic complaint?"

"Only one, very minor in late summer… let me check my notes," he said and flipped back a few pages on his yellow legal pad. "Yeah, here it is. Late May of 1981 and it wasn't filed by Teddie, but by a neighbor," Clark replied. "Portland cops appeared at the door, and asked the predictable questions of the husband and wife. The report says they claimed that it was nothing more than a highly spirited shouting match that got out of control. Big Mo also claimed that the neighbors were nosy busybodies who let their dog roam and shit on his lawn, and had always had it in for them. Nonetheless, he apologized and they promised to keep it down. The cops left and there was nothing after that."

"Except for the fact that Teddie's days were numbered," Jenna said.

"Less than three months later, Teddie Biggs was dead. How and where did it happen, Clark?" Kiki asked.

"She died after a fall, in a public park."

"What happened?" The two girls asked at the same time.

"You know the old stone staircases amidst the trails that go up into Washington Park above downtown Portland?" He asked.

"I've spent a lot of time in Washington Park over the years," Kiki said. "Mom and I used to drive up to see the roses every year." Kiki said in a voice that was barely audible and sounded wounded by the memory. Jenna reached over and put her hand on Kiki's shoulder. "She and Dad took me to see Boz Scaggs in concert there last summer. I …"

"One of my favorite places, too," Clark said, adding, "And where Teddie Biggs died."

"How did she die?"

"Big Mo and Teddie had apparently been picnicking on Sunday afternoon. In a spot you reached using an old stone staircase. An absolutely gorgeous spot, but it's dangerous to get to. It's closed now and has been for a long time. At the end of the day, on their way up, she slipped and tumbled down the staircase, falling to the valley floor below. She broke her neck, and died at the scene, never regaining consciousness. It was tragic."

"Yeah, tragic, *and* convenient," Kiki said quietly.

Chapter Twelve

KIKI HAD ALWAYS SLEPT DEEPLY and well, often having wild and crazy dreams.
Often breathless upon awaking, and wondering where all *that* could have come from, she'd either be thankful for the entertainment or relieved to have finally escaped the show.

Not anymore. That was before.

At this moment, she thought, how ironic it was not to dream.

After coming home to a nightmare, she'd been living a dream ever since.

Now she felt trapped, like a stranger in her own sleep.

Sleep that, like everything else, had been redefined by the stunning cosmic shift delivered by Little Mo Biggs. These days she slept neither deeply or well. It was a restless and dreamless sleep that featured an undeniable tactile quality, full of vivid images, some of them familiar, others only vaguely so. Missing were the madcap events that used to entertain or frighten her. It made no sense, but at times she felt part of something greater that she didn't understand and couldn't understand.

All this she credited to The Guardian, to the remarkable bracelet around her left wrist, and how they connected her to something utterly fantastic: the opportunity for a second chance by leaving all that she knew. As much as she believed it, and wanted it, she couldn't shake her doubts. The promise of it suspended reality leaving her in a perpetual state of emotional limbo.

The responsibility was as overwhelming as the stakes were humbling and daunting. What Kiki did, or failed to do, would determine the future for so many. She welcomed the chance but had no confidence she was ready for it. How could she be? For Clark and Jenna she put on a brave, confident front. If only she felt way.

After the First Visitation her natural skepticism refused to allow her to totally buy in; instead challenging it, fighting it, and denying it. Her rational side stubbornly insisted losing her grip was a far more *reasonable* explanation: The attack, the injuries she sustained and the drugs used to treat them, the shock, and the horror were more likely the cause. There was more than ample reason to chalk it up to that in some combination contributing to a temporary insanity.

Then the Second Visitation changed everything.

After that, Kiki had no choice but to accept many things.

She did. But despite this, her doubts and fears refused to be permanently silenced.

One thing was inarguable: Her old life was gone, and along with it whatever innocence she might have still clung to. Plus, everything that would happen was beyond her life experience. Her old life had been constructed upon logical, unshakable pillars of truth, in a world that was comfortable, cozy, without mystery, allowing her to believe easily, even fiercely at times.

But all that was gone, replaced by new rules and new possibilities.

The starting point was total acceptance that what couldn't possibly be, absolutely was. It was hard to think about it and she tried not to. Thank God there was so much to do. It kept her from dwelling on things that she couldn't answer and added to her confusion and frustration.

She couldn't know how long she'd been asleep.

It might have been minutes, or hours, when she became aware of the arrival, sensing the presence, a change in the fabric, almost a subtle vibration perceived as much, or more, than it was felt.

She'd never *seen* The Guardian. Similarly, she was never quite sure if she was hearing him or if this was some sort of seamless, non-verbal psychic connection. Not that it mattered; The Guardian was here for her now.

"Hello Kiki. You've done well," The Guardian began, "and without any help from us. This is as it should be. We never know exactly what to expect of any of you, but I confess to my never doubting you."

She didn't know how to respond to that, and finally said, "Thank you. Something is bothering me," she began. "Actually, many things are bothering me but one thing in particular, so may I ask a question?"

"Of course. We can discuss anything you like."

"Okay ... I've never seen you."

"Don't be troubled by that, we're not ... physical."

"Okay," she said warily, not meaning it and sounding disappointed.

"How would you like me to appear? Like Charlton Heston in one of the old biblical movies, or as an older man in a long robe with a staff and flowing white hair and beard?"

"I just love it when my questions are answered with questions. Let me say I can't think of much that would make all of this less surreal, other than that. You understand it's a leap of faith for me to get this far, right?"

"Of course, I do."

"I want to ask another question ... Am I actually hearing you, or is it something else?" she asked.

"There is no speech. No one can hear our conversation."

Kiki sighed. "I get that I can't understand you and that's by design and your rules, or whatever. But I don't know what the rules are, who you are, what I can say or do or not, but, I want you to understand me."

When The Guardian didn't respond, she continued.

"Faith has never been a given for me, it's always been a mystery I couldn't quite figure out. Unsure more than unwilling, you could fairly say. Not that I don't appreciate The Gift. I do. Totally. If you insist that I believe in you, I will, I guess have to. What that means I don't know. If I never know, that's okay. You've never said anything. You never asked anything of me."

"And I won't. Nothing is demanded or required of you," The Guardian replied, "freely means freely, and is universally applied. Your faith, or whatever you choose to call it, whatever it is or isn't, however you apply it or don't, is your affair. The Gift comes to you without strings or conditions, physical or metaphysical."

She remembered feeling like this at times during the Second Visitation.

Like in some fashion he was unpeeling new layers of understanding. While at times that was encouraging, satisfaction always stopped short because it always led to still more layers.

"I don't want to appear ungrateful. Perhaps I should be glad you think I'm doing well, but instead what I feel is mixed up and horribly dissatisfied."

"You want an owner's manual, and, for lack of one, believe that in the very least you deserve instructions, a little guidance."

"Yes! That's it, exactly," she answered.

The Guardian had summed it up perfectly, and she was encouraged.

"There are forces that are beyond you, forces that are beyond all things. Forces in the universe that are accepted more than understood. Much of your frustration stems from your assumption that I transcend them, and transcend everything. I don't, nothing does. It's not like that. But don't be distraught by your natural predisposition for superpowers and supermen, for a storybook ending, and a magic bullet to cure the ills and evils of the universe. The fact that I've appeared to you with a second chance, isn't meant to signify anything greater than that."

"Sometimes I feel like I must be amusing entertainment for you guys."

"No offense was intended," was all he said in response to that.

"Well, just what am I supposed to do? I'd like to know, I need to know, what to expect. It seems a small and reasonable request."

"We can't help you with that, because it isn't known, it can't be known. There are some things that aren't meant to be known, what you think of as faith."

"I can't believe that you leave it all up to me."

"What will be is entirely up to you. You'll define it with your actions, and you'll act without any help from us."

Her eyes closed, Kiki wondered if The Guardian had said that with a celestial shrug

"Huh! I suppose that I have to hear this as your cryptic way of telling me that there's no Owner's Manual?

"That's one way to put it," The Guardian said, and she thought he almost chuckled, "as there are no rules, or limitations, either."

"I don't know how you expect me to react to that, but I'll tell you it doesn't help me."

He remained silent, and Kiki pressed. "Just what am I supposed to do?" She repeated, making no effort to conceal the exasperation she felt.

"Your heart and brain will sort that out."

"Not that I can do anything about it, but I feel like you talk in riddles, and my life – many lives – hang in in the balance, depending upon me. Again, I'm very grateful for the chance, I truly am. But how will I know what's right? Can't you give me a hint or two, a little nudge in the right direction? Is that really asking so much?"

"You'll discover that all you need to know will be revealed by the living of your life. Our role is only to provide you a chance, with a tool, and nothing more."

"I don't want to blow it. I've already lost my family once. The idea of losing them again because of my failure is terrifying," Kiki said in a tiny voice. "I'm not calling wolf. I know you won't – or can't – tell me who or what you are, but please, I need a little help."

"What you do, will be right."

"I wish I believed that."

"You can and you will."

"I just don't understand," she said shaking her head slowly.

"The natural order is that the Children of the Earth be allowed to live their lives freely, this means unfettered and not to be interfered with – especially by us."

"Why?"

"Man was given a world that he could mold to suit his hopes, dreams and ambitions. That world is today the product of countless generations, molding it to suit over all the past generations to suit, for better or worse. What humans have created, we can't fix. Your world is far too complex now and beyond our capacity or charge. You may fairly perceive this as a sad commentary on our capabilities, but that is true only in the narrowest of bands. Look beyond that to a reaffirmation of our commitment to mankind's unencumbered destiny."

"But, if you have a hands-off policy, what's the point? Why appear at all? Why not just leave it like that, like you said, to living our lives?"

"Mankind's missteps notwithstanding, we ultimately have high hopes. But despite our genuine affection, regrettably, it comes with

the certainty of a lottery ticket. The world man has invented invites abundant good and evil, and sadly, there is nothing we can do about that."

"At least we can agree that we've made a mess of it," Kiki said softly.

"I'm sure we'll find common ground on much more than that."

"Hopefully so," Kiki agreed.

The Guardian continued. "You must accept there are reasons that bad things happen, and those reasons are often not understood. Good, evil and indifference aside, life's quixotic nature affects so many disproportionately. It is both random and unjust. And while we can't eliminate that, or transform the world into paradise, we can do more than simply sit back and watch idly."

"At times it's hard to have faith, I hope you understand that. So you do what you can?" Kiki asked.

"We discovered long ago our ability to assist in a small way, offering a few deserving souls a second chance. Confident when we did, that those chosen will make the most of being given a second chance. We tip the balance, so to speak, to help without interfering unduly. It's a small thing, actually."

"Not to me, it isn't. This is a very, very big thing, and the best thing that could ever happen to me."

"Of course, Kiki, I was referring to the larger context ... of the race, not the individual."

"Right, so how do you choose? Why me?"

"We selectively choose to assist those that, like you are deserving of a second chance; and if given one can a make a difference for many. Those few – like you – will."

"But you offer something that could make using it for personal gain such an easy, trivial thing. Wouldn't some people simply use it and amass wealth and power?"

"It's possible of course, but has never happened that way."

Kiki was incredulous and said so.

"You must know how hard it is for me to believe that. However great your affection and respect for the human race may be – and I'll take this opportunity to thank you on behalf of all of us – it's hardly what I'd call human nature. Very little in life would suggest that to be the case. The temptation would seem to be too great."

"You're wondering how that can possibly be."

"Yes. I am. I wonder how it's possible," Kiki confessed, "to ignore such a temptation."

"Two reasons. First, if you were so inclined, it is unlikely you would make it this far."

"And what else?" Kiki asked, flushing slightly.

"Having come this far, you already know that life is about much more than money."

Chapter Thirteen

THE GIRL IN THE MIRROR **had been replaced by a woman.**

Beautiful had never been how Kiki thought of herself, but knew she was attractive, and as far as that went, had never looked better and was trending the right way.

"Peaking at the right time," as her dad liked to say.

Beauty, she knew, is randomly distributed, but age is the universal enemy.

Fortunately, beauty had never been either a primary focus or a source of confidence, and certainly never an asset when it came to dealing with men. In fact, it was only relatively recently, perhaps in the last year or two, that she'd felt more comfortable and in control with not just men, but people of all kinds and in most any situation. She was now, for the first time, tapping the growing confidence of a young woman nearing her physical peak.

She really was the *late bloomer* mom had always said she'd be, and a woman who would hopefully look better as she grew older. Maybe she'd be luckier still and her youth would make a graceful exit when the time came. None of this went to her head, she wasn't one to mistake good fortune for entitlement, but it strengthened her, and for the first time in her life, Kiki felt truly capable.

For this she was grateful, she'd need all that and more.

It was prudent to assume that what lay before her might well demand everything she could possibly give, and more. She might get farther, or have more options if she looked good and appeared confident and sure of herself. This not unpleasant reality check was followed by a grave realization.

With everything at stake, she was nowhere near the top of her game, not even close.

Earlier today, after a quick glance in the rear-view mirror she'd paused to briefly inspect her reflection in a shop window, and it stopped her cold. Kiki barely recognized the profoundly changed face gazing back.

The strain was evident in her drawn face and slumping carriage.

She looked wounded, vulnerable and battle-weary. Mental and physical fatigue had usurped her customary high spirits, stealing away her healthy glow and compromising her positive attitude. Once flawless skin now appeared sallow and populated with new worry lines taking up residence around her eyes. Sagging shoulders spoke to her invisible burden that weighing her down was too much to bear. Even the naturally thick, lustrous hair her mom had always called her best feature – and increasingly turned male heads – now hung limply looking lifeless, its sheen gone.

There was no mystery about any of it. Shock and pain had taken her on, beaten her down and won convincingly. Somewhere a pretty young woman was hidden away inside a shell-shocked body. This concerned her, not for its assault on her vanity, but how it might impact her in the days, weeks and months ahead.

But seeing herself as a weakened, defeated, and dispirited woman got her attention, and she bristled at the idea, rejecting it as unacceptable, determined do something about it. She resolved to get herself back on-track, At home, slowing her breathing, she moved to her favorite spot on the couch to think it through, to take personal inventory and to do something about it because she could. Finally, something she could actually control, but two things hit her hard.

First, in her zeal to get going, key elements of preparation had been ignored.

Second, she looked like she felt – pretty lousy.

That was a huge problem.

It occurred to her that the two seemingly disparate items were actually interconnected. She'd been so single-minded and focused on the task at hand that she'd overlooked the obvious and gone plunging ahead attacking every item in a gut-busting sprint. It's time to slow down.

Some of her choices needed to be reconsidered and her priorities reassessed.

Wrong ones would only make tough times tougher and the worst case more likely. Pushing on through her personal challenges might be admirable on some levels, but doing it at her own expense made no sense and worked against her. Kiki scolded herself because she knew better. How could she have failed to consider taking the time she needed? Could she have been more short-sighted? Thankfully, she'd caught herself in time. Kiki resolved to be smarter.

Why have I been in such a hurry? She asked aloud.

The past isn't going anywhere.

A measure of relief came with this knowledge.

It brought a tentative giggle that before long grew into a deep, uninhibited belly-laugh. She was laughing in a way she hadn't since this all began. It felt good. The weight began to lift, her spirits rose and her outlook brightened. The world, the future, didn't seem quite so bleak.

For the first time she believed it might be okay, that she could actually pull it off.

The past isn't going anywhere.

Other than the meaningless deadlines that she'd chosen to self-impose, arbitrarily and needlessly, there was really no time-sensitive urgency to the undertaking. That was all in her head. Much of what she'd been doing, she realized, worked against her objectives. What she needed to do was slow down a little, catch her breath, and think things through.

Why make it harder than it already is?

Noble intentions didn't excuse it and she resisted scolding herself again.

She got it, would make the correction, and get on with it.

To succeed, she would have to be at her best, healthy and strong in mind and body. Not getting the rest and nutrition she needed begged trouble and invited failure, and that made recovering her health and regaining her strength the highest priority. If it meant pushing back the schedule, so be it, there was no choice.

Her journey would be much more than a simple trip to the Portland, Oregon of thirty-one years ago. She wouldn't be a tourist or a casual visitor observing anonymously from a safe distance. The world she'd find in 1981 would require much of her. She would be challenged to become engaged, a pro-active participant orchestrating change, all while living among people of that time. She would also be an active interloper. She would be posing as one of them, as a peer, an equal, an ordinary woman, and needed to give the performance of her life.

Her hidden agenda would manipulate events and change lives.

Some people's future, and there was no way to know of how many, was in her hands.

Exactly what that meant, and what might be required, she couldn't know.

Gaining their trust.

She repeated the words, but they sounded disingenuous and caught in her throat.

The truth, she knew was something else: She'd repay their trust with deceit.

There was no way around that.

Reflecting on this, Kiki vowed to consider the interests, and the well-being, of everyone whose life her actions would impact. She wanted her family back more than anything; that was understood. That fact didn't exempt her from a compassionate responsibility to draw the line correctly where it fairly should be drawn. To get what she wanted at the expense of others couldn't be right, she knew it wasn't.

Kiki had arrived at a critical turning point.

She would take whatever time was necessary to heal and get ready, to rest and get healthy, to get stronger, physically and spiritually. And while doing that, to learn more about the past world that held their futures, and how to affect the greatest good for the greatest number.

~~~

Kiki used the time wisely and put it to good use.

Meeting regularly with Jenna, they constructed the details of the life history of Lainie McCann, and role-played over lunches and dinners until Kiki became comfortable and at ease with it.

"I almost believe it, myself," Kiki said lightly.

"When I start calling you "Lainie" is when *I'll* worry," Jenna retorted.

Kiki committed to a disciplined training and conditioning regimen.

Diligently, she watched what she ate to get proper nutrition. She returned to the gym at the neighborhood Rec Center, resumed running three-miles four mornings a week, a complement to her weight lifting regimen and added occasional extra cardio on the elliptical trainers.

With better health came more restful sleep and clearer, sharper mental faculties.

She spent afternoons researching the life and times of Portland, Oregon in 1981. Much of it she found online. More and more had been recently archived and she was always thrilled by what she stumbled across.

On two occasions she had dinner with Clark and enjoyed his company immensely. As their friendship deepened, he revealed more of his private side than she'd ever seen. She found that she genuinely enjoyed his company and looked forward to their time together.

As he opened up to her, she saw him appraising her as a woman, not a child, and realized that she had begun thinking of him more as a man. Clark Bannion was more than the lawyer, more than the trusted family friend and her dad's longtime pal. They'd become genuine friends.

He's smart, charming, clever and still quite handsome, attractive and single.

She flushed at that thought, embarrassed and a little guilty thinking of him in that way.

Clark provided more information about Morris Biggs Sr. Elliot Rose, unofficially, shared the few police reports he'd dug up that involved him. This gave Kiki even greater insight into the man, and the fabric of his family. She next returned to Little Mo's medical records, probing deeper, and researching the hospital personnel.

These were people she would seek out and work with – or work around.

One afternoon while strolling downtown, Kiki passed the Oregon Historical Society and went inside. It was a wise decision, the library, exhibits and collections were interesting and helpful, but, even better was that exposure to them pointed her to an even more valuable source for additional information and background.

The library.

Multnomah County's historic Central Library is located on SW 10th, and from the outside is a rather impressive edifice. Looking the part of serious big city library, it was first opened in 1913, but in the years between 1994 and 1997, underwent extensive renovation and expansion. Today it boasts more than seventeen miles of bookshelves inside, and an impressive complement of services and resources.

One, in particular, was of value, and help, to Kiki:

The digital archives of *The Oregonian.*

Starting with the papers published in December of 1980 – more than six months before her arrival date – she spent long afternoons reading old editions, occasionally making notes. Working her way forward through the first half of 1981, she considered the exercise to be a fruitful immersion in the world of the times.

It was more than local news stories and the national and international events of the day. She paid particular attention to the ads, gaining a familiarity with products, styles, trends, fads and prices. There was also a lot to learn by reading movie listings, and the *NY Times* Best Seller lists. She found a few well-read copies of some of the most popular ones at a used bookstore. At night, thanks to Netflix, she downloaded a number of hit movies and television shows of the day.

The final item was a visit to her hair stylist.

She'd thought about going with a big hair perm, but drew the line there. Her hair was long, and mostly straight, and of a style that while never the height of fashion, had always been fashionable.

It would have to do.

Chapter Fourteen

THE NIGHT BEFORE she'd make The Journey, Kiki met Clark Bannion for dinner.

It was a special night, and in honor of it, he'd made a reservation at Tulee's, a steakhouse in downtown Portland. Tulee's had been there for more than thirty years, and was not only his favorite, but Kiki's, as well. For the Kinsler family it was their special occasion place. As long as she could remember, her parents had taken the family there for dinner during the Holidays. On the eve of her departure, returning to it delivered a flood of memories, mostly happy ones

Clark had also invited Jenna, but she was unable to join them.

"Jenna called a little while ago. She told me she's sorry she couldn't be with us, but thanked me for the invitation," Clark told her. "She's played quite a role and does great work. You –we – we're lucky to have her, and wouldn't be so far along without her. I've enjoyed getting to know her better. Is she okay?"

"Jenna's fine," Kiki explained, "whatever that means. Everything you said is true, there's no one quite like her. We've always been there for each other, always, I don't know where I'd be without her. About tonight, she said something about her *regular life needing attention*, that she'd been neglecting it lately and had some things she had to do. I'll take what's left of my rib-eye home and leave it for her. I've never been able to finish one."

"Umm, hmm."

"I can barely remember my regular life," Kiki joked.

"Maybe you'll rediscover it?"

"That's the plan, isn't it? Although there's a long way to go and so much to do before I get to that place."

"Would you like a drink?" Clark asked, changing the subject.

Kiki nodded yes, and ordered a dirty vodka martini, up with two olives and ice on the side.

"You aren't worried about the effects … tomorrow, I mean?" He asked.

She shook her head. "No, I'm not, not at all."

"Why is that?"

"It seems like a lousy time to deprive myself, so I won't. Instead, I'm living it up. For all I know, I could be having my last drink," she said lightly.

"Unlikely."

"Maybe the device won't work at all. Or it malfunctions, or I screw it up somehow and I get lost back in time. Like an episode in a short-lived and forgettable TV show."

"I doubt The Guardian had a *Last Supper* in mind for you," Clark dead-panned, and sipped his Scotch, nodding his head approvingly. "Great whisky," he said. "At times I miss Bourbon's bite, but these single-malts are so smooth, and the flavor is so … complex, and Scotch reminds me of your dad … How's your martini?"

"Perfect. I may have another."

"As you said, there's no reason not to. Jenna did really well. You know, the documents she created are simply outstanding. They'll pass, I'm sure of it. Combined with the transcript and resume, you'll get a job as a social worker for the medical center."

"I've given Jenna an exciting new career possibility," Kiki joked.

"How so?" Clark asked.

"If law school doesn't go as she hopes and her plan to get hired by the FBI doesn't pan out, the girl has got a real future in Identity Theft, given her gift for document manipulation and creation," Kiki laughed. "Now there's a cottage industry with upside."

Clark stayed on point. "You're convinced the Social Worker path is your best shot?"

"I do, and ideally with the Medical Center. By the way, congratulations are in order. I'm a college graduate. Jenna gave me a degree, although two years ahead of schedule; so much for my junior and senior years at U of O. If for any reason the medical center doesn't work out, Plan B is to volunteer as an aid or an intern. I'm counting on the fact that free labor is hard to turn down, should it come to that. If all else fails, I'll have to work something out ... there's always Plan C."

"Which is?"

"I could try and get work for Mo Biggs' landscaping company. That would get me close to the family and Little Mo."

Clark frowned. "I don't like that idea. I'd rather you didn't go there."

"It's Plan C, a last resort ... what bothers you about it?"

Clark leaned forward. "The evidence is rather thin and certainly inconclusive, but ... my gut tells me he had something to do with his wife's death," he said, and grew pensive.

"Don't stop there, Clark," Kiki pressed

"Whatever your opinion of the evidence, there is more than enough for me to suspect him. I think it's a more than a possibility, I see it as likely. What we do know, is that by all accounts, he's bad news and capable of violence. Be careful."

"I will."

"I mean it, Kiki. If Morris Biggs Sr. did kill his wife, you're walking – or time-traveling – right into the midst of it. He was agitated or worse, and you're arriving not long before he snaps, by design. It's reasonable to think that murdering Teddie wasn't a spur of the moment crime of passion, but a premeditated act of violence. And, if that's the case, he may not think twice about dealing with you if you get in his way."

"I'll be careful. Don't worry about me."

"I do worry about you, Kiki ... I care about you ... very much," Clark said, and looked a little awkward saying it, hiding behind his drink after he did.

Kiki reached across the table and laid her hand lightly atop his. Along with everything else in her life, her relationship with Clark had changed.

He flushed again, deeper this time. This was a young woman he'd known all her life. In the early days, shortly after she was born, in a pinch Clark had even babysat a time or two, and remembered changing her diapers, feeding and burping her. Beyond the friendship with her father, they had shared a special bond. Kiki loved him, and had always looked upon him as extended family, somewhere between a godfather and a favorite uncle.

He no longer saw her as a child.

And she no longer looked at him through a child's eyes.

"Are you frightened?" he asked.

"A little, I guess."

"Of what?"

"I can't help wondering what might happen. And I worry if this, somehow, could go wrong and might be … goodbye." She looked away, confused by feelings which couldn't have been more vividly contradictory, orderly yet confused.

"I've got a good feeling about it. I really do," he said, nodding to add emphasis.

"You wouldn't say so if you didn't mean it, right?" Kiki knew the answer, but realized as the words came out, she needed to hear it from him directly.

"I do mean it," he assured her.

The rest of the evening was easy and pleasant. As always, dinner at Tulee's, was perfect. Over coffee she remarked it was getting late, and she should be going.

"Thank you for a wonderful send-off, Clark. I'm sorry to see the evening end, but I've got quite a day tomorrow," she said with a small smile. She felt friendship, respect, gratitude and deep affection for him. In his late fifties Clark still cut quite a dashing figure. He was comfortable to be with, remarkably intelligent and kind.

Amazing that no one lassoed him back in the day.

And realized she would soon meet him … back in the day.

As she prepared to leave Clark looked at her, his eyes seeing deeply, never leaving her face, reflecting both his knowledge and his deep feelings for her. She held his eyes with her own, and watched as he removed an envelope from the inside pocket of his suit coat, and handed it to her.

Grinning a little sheepishly, he said, "You'll need this, I think. It's the letter from me, to me. Some items will erase his doubts, and more than counter my well-known and much admired incredulous nature."

"Dad always blamed it on your inner-lawyer. He called you the *Original Doubting Thomas*," she teased.

"Yeah, among other things. Still, I know me, and you'll need this letter."

"Great minds," she joked. "I do need it and was about to ask if you'd brought it."

Waiting for the valet to retrieve Clark's car, they embraced. With a hand on each shoulder he kissed her on both cheeks, and then hugged her fiercely. She felt his heat, breathed in his male scent, and was reminded of both her father and how it felt to be held by a lover.

"I know you'll be able to send things, or update us, using the box. I wish there was a way to respond, to help you, but there isn't. Unfortunately, it is that one-way street thing."

Kiki heard the regret, almost an apology, in his voice, and shrugged it off.

"I'll make do. What limitations there are, they're just the rules for this game. You've been wonderful, Clark. I couldn't have asked for more than you've given me, your friendship and support. I'll never forget it. And I'll be fine, I really will," Kiki said, and meant it.

"I suppose," he said softly. "There is still another unknown to add to the ever-growing list of unknowns … "

"What's that?"

"How what you'll do, changes things, everything, and us. The impact on us, and what it does to our relationship, is anything but a certainty."

"I haven't had much time to consider that, but certainly would have come to it before long. What should I call it? I guess it's the *afterwards* of all this, the back-end. If I'm honest about it, as far as the two of us, I didn't want to think about or dwell on it. I don't like thinking about it. You know how much you mean to me," she said, and the truth of it showed in eyes that welled-up with tears, and a choked voice that broke and tailed-off into silence.

"I just had this terrible thought, Kiki," he said, gathering his thoughts and his lightened the mood. "Whatever I say now is likely to sound like cheap philosophy."

"Don't let that stop you. I'd say this is a pretty good time for a little philosophy, cheap or not."

"Okay, here goes. What's ahead, we can't really know, can we? But I have to think the interdependency of past, present and future would seem to require the yang reacting to the yin, the cause and effect, or whatever. The best course, your only course, is to do the right thing."

Kiki was quick to agree. "That's just what I've come to. In some ways not knowing what I'll return to is as unnerving as not knowing what I'm going into. I have to trust that good can only come from good. I have to have … faith. I'm sorry if that sounds corny, but all this runs that way … you know, it's during times like this that I always had Dad to talk to …"

Clark nodded his understanding, but didn't speak. He knew Kiki had more to say.

"There are so many things I wanted The Guardian to tell me. I was hoping for a little help, an idea of what to expect, what not to expect, stuff I should know, and he kept throwing it back to me. I understand so little, anything would help, and believe me, I tried everything, but still got nowhere. He claims he doesn't know, he *can't know*. I have no choice but to accept it."

"All we can do is hope for the best, I guess," Clark said at last, and brought her back into his arms. "Whatever comes has to be better than the nightmare we've been living."

"I hope so. I just wish I knew what …"

Clark interrupted her, placing two fingers over her lips to quiet her.

"It's really not surprising at all, that we can't know, I mean," he began. "On this topic I have to side with The Guardian."

"And why is that?" Kiki asked.

"It's only logical when you think about it. If you change what is, by reinventing what was, how can we possibly know *what might be?*"

Kiki had no answer.

The path to finding the answer would begin in the morning.

Chapter Fifteen

RETURNING HOME, Kiki heard the phone ringing as she was about to open the door and hurried inside to answer it. The classic late Twentieth Century ringtone trilled urgently as it announced a call on the landline her parents had stubbornly refused to give up. This despite both of them having had wireless phones for years. Reaching for the handset was a reminder of the different world she'd find in the morning. Thirty-one years ago payphones were the only available on-the-go option. She knew they'd be nearly everywhere, and wise planning meant having a ready supply of dimes and quarters.

Who could be calling so late? And immediately realized it had to be Jenna.

Her friend was calling to apologize for not saying goodbye in person.

"I planned on coming over … to say goodbye and wish you well," Jenna said, "but I sat in my car and just couldn't turn the key. I just didn't know what I'd say or how I'd react when I saw you. If I'd break down and get weepy. What do I say? Goodbye? Farewell? Good luck? Bon Voyage? And the longer I thought about it, nothing seemed right and the last thing I wanted to do was say something dumb and make things harder or more emotional for you than they already are. So, with all of that, I took the cowardly way out, but I had to call. You understand, don't you? Does this make any sense?"

"Of course it does, and you know I understand. We've said all that needs saying and coming by just to make an appearance isn't necessary, although I do appreciate the sentiment, isn't necessary with us. I am glad you called, though. It would have been weird to take-off without hearing from you."

"Things are weird enough ... could they get any weirder?" Jenna asked.

"Let's hope not," Kiki answered, and for a moment neither said any more.

"I do have a good feeling, Kiki. I know you'll be fine and can do this. And I love you. You're the sister I never had," Jenna said in a voice that trailed off. "Listen. I have to say it again ... Big Mo scares me, a lot. So remember to be very careful, very smart and patient, too. Take your time, and do it right. Make sure you're seeing what really is and choose the best path. And send us messages through the box in Clark's office ... so we have some idea ..."

"I will," Kiki said. "Jenna?"

"What?"

"I love you, too. I couldn't do this without you, I mean that. It's not just the docs and the research, but your friendship, the moral support, and the fact that you believe in me. You're a once-in-a-lifetime friend. We're going to have a lot to talk about when I'm back."

"I'll be counting the days. Until then, Kiki," Jenna said simply.

"Until then," Kiki answered, and ended the call.

~~~~~

As she got ready for bed, the enormity of what lay ahead seemed less daunting.

Whatever the reasons, the relief was real and welcomed as she slipped into bed.

Nights had been the worst, when insecurities and fears abound, but not tonight.

The murders of her family, more than a personal tragedy, had stolen her past and redefined her future. Remarkably, and for the first time in many weeks, she felt less conflicted, not as stricken and panicked. As if an unexpected spiritual cleansing had washed over her like salve for the still raw wounds. So many lessons had been learned in these past few weeks. Most she'd never imagined having any relevance in her life, but she saw two as life-defining.

Pain, however grievous, is only the beginning. What happens next is up to us.

And, incredibly, the details are only details. What's really at stake is far bigger.

Good and evil, fighting it out like heavyweights for my soul, for my spirit.

She had no guarantee of success, but could be no passive observer in the battle.

Do what's right, do your best, what you can, and accept whatever happens.

No one can do more than that.

Choices become both clearer and fewer when the heart is brutalized and Kiki made hers with confidence. She saw the choice between good and evil as a choice between life and death. If in the end, it all came to nothing, and was no more than a long and insidiously perverse dream, none of it real, except for the deaths, she would still have made the very same choices.

If next morning is simply tomorrow, the tomorrow of the here and now, and not long ago, it's the same choice. If she awakened having gone nowhere, having changed nothing and no longer on a mission with crazy expectations of what could never be, still the same choice. She would simply carry on. Tonight, knowing that now boosted her spirits and encouraged her.

There are worse consolation prizes than resurrecting and reclaiming my life.

More than an emotional hedge against the potential non-event, it was a vital grounding. The attack on her family had struck directly at her love of life, vilifying her will to live with a blistering assault undermining her once indomitable spirit. All she believed to be good and true had been malignantly denounced, but out of it came one truth that stood apart from all others.

Only she could rekindle her spirit and safeguard her soul. It was up to her.

Whatever life brings, we either give in and give up or hold on and carry on.

Second chance or not, giving up would never be her way and tapping an inner reservoir of strength, her spirits soared with a renewed confidence and a humbled hopefulness. She was at peace and more than ready, accepting and acknowledging her ultimate responsibility.

Silently, she thanked The Guardian, again.

It is up to me, just as he said.

Her burden seemed lighter, the future, while unknown, brighter, and her resolve, stronger. Calmer than she'd felt in weeks and astounded that it was possible, she understood why it was.

Because I've already been tested ... what's to come is the next test, not the first.

The simple truth was that her predictable life had been obliterated. The virtual rug had been yanked and reality violently morphed. Everything precious swept away by a random and indifferently churning universe. A montage of chaotic contradictions now orchestrated a total transformation, leaving her to fend, as best she could, alone and on her own. The old rules no longer applied, they'd been marginalized as a matter of course, and now seemed barely relevant.

Trust in the world of new possibilities.

The emotional rollercoaster ride of the past month had exacted a steep toll. She'd crested terrifying peaks, followed by suicidal dives into the deepest valleys of darkest despair. The last vestiges of her youth lay littered along the tracks of that manic ride. Scariest of all had been staring into the emotional abyss, with no idea how to avoid sliding into it.

She had even prayed, in her way, for release from a life unfairly ganging up on her, and in protest of the unjust betrayal of her faith that had cast her out, naked, vulnerable and alone. Thankfully, at her lowest moments, Kiki had been buoyed and buttressed by Jenna and Clark. Their love and friendship meant the world to her, and that they'd given freely and selflessly.

She'd survived, prepared as best she could, and now it came down to just doing it.

The instructions, sparse as they might be, were clear enough.

Enter the information to set the date, time and location; then go to sleep.

Sleep was her portal to the past.

Somehow, when she awoke, it would be ... *then.* She hoped.

With everything ready, she decided to do something she'd never done for herself.

In the kitchen she fixed a *google-moogle*, and sipped it on the way to her bedroom.

Her mother had often made the simple concoction of warm milk, a little butter and honey, when Kiki was a child. A mug appeared nights when she had trouble falling asleep, or had been awakened by a nightmare and was too frightened to return to bed. It was no magic potion. The magic was in the loving woman who tendered it. The hot frothy brew brought Mom to mind, triggering a warm wave of pleasant memories, sweeter still filtered by her adult emotions and experiences. Kiki ached to see her mother again, to talk with her, for even the briefest time.

There was so much she'd tell her.

The Kinsler family home had originally been built by her grandparents in 1971. Land was cheap, and they purchased 12 wooded acres on the fringes of what was then Portland's urban growth boundary. Over the next decade, harvesting the timber, and selling off most of the acreage to developers, made them a tidy profit. Their almost-rural home ten minutes from the heart of the city became part of a highly desirable Southwest Portland suburban neighborhood.

Kiki barely remembered her grandparents, they'd died when she was very young, but she knew they'd struggle recognizing the area today. They'd lived there for only ten years before moving to Arizona. Her dad explained that his mother had suffered all her life with asthma and severe grass allergies. Her grandfather hoped both would be mitigated by the dry desert climate and Kiki remembered her father talking about it, how happy his parents were that they had.

"There are urban legends that say the Indians who first inhabited the Willamette Valley called it the Valley of Sickness and Death. Historians debate it, but true or not, one thing is true. If you have seasonal grass allergies the Willamette Valley might be where you don't want to live," he said. "Damp Oregon winters can be especially hard on folks with those health issues."

The home had stood furnished but uninhabited for two years as they decided whether to return to Portland or settle permanently in the desert. Attending her parent's wedding in 1983, after

Dad's residency at Johns Hopkins, proved to be their only trip back to Oregon. They made the house in Southwest Portland their wedding gift to their son and his bride. Kiki was born in December of 1990 and her grandparents died within a month of each other in 1994.

The house on Southwest Radford Drive had been the Kinslers' home ever since.

They were a happy family, and it was a happy home, warm, loving and secure.

The room had been Kiki's since she was a baby, her personal base and sanctuary from childhood to adulthood, bearing witness and providing safe haven through every milestone and cataclysmic coming-of-age event. Witness to all the triumphs and failures, laughs and tears, countless hopes and dreams and even her most carefully guarded and secret fears. Those few of us are spared, however loving and nurturing our environment.

She lay on her back in bed, staring up.

No matter how hard she tried, Kiki had never actually been able to sleep on her back, but stubbornly always started out that way, part of the flawed personal ritual it was. Before long she'd get restless, give it up with a roll onto her right side and get down to serious sleeping, but first, and always, on her back. Even on this night, her last night in her bed, at least for a while.

The night sky was clear, the air fresh, cool and comfortable, with a low humidity people who don't live in the West can only envy. After a glorious summer day reaching the mid-eighties, the temperatures overnight would plummet into the low fifties. Windows could be raised, taking advantage of perfect sleeping weather where air conditioning wasn't needed.

A soft but steady breeze gusted now and again, urging the ancient maple tree outside her window to drag its branches against the glass and siding in-tune with the rhythm of the wind. A nearly full moon bathed the night in yellow moonlight fighting to pierce the lush leaves. Tiny determined points of light found a path through them, and celebrated their arrival by dancing with the breeze and playing gaily upon her ceiling.

A private performance, given by a piece of starry sky, she shared with no one.

The bracelet around Kiki's wrist, as always cool and smooth to the touch, seemed to have come alive. There was no physical change she could point to, but everything seemed different. Nothing she could hear, or smell, or even feel, it was more sensation she couldn't describe, but even that didn't properly characterize it.

She understood without understanding, more a knowing.

Looking closely at the band, gliding a fingertip across its glass-like surface, the inanimate object now seemed animated ... and connected. To what, she couldn't know, but sensed it was linked, or perhaps reunited and again part of something more, something greater.

Kiki had played with the band countless times, but until now had never used it.

Running her index finger along it she let it linger where the face would appear. A virtual control panel rose up above the surface of the band, many times its size. Buttons controlling key functions she could only hope she understood were muted and blinking. The current time, date and year were displayed prominently in a series of boxes. Just under it was an identical display.

For now, those boxes were blank.

Next to these boxes, one button seemed more conspicuous than the others.

It was larger and backlit by a pale, lime green light that seemed to flash every few seconds, almost expectantly, as if anticipating something. Kiki believed this was the button she would use to begin the process of inputting the parameters of her destination.

Kiki took a deep breath and entered:

5:30 a.m.   **Saturday**   **June 13**   **1981**

With the data entered, a second green button appeared, larger still, significantly darker but with a distinctly fiery quality to it. Intuitively, Kiki suspected this would enable her to "Confirm" the data she'd entered. She pressed it, and the data appeared to have been accepted.

Now the empty spaces under the current time, date and year, were populated.

5:30 a.m.   **Saturday**   **June 13**   **1981**

The data was now apparently locked and loaded, looking like it belonged.

The very idea brought a giggle, and the giggle a smile, and then she was laughing out loud, amazed to be doing it at a moment like this. There was now nothing left to do but close her eyes and drift-off to sleep.

Her eyes were heavy and she yawned.

Stretching her legs, she rolled onto her right side.

Kiki clutched Friendly Friend, the stuffed elephant she'd prized since she was born, tight to her breast. This well-worn and well-loved constant companion had always graced her bed, and for years served as a first pillow. Friendly Friend had been with even during her college years in the dorm and her apartment in Eugene. She held her old friend tighter still, rubbing her lips with his trunk, as she had as a child.

Sleep provided the gateway.

Her eyes grew heavier still, and she closed them without a fight.

Eager to get on with it, Kiki was ready and wouldn't contest sleep this night.

Feeling both exhilaration and trepidation, she gave silent thanks for her second chance.

With no idea what to expect, she was untroubled. Would it be like climbing aboard a carnival ride or stepping through the entry-way into a fun house? Did spirits or demons await her? Would she feel or be aware of anything? Did any of that matter? Probably not at all.

She would later use a single word to describe the experience: contradictions.

Sleep at first was a shallow dreamless state cached just beyond consciousness.

A safe and familiar realm that was simultaneously foreign and unknown.

There was a slight sense of movement, but she knew that she remained in her bed. She was not quite asleep but not fully awake, still, but somehow in motion, energized but at peace, eager but patient, and excited but fearful at what she'd encounter upon awaking.

Floating, drifting, gliding through a pool of cool, fresh water, but her skin was dry and there was no sensation of moisture. She was comfortable, more than warm enough, her breathing relaxed and even, allowing herself to be swept along, one with the unknown forces ferrying her. She gave in, freely and completely, to things beyond her comprehension.

Deep in her consciousness was an awareness of a passage.

Dreamless and unthinking, it was more a *knowing*, and in no way unpleasant.

There was no fanfare or bright lights, no Star Wars-like cinematic jump to hyper-space. Instead, it was a rather subtle and barely conscious realization of having made a smooth and fluid transition. Her ties to the conscious and physical world of the present had been severed.

Slipping into still deeper sleep she completed her improbable passage.

This was a passage not only to another place, but to another time.

Chapter Sixteen

THE NIGHT BEFORE, Kiki had raised the bedroom window halfway as was her custom any time of year. She loved the fresh coolness in the room, and was convinced she slept better for it. Apparently, overnight it had once again worked its magic, but last night was like no other.

Birds in the trees just outside her window were busily welcoming the new day.

It was their song that gently and lyrically, roused her.

Kiki was shocked at how well she'd slept.

She felt ... great; actually, rested and refreshed.

Her mind was clear and alert, another surprise, because Kiki had never been a morning person. Typically, she liked lazing in bed, delaying opening her eyes, tarrying a little longer and waking-up slowly, relishing the not quite awake time. As a rule, her brain didn't kick-on and kick-in instantly. She stretched languidly, feeling almost guilty for it. Indulging herself, as if there was no rush or hurry to start the day, until her brain sent a wake-up call of its own, delivered with a physical jolt.

The Journey, I made it!

Did I sleep so well I forgot where I am, when it is and why I'm here?

Or was it the physical toll of making The Journey?

Whatever the explanation, the fact was that she hadn't slept like that since it all began, and under the circumstances, had doubts she ever would again. Before last night there hadn't had a single moment's relief from a nightmare that played nightly and lingered all day. For the last month she'd been living like a stranger in her own skin, searching, without success, for her old life, in denial that it was gone, permanently displaced. Hardly the recipe for sweet dreams and blissful sleep, except last night, of all nights, it was. She wondered how it was possible.

Did I leave all that baggage behind in the future?

Or have I completed something and crossed a threshold?

At this moment she felt none of the doubts or lack of confidence she'd worked so hard to keep hidden from Jenna and Clark. Fearing she lacked the strength and the will to do much beyond reliving the nightmare, over and over. For weeks an endless loop coloring every day and every night. Reopening her demoralizing soul-crushing wounds, her dread that no magic band, or whatever The Gift turned out to be, was enough to save her, or anything or anyone, and that the work to be done was beyond her capabilities.

But that was yesterday.

Today, this morning, everything seemed … *possible*.

The Work, how she thought of it now, was important and good work if done right.

Preparing for it had been desperately needed therapy and she'd dubbed the process *My 3 P's: Her path from pain to purpose to possibilities.* Getting ready more than got her through the harshest early days and over the hump, but in truth, she had prepared without really believing. Her skeptical mind wouldn't allow it, but inexplicably, at this moment, she did.

Did I leave my doubts behind with my old life?

Or am I getting way ahead of myself?

Slow down, get up and find out.

She started to, but the idea stopped her cold, and made her think.

Once she opened her eyes and looked around it would real, her exit from sleep's snug, safe cocoon complete. Replaced by … what? All too familiar doubts resurfaced, vying to inject apprehension and uncertainty into a peaceful morning. With her eyes still closed tightly, licking her lips, her chest constricted, it became suffocating, almost painful to breathe. Despite the cool early morning, she felt suddenly overheated, and struggled to relax and calm a rising panic.

This is what I prepared for. There is nothing to fear.
Only she was no longer so sure.

Preparations, neatly made in a vacuum, had then seemed reasonable and manageable enough, but now appeared almost comical. This was no vacuum. When she opened her eyes it would be the real world of 1981, thirty-one years in the past.

Whatever that meant, it was time to take a look, and warily, Kiki opened her eyes.

At this early hour there was barely enough light to see. The first rays of daylight were dim, not yet established or strong enough to fully dispense night's fiercest shadows. Dawn was still hinting at what would soon bring the world the light of day.

She would begin with a visual survey of her room and then the house to get her bearings. Later, when she was ready, with a solid plan for this first day, she'd venture out into the world.

With Kiki's first look about, she recognized the room, but nothing in it.

For all her preparations, she discovered she was totally unprepared for how it *felt*.

Not what she'd expected, Kiki wanted to process it, to define it by putting her feelings into words, but couldn't. Overloaded by contradictory elements conflicting and contesting each other, the house that had been her home all her life wasn't hers, yet. It was just the opposite.

She had awakened in a strange house, a place she had never been, filled with things she had never seen. What she saw at every turn reinforced her feelings of detachment, of separation, and of not belonging. She tried to calm herself by taking another deep breath.

The room was familiar, but its contents lent an unreality to it, as if gazing through some sort of filter or prism. Or having been transported to an alternate universe and waiting for Rod Serling to introduce a *Twilight Zone* episode she happened to be starring in. Not long ago she would have scoffed at such a cockeyed idea, and blamed it on too much SciFi Channel. Now it didn't seem crazy at all, it actually made a lot of sense.

There was a black rotary phone atop a small, wooden desk against the far wall. It looked like an antique plucked out of a museum exhibit. A desk calendar from an insurance agency showed November 1980. The month and year her grandparents had left for Arizona.

This is my room before it was my room, before Mom and Dad, before everything.

Long before there was a 'me'.

Slipping out of bed she padded across the floor to the bathroom just down the hall as she'd done countless times. She could have made it there with her eyes closed. Hoping she'd get lucky and find soap and a towel her grandparents might have left behind, and take a shower before going out. In one of the drawers she discovered a few complementary bottles of shampoo and conditioner from hotels they had visited.

Her dad had often talked about how they loved to travel. She remembered the two of them looking at their album of photographs of their big trip, a three-month dream tour of Europe they'd taken the summer after moving to Arizona.

They'd be there now, she realized.

A small linen closet in the hallway had a modest selection of sheets, as well as towels and washcloths. An old robe hung on a hook on the back of the bathroom door. A small thing but it cheered her.

The shower coughed and spit at first. For half-a-minute water ran a rusty brownish color from lack of use before it finally cleared. The water pressure was impressive. Kiki had always liked long showers. Contentedly, she stood under the hot water letting it pelt her like a *poor man's massage*.

After her shower she toweled off, slipped into the robe, and gathered the clothes she'd slept in, unsure what else, if anything, had actually made the passage with her. She carried her clothes to the laundry room. If they were all she had, she wanted them to be clean enough when she went out later to do what she hoped to do.

Kiki knew she had a full day ahead. She planned on stops at DMV, the bank, the grocery store, and if time, to do a little clothes shopping. And then there was Clark. He'd come later.

In the kitchen she looked through the pantry, and while not bulging with goodies, it was far from empty. The freezer had a few items, including some TV dinners and a frozen lasagna. Cupboards had the pots and pans that hadn't made the trip to Arizona. On its own cart, like it was a place of honor, was an old-fashioned microwave oven. All of these finds exhilarated her, but none more than a nearly-full jar of *Tasters Choice* instant coffee.

She laughed picturing Clark's reaction. A coffee aficionado reduced to a cup of it.

But it was available and better than nothing.

Kiki rinsed a mug, wiped it out, and dropped two heaping tablespoons of the dark crystals the label bragged were *freeze-dried for fresh-brewed flavor*. Instant coffee three decades ago, right. Maybe if she made it strong enough. Or maybe instant coffee was one of those things that were better back then. Pointless trying to rationalize the irrational, Kiki realized it made more sense to give it up and accept where she was. That thought triggered two things that hit hard.

For me, there is no *back then*, for me it is *here and now*.

This realization underscored what Jenna and Clark had emphasized many times over the past weeks: The urgency for her to adapt by changing her mind-set in not one, but two ways.

My name is Lainie McCann.

1981 is my time.

The faucet at the kitchen sink behaved much like the shower, but after sputtering briefly, the halting water turned steady and clear. It was a well-built home with Portland's good water. She boiled some in a saucepan, and made a unique cup of coffee. It was drinkable, barely. Wincing with every sip, real coffee instantly became her top household priority.

Mug in hand, in less than half an hour she'd peeked into the other rooms and garage.

The house was dusty but fully equipped. She'd found nearly everything she needed.

Even a pair of her grandmother's jeans and a couple tops she could wear in a pinch.

But what thrilled her most was a bicycle in the garage: She was mobile.

This was fantastic luck. She'd never been a fan of riding a bike in city traffic, but at least there would be less of it to contend with. In her mind she began considering the route she'd take. Now, what she felt more than anything was a growing excitement.

Suddenly it hit her:

I'm here, I'm really here.

Chapter Seventeen

THE BICYCLE WAS IN EXCELLENT CONDITION **but the rear tire was low.**
     With a pump hanging on a hook among an impressive selection of tools populating a peg board taking up the entire back wall, Kiki topped it off. The height of the seat was fine. The bike was a woman's model, her grandmother's and it felt right. She climbed up onto the bike and made a mental note to stop and buy a bicycle helmet when she passed a sporting goods store or a Fred Meyer.

She had what she needed in the backpack that, happily, had made the journey with her. Before heading out, she'd taken inventory of the items Jenna had armed her with, making a point of leaving Clark's letter and gray metal box she planned to leave with him at home for now. It would be safe there, and she didn't need it yet, not today. She reviewed her plan for the day.

The California Driver's License she'd turn into DMV, the Social Security card, college transcripts, and an artfully forged letter from her grandfather, were safely stowed in a file folder inside a manila envelope. This letter explained who she was and why she was there, and would answer any questions about her right to be living in the house. A top priority was to get out and meet the neighbors, something she planned on doing right away.

Reviewing her back story for her before she left, Clark declared it *solid and air-tight*.

The memory of it was pleasantly reassuring and made her feel closer to him.

"Your right to be in the home may never be questioned, Kiki, I mean, "Lainie". But if you are asked about it, I think this letter will answer any questions."

"I hope so," she'd replied, "I wish there was something more, just in case."

"Like what?" he'd asked.

"I don't know … another layer. Something … I don't know what exactly."

Clark had soon come up with it, handing her an amended version of Dr. Kinsler's letter.

"Read it through. I've also added something to my letter, the one to me … it's hard to know what to call it," he sighed. "Okay, here goes. Jenna made you the daughter of a woman who recently passed away. According to the Death Certificate, she had no children and no family.

"I like that," she said, and listened as he summarized the rationale.

"To escape the damp Northwest climate, your grandparents, Robert and Ruth Kinsler, moved to Arizona the previous November. Happily for them, the drier desert air and warmer climate appeared to have agreed with your grandmother, and they plan to settle in the desert permanently. To celebrate the happy outcome, Dr. Kinsler, who is now retired from his pediatric practice, surprised his wife with the gift of a three-month European tour. This had always been the trip of her dreams, but between the demands of his practice and his dedication and devotion to his patients over the years, he was always too busy to make it."

"All true, consistent with what Dad told me many times," Kiki said enthusiastically.

Clark nodded. *"That they actually made the trip at this time really helps us. Now, the letter introduces you as Lainie McCann, the daughter and only child of your grandmother's college friend, Markie McCann of Sacramento, California. Markie had recently passed away but just before she died, Ruth Kinsler was able to visit her old friend on their way to Arizona. Markie imposed upon her old friend for a favor, asking her to assist her daughter Lainie's move from Sacramento to Oregon. Ruth Kinsler was more than happy to help in any way she could, and, as it turned out, the timing of the request couldn't have been more perfect for all of them."*

"How so?"

"Needing a house sitter while they were away, Dr. and Mrs. Kinsler offered their home to Markie's daughter, rent free, for as long as she needs it. An ideal arrangement perfectly suited for everyone concerned. Lainie – you – use it while getting settled and pursing your career in Social Work, and keep an eye on the property for them. Lainie's long-term plan is to move into her own apartment by late summer or early fall."

"What if someone wants to confirm this with Dr. Kinsler?" Kiki asked, frowning slightly.

"Unfortunately, there's no way to reach them while they're abroad."

"Convenient," Kiki mused.

"They have no fixed itinerary, because Dr. Kinsler prefers to 'Play it by ear and go where the spirit moves us.'" That being the case, Lainie can only offer the letter, and point out that they had already taken steps for all recurring household bills to be paid automatically, adding – honestly and genuinely – that she does expect them to call at some point to check-in – unless they're having too much fun. Which they were when you last heard from them."

Kiki smiled, "You're holding the last bit back, aren't you?"

"I am," he said, smiling broadly. "If anyone needs or insists on external confirmation, we'll make me, back then, an attorney in Portland who, as it happens, is a friend hired to assist Lainie with any legal issues that might arise from her mother's estate, and facilitate her move to Oregon. He knows the Kinslers and can vouch for you."

"I'm losing track of how many laws we're breaking," Kiki dead-panned.

"I'm trying not to think about that," Clark shot back, grinning. "Luckily, the long arm of the law isn't long enough to reach me, here, now. I said from the very beginning that I don't expect the documents, given what you're doing, will be checked all that thoroughly. Even if they are, the docs are good, and should pass. Besides, you're exactly who you appear to be doing exactly what you're supposed to be doing."

"That's true, but ..."

Clark interrupted her.

"The exception may be the medical center, the more I think about it. It's possible, maybe even likely, that even back then they may have vetted employees more aggressively, but that's fine, I see a social services agency as a better bet anyway. And it fits, because we know that the Biggs family is paid a visit by the police not long before she dies."

"And you're recommending what?" Kiki asked.

"Here's my advice when you get there: First, deal with DMV, and then the bank. Gather basic information about employment at the medical center if you want, but without actually applying. Better opportunities, I think, with Family Services. Once you've finished with all that, schedule a time to visit with me, and we'll, well the two of you, will see where you are."

"Saving the best for last?"

"You'll have to judge for yourself," Clark said, chuckling as he said it. "By the way, I'm smarter now, but I was much better looking thirty years ago."

Kiki eyed him critically and realized she was looking forward to finding out.

More than smart, Clark was organized and had thought things through completely.

She was so lucky to have him on her side.

There were things she'd missed, overlooked, credit the emotional beating she'd endured and her relative inexperience. Not Clark, he kept zeroing-in on details she might otherwise have missed, things large and small that might have made things more difficult. Methodically, he'd thought of nearly everything, down to a small envelope he pressed into her hand at the last minute, the kind of envelope that banks use for customers requesting large amounts of currency.

Inside it were three hundred dollar bills, two fifties and five twenties.

"What's this about?"

"Something we talked about, but never got around to. You'll need a little cash, some working capital until you can get to the bank and, when you do, you'll need to make a deposit to open an account. It occurred to me it may be a while before you can sell the jewelry."

"Well, it's very thoughtful – and generous. $500 should go far in 1981, but I'm curious, where on earth did you get these?" she asked.

She was holding one bill after another up to the light, examining them closely.

They were strange looking, she barely recognized them. She was holding outdated paper money that had been replaced and was no longer in circulation, and these were large bills that kids weren't likely to see. In 2003, beginning with the Twenty, The U.S. Treasury had introduced redesigned currency that included enhanced security features to combat counterfeiters.

"What paper money used to look like, I'd forgotten."

"Some people collect coins," Clark began. "My dad collected currency, and not only U.S. currency, but paper money from every country that he visited and that man did love to travel. Bills from Europe, Asia, even Africa. He left it to me, and I raided the collection last night."

"But your collection, I hate for you to spoil it," she said, feeling a little guilty.

"Not to worry, I'm not. There's plenty more where that came from."

"Plenty more? From where? She asked. "They're long out of circulation."

"Yeah, but I'm counting on being paid back. You are planning on coming back, aren't you?" he asked with a wink. "Where you're going, just stop in a bank and bring me some nice, crisp replacements!"

Climbing up on the bike and remembering how they'd laughed about it brought a smile.

She couldn't have asked for a more perfect day to ride around Portland.

Morning clouds had hung-on persistently before burning off in late morning. Today the temperature would struggle to make it out of the seventies. Kiki noticed everything seemed down-sized, slower, more peaceful and quiet, safer, too. She was gazing upon Oregon before it was "discovered" in the last decades of the Twentieth Century. It would be two years before her parents returned to Portland and her dad began to practice. Kiki found herself envious of the slower paced, quieter Oregon that had been theirs then. It was hers, now, for a little while.

Areas that she knew as fully developed with office parks, strip centers and subdivisions, were open spaces. The intersection of Scholls Ferry Road and Hall Boulevard, just before Washington Square, Oregon's largest shopping center, seemed almost rural, and looking down the hill she could see that only a Toys 'r Us and a Levitz Furniture dotted otherwise empty land. She suspected Murray Hill, where so much residential growth would explode in coming years, at this point was little more than a gleam in hungry developer's eyes.

On the roads there was less traffic than she was accustomed to, because there were fewer people, which meant fewer cars. The sky seemed bluer, the air clearer, the living more relaxed and less frenetic. Her pleasure was muted by what her unusual perspective reminded her lay ahead.

How different life was. When you live through the changes you barely noticed them.

The day had been a successful one.

She'd ridden past a bike shop on Beaverton-Hillsdale Highway. Walking her bike in, fearful of it being stolen, she'd checked her tires and purchased a helmet and a lock. The fashion statement didn't thrill her, but the safety the helmet provided was important. A friend in high school had lost her life riding without one and she'd never forgotten or gotten over the shock.

Other than waiting for an hour at the DMV on Allen Boulevard, things couldn't have been easier. A bored employee appeared and began going through the motions, barely glancing at the California license she turned in and the Social Security card she offered as proof of her identity. She was given a vision test that she passed with flying colors, and after paying a fee that seemed more than reasonable, was photographed and given a temporary paper license until her permanent one arrived by mail in a couple of weeks.

Sheila, a friendly young woman about her own age, opened her account at First National Bank of Oregon. She couldn't know that First National would become First Interstate before ultimately being purchased by Wells Fargo. Sheila accepted all her identification without question. She opened the account with two of the three hundreds Clark had given her, and changed the third into twenties. Kiki caught herself before she asked about a Bank Card, remembering that it would be a few years before they became commonplace.

She rode by the offices of the Family Services agency but hesitated going in, fearing she was under dressed. If time permitted, she'd do a little clothes shopping later.

Her final stop before heading home was at the Fred Meyer in Raleigh Hills. It was *her Freddie's,* but so much smaller and older looking; remodeling and expansion was decades away.

She bought a half gallon of milk, bread, cheese, eggs and sliced lunch meat from the deli. She almost bought a six-pack of Tab, Diet Coke hadn't yet been introduced, still a year or two off, but in the end decided she deserved *The Real Thing* and went with real Coke before it was *Classic Coke.* The New Coke fiasco was years away. A can of coffee was her final purchase. It would have to do, beans weren't yet readily available. Anything would be better than instant.

A good day; once home, she'd call Clark Bannion's office and make an appointment.

He would play an important role in coming days, if he believed her impossible story.

Chapter Eighteen

"WOULD YOU LIKE SOME COFFEE?" Clark asked. "Believe me when I say it's the best in town, I order beans from Graffeo, an Italian Roaster in San Francisco. Wonderful stuff, it beats anything else around."

"I'd love a cup. Yesterday, I was reduced to a jar of Taster's Choice I found in the house. It was dreadful. Then I bought coffee at Freddie's, but it really wasn't much better."

"Coffee is a passion, but Portland is still a step behind the big cities, we're limited. There's a new chain out of Seattle called Starbucks? Have you heard of them? They haven't made it down here, yet."

"Yes," Kiki answered, "I've heard of Starbucks," she said, careful not to show her amusement.

If you only knew what was coming...before long they'll be on every corner.

"Your message, when you called yesterday to schedule an appointment," he began, "was a little vague, even a bit ..." He hesitated, as if searching for the right words. Kiki stepped in and finished the thought for him.

"Cryptic," she offered, "is that what you were about to say?"

"Ah, yes, that might be right."

The attorney eyed the young woman seated across his desk in one of two visitor's chairs. She wasn't exactly beautiful, but very attractive, he thought. She was fit, had a nice figure and flawless skin with just a hint of recent time in the sun. Her demeanor featured a vitality and energy that he found very engaging. But it was the deep blue eyes, bright and holding his with an unabashed confidence, that he found genuinely appealing. He had to admit he liked the way this girl presented herself.

"According to your message, you have some estate issues you need help with. You also claim that we have an old friend in common, but declined to say who, preferring to tell me when we met. Is that correct, Ms. McCann?"

"Call me Lainie, please, I hate formality. But, yes, that's about right, what I said, I mean."

"Well?" Expecting more, he asked, "I'm intrigued, why don't you enlighten me?"

"I will, but if it's alright, I'd like to start with a brief explanation to set the stage. Then, I'm going to give you a letter from … our mutual friend. Would that be okay?"

Clark Bannion titled his head in assent, and turned his hands palm up, a signal of his willingness to play along and hear her out. "Go right ahead, Lainie, and please, call me, Clark."

He leaned back, settling into his high-back leather executive chair. The same chair, she noted with amusement, albeit over thirty years newer, that Clark still used.

"Okay. Without the letter to explain who I am, really am, what brings me here, and our connection, I wouldn't blame you for thinking I'm out of my mind and either showing me the door or calling for the men in white coats to come and collect me. It's quite a story."

"It's an ominous beginning, Lainie."

She nodded. "I know it is. The letter should be enough to satisfy you, but if for some reason it's not, and you're unwilling to make the leap of faith and believe me, I do have more … proof."

The attorney narrowed his eyes, not in a frown, but reflecting on her words.

"And this letter is written by?" he asked.

Kiki, as Lainie McCann, reached into her backpack and withdrew the manila envelope, and from it the letter. She handed it to him without answering his question.

"Please just read the letter first. After you do, I'll answer any questions you may have. Inside the envelope is a smaller envelope with a photograph. Take note of the letterhead and, although I've hand-delivered the letter, the first-class stamp I stuck on it for dramatic effect."

"As you wish," he shrugged good-naturedly.

He'd been drumming the fingers of his right hand softly on the desk, but stopped, and looked more closely at the letter. Eyes wide, puzzled but curious, he examined the envelope. Whatever his thoughts, about gazing at a future version of his letterhead, he kept to himself.

"The stamp has no price … it says *Forever*," he observed. "What's that about?"

"I'll try to explain everything after you've read."

He sighed deeply again, exhaled a breath he'd been holding, and reached for a gold letter opener that was part of an expensive pen and pencil set prominently placed on his desk. She recognized it, because thirty-one years later, he still used it. Clark had told her it was a gift from his parents when he'd passed the Bar Exam, and one of his most prized possessions.

The tension between the two had grown palpably. Clark tried to lighten the mood and said, "Relax, I promise to hold off calling for the cavalry until *after* I've read it."

"Thanks," she said, with a small, tight smile. "That's a good idea."

Clark slit open the envelope, removed the two typed pages and began to read.

He was soon absorbed and she studied him with great interest.

This Clark Bannion was twenty-seven years old, six years older than she.

Just over six feet, but thinner, and more fit, in what was his physical prime. Almost handsome, strong but not overly muscular, she knew from her father he'd been a runner until achy knees ended that in his late forties. Self-assured, his confidence seemed natural. His dark brown eyes were warm, active and alert, and seemed to take in everything. A generous mouth found its way to a smile easily and often. It was a very nice smile. She liked this Clark Bannion a lot.

After reading the letter he sat staring at it for what seemed like forever.

She continued studying him, until her reverie was interrupted as he cleared his throat.

"Have you read this letter?" He asked, visibly shaken by what he'd read.

"No," she answered, shaking her head, "I haven't."

"I'm surprised," he said simply.

"Why? It's personal, at least that's the impression he, er, *you*, gave me. I respected that."

Clark nodded. "Still, I wouldn't have blamed you for reading it. Look, this is simply unbelievable, but I'm going to try to go with it. There is an underlying truth in this information, an undeniable truth. And, I'm sorry for your loss, an unimaginable tragedy. I can't believe your family was murdered."

"I still struggle with it," she admitted, "every day."

For a brief time neither spoke, then Kiki asked, "I assume that the letter convinced you?"

He didn't answer right away. She saw that he'd drifted away for a moment, and sensed that he had lost himself somewhere in something intensely painful, personal and private."

"It reminded me of something I haven't thought of in some time, a childhood memory, a secret between my brother and me. He's gone now, one of the last to die in Nam. God, such a waste. I kept his secret, I never told a soul. No one ever knew, or ever will. After John died, well, there was rarely reason to ever think of it. I guess I buried it deep in my memory."

She saw a hint of tears in his eyes and, touched by it, could nearly feel his pain. "Still no reason to talk about it," she said, "I don't need to know. Some things should remain secrets. I'm sorry if I've forced you to relive it, I wish that wasn't necessary."

He dismissed that with a wave of his hand.

"So, your name isn't Lainie McCann, you're Kiki Kinsler. Your dad and I were friends back in high school; a good guy, he's doing a specialized pediatric residency now, in Baltimore at Johns Hopkins, isn't it? Apparently, we're going to become best friends, and I'm meeting his older daughter long before he does."

"That's right," she said. "This might be a good time to take a look at the picture."

He did and gasped audibly, stunned by what he saw.

This photograph had been taken in front of his office – the only office he'd ever known. Two people were in the photograph:

The young woman he was meeting with now, and a much older version of himself.

"This is fucking incredible, forgive my language."

"Not a problem, considering."

"Can I see the band?" he asked. "I don't want a peek into the future – not yet at least – I'm not ready for that, but maybe later."

She extended her left wrist to him.

He studied it, and then felt it, raising his eyes at the smooth, coolness. Whens the odd control panel rose up and out of its face, he whistled softly. Clark picked up the phone on his desk, and buzzed Tracie. Speaking into it, he said, "Please cancel my appointments for the rest of day, Ms. McCann and I are not to be disturbed."

"What do we do next, Clark?" She asked.

"The letter gives me an overview, but I want the details. I'd like you to start at the very beginning and tell me *everything*. Take your time, Kiki; I need to hear it all."

Taking a deep breath, she began.

~~~~~

Two hours later, Kiki had related all of it, Clark asking questions throughout.

She began with a snapshot of her childhood and her family life, her years at U of O, and the ill-fated return to Portland little over a month ago. She stepped him through her arrival at home, the horror that she'd walked into, the attack by Little Mo Biggs and her time in the hospital. She recounted the three Visitations by the force, or presence, she'd come to call The Guardian.

After that, how she'd told her friend Jenna, and then Clark Bannion, what had occurred, and enlisting their help in her attempt to un-do the wrong, to *correct it*, as The Guardian termed it. How wonderfully supportive they'd both been, and how grateful she was for them. They'd helped her to learn about the history of the Biggs family, and how that pointed her on this path, with a plan to spare Little Mo from his fate, and in so doing, save her family from theirs. Then, she confessed the days and nights filled with doubts and fears, and the emotional whirlwind that had led up to The Journey and brought her to him today.

He listened without questions or comments, filling a legal page with notes.

When she was finished, she asked, "Do you believe me?"

"To tell you the truth, this is the craziest most impossible story I've ever heard. What it sounds like is something out of a science fiction movie, not real life. It's beyond incredible, but, yes, I do believe you. It's not as if you've given me much choice in the matter," he said wryly. "And, of course, I'll help you in any way I can, so let's talk about what you need, prioritize those things and get on with it."

"I need to get my living situation in order, sell the diamonds, and get to work."

Clark's chin rested on hands he'd steepled under it, carefully considering his answer.

She recognized the mannerism: Clark Bannion, attorney, in his legally pensive mode.

Impressed, he said, "You're absolutely right. We address logistical requirements first, what you need in place to operate comfortably and easily. May I make a few suggestions?"

"Of course, that's why I'm here."

"From now on, I am your attorney – *Lainie McCann's* attorney – representing you in the liquidation of assets inherited from your mother's estate. In that capacity, I'll assist as needed, and help you sell the jewelry. From your description, they're quite valuable. Reputable jewelers might question your possession of them, as they would any young woman. We may ask for a Cashiers Check, so such a sizeable deposit doesn't raise eyebrows at the bank. This should give you more than enough capital to live comfortably and do whatever it is you need to do."

"That's perfect."

"Now, let's discuss the house. I know Dr. Kinsler, played golf with him once. He kicked my ass by the way, I'm a lousy golfer ... tell me, is it worthwhile for me to keep playing?"

"I could extend your misery, but won't. I don't think you play much when you're older."

"Actually, that's a relief. Setting me free from something that brings me more pain than pleasure. The truth is I stink, don't have the patience, time or talent for the game, and don't love it, anyway. Okay, introduce yourself to the neighbors. Tonight, don't put it off.

Your cover story is fine, so give 'em a quick summary. If they have doubts, or you run into any problems, you can refer them to me. Here, take these," he said, handing her a small stack of his business cards. "Tell them to call me, they won't, suggesting they do should be enough."

"I really do appreciate the legal cover."

"You know, for all the lawyer jokes, we're handy folks when you need us."

"I'll visit them right away, as soon as I get home," Kiki said enthusiastically.

"I can also help you with the Family Services," he said confidently.

'Really? How?"

"Lucky for you, you've came to the right lawyer. I've done some work for them, until recently, mostly pro bono stuff. If we can't get you a paid job, I'm sure a referral from me will get you an internship."

"Fantastic ... is there anything else?"

"Other than lunch, I can't think of anything. Are you hungry?"

"Starved, I haven't eaten much."

"There's a great pizza by the slice joint around the corner, we'll talk more while we eat."

"That sound wonderful, but I do have one more thing," she said, and reached into her backpack and pulling out the box she'd brought with her."

"More surprises? What's in it?" Clark asked.

"Nothing yet," and from the backpack she withdrew a Polaroid camera she'd purchased at Fred Meyer yesterday afternoon. "For a while, in my time they stopped making these," Kiki told Clark, "but fortunately they're still popular here, and it's just what I need."

"What's the plan?"

"Could Tracie snap a picture of the two of us?" she asked.

"Sure, what's it for?"

"For now, just put it in the box and keep it in the floor safe under your desk. Yeah, your trusty safe is still there, I've seen it. This is my way of sending a message back, forward, whatever. It's so confusing. The people I left behind will be wondering if I actually made it. This lets them know I'm alive and well ... and here. You know what they say: A picture is worth a thousand words."

Chapter Nineteen

"THERE'S NEWS, GOOD NEWS," Clark told Jenna. "Something you'll want to see."

"You've *heard* from her?" She asked, excitement bubbling up in her voice.

"From *them* is more like it," he laughed. "Stop by any time, I'm here all day."

Jenna wasted no time hurrying over to Clark's office, and Tracie waved her right in. Clark beamed at her, pointed to the ever-present pot of coffee. Jenna poured herself a cup and sat down with it across from him.

"I have to admit I've been a little worried, even though it's only been two days," she said. "We expected it could be a few days or longer before she had the box in place and contacted us. So, you've got a message of some kind to show me? I can't wait to see it!"

"I had a feeling you'd rush right over. To tell you the truth, I've been a little nervous myself, but we can relax now. All this actually works, imagine that!"

He brought the box to his desk, set it down and opened. Inside it was a photograph and a yellowed envelope of his original letterhead with 'Jenna' written on it. Clark handed her the photograph, and said, "It's from a Polaroid instant camera."

She nodded, recognizing the photograph's unusual rectangular shape.

"My dad has an old Sun 600 model he's kept going for years. He's old school and loves instant photography, but they stopped making the film a few years ago, then about a year later they started again on a smaller scale. According to him, 'the niche refused to go quietly and was making a comeback, albeit a small one, and he was thrilled about it. Polaroid cameras were on the other side of the generational divide, but I know they still have their fans, like my dad. Digital cameras killed them, along with much of the conventional photography industry, chemicals and processing," Jenna said.

"For our purposes, Kiki made a shrewd choice. I look pretty good, wouldn't you say?"

The photograph was of two people: A smiling Kiki Kinsler and a younger Clark Bannion, and had been taken in his office. They were standing side-by-side, leaning back against the edge of his desk, with Kiki holding up the June 15th, 1981 edition of *The Oregonian*. Close in age, it occurred to Jenna they made a nice looking couple. Surprised by such a ridiculous thought, and blushing a little for it, she kept it to herself.

"Yes, you do, no argument about that," Jenna said. "The ladies must have loved you back then – not that they don't today, of course. But check-out the suit and tie, not to mention the hair! Wow, have styles changed!"

"Yeah, the hair, I really miss my hair. Not only was it black, I still had all of it! Long was the fashion back in the day, you know. *Everyone*, well, most everyone, wore it long. *Big hair* was big, hence Big-Hair bands. Let me confess something to you. When I'm alone in my car, I still have a fondness for *Hair Nation*, a satellite radio channel with 80s metal bands. I like to crank it up in the car, especially on the freeway. It's unbeatable cruising music!"

"Timeless, classic stuff, it is the best cruising music. *I* like a lot of it," she agreed, and changed the subject. "Kiki looks well, happy, wouldn't you say? I'm relieved to see it."

"We didn't talk about it much, but it was hard not to have my doubts. I know we all had a few, it was hard not to. Let's face it; a few weeks ago, the very idea of this was insane. And even after I was convinced, who knew what would happen once she actually did it. So much was unknown in all of this was, it was overwhelming, wasn't it? Part of me feared she'd get lost in some in-between realm never to be heard from again."

"I guess we were both thinking about it but neither one of us wanted to talk about it," Jenna agreed. "The newspaper is a nice touch, as is the Polaroid photo."

"These items are much more than a nice touch, they fall into the category of conclusive and indisputable evidence, not that I imagine we'll ever need it. But they offer real proof of where she is and when it is. Between us, I'm thrilled to have it. This is the kind of proof that gives me confidence that we're not all out of our minds and in the middle of some sort of shared delusion … and that what she's set off to do, is real and possible. Even now, hearing those words come out of my mouth, I have trouble believing them."

"I know. When she first told me the story after the funeral, I didn't know what to think. Then she showed me the band around her wrist, and my doubts quickly went away. Have you read the letter?" She asked.

Clark shook his head. "It's to you. Why don't you read it and tell me about it?"

The letter was two typed pages, single-spaced on Clark's old letterhead.

My Dear Friend –

I hope you're well and want you to know that I'm fine. I'm confident that this will reach you, because, at least so far, everything we hoped would happen has happened.

How crazy is that???

This is the afternoon of my second day, and I've been busy. After you read this letter, please pass it along to Clark.

As you can see from the picture I've enclosed, I'm with him in his office.

I called late yesterday afternoon and scheduled an appointment for this morning.

He's been terrific – charming and handsome, too – kind and supportive, just as I expected him to be. No surprise that he has agreed to help me in every way he can. The letter, and the photograph that I brought with me, convinced him that I am who I say I am, and where I'm from, and when.

Thankfully, I'm feeling no ill effects of The Journey.

In fact, the experience was rather pleasant, although finding the words to describe it is beyond me for now. I awoke yesterday morning having slept better than I have in weeks.

For the most part, I'm feeling comfortable here, although not like I belong. That may change, I hope it does, but we'll have to see. The world seems smaller, calmer and less chaotic. The rhythm or the force of now seems more relaxed. The roads are smaller and there is far less traffic on them. There are fewer people so there is more undeveloped land and more open Green Spaces with far fewer houses. It's nice. What's missing is all of the development we grew up with and took for granted, like the wallpaper of our time. The slower and smaller world of 1981 has its charm.

I like it.

The lifestyle seems less frenetic, and the problems of this world notwithstanding, it is a more relaxed and gentle place than the world I left behind. Maybe it's all the cell phones, computers, microwave transmission lines, fiber optic cables and electro-magnetic do-dads we've come to take for granted. I've often wondered if they create some kind of aggregated background noise we accept as normal, stimulating us, killing us, or making us crazy, while satisfying our insatiable communication and entertainment demands.

I don't sense that now, at least not nearly so much of it. Another good thing, I think, a pleasant thing, rather than being overwhelmed and confused, I'm finding it comforting and soothing considering I'm a fish – or is it a time traveler? – Out of water! I feel like it is giving me time to adjust.

I suppose whatever era we call "our time" becomes second nature to us. We accept it unconditionally and without thinking much about it. It simply is. It's our normal, what we know, and call home. The funny thing is that I always thought of home as a place.

Now I know that's only part of it. Home is also a time.

The house is everything I could have hoped for. It's empty of people but full of all the things I need to help me get along. If you can believe it, I even found a bicycle in the garage enabling me to travel around the city without a car.

Part of me wishes my grandparents were here, because I never really got to know them. I was so young when they passed on. At the same time, if they were here it would complicate matters considerably. With the work I have ahead of me, the last thing I need is for things to be more complicated than they already are.

Let me tell you about yesterday, my first day.

I said I slept well, better than I have since the attack, which delights and amazes me.

My first stop was a bike shop on Beaverton-Hillsdale Highway for a helmet and a lock. Next, I went to DMV and got my Driver's License, and then to First National Bank (Wells Fargo in our time) and opened an account. On the way home, I made a final stop at the Fred Meyer in Raleigh Hills. I'd forgotten how small Freddie's was before they remodeled it a few years ago. I picked up a pair of slacks and a top – in case I needed to look more presentable in a hurry – a few groceries and some real coffee. I was desperate.

Especially after choking down a cup of Taster's Choice yesterday morning.

Ugh! Instant coffee! Clark would have been absolutely horrified by it!

On the subject of coffee, two more things –

Can you imagine Portland – or anywhere – without a Starbucks or twenty? It will be years before they expand here from Seattle. For now, coffee-wise it's slim pickings.

Clark rescued me this morning with what he claims is the best coffee in town. Few people get beans yet, but he gets his from Graffeo's in San Francisco, a great Italian Roast.

This gives me further insight into the Clark Bannion we know and love.

No jumping on the coffee bandwagon, he came by his passion honestly and early.

Anyway, back to business.

Clark's going to help me sell the ring and earrings, and as fate would have it, he has a professional relationship with the Family Services agency, having done some recent work for them. It's amazing how things just work out sometimes. He suggested, and I know our Clark will agree, that it will be simpler to get hired there, probably safer, too. I'll still have ready access to Teddie Biggs and the Biggs family. It's a tremendous relief to have already found a path that avoids the bureaucracy of the Medical Center. I worried about that.

Oh, one more thing!

One night soon, we're going out for Chinese and to see Raiders of the Lost Ark.

On the big screen, I can't wait!

That's it for now, so be well, take care, I love you and will see you soon.

Know that you and Clark mean everything to me.

I couldn't do this without you.

Fondly,

Kiki
June 14, 1981

When she'd finished, Jenna sat quietly and waited patiently while Clark read the letter.

After he'd read it, he carefully refolded the pages and returned them to the envelope.

Smiling, he sank back in his chair, his hands steepled under his chin.

"What are you thinking?" Jenna asked.

"Words fail me."

Chapter Twenty

ITWAS TWO DAYS LATER when "Lainie McCann" received an early-morning call from Joyce Buckman, the founder and long-time Executive Director of the Community and Family Services Consortium of Washington County. Clark had explained that the agency was a non-profit and not formally associated with the State of Oregon.

"CFSC is as protective of its independence as it is dedicated to its civic mission," he'd told her.

Kiki liked the sound of that.

"Clark Bannion called me yesterday," Joyce began, "and I'd very much like to meet you. Would you be available to come into our office sometime in the next day or two to interview? I know this is terribly short notice, but I happen to have some time open today," she added hopefully.

Kiki thanked her for the call and they agreed to meet that afternoon.

Persistent morning clouds again hadn't burned off until after Noon. Temperatures might not make it *into* the seventies today. Kiki wondered if she should toss the U of O windbreaker she'd found in her grandmother's closet into her backpack when she left the house to meet Joyce.

Yesterday, she'd spent much of the late afternoon and early evening making the rounds through the neighborhood introducing herself to everyone she found at home. Most people were, and she discovered that her neighbors thought highly of her grandparents, and proved to be friendly folks; welcoming her, wishing her well, and offering help should she need anything.

She showered, and put on a little make-up, very little, found her grandmother's iron and ironing board, pressing her new clothes before riding to the interview. If she were lucky enough to be hired, the new job would make clothes shopping an instant priority. Kiki loved shopping, and looked forward to what would be fun, the low prices amazing.

She thumbed through the papers she would take with her. Her college transcript, the references she hoped wouldn't be necessary to call although one of them was Clark should anyone insist, her Social Security card and temporary driver's license.

Sun breaks were just starting to punctuate the sky.

The transition from morning clouds to a sunny summer afternoon was a slow one today. She rode in and out of sun and clouds, sometimes almost too warm, and minutes later nearly too cold. Oregon weather, she thought, even in the summer so unpredictable. But in an hour or two, when the strong summer sun had finally vanquished the clouds until their next assault, next morning, it would be a perfect afternoon, the best Northwest summer had to offer. Summer, she thought, doesn't get any better than right here in Portland, Oregon. This beautiful city is simply extraordinary when the sun is shining. The less than ten-minute ride was pleasant, uneventful, and Kiki sighed, relieved at never breaking a sweat.

The Community and Family Services Consortium office and administrative headquarters were in an old building in downtown Beaverton, one of Portland's original southwest suburbs and the unofficial capitol of Washington County. The building had been something else, before, and would become something else yet again, after CFSC. It occupied a corner of a block on a side street off Lombard with a smattering of commercial enterprises amid modest, older homes. A UPS truck making a delivery slowed, patiently picking its way around local children playing in the street, unhurried and content to wait for them, almost like it was still a small town.

Everywhere Kiki went, and everything she saw, was smaller, older, and as a result felt much more personal. Most of the people she met seemed more open, relaxed, friendly and trusting, rather than standoffish and wary. People were so different, and Kiki wondered if it was 9-11, or social media that thirty-one years later had changed us so fundamentally. How socially guarded we've become, one step removed from each other, connecting without connecting, an illusion of connection behind the safety of a constantly reinforced insulation of cyber-barriers.

The offices were professional, functional and neat, unpretentious, non-threatening and welcoming. She liked it right away. A middle-aged receptionist with impossibly long black hair going to gray, and wire-rim hippie glasses that when she got a closer look Kiki realized were bifocals, greeted her warmly.

"I'm guessing that you would be Lainie McCann. Good Morning and Welcome to our little shelter from the storm!"

"Thank you, I'm happy to be here and it's nice to meet you," Kiki replied.

She reached her hand across as the two women exchanged smiles and firm handshakes, "Emma," Kiki said, noting the name badge that had fought its way out of the cover of her long hair. Eyeing the wall clock she added, "I'm a little early, I know. I really overestimated the time it would take to ride over from Raleigh Hills, I'm happy to wait."

"I'm afraid you'll have to. Joyce has someone with her now, but it shouldn't be too long. Can I offer you coffee or tea? We also have iced tea today that Joyce brought from home for us. I don't know what she does exactly, but it's some kind of magical sun tea. She adds citrus and mint. We look forward to it every summer."

"I'd love some, thank you."

The tea was as advertised, and Kiki was happy to have made the right decision. "I'm not usually an iced tea drinker, Emma," she confided, "but this is wonderful ... you've worked here long?"

"Ten years in September," Emma answered, "I was one of Joyce's original clients. She saved my life, gave my kids a chance at theirs with a mother to love and support them. The truth is that I owe Joyce everything. There's nothing I wouldn't do for that woman. And I'm not the only one who feels that way, most of her clients do, you can ask 'em yourself."

Kiki could see that Emma meant every word and was about to say something when her phone console buzzed twice, signaling a call that was coming from within the office. Emma answered the line, and after listening for a brief time, said, "Yes, Ma'am, she's here with me now. Right, I'll send her right in."

Emma ended the call, and turning to said, "She's ready for you, Lainie. Straight down the hall, last door on your left." With a big smile, she pointed the way. "Good luck, I know you'll like her!" she added, encouragingly.

"It was nice meeting you, Emma, I hope to see you again," Kiki replied, returning the smile and heading towards the office.

The door to Joyce Buckman's office was open. The Executive Director of CFSC of Washington County was standing up behind her desk and welcomed Kiki with a smile.

"Come in, come in," she said, pointing to a chair, "ever since I spoke with Clark, I've been excited to meet you!"

Joyce was an attractive, vivacious woman with a ready smile who looked to be in her late forties, no older than early fifties, Kiki guessed. Short and slightly overweight, she carried it well. She had short, curly red hair, shocking green eyes that seemed to scream *I'm Irish*, with freckles across the bridge of her nose spilling down her cheeks. She spoke first.

"I see you got the dress code memo," she said with a playfully serious look.

Kiki was puzzled by this at first, then put it together and groaned when she had.

"Oh, my God," she said, "How is *this* possible?"

She and Joyce were wearing virtually identical slacks and tops.

This time, Kiki spoke. "It's one of two things. Either I'm showing great taste, or there is a soon-to-be-announced dress code that I've intuited."

At this, Joyce exploded in a fit of genuine laughter that soon had Kiki laughing.

"Clark told me you have a winning personality and a sense of humor," she said. "Have you known him long?"

She smiled, well prepared for this question and answered in a way that avoided details, saying, "You know, Clark. He's one of those men you feel like you've known all your life, isn't he?" Kiki expected the answer was vague enough *and* positive enough to mask her evasiveness while satisfying Joyce's question.

"He is that," Joyce agreed, to Kiki's relief. "By chance, did he tell you how he helped us? I'll bet he didn't, it's not his way, so I'll tell you how he won me over. When no one else cared, he went to bat for us, and did it pro bono. If you ask me, he's one of the smartest and toughest – don't let his friendly and outgoing manner fool you – young attorneys in Portland. Add to that he's not afraid of a fight and will do what's right, even when it's harder, unpopular or contrary to the safe political tide. If Clark Bannion vouches for you, that's good enough for me. Okay? So, let me tell you our story, Lainie. Then you can tell me yours, and we'll see if our heads and hearts are heading down the same path. Sound good?"

"I can't tell you how good," Kiki answered, and folding her hands together in her lap, listened attentively to the story of one woman's dream of saving families, one at a time.

Joyce spoke articulately and passionately about her work and their mission. She was a Social Worker by training, noting that she and Lainie had that in common. Leadership of CFSC had required her to wear an administrative hat, learn to sell, promote, fundraise and defend against doubters, skeptics, competing agencies, and a world of critics certain they knew better.

"Corny as it sounds, there aren't enough hours in the day," she said.

Kiki realized Joyce was a classic multi-tasker, another term that didn't yet exist.

"We've got a reputation I've fought long and hard for, no, that's not right, we've fought long and hard for. We're a team and I'd like to think that we've earned our success and all we've achieved honestly," Joyce continued. "We're advocates for family, and the root of that is a respect for abused wives and mothers who have no one to stand with them. That's what I think of as our mission. We do what we can, and I'd like to think we can do a lot."

"In the few moments I had with Emma, I learned she was one of your first clients," Kiki began softly. "I saw right away how passionate, proud, and committed she is, and that really impressed me. I know I'm young and don't have a lot of experience, but I'm old enough to know how rare that is, and what it says about an organization and its people."

Joyce Buckman arched an eyebrow, apprising the young woman in her office, allowing her to continue.

"I'm grateful that Clark spoke well of me, I really appreciate that. You should know he told me many wonderful things about you, how he respects you, and the work you do, and felt I'd fit right in. In the time I've spent here, I can see why and agree."

"Tell me a little about Lainie," Joyce encouraged. "What are you looking for?"

"As you know, I've earned my degree in Social Work, and like you, my primary interest is working with families. I believe I can help make a difference. I don't know if Clark told you that my parents are gone. I lost mom not long ago and decided to leave California and move to Portland."

"I'm sorry for your loss," Joyce said, and Kiki could see the genuine empathy in her face, "but perhaps Sacramento's loss is our gain," she added on an upbeat note.

"That's very kind, I hope so," Kiki said, touched by the woman's words she knew were genuinely offered. "It's been hard. Losing a parent is never easy, but I'm working through it, it just takes a while. One day I woke up and realized that without being aware of it, the painful part wasn't so close anymore, and the hurt was no longer so raw. In their place I'd been left the memories of the good things and the happy times. It's nice when experiences you're unprepared for teach invaluable life lessons. It did for me. Because of it, I think I'm better prepared to help others. It's wonderful to be feeling healthy and strong and I'm truly glad I'm here. I really like Oregon; Mom and I visited many times over the years, such an easy drive from the Bay Area. Mom's college friend lives here, or did until recently. They're in Europe now, and have been living in Arizona since fall, so I'm staying in her house while they're away. Housesitting for them and saving money, making my transition easier than it otherwise would be.

"I'm confident in my abilities and skills, but wouldn't in anyway overstate them. I have a lot to offer but much more to learn, and I know that. The opportunity to do that here, with you and your team, is something I'd take very seriously. You could count on me to give you my best, to take responsibility, and add to the team."

Telling her fabricated story to such a good person left Kiki a little uncomfortable, but there were good reasons to ignore that and press ahead. The truth wasn't an option, how could she tell Joyce *that* story? And her objectives were pure, weren't they? She thought so. Her only agenda was saving a young boy and his mother – as well as her own family – from fates that were catastrophically intertwined. She intended to do good and right by people to accomplish that. Left to rely upon her heart and head, trusting that she would do the right thing, but never having the luxury of actually knowing what the right thing was, she would do her very best.

She'd seen moments like this one coming from the beginning, so a moment of doubt and indecision wasn't unexpected. That was the very reason she'd pressed The Guardian, albeit without success, for any direction, help, or hint of a moral compass to navigate the unknown.

But it wasn't to be, and not part of the deal.

At first, forced to accept it, Kiki felt a little let-down, even miffed. To her it seemed cold, indifferent and distant. With time her view of it changed. The Guardian believed she would *know* what was right, so shouldn't she trust herself? And wouldn't CFSC offer an ideal environment and platform to do just that?

From the look on Joyce Buckman's face, she liked all she'd heard. Smiling broadly, she leaned forward and said so.

"Clark was right about you, from what I can see. I'd like you to join us, Lainie. We can work together and I'd like to think we learn from each other. Shall we talk about what that might look like?"

"I'd like that very much, Joyce, I really would."

Later, she biked home happy and gainfully employed at $400 per week with paid medical which she prayed she'd never need to use. That would cause problems.

"Lainie McCann", CFSC's newest counselor and family advocate caseworker.

Chapter Twenty-One

JOYCE BUCKMAN WAS TRAVELING to San Francisco to attend a conference and would be out of the office the balance of the week. Because of this, she asked Lainie to come in the following Monday to begin orientation and training. Kiki happily agreed; the extra time would allow her to take her time assembling a wardrobe for work, putter around the house, and, equally important, continue acclimating herself to her new world. She called Clark to tell him the good news.

"Joyce already called me," he told her, clearly pleased by it, "and thanked me for referring you to her. She was very impressed, obviously, and excited about what you bring to CFSC. It seems you made quite the impression, not that I'm surprised by that in the least," he finished.

"It was mutual. I really liked her; she made me feel right at home. It's easy to see why her staff loves her and CFSC has had such success."

"What are you going to do with your free time until you start?" He asked.

I thought I'd drop into Biggs and Sons in the late afternoon. I'd like to get a feel for them, he might be around then."

"Hmm," was all Clark said, and for a few moments neither spoke.

"You aren't wild about the idea?" She asked finally, sensing there was something he wasn't saying.

"Not necessarily, it's not that … although I think there is risk in being too bold. You need a reason for going there, let me think about this for minute."

"What if I'm looking for someone to take care of my grandparent's yard?"

"No, I don't think so. They have something in place already, so why rock that boat? Whoever currently cares for their property may have been doing so for some time. Losing an old and valued customer is something he might not take kindly to and, for all we know, he may even contact Biggs. Why take that chance? Why take any risk at all if it can be avoided?"

"I never considered that," she admitted, a little embarrassed by her oversight.

"Safety first, we know Morris Biggs Sr. is unstable, and that he's capable of violence. You shouldn't underestimate what that might mean, so let's be as careful as possible in dealing with him. How does this sound? You can visit on my behalf, inquiring about services for my property. I've been cutting my own grass and raking my own leaves. The beds are a mess, and I don't like the message it sends clients. Plus, I no longer have the time – or the energy – for it. The truth is I am looking for someone to take it off my hands, and do it right."

"That is better," Kiki agreed.

"Give him one of my cards, and ask that he stop by at his convenience, take a look, and give me a bid. A lawyer's card might keep him honest. He's flirted with the law in the past."

At home, she emptied her backpack, before going back out to spend the afternoon clothes shopping. Her first stop was the mall, but prices at Meier and Frank, not yet Macy's, and Nordstrom, posed a problem, threatening to put a serious dent into her available cash which was limited and dwindling rapidly. Kiki reminded herself to watch her spending until she and Clark sold the jewelry. She was about to leave when Betsy, a helpful and sympathetic sales clerk at Nordstrom, sensing her frustration, quietly suggested visiting a thrift store in Tigard.

"My manager would throw a fit if she heard me telling you about this store, but it's a real gem, with upscale clothing at bargain prices. Between us, I buy a lot of my clothes there. It's where wealthy women from Lake Oswego and some of the ritzy suburbs take beautiful clothes when they tire of them, so more often than not they're in excellent condition. You'll be amazed at the selection and the quality compared to most of the consignment and resale stores. For the cost of a couple of items here, you may walk out of there with a wardrobe makeover," the young woman confided excitedly but in a hushed tone. "It's a fun shop, too. You never know what you can find if you hit it at the right time. Maybe you'll get lucky!"

"Thanks, that's so nice of you," Kiki told her, "I'm on a tight budget, and every little bit helps!" She added with a conspiratorial air. "I start a new job on Monday and need some things."

"When you're rich and successful come back and see me," Betsy told her with a knowing smile, "we'll have some fun. You have a great figure for clothes and look great in everything!"

Kiki rode right over and her timing couldn't have been better.

An hour later, with her backpack crammed, she returned home with enough new clothes to get started. She'd ask Clark to borrow his car one day, unless he was willing to accompany her, and make a return trip. The place had been a real find, everything Betsy said it would be, and more.

It was nearly five p.m. when she reached home. Kiki removed her purchases from the backpack and hung them hoping to coax the wrinkles away and avoid having to iron them before she wore them. She'd stopped at a Chevron station riding home and picked up two maps, one of the Portland Metropolitan Area, the other of Oregon-Washington, astounded that they actually gave them away just for asking, no purchase required.

In my time, she thought, no one gives anything away.

She had the address for Biggs and Sons Landscaping and the map made it easy to find.

The property, serving as both their home and business base, was just off Greenburg Road across Highway 217, on a short street that spurred west off SW Tiedeman. This was an area she knew well, but in its more developed state years in the future. Now, it had the look of one of those forgettable stretches of no man's land in what might have been Beaverton, Tigard or unincorporated Washington County. Tucked away as it was, she couldn't be sure. Reaching it in less than a fifteen minute bike ride, she was surprised to find it already combined light industrial with old residential that, even more than thirty years earlier, had already seen better days.

Biggs and Sons was at the end of the street, with the house in front, and a pole building perhaps thirty yards behind it backing up on a field with two old horses grazing in it. An arrow on a crudely painted sign pointed to the business office, identified only as "Office" painted by hand in white letters on a door that, compared to the rest of the structure, looked comparatively new. Around the right side leaning up against the wall, was a heap of discarded tools and rusted, antique farm implements. Kiki wondered if they'd already been retired when the Biggs clan had arrived. The ones on top were covered with thick Northwest moss. Along the left side of the building was a stack of old tires that had tipped over. Some were standing on end, others haphazardly rested atop each other, and a few had rolled unencumbered until stopping against a cyclone fence that looked like it might be down for the count and considering giving up.

Two trucks were parked in front, loaded with lawn mowers, edging tools, gas blowers, and overflowing mounds of clippings and yard debris, apparently removed from the grounds of that day's customers. Like everything else she saw, the trucks were tired and beat-up, full of scratches, dents and caked mud, looking as if they hadn't been washed in years, if ever. On one truck, a magnetic signs on the door with "Biggs" in red letters had slipped to an odd angle.

It appeared Big Mo was in the house.

Kiki took a deep breath, walked up to the door, knocked sharply, waited a moment, opened it and walked in.

A small office area was just inside on the immediate left, separated by a roughly-hewn counter constructed with an eye for speed and budget but not appearance. Behind it were two surplus metal desks and three ancient filing cabinets. To the right was a small office, unoccupied, and beyond it through a closed door, what she assumed was the working shop and a storage area. A woman in her early to mid- thirties, Kiki couldn't easily tell, looked up from one of the desks and offered a weak smile that seemed to apologize and ask forgiveness for the clutter and the mayhem.

Kiki returned the woman's smile, mindful to strip it of anything that might be construed as disapproving or condescending.

She knew this was Teddie Biggs, Little Mo's mother. Other than her desk, which was orderly and neat, chaos ruled, the place was a mess. A dim fluorescent light cast an odd shadow on a once pretty face that now, at the end of the day, looked exhausted and dispirited. Kiki wondered if this woman looked any happier at the beginning of the day, or if such looks of defeat and despair had become her constant companions.

"May I help you?" Teddie asked politely.

"Yes, thank you, I hope so," Kiki answered amiably. "My name is Lainie McCann, and I'd like a bid on weekly services."

"Residential or commercial," Teddie Biggs replied, "would this be for your home?"

"No, it's not for me, but for a friend, an attorney who owns a small office building in Southwest Portland. I was in the area, and when I saw the sign on Greenburg, and decided to stop in and ask if you're taking on new customers. The grounds of his building aren't huge, but need more attention than he can give them. To be honest, he's shopping around, getting bids – you know how lawyers are," she added with a wink. "So, I'm helping him out, inquiring at a few places. If you're interested, I'll leave his card so someone can run over there, take a look and get back to him with an estimate and service options."

Kiki was now close enough to Teddie to get a better look at her, and it was troubling.

The woman's eyes were red-rimmed, and while for many this was peak allergy season, Kiki suspected that crying, not pollen was the culprit. But there was more to it than allergies or tears. Behind tortoise shell glasses, her right eye appeared to have almost recovered from being blackened, bruising gone to yellow, but not quite faded away. Her lower lip had been split, evidenced by a scab that still looked angry. Teddie was wearing jeans and a sleeveless blouse that, while clean was threadbare, and didn't conceal a large bruise just above her left elbow.

Just then a young boy rushed in, frightened and wailing, tears flowing down his chubby cheeks. "Mommy, Mommy, don't let Daddy spank me anymore," he cried, and trembling, buried his face against his mother's breast, chest heaving, unable to stop crying.

His mother wiped his eyes, and moved to calm him. Patting his back, whispering softly, planting kisses on his cheek while murmuring endearments tenderly into his ear.

Little Mo Biggs, Kiki knew, terrorized by his father even while his mother lived.

A door slammed in the back shop, hard enough to rattle the walls in the front office.

"Little Mo!" a deep voice bellowed. God dammit, where is that fuckin' kid?"

Seconds later, the man who owned the voice appeared in the office. Seeing Kiki, the look on his face expressed no regret for raging at the child in front of a prospective customer, but left no doubt how displeased he was to be inconvenienced by an unexpected stranger's intrusion.

The huge man was wild-eyed, filthy and smelled like sweat and dirty clothes. He nodded at Kiki, and grumbled something under his breath she couldn't quite hear. He glared at his small son, wrapped tighter in his mother's embrace, whimpering and shaking uncontrollably.

"Mo, this is Lainie McCann. An attorney in town would like us to estimate the costs for doing the grounds of his building," she said brightly, hoping that the prospect of new business might cool his hot temper and encourage him to behave in front of a prospect.

"Yeah?" He asked. "Could take a look next time we're over that way, I guess," he said. The look on his face wasn't quite contrite, but Kiki suspected this might be what passed for civil and courteous with Morris Biggs Sr. "Anything special I should know before I do?" He asked, eyeing her more closely. The fact that she was an attractive young woman had just registered. His eyes took her in, looking her up and down, locking on her breasts and undressing her, until, grunting with approval, he looked away and down at the ground.

Kiki couldn't help feeling embarrassed for his wife and cheapened by his invasive stare. Despite having expected that and worse, being confronted, first-hand with such brutish behavior was appalling, leaving unprepared for the sudden boiling-up of anger and hatred she harbored for him. Then she was rescued by a calming awareness enabling her to relax, and endure the moment without losing her head. Big Mo Biggs deserved whatever he'd get and she was committed to giving him all that he deserved. The man was a pig. Teddie handed him Clark's business card. Big Mo nodded, grunted a goodbye, and disappeared back into the shop.

At his departure, Kiki saw Teddie heave a silent sigh of relief.

"He's had a long hard day," Teddie explained in a robotic voice that sounded like she was going through the motions, mouthing the words out of habit. Kiki was certain Teddie had said them so many times before she no longer had the strength, or the will, to believe them.

Kiki nodded slowly, indicating she understood, and that it was okay.

"Here's another card," she said to Teddie, placing it on the desk. "I know how easy it is to misplace them when you're busy. I can see your husband is very busy," she added.

"Thank you," Teddie told her, grateful for the unspoken solidarity Kiki had offered.

"Oh, one more thing," Kiki said, and picking up Clark's card, turned it over writing on the back of it. "I'm also going to give you my contact numbers. At times, Mr. Bannion is very hard to reach. He's often tied up in court and difficult to catch-up with. This way, you'll be able to reach me at my home number and at work."

Teddie looked surprised by this. "You don't work for the lawyer?" She asked.

"Oh, no, I'm doing him a favor. Clark Bannion is a friend, and he represents me, I'm a client. He's helping me with my mother's estate. I work for the Community Family Services Consortium. I'm a Family Services Counselor, Mrs. Biggs. We're advocates for mothers, children and families," she said pointedly. "Some women need aid, others need shelter, and many just need someone they can talk to."

A flicker of awareness crossed Teddie Biggs' face disappearing almost as quickly as it had appeared, and quickly followed by a series of emotions as she processed the information. Confusion, fear and hope each made a fleeting visit to the beleaguered woman's face. Kiki's heart went out to a mother trapped in a dangerous situation and desperately needing help had no idea how to get it.

Teddie held Kiki's eyes, searching for something and without speaking the two women communicated a non-verbal understanding that each recognized as significant. There was no need for Kiki to say more, she'd merely casted an idea hoping to set the hook. If she had, it might result in a woman looking for sanctuary when things got too much bear, and reached a tipping point, searching for a way out of her domestic prison.

Little Mo had finally stopped crying, and Teddie held a tissue to his nose.

"Blow," she told him, and he did, surprisingly loud, and the two women smiled at it.

"Goodbye, Little Mo, I hope to see you again," Kiki said kindly, turning and reaching for the door. "It was nice meeting you, Mrs. Biggs," she said to Teddie.

"Teddie, please," she corrected.

"And I'm, Lainie," Kiki replied. "Have a nice evening," she said, and walked out the door, closing it softly behind her, wondering what the evening might hold for the Biggs family that could possibly be good.

Chapter Twenty-Two

❝IS YOUR DINNER ALRIGHT?" Teddie asked Big Mo timidly, hoping the stew that had cooked all day in the crock pot would meet with his approval. These days, few things did meet with his approval, despite her every effort to make him happy and going to extraordinary lengths to avoid setting him off.

Her husband was on his fourth beer, well on his way to drunk, and he was a mean drunk.

"It's all right," he said curtly. "Is there more bread?"

Teddie winced, knowing he wouldn't like the answer. "No, that's it. I'm sorry."

"Fuck, woman, is it too much to ask for a little bread with dinner, for Christ's sake? What the hell am I supposed to use to mop up the gravy? God damn, can't you get anything right?"

Little Mo was poking listlessly at his dinner, shrinking into his chair, wishing he could disappear and make himself invisible. Looking around for a place to hide but finding none, cringing at the exchange, his breathing quickened and he began to whimper.

"What's your fuckin' problem?" Big Mo demanded, glowering at the young boy.

"If you're mad at me, there's no reason to take it out on the child, Morris," Teddie said, hoping to deflect her husband's distemper away from their son, doubtful that she could.

"Not talking to you, this is between me and Little Mo," he advised his wife with a menacing eye, and jabbing a finger at him to accent his point. "If you have a brain in your head – which I doubt more and more – shut your fuckin' trap, and quit your sniveling," he warned coldly.

Teddie knew better than to answer, but also where this was heading. What passed for dinner conversation these days and it had become an ugly nightly ritual.

The man turned back to the boy. "Why aren't you eating? Food costs money."

Before he could pursue the brow-beating grilling, Teddie intervened.

"Please, Morris," she pleaded. "Little Mo is five years-old, and you're frightening him. There's no reason to abuse him this way. He's done nothing wrong."

Big Mo stopped, thought about it for a minute, and slowly nodded his head in agreement.

"You're right," he admitted.

Without warning he reached over to his wife and backhanded her across the mouth. The act reopened the scab recently healed on her lip and it began bleeding freely. Tears welled-up in Teddie's eyes and Little Mo began to cry.

"Aw, fuck this shit," Big Mo spat, disgusted by his wife and son. "I'm goin' out to the Barn," he said and pushed back from the table. "Things better change around here with you two," he told them, and lifting a six-pack from the refrigerator, went out the back door.

Teddie Biggs sat unmoving in her chair at the table, numbed by another happy family dinner. How did I end up with this monster? And how on earth could I ever believe a child would make things better? It's made things worse, if that's possible, and Little Mo is an angel.

She sighed forlornly, overrun by futility, resignation, fear and dread.

One thing was clear: she needed to be strong for her child. Teddie wiped her eyes with her napkin, and dabbed at the blood on her lips. Looking down, she saw that a few drops had found their way to the tablecloth. She frowned at this but feeling her small son's eyes upon her, watching her intently, forced a cheery and upbeat smile. Kids miss so little, she thought, and on some level they understand things that are way beyond their experience.

She beckoned to Little Mo, inviting him to her. He gratefully crawled up into her lap and lost himself in his mother's loving embrace.

"Shh. Shh," she cooed, "it'll be alright little man, there's nothing to worry about."

Little Mo looked up into his mother's eyes wanting – and willing – to believe her.

She knew her son, even at five years old, really didn't believe her words.

Teddie Biggs had stopped believing them long ago.

~~~~~

Kiki was at home, inspecting her new clothes, considering the outfits and pairing them into different combinations. Thanks to some wise selections, she could stretch the day's haul much farther than she had first imagined. It was a great start; she liked to shop and when she did, success always thrilled her. Like winning a game, the one thing that could make it better, make it perfect, was to have also found the deal of deals. And she had.

Professional shoppers like her mother and Jenna would have been suitably impressed.

Saddened by those thoughts, forcing them away, she banished for another time.

An inspection of the cupboards and pantry was not encouraging. Uninspired by what she'd found, with little to choose from it was time to do some real grocery shopping. She briefly considered ordering a pizza, but didn't want to spend the money for a nothing-special pizza. Equally unappealing was the prospect of heading out again on her bike.

She'd ridden a bicycle more in the last few days than she had in all the years since learning to drive combined. Wonderful exercise, but her legs were barking and her butt was more than a little tender. A break was needed and well-deserved. Maybe she'd settle for a bowl of cereal and a couple cookies. After a long bath, she'd crawl into bed with a good book and get a good night's sleep.

Her grandfather had been an insatiable reader. He loved fiction, her dad used to say, *with enough action, intrigue, suspense, mystery, sex and well-turned phrases to keep the pages turning and him awake and reading late into the night.* Combing through book shelves and boxes, she'd found one of his all-time favorites, a well-read paperback copy of *Tai- Pan*, the James Clavell epic about Hong Kong during the Opium Trading days. People were talking about *Noble House*, one of the year's biggest books and the smash best-seller that continued the story, so she decided to read them in order. In high school she'd read *Sho-Gun*, and loved it, but that novel had been written years later and for her was more contemporary. To read the earlier ones, now, during their time, seemed like a wonderful idea, and in an odd way brought her closer to the grandfather she'd never really known.

Kiki decided to take a bath first, and eat later. After losing the dust and sweat from riding around all day in a good soak, everything would be more appetizing. Stripping off her clothes and slipping into her grandmother's robe, she ran the tub. Just as she was about to step into it, the extension on the night table in the bedroom rang. She smiled at the old-fashioned sound of it. In a way, she thought, that's how phones ought to sound, and made a mental note to search out a ringtone like it for her cell, when she returned, to her time.

"Hello."

"It's Clark, Kiki. Have I caught you at a bad time? Say so if I have," he said, almost too emphatically.

"No, not a bad time at all. I'm glad to hear from you. What's up?"

"Have you eaten? No big deal if you have, but here's what I'm thinking. The jeweler I think should see about your stuff is open 'til nine tonight. My schedule is tight the rest of the week, but I could do it tonight, if that works for you. And if you haven't had dinner, we could grab a bite, before or after. What do you think? How's that sound?"

"Like an offer I can't refuse," Kiki said. "Could you give me half an hour?" She asked.

"Sure, let's see. It's almost seven now. I'll come by around seven-thirty."

"I'll be watching for you," she said.

Thirty minutes; the bath turned into a shower. She had to get clean, but there was no time to wash her hair. Just put on a little make-up, figure out what to wear, hope that it worked well enough and was presentable enough, although this was Oregon, and Oregon had always been an *anything works if it works* place when it came to fashion, so she thought she'd be okay there. And what was the big deal? There was no big deal. This wasn't a date or anything, nothing social about it. It was just a friendly bit of business with an old friend, someone she'd known all her life, her dad's best friend.

With two minutes to spare she saw Clark drive up in his '81 Datsun 280Z. He smiled and when she nodded approvingly at the car he was absolutely beaming. Walking around to the passenger side he opened the door for her and she climbed in.

"Nice Z," she said. "You look good in it!"

"My one and only vice, I love this car," he confessed.

"*Nissan* is still making Z's and they're better than ever."

"Nissan, I just read about the name change," he answered. "I really don't get it, not that it matters. Still, it's going to take some getting used to. This is my third Z, and they've all been *Datsuns*, except now I have to call them something else."

"You'll get over it," she assured him, "and even if you don't, get used it. The future is full of name changes and consolidations, old favorites popping up on the endangered species list and new favorites getting so big, so fast, your head will spin like Linda Blair."

"Glad I called, Little Miss Sunshine from the Future," he said as he stepped on the gas hard enough to almost roar off with a look on his face that said you don't mess with me.

Goodhal's Jewelers was virtually on the doorstep of Washington Square, not in the mall, but in a small strip center that was essentially next door. The owner had been a friend of Clark's dad since their days together in the Korean War, and Roger Goodhal was always thrilled to see the young man he loved like a favored nephew, winking at him when Kiki wasn't looking, and indicating his enthusiastic approval of the young man's female companion.

"Hi Uncle Roger," Clark said. "I'd like you to meet Lainie McCann; I'm assisting her with the disposition of some assets she recently inherited, her mother's jewelry."

"I'd be happy to take a look," he said, showering Kiki with his most dazzling smile.

"Don't let that smile lull you into settling for a lower price, Lainie," Clark advised soberly. "Roger has perfected that smile over the years. It's a lethal negotiating weapon."

"Duly warned," Kiki replied brightly, returning Roger's smile with one of her own that matched his and nearly melted him.

"Wow, you're good," Roger said admiringly. "Better watch yourself, Clark. Okay, here's what I see. At a glance, these are gorgeous pieces, exceptional in many ways, so quite valuable. I can't tell you, tonight, though, how valuable. I want our senior appraiser to look at them in the morning. I could call you then, certainly no later than noon. Would that be satisfactory?"

"That's fine," Clark said. Offering his hand he was pulled into a bear hug

When Roger released him from it he held him at arms-length, looking into his eyes.

"I still miss your old man, kid," he said with a weak grin.

"I know, me, too," Clark replied, "I miss him every day."

"Nice girl," Roger said in an even softer voice, tilting his head towards her, "You, uh …? You need to settle down with a good woman."

"No, nothing like that, Lainie is a client," Clark said, a little embarrassed at the exchange.

Roger nodded and then shrugged. It came off with a non-verbal message that said *that's a shame.* "I'll talk to you tomorrow. A pleasure meeting you, Lainie," he said, smiling again.

On their way out, Clark said, "That couldn't have gone better, I think you're going to do really well," and then asked, "Say, you aren't a vegetarian or anything, are you?"

"Always hunting for the ultimate burger and fries," she huffed with mock indignity.

"Then you're in luck. Not far from here, in Aloha, almost to Hillsboro on Farmington, there's a great one. Are you up for a little ride?"

"In a Z with a great burger waiting at the end of it, are you kidding?"

"It's a cool place, you'll like it. This owner comes from Chicago; it's full of Cubs, Bears, White Sox, Bulls and Black Hawks stuff, lots of television screens, too. It's like a bar for sports fans with the kind of food a sports fan loves. Helluva great idea, I think it could be big," he said, and saying it caused him to stop and think. "Do sports bars catch-on?" he asked.

She smiled. "You could call sports lovers and food lovers a marriage made in heaven." She didn't say that while sports bars thrived, Heidi's hadn't survived.

Clark loved to drive and the Z was a driver's car. Kiki was familiar with this part of Farmington Road, but couldn't believe how rural it still was. Heidi's was on the left, just past Kinnaman, about ten blocks before 185th. Clark told her everything was good, including the hot dogs, but the burgers were simply great – big, thick, hand-formed patties, charred just right.

"Sound great to me," she said, "is that what you're having?"

"What I always have," he said seriously, "although when I'm alone, with no one watching, I sometimes indulge myself in their *big* burger. It's really big, really good, and really depraved. I shouldn't talk about it and reveal my secret side, the weak and gluttonous me."

"I don't see it listed," she said, puzzled she saw nothing about it on the menu.

Pointing to it, he said, "Here it is. They give it its own section, The *One-Pound Mound of Ground Round.* See?"

"That's a burger? Wow, a one-pound burger ... you've actually eaten all that?"

"More than once, I'm a growing boy – or was. I know it's not something to be proud of, but I will also admit, and *proudly*, that I enjoyed every bite. For the record, it's the only burger I've ever eaten – anywhere – that had me in pain and questioning my sanity afterwards."

"I believe it. Was it painful enough not to order it ever again?"

"Not quite. But it was painful enough to make me think about twice before ordering it again. So now, if I'm going to have one, I train for it, by fasting all day before I go for it. "

They each ordered the regular bacon cheeseburgers that when they arrived Kiki noted were plenty big enough. They shared orders of fries and fried mozzarella sticks dipped in marinara sauce, and sipped draft beers. Kiki agreed the food was great, but knowing Heidi's was gone in her time left her a little sad, fearing many more such memories lay ahead for her.

Their conversation covered practically every possible topic. Without having to try, they were comfortable with each other, relaxed and unpressured, speaking openly, freely and without pretense. Kiki found herself enjoying Clark Bannion thoroughly. A man her mother would have liked, did like, actually, smart, kind, and well-mannered, attractive inside and out.

She liked him a lot.

But then she always had.

And there was no question he liked her, men being so obvious that way, and, wanting to make a good impression, was working hard at it and succeeding. That realization caught her off-guard because its significance was so startling. Here they were, chattering non-stop, genuinely enjoying each other's company as they shared their life stories, the way strangers that had just met would; strangers knowing little about the other, eager to learn all they could.

All well and good, Kiki thought, except I've known him all my life, in another life.

And this is his time, the time of his youth, but not the time of mine.

"Have I lost you, Kiki?" Clark asked. "Or am I so painfully boring that you've tuned me out in an act of self-preservation?"

"Boring? Not you! I'm sorry. I'm having a wonderful time, and hope I'm not boring you. Something you said got me thinking, and these days when something gets me thinking I get lost on my own just fine, thank you. But it was rude of me, and I apologize for drifting away when I should have been listening. Do you forgive me?"

"Of course. So, are you going to answer my question?"

"The one I didn't hear, apparently. Would you mind repeating it?" She asked contritely.

"Are you involved with any one, back in 2012?"

"Not at the moment. I did have a boyfriend at school, for most of my freshman year and all of my sophomore year, until the very end. He was older, a senior from LA on his way to med school at USC. We broke up just before I came home for the summer."

"Was the break-up mutual?"

"No, for once it was me. I thought I loved him, but I think it was more being in love with the idea of being in love, the magic of that. Doesn't everyone want that? I did, but one day I woke up and realized I didn't love him, or even like him very much. Rather than heartbreaking, it was liberating, and the best thing that could have happened. But you know what was really incredible? The more

I really got to know him, the clearer it became that he was what I *didn't* want. I realized that I wanted much more, if that makes sense."

"Now I'm really curious," he said and waited for her to explain.

"With Justin, it was all about Justin. He could say the right things, take me nice places, give me occasional gifts, and was thoughtful enough, but there was no depth to our relationship, and it was all sizzle without the steak. When it really mattered, there was no *me* and no *us*, only *him*. When I saw my future as a trophy wife, I couldn't run away fast enough."

"His loss," Clark said, "but good for you, figuring it out before you made a mistake. Some mistakes are harder to unwind than others; that's the lawyer in me talking."

Kiki nodded. "Okay, now it's your turn. What's a handsome, successful young attorney doing unattached when I happen to know that a bevy of attractive women would love to meet you and try to cut you out of the herd, so to speak."

He blushed slightly and Kiki thought it was cute, glimpsing his almost little-boy shyness. Something she suspected he kept well hidden and rarely showed. That he had, touched her.

"Okay, my turn. I've had girlfriends, and a relationship or two over the years that were more than casual. Law school isn't the ideal time for dating, and it's the worst for relationships if you're in one. Romantically, in law school nobody wins or goes home happy. It's a well-known relationship killer, actually. I saw it over and over again, always glad it wasn't me. I've been practicing for three years, and my practice consumes my time. Not to say I'm a monk, but I'm no hunter, either. I want what my parents had, I guess."

"And what was that?"

"My mom and dad were happily married, really happily married. They weren't one of those lovey-dovey couples, touchy-feely all the time, nothing like that. They liked each other. And they talked to each other, really talked, because they liked talking to each other. I think they were friends first, and that made being lovers even sweeter. The love they felt for each other all their lives was built upon that friendship."

Clark glanced at his watch, it was late. They'd been talking for over two hours.

"Better get you home before you turn into a pumpkin, Cinderella," he said and picked up the check. "I've enjoyed this, very much."

"I have, too, Clark. I loved dinner, and thank you again for all of your help, but most of all for the wonderful conversation."

Chapter Twenty-Three

THE NEXT DAY, Clark called around noon with good news about the jewelry.

"I just heard from Roger. His appraiser loved the ring and earrings, so here's the deal. They'll pay $14,800 for them. A lot of money, maybe much more than you need. If you don't want to sell both, the numbers are $8,200 for the ring and $6600 for the earrings. He said both pieces are very nice, but the earrings, the size of the stones makes 'em rare."

Kiki did some quick math in her head.

A dollar in 1981 had the buying power of thirty-five to forty cents in 2012. Selling both pieces meant she was looking at the equivalent of $35-40,000, which was much more than she needed. The earrings, supplemented by the earnings of her new job, would net her enough to get along comfortably. Additionally, it would spare her having to part with the diamond ring her mother had inherited from her mother, who had worn it all her life.

More than a connection to her mother, Kiki hoped to wear it herself one day.

"I'll sell the earrings and hold on to the ring," she told Clark.

"Give Roger a call, he's waiting to hear from you."

"I will right away. I'd like to stop by for the ring and the check later this afternoon."

"Is the money burning a hole in your pocket already?" He asked, teasing her playfully. "What are you planning?"

"I need a used car," she said. "I don't suppose you …"

"Actually, I represent a dealer. A good guy, a straight-shooter, let me make a call."

By the end of the day, Kiki had deposited the check and purchased a red '78 Honda Accord four-door from Gates Honda, the dealership owned by Clark's client for $2100. The price was a real bargain, and the great deal was explained to her as "something I'd like to do for Clark, I owe him a favor," Randy Gates said.

The mileage was low and the car was in excellent condition. Kiki asked him about it.

"It was my mother's car," he'd explained, "and at her age she really didn't drive all that much."

"Are you telling me that this is the proverbial *little old lady's car?*" Kiki asked.

"Believe it or not, that's exactly what it is. I know you'll love this car, but if you don't, bring it back, Lainie, no problem."

On her way home she stopped for some serious grocery shopping.

It was nice to be able to buy more than she could fit in a backpack.

She had fun leisurely making her way up and down the aisles, inspecting brands and packages she'd never seen before. Most everything was both unknown but vaguely familiar. Tomorrow was Saturday, she planned to make a return trip to the thrift store and see if she could find more clothes. And, if time permitted, she'd visit Betsy at Nordstrom to thank her properly and look for some more suitable shoes for work on Monday.

~~~~~

Kiki didn't see Clark over the weekend, but hadn't expected to. After purchasing the car she'd called his office to thank him for his help but he was in court that afternoon. She left a message with Tracie who congratulated her on the great buy.

"Everyone loves Accords," she told Kiki, "Japanese cars may take over some day!"

If you only knew, Kiki thought.

Leaving a message with a real, live person, who would write it down and hand a physical piece of paper to the intended recipient, seemed such a foreign thing. She came from the time of instant, digital communication, where everyone depended upon email, voicemail, text messages, Facebook and Twitter. When you wanted to know about something – anything – you went online, rather than paying a visit to the library.

At first, it was strange getting used to being cut-off from all of that. Consciously gearing down wasn't as easy as she'd persuaded herself it would be. Everything looked different from thirty-one years in the future, but this world came with benefits that were pleasing. Connecting with people in a real, flesh and blood way was satisfying. Hearing a live voice rather than a recorded greeting when she made a call wasn't hard to get used to at all. She liked it a lot.

After a long and wet rainy season, the perfect summer weather was everything soggy Oregonians hope for, practically crying out for cooking something on the grill and eating outside. Kiki spent part of Sunday afternoon getting her grandparents' old Weber kettle into barbeque-shape. Then, she grilled a chicken breast and an ear of sweet corn over the coals for dinner, complementing it with a salad and some watermelon. Eating at the table on the patio in the back yard, sipping iced tea until the sun set. She took a stab at brewing a pitcher of sun tea, and while it wasn't bad, it didn't come close to Joyce's magical concoction at CFSC.

"I've got to learn how she does it," Kiki told herself, and standing up, stretched, yawned and carried her dishes back to the house into the kitchen.

After scraping and rinsing them off, she loaded them into the dishwasher, wondering how long it would take her to use enough of anything to run a full load. Cooking for one, especially if she grilled, didn't use many pots, pans and dishes, it could take an entire week before it was full. Not that such a trivial and insignificant thing mattered much. Still, in an odd way, it affected her to a degree which she was unprepared for.

Intensifying the distance and separation she felt from her world, her home.

Inside the empty house, alone and getting ready for bed, she was lonely.

Work is what I need and will be good for me, she thought, dropping off to sleep.

It was what she needed in more ways than one.

~~~~

It rained unexpectedly overnight, courtesy of a summer thunderstorm that passed through quickly dumping a lot of water in a hurry. This was the first measureable rainfall in nearly a month, *The Oregonian* reported, neatly clearing the air and washing away the summer dust. The grass and flowers seemed to have perked-up as a result, and birds chattered happily on a beautiful summer morning that dawned without a cloud in the sky.

She wore a long skirt, peasant-style blouse with impressive beading, and pair of sandals she'd fallen in love with that Betsy had recommended. Ready to leave for her first day at her new job, she briefly debated whether to drive or bike to work, and opted to drive. Why take any chances, she reasoned. Better to ensure arriving on time and looking her best. What's more, the excitement of a new car, albeit an antique by her standards, was hard to argue with and she was grateful for the freedom it afforded her.

Parking wasn't a problem. CFSC had ample on-street parking without meters and a small lot behind the building that was available to its staff on a first-come, first-served basis. Kiki was early, it was not yet eight and office hours were 8:30 – 5:00, so she'd have plenty of time to visit with Emma and have another cup of coffee before her scheduled meeting with Joyce at nine. Checking herself in the rear-view mirror, she took a deep breath, hopped out of her car, and walked briskly into the office.

"Lainie! Good morning and welcome!" Emma called, seeing her come through the door.

"Thank you, Emma," she replied. "I'm happy to be here, but I'm a little nervous, too," she said, her voice lowering to an almost whisper, "with it being my first day and all."

"Trust me, that won't last long. We're easy to get along with and we've all had first days of our own, you know. There's coffee in the break room down the hall," she said, "just past Joyce's office. Why don't you grab a cup, and come back here. I've got a packet of New Employee stuff HR left with me for you to complete. I'll point you to your office – it's actually more a mostly private cubicle, but not bad – and you can either work on these things back there, or sit with me … in case you have questions. Most people do. So, go grab your coffee, there's tea if you'd rather, and we'll get started and get this stuff knocked out before Joyce gets in. Sound good?" Emma asked.

"Sounds great, Emma. Thanks to you, I'm already starting to feel at home!"

The smell of freshly brewed coffee grew stronger and more inviting as she neared the break room and it tasted even better, reminding her of Clark's Graffeo. She wondered if he'd sent the beans over, or if he'd made Joyce a disciple of his beloved Bay Area java supplier.

She whipped through the generic application, concentrating on her fictional information, filled out forms for payroll deductions and insurance, and included crisp copies of her cover letter, transcript, resume and professional and personal references, making sure that Clark's was prominently displayed, first. Hopefully, there would be no reason or inclination to dig deeper. She felt confident there wouldn't be.

The final item was an Employee Profile card for CFSC use. This was used to capture everything from personal interests, hobbies, birthday, and next of kin to emergency contacts. Leaving Next of Kin blank made her uncomfortable, but she had no one. Per her back story, and for her, now in 1981, it was the truth, but she did list Clark Bannion as her emergency contact.

Just as she'd finished, Joyce walked in and greeted her warmly.

"Good Morning, Emma and Welcome, Lainie! Thrilled you're here and can't wait to get started," she said. "Give me ten minutes and meet me in my office. I've got a couple of phone calls to make. After that, I'm clear for as long we need." Without waiting for an answer, she breezed down the hall and closed the door to her office behind her.

Emma glanced at her phone console. A line lit-up and she smiled knowingly.

"Now that's a peek at what you'll come to recognize as classic Joyce. She's making her first call before she even sits down. C'mon, I'll show you to your desk, introduce you to any co-workers that are already here – most of them come in through the back door, but you need a key card," she explained, and handed one to her. "Use it for the back door, it's always locked, and for the front door after hours or on weekends."

The desk and her cubicle were fine, and the people working with her in that part of the office seemed friendly and professional. So far, Kiki liked everything she'd seen and everyone she'd met at CFSC. That was rare, she knew, even for a first day, when eager to make a good first impression, everyone would be on their best behavior. Everyone seemed genuine. Emma turned to leave and return to her station when she stopped abruptly.

"One more thing, I almost forgot!"

"What's that?" Kiki asked.

"We're getting voice mail, which I'm told is part of our new phone system I hope won't drive us all crazy. Voice mail is pretty snazzy, but it's not really installed yet, which is good because I have no idea how it works and couldn't explain it if I had to … I don't suppose you have any experience with voice mail systems?" Emma asked with a troubled look on her face.

"As a matter of fact, I do," Kiki said, delighted by Emma's look of sheer relief, "and I'd be happy to try to help when the time comes!"

"You know something, Lainie? I think we're going to be great friends!" Emma said.

In Joyce's office, her boss wasted no time jumping right in, which, as Kiki was learning, was the Joyce Buckman way; hands-on, full-speed, and with maximum effort. She liked that.

"Here is your copy of the Employee Manual," Joyce said, plopping it down halfway between them on top of her on her desk. "But don't read it now; later, tonight, whenever. Now is for talking. Don't hold back with any questions or comments. Nothing is off-limits so don't be afraid to speak your mind and don't worry about what I think. I'll usually tell you.

"Rule One: Everyone makes mistakes, we're human. Take responsibility, own it, learn from it and move on.

"Rule Two: The truth will set you free, but lies will enslave you and corrupt your soul. I'll never crucify you for giving me the straight shit.

"Rule Three: We're advocates for our clients; they need us and count on us. Put your interests above theirs and we undermine our mission. Client relationships are everything.

"Rule Four: Don't be afraid to think outside the box. We're under-funded, under-supported and under-respected, so we have to find a way when everyone tells us there is no way.

"Rule Five: Have a life, there's more to life than work and I really mean it, Lainie. You'd be amazed how many people forget that and I've come to believe there's no bigger mistake any of us can make.

"You'll be given a case load. Your job is to ascertain what your clients need and how to best serve them. We have meetings Tuesdays and Fridays to touch base, they're required. If you need to run something by me, I'm available anytime, schedules permitting," she said, with a grin.

"We work with state and federal agencies. We *need* them, but I don't exactly trust them because government agencies, from Child Services to Welfare, have agendas that are different from ours. We have legal aid lawyers that are *unofficially* on staff, but they're often young and green. Because of this, there are times when we go outside for help – like I've done with Clark lately – usually if we encounter something that is beyond our internal expertise or need to adopt a more neutral posture. This can be very helpful, especially when the courts are involved. The media has been good to us – mostly – but the truth is I don't trust them completely, either. It's always good practice to watch what you say and say as little as possible most of the time.

"Finally, a word about the cops, and listen carefully. We need them, but they view us through the same lenses they use to view our clients. Our clients are poor, often uneducated, and many have legal histories. Cops see the worst in them, not the best, but in fairness, by definition, the nature of their interaction with our clients makes them understandably cynical, if not jaded.

"Here are a few of my cards. You'll find my home number on the back and I'm giving you permission to call me anytime, anytime you need me. You're well-trained Lainie, I can see that in your transcript and in your eyes. If you didn't care and weren't a good person, Clark wouldn't have referred you. We can do good things. Our best work comes by working together as a team. Your case files," she said, abruptly dropping a thick stack of folders on a corner of the desk. "A good start would be reading through them. Okay, I'm sure you must have questions, so fire away."

Kiki had many and asked them, in a well-ordered and methodical fashion. She began with the procedural policies, moving next to a hypothetical timeline of a case from start to finish, and then asked for best case, worst case examples to use as a frame of reference. Joyce was clearly impressed with the organized approach her new hire was taking. Kiki was actually biding time, scoring points, and trying not to think of *Rule Two*; that honesty thing, the fact that she wasn't who she purported to be and had an agenda. God, she had an agenda. Hers was an honorable, even a noble agenda, perhaps, one that, had Joyce known of it she might support, but an agenda nonetheless and outside the domain of CFSC.

Joyce's answers helped her, but she had withheld one last question, the biggie.

"One last question, Joyce?"

"Of course, shoot."

"I'm not exactly sure of the best way to ask this, but my question is how to proceed, how to handle, situations which don't fit the usual matrix. I think what I mean are the dysfunctional families where a mother, perhaps with a young child, are victims in an abusive situation, both physically and emotionally, and paralyzed with fear are unable to act. Families at risk, in the largest sense, that may not have taken the step to seek help, but needing help desperately, may wait too long, maybe until it's too late. What can we do?" Kiki asked.

"There is no answer, Lainie," Joyce said simply. "You listen to your heart and follow it, use your gut, your instincts and your brain and do what's right."

Kiki sighed. "But that's the dilemma, and what to me seems so daunting and confusing. How will we *know* what's right?"

"You'll know, Lainie. My advice is to listen to your heart and you'll do what's right, I know you will."

Kiki recalled a similar conversation on this subject a few weeks ago.

The Guardian, when asked this very question had given her the same answer.

Chapter Twenty-Four

KIKI IMMERSED HERSELF in the new job, attacking it with passion and purpose.
To her delight, she found that she genuinely enjoyed the work and earnestly applied the knowledge she'd gained in college to what she was learning in the real world each day. This was considerable. There was no going through the motions for her, never a sense that every day was like the one before it or that tomorrow would blur anonymously with those which followed.

The job in so many ways was another gift, and Kiki couldn't escape acknowledging how lucky she was for it. At CSFC, integrity, of the mission and its people, was real. That was a rare thing, and she was living it. Still, despite loving the work, she felt guilty at being dropped into a dream working environment more like grad school before completing her undergraduate studies. Knowing there were people more qualified motivated her even more to give it all she had.

Could I ever be so fortunate to find a career like this in my own time?

She hoped so.

Life, as she was learning, so often came with painful, poignant choices, bittersweet compromises and unpleasant trade-offs. But this job, she realized, was one of the things she'd sorely miss. But, you can't have it all, isn't that what they say?

What you can do is hope to make the best of what you have and waste as little time as possible pining for what you don't have and wasn't meant to be. Can anyone ever know what that is?

What's meant to be, according to whom? Who makes that determination? Or is it just destiny? If it is destiny, does anyone have the right to alter it, however justified or entitled we think we are? Since arriving in 1981 she'd struggled coming to terms with this dilemma.

But this morning she rose to her own defense.

The circumstances bringing me here allow me to make the call.
The Guardian gave me the chance and the freedom to make it.

Even so, it wasn't enough. In asking her mind to process experiences in an entirely new way, by inventing a new perspective looking first at everything see how it fit in her dual realities, she'd unleashed a monster. There was simply too much to consider her mind was never at rest, always on, locked in an endless debate, struggling with an endless series of questions and contradictions. Before The Journey she'd been plagued by not quite believing. Now, after arriving, she challenged her own right to do what she'd come so far to do. It's not fair.

Spontaneity and freedom are the first casualties, she realized, picking listlessly at a salad she'd thrown together for dinner. Thank God for work; immersed in it, I almost forget.

Almost.

Her respect and admiration for Joyce Buckman and CFSC continued to grow.

Kiki liked and appreciated the other caseworkers, especially Lynne, a young woman from Chicago about her age, and Terrance, a quiet and introspective man in his late twenties who was taking law school classes at night. They became friends, although Kiki rarely joined them for a drink after work or socialized with them on weekends, guarding herself by maintaining her distance. She feared the pain she'd feel saying goodbye, and the hurt she might inflict upon good and decent people when one day she simply disappeared. Not to mention getting caught off guard and saying the wrong thing after a drink or two.

There were a few exceptions.

She attended a Fourth of July barbeque Joyce hosted for the staff at her home in the West Hills, and while getting along splendidly with everyone, maintained her distance and didn't allow them to get closer. Instead, she joined her co-workers for an occasional lunch, and Happy Hour on Fridays, a couple of times a month, for a quick drink, not wanting to appear unsociable.

At the end of the day, she returned home exhausted but happy, excited and professionally satisfied. Such a gratifying feeling, but one she knew couldn't last. How could it? Her time was limited. Each day that passed rushed her day of destiny nearer, the day when her past, present and future intersected. When that happened it would change everything and this would be over.

There was no way to know just how things would change. She had to trust, and despite her inability to quantify the wholly inexplicable, what made faith a tangible commodity for many, she had to have faith. Forces she couldn't understand propelling her forward.

So far, so good, she thought.

She trusted that love, hope, goodness, and righteousness, in some incomprehensible fashion were guiding her actions. There had to be more to all of this than her own dream of redemption. Didn't there? The *correction*, as The Guardian called it, had to be bigger than she, if, because of her efforts, or despite them, the mysteriously capricious ingredients of the human stew of heart and mind would align and reorder the world as it was meant to be.

There was that *meant to be* thing again, demanding attention and refusing to be dismissed or ignored. As best she could, Kiki forced it away, focusing instead on a more pleasant thought. Tomorrow was Saturday, and Clark was taking her to dinner and a movie. In the past month, they'd had lunch about once a week, but there had been no follow-up to dinner after their visit to Goodhal's Jewelers.

Not that she'd expected there to be something more, it hadn't been a date.

And there was no reason to think of tomorrow night as one.

Or think of Clark Bannion in some sort of romantic light.

That was absurd, wasn't it?

Of course it was, but …

Since arriving a month ago, there were many things she now questioned. Some were difficult, but not impossible, others were staggering in their implications, ushering in entirely new sets of questions, new possibilities, and still more questions.

A few lessons were invaluable.

Making another time your time came with real costs and consequences.

Overconfidence in the ability to shed the consequences of living is its own mistake.

Life, Kiki was learning, offered no such immunity and came with no guarantees.

Whether this time was her time, or not, she was no guest. She had no free pass.

Living, wherever you are and whenever it may be, has its own rules and is indifferent to our preferences, prior experiences or convenience, and this knowledge was fundamentally changing her. Every day she was growing more mindful of how the present, because of its *presence*, dimmed her memories of her future and distanced her further from them.

Each day in 1981 seemed to ramp-up its subtle seduction as it lobbied for the now.

~~~~~

It had been two weeks since she'd seen Clark. They'd had brief chats on the phone, but both had been busy with work, and he'd been out of town the past two weekends. First was a fly fishing trip with Roger on the Deschutes River in Central Oregon, and then last weekend, a gambling mecca to Reno with a law school buddy, an annual trek for two old friends.

She'd missed him and realized how anxious and excited she was to see him tonight.

In the hour before he would call for her, Kiki had changed clothes three times, not at all satisfied with how she looked, frustrated with her hair that wouldn't quite get to behave, tinkering with her make-up and unsure whether a little touch Sung behind her ears might be too much.

They caught an early showing of *Raiders of the Lost Ark* at the Washington Square cinemas. In the future, what had been a popular and convenient venue had been abandoned, replaced by newer and larger multi-screen theaters.

"I make it a point to avoid the movie crowds on Saturday nights," he'd told her, "it's date night, you know."

Clark loved the film, and she did, too, enjoying seeing *Raiders* on the big screen with a theater full of first-timers captivated by Steven Spielberg's masterfully entertaining tour de force.

"You've seen it before, haven't you?" He asked.

"Yes, but never like this," she answered. "Does it bother you that I have?"

"Not at all, as long as you don't mind seeing it again, and putting up with me behaving like a kid. But it's strange, like so many things are when we're together. Nothing is quite what it seems. Everything has a back story, a hidden story."

"I'm sorry for that."

"Don't be, it's not your fault and it's not a problem. Consider it an innocent observation, not a complaint. I enjoy our time together, very much. The quirks of the circumstances are a fair price to pay for the pleasure of your company, Kiki."

She blushed at that. "You're a good guy, Clark, but you always have been. I can't imagine being here, now, without the safety net of our friendship."

He didn't comment on that, but asked, "Where would you like to eat?"

"I'm glad we waited until after the movie, but now I'm starved, so anywhere is fine with me and the sooner the better! I hear my stomach growling." Across the parking lot, she saw a TGI Fridays. It hadn't been open long and was an instant hit, and usually had long lines to get in. Pointing to it, she said, "Fridays sounds good, I can't remember the last time I was there ..."

"See, that's what I meant. Every conversation is complicated. Was the *last time* years ago or years from now, or both?"

"Whatever it is – or was – its right here, *now*, and I'm hungry!"

"We've picked a good time, it doesn't look crowded yet, there are still some open tables on the patio. It would be a shame to eat inside and pass up a warm summer night in Oregon!"

"We should grab a table," she said, and taking him by the arm steered him towards the restaurant.

An ebullient young hostess, fancifully made up in unknown character complete with a wild wig and hat, showed them to a far table under an umbrella. An almost intimate setting away from the crowds inside, and sheltered outside from the noise of the street, the theaters and the parking lot.

"I'm glad we're out here," Kiki said, "it gets so noisy inside."

"True, but I've always thought that was a fair price to pay for the potato skins. I love 'em, and can't get enough of them."

"Just remember you're entitled to *half* of them, the others are mine, and I'll show you my mean side if you make a move on them," she warned and he smiled at that. She blushed again, and looked down, feeling his eyes remaining on her, and when she looked up and saw they hadn't left her face.

"I've missed you," he said, and left it at that, the words hanging in the air between them.

"I've missed you, too," she admitted softly.

While true for both of them, it didn't the situation less awkward. Their time apart, forced by work and his travel, had temporarily allowed them close their eyes to a growing tension each felt when they were together.

Something that was increasingly harder to ignore.

Not a sexual tension, at least not exactly, although that was surely one component of it. Clark was twenty-seven, Kiki twenty-one, they were virtually peers. Sharing similar interests and world views, they'd fast become friends, genuinely liked each other, respected each other, and enjoyed spending time together, but so much was left unsaid.

In good part, neither knew what to say, so they tried to keep it light.

Only to find that light chatter made it harder, not easier.

Feeling a stronger attraction each time they were together, thinking of him when they were apart, knowing she shouldn't but unable not to. This helpless inability to control her feelings frustrated her. But nothing in life is harder to control than feelings like these and, at times, she wasn't sure she wanted to.

Sometimes she wanted just the opposite.

And take the risk, however ill-advised.

To give in to her feelings, and grant them free will. But how could she? Doing so would mean embarking on that dangerously vulnerable journey, where he might reveal his feelings. Together they'd discover what they had or might have.

He was so handsome, and charming, and kind, and intelligent, and despite all this, it was so wrong. She knew that, it was obvious. That something seeming so right could be so wrong couldn't have been more cruel and unfair. If she allowed herself, it would be easy to fall in love with this man.

Had she already? The answer terrified her.

If she was honest about it, she knew his feelings without him ever saying a word.

Over these past weeks she'd learned to read him.

That he couldn't disguise his feeling from her, that he displayed them so transparently while smugly believing he didn't, only served to endear him even more to her. The look in his eyes said it all, and when their eyes met, locking briefly, neither of them able, or choosing, to tear away, her heart rate ratcheted up uncontrollably. It was then that she feared she was lost, and that he saw in her eyes what she saw in his.

Until tonight, until a movie and a casual dinner, none of this had been a problem.

In fact, she'd congratulated herself on keeping these forbidden feelings and emotions at bay. Safe knowing that, within a matter of weeks, a couple of months at best, it would be over and she'd be gone. Fleeing Clark Bannion for the refuge of a future where he played an entirely different role. Sadly, that idea offered little comfort and no consolation.

Tonight that thought pained her so deeply she felt mortally wounded.

After dinner, they shared a dessert. A monstrosity of a hot fudge ice cream cake they agreed was as delicious as it was decadently sinful. Taking a too-large mouthful, some errant hot fudge escaped the corner of her mouth. He reached to her, capturing it with his spoon, feeding it to her, then wiping her mouth with his napkin and licking the spoon.

Her eyes filled with tears.

"Kiki, what's wrong? " He looked stricken.

"I'm sorry. I guess I'm in a funny mood," she sighed. "It's been a wonderful night. I've had such a great time, but I think you better take me home now," she said, looking away before he could see the pain the words carried for her.

She took his arm on the way to car, leaning into him, feeling his warmth and strength.

"Some things about this time traveling are wonderful," she said softly, "but others are something else again. My emotions, I feel out of control at times, and don't know what to say, or do. I'm sorry. This is one of those times," she said, leaning into him again.

"I know," he said, and hugging her chastely, said no more.

Chapter Twenty-Five

WEEKS LATER, on a beautiful August morning, Kiki's phone buzzed. Emma.

"You have someone here to see you, Lainie," Emma told her.

"A client?"

"No, but she says she knows you."

"Really? Who is it?"

"Her name is Teddie Biggs," Emma answered, "and she has the most adorable young man with her!" She added enthusiastically.

"I'll be right up," Kiki said, knowing the reason why she was here immediately.

It had begun.

Making her way to the reception area, Kiki hung back, remaining out of sight getting a glance at her visitors before she greeted them. Teddie Biggs was sitting quietly, hands folded in her lap, eyes closed, shoulders slumping, combining to give her a thoroughly defeated look.

Kiki's heart ached to see this woman, understanding the painful reality of her life.

Nearby, Little Mo Biggs sat at children's table, happily playing with puzzles and eyeing an impressive array of toys overflowing from brightly colored plastic crates against the wall.

"Hello, Teddie," Kiki said, "I'm surprised but glad to see you. Would you like to come back and talk?"

Smiling gamely, Teddie nodded, and looked at Little Mo, now engrossed in Star Wars action figures he was arranging on the table.

"Hi, Little Mo," Kiki said brightly. "If you'd like to play with the toys, I'm sure Emma will be happy to watch you while your mom and I visit." Emma nodded that this was fine, and the boy beamed his approval, returning happily to Darth Vader and Han Solo.

"Let's go to my office," Kiki suggested to Teddie. "Emma will let us know if Little Mo needs anything. Would that be okay?"

Teddie nodded again, and stood up, stopping to tousle her son's hair affectionately before following Kiki down the hallway.

"Would you like something to drink, Teddie?"

The woman shook her head, "No, thank you, maybe later."

Kiki sat quietly, waiting patiently without speaking.

She had learned it was best not to rush clients, always better to let them begin these initial conversations, allowing them the time and space to get comfortable and choose their time. For most, coming to see her, coming to see anyone, and then opening up and unburdening, was a difficult step, a painful and frightening step.

Teddie Biggs looked haggard, and make-up heavily applied couldn't hide bruises on the side of her face. Her eyes seemed vacant, but darted around the cubicle as if expecting someone to burst in upon them. She gave Kiki a helpless look, appealing for an opening, for direction and a way to begin.

Kiki broke the silence, sensing the need to do so.

"You can tell me anything, Teddie," she began gently. "Whatever you choose to tell me goes no further, it's totally confidential. If you have questions, I'll try to answer them, and if I don't know the answers, we'll find them together. If you're in trouble, I'll try to help. And if you just want to talk, and just need a friend to listen that won't judge you, it's fine. Whatever you want, you tell me, okay?"

"I really don't know what I need," Teddie said dully, "or why I'm here. Maybe I shouldn't have come ... I'm sorry, I don't want to waste your time, Lainie," and saying this she looked around furtively, clutching her purse to her breast and preparing to stand and leave.

"You aren't wasting my time. I think you're here because you need a friend," Kiki said. "Isn't that it?"

"Yes," she answered in a choked voice that was barely audible, and collapsed back into the guest chair.

"Take your time, there's no hurry," Kiki encouraged soothingly, "I'm a good listener, I'd like to help, and there's nothing you can tell me that will shock me." She waited to let that sink in, and then asked, "There's trouble at home?"

"Yes."

"Can you tell me about it?"

"Yes, I ..."

"Are you afraid?"

"Yes."

"Can you tell me what you're afraid of? Is it being here, or being at home? For yourself, or is it for Little Mo?"

"All of that, I guess."

"I see. I know it's hard. Why don't you start at the beginning, whatever you think I need to know, whatever you're comfortable sharing, and we'll think it through, together. You're safe here, Teddie, and you're not alone."

"When people come to you, Lainie," Teddie said in quiet voice, "and you try to help them, do you, I mean, can you, protect them?"

"Yes, we can help, you have resources. But every situation is unique and the steps are tailored to yours. Tell me more and the two of us can decide what's best for you and Little Mo."

"I think Mo wants to kill me," Teddie said, and began to cry.

Kiki rose from her chair and walked around the desk sitting in the visitors chair next to Teddie. She reached over and took her hand, squeezing it gently but firmly.

"He hurts you, doesn't he? I saw the bruises when we met, and wondered about it. I see them now. Does he hit you regularly? Does he hit the child?"

Teddie Biggs' breathing was verging on convulsive and Kiki wanted to calm her.

"We could both use a nice cup of tea, would you like some now?" Kiki asked, and when the woman nodded, promised she'd be right back with it.

She ran into Joyce in the break room. "What's up?" Joyce asked, surprised by the tea.

"I think it will help a friend relax," Kiki said.

"Can I help?"

"No, but I'll holler if I need you," Kiki said, and hurried back to Teddie Biggs who took the mug with both hands.

"Thank you, Lainie, this is nice. You're so easy to talk to, I saw that right away when you came to the shop, that's why I knew I could come," she said, and as she sipped the tea, and sat up straighter, regaining her composure. "Mmm, this is good!"

"I'm a coffee girl, usually, but there are times when there's nothing like a cup of tea. This is my favorite, it's an herbal tea but with guts!" She said with a small laugh, but saw Teddie had sobered.

"I was a fool to marry him."

"Did you love him?" Kiki asked.

"I thought I did. He was handsome, and I was lonely. I guess you could say I was on the rebound. I'd just broken up with a boyfriend after five years, and Mo treated me nicely, fussed over me and told me he loved me. Then I got pregnant. I thought about an abortion, but just couldn't. Now, with Little Mo, I'm so glad. My boy means the world to me, Lainie; he's a good and sweet child. He deserves a father who loves him, and is good to him, not a man like Morris Biggs. There are times I swear Little Mo would be better off without a father."

"When did he start hitting you, Teddie?"

"Not long after the baby came. Mo hates children. The man has no patience for them."

"Was it ever serious enough to go to the hospital, the ER or anything like that?"

"A couple of times, but he's smart. He knows how to hit me in ways that aren't so obvious, that looks like an accident, you know?"

"I do, but tell me about the hospital visits. Did doctors question you about it? These days they're sensitive to these things, and often are suspicious. Were they?"

"Maybe, it was a few years ago, it's hard to remember the details. I made excuses, and if they knew better, they accepted what I told them. Mo had taken me to the ER. My arm was broken, and he was waiting. I was afraid to tell them the truth, and afraid of what he'd do if he knew I had. And Little Mo, if I wasn't around, if all he had was his father, what would happen to him? All his father does is drink beer all day and night. What kind of future would my son have?"

Kiki had been living with the answer to that question for what seemed an eternity.

She paused to choose her words carefully before speaking.

"Your first priority, of course, is Little Mo's safety and his future. Anything we decide puts that first. Let me ask something else, about the police. Have you ever filed a complaint against your husband? Have they ever been called to the house, perhaps a domestic complaint from one of neighbors?"

"I've never called them, although I've been tempted often enough. They did come to the house once, two years ago, no three, yeah, that's right, three years ago. We were struggling with Little Mo, toilet training, and he had an accident and Big Mo went crazy, and screamed his head off at the child. One of the neighbors, an older couple down the street, must have thought he was going to kill someone – or had. When the cops came to door, Mo talked his way out of it, made like it was kind of a joke, one of those crazy things every parent understands. The cops asked to see me and the baby, and since we were fine, that satisfied them and they left."

"Okay, now another question, a hard one to ask and for you to answer, Teddie, but I have to. There is no right or wrong answer, just your answer, however you feel. Do you want to stay with your husband, or leave him? And if you left, do you have anywhere to go, do you have family nearby?"

"No, I don't want to leave him, at least not yet. I have no one, well, a step-sister on the East Coast. We aren't close. I haven't seen her or talked to her in years. She doesn't like Mo."

"I see."

"And another problem, about leaving, I mean, is that my husband is also my job. What would I do? How would I support Little Mo and me?

"Well, you wouldn't be alone, and there are resources to assist if it came to it. I'm not suggesting what to do or not do, that decision is yours alone. My job is to remind you that you have every right to feel however you feel and help you understand your options. I'll explain the different kinds of assistance available. What we do, if we do anything, only happens when you decide it's time. Okay?"

"Yes, I understand."

"Now, I have a final question for you. May I ask it?" When Teddie nodded, Kiki asked, "What happened to bring you here today, Teddie?"

"Last night," she said in a tiny voice, "he hit me, pointed a gun at me and said he was going to kill me."

Chapter Twenty-Six

AFTER THE MEETING WITH TEDDIE BIGGS, Kiki remained at her desk considering how to best proceed. Teddie was a woman of good heart trapped in a disastrous marriage. Kiki genuinely liked her. Given Kiki's unique perspective, she knew how well-founded Teddie's fears actually were. The woman's reluctance to take the next steps was understandable.

Many women pushed to the brink stopped short of doing what signaled their capitulation and defeat. Relationship failure is hard to accept. Add to that fears of starting over, the social stigma accompanying that choice, and the economic hardships sure to follow. More than enough to encourage many to ignore the truth and persevere, despite the realities of the lives they lived every day. Others never got past denial, clinging to false hope, stubbornly determined to go to the grave before giving up and cashing-out of their biggest emotional investment. In the end, some paid a tragic price for unfounded hope.

Kiki would intervene and not allow that happen to Teddie.

That's why she was here, and the time had come to develop her plan

Teddie had left the offices of CFSC with Kiki's pledge of complete confidentiality, which was another reason not to open a new case and start a file. Joyce Buckman was curious, way too curious, but Kiki anticipated that. When asked about the meeting, Kiki deflected her questions with a half-truth that she had first met Teddie weeks ago, inquiring about landscaping services for Clark's building, and the two women had liked each other. Adding that Teddie and her son had been in the neighborhood, and had simply taken advantage of the opportunity to stop in and say hello.

Joyce's eyes said she bought it, mostly. "So, there's nothing more here?" She asked.

"There could be, but I'm not really sure," Kiki said. "She's slow to open up, and unsure she can trust anyone with secrets she's never shared. I'm earning her trust, giving her room and plan to stay in touch," she added. "It may be nothing, but if circumstances change I'll be prepared for it. I won't be caught off guard."

"I like the sound of that," Joyce said, and seemed satisfied. "Let me know if I can help."

Kiki pulled a thin manila folder from her satchel and from it a copy of a police report. The two-page document was yellowed with age dated September 10, 1981, only a few weeks from now. It detailed the investigation into the death of Theodora Jane Biggs, age thirty-six. The death, late in the day after a picnic with her husband in Washington Park, was ruled accidental. One of the detectives with a dissenting view authored an addendum expressing, in what Kiki thought was guarded language with a mild bite, "some doubts and discomfort with the veracity of her husband's explanations, despite the lack of hard evidence to support my suspicions."

She'd read this portion of the report many times before, but focused again on the location where "the accident" had occurred. Washington Park is a 410 acre city park, easily accessible from the downtown core in Southwest Portland. It is home to the International Rose Test Gardens, the Hoyt Arboretum, the Oregon Zoo, Children's Museum, Forestry Museum, amphitheaters, playgrounds, tennis courts and picnic areas. Additionally, there are fifteen miles of trails for hikers and cyclists winding through it and connecting with Forest Park, which is unique in other ways.

The scale of Forest Park, and its proximity to the metropolitan area, is extraordinary.

At 5100 acres, it is one of the largest protected urban forest reserves in the country. Old growth forests exist where conifers reach well over two-hundred feet and live for up to 750 years. Its home is the Tualatin Mountains, locally known as Portland's West Hills, which form a natural boundary between the city and its western suburbs. These are deeply forested hills of Douglas fir,

Western Hemlock and Western Red Cedar, with stands of Grand Fir, Black Cottonwoods, Red Alder and Big Leaf Maple trees worthy of their name. Each fall, school children collect some of their platter-sized leaves for *show and tell* in their classrooms.

Forest Park has over seventy miles of trails. The Wildwood Trail, starting near the zoo in Washington Park, connects it to Forest Park.

On August 30th, a sunny and pleasant late summer Sunday afternoon in 1981, Teddie Biggs would die after falling down an old stone staircase on a remote stretch of an old trail that was closed not long after the tragedy ensued. Kiki had visited the area before journeying back. Now, thirty-one years earlier, despite its regular usage, it was a secluded, almost hidden spot.

When Kiki visited in in2012 it had been nearly forgotten.

She planned to hike up to it on Saturday, and see it again.

~~~~~

Early Saturday morning, Kiki parked her car near the zoo parking lot. She had no trouble finding a space, but on a summer weekend day like this one, that would change in a hurry. She shrugged into her backpack, checked that she had water and some trail mix, and hiked over to the trail heads. Again, as she was becoming accustomed, she was struck by the absence of features she remembered but knew were years off. Everything looked almost, but not quite, familiar.

Real progress and big-time development would arrive soon, transforming the state over the next three decades, but Oregonians had bargained hard. When it did come, it came with a corresponding commitment to protect green space, especially when it fell within the city limits.

Pro-growth had to also be pro-Oregon. Development was expected to keep faith with that ideal. For many, growth never came fast enough or was big enough, and the environmental concessions appalled their critics, but in the end it worked well enough so that Oregon was still *Oregon*.

Parks like these were part of Portland's cultural fabric, carved out of natural treasures many years ago. Thoughtful stewardship would ensure generations to come would enjoy them. As it had always been, maintenance was an enormous undertaking. Many of the oldest trails were no longer safe and sorely needed work. City parks, like most popular public venues, aren't static entities but change over the years. Their utility and life expectancies vary. Over time they might be moved, expanded, closed or abandoned.

Council Crest was an example. In the early Twentieth Century, an amusement park had been a major attraction atop Council Crest, until closing in 1929. Similarly, the Portland Zoo, later the Oregon Zoo, was moved after outgrowing earlier homes and undergone multiple expansions. In 1981, its Washington Park neighbor, OMSI, the Oregon Museum of Science and Industry Museum, in 1992 would move to impressive new digs downtown along the east bank of the Willamette River that flows through the city and divides it east and west.

Other attractions, even those once wildly popular, had very different fates.

Many were replaced by newer, bigger, venues with greater capacity, but others outlived their usefulness. With dollars always in short supply, some became lower priorities, which made starting fresh easier and cheaper because the land was plentiful. In some cases it was easier and far less costly to just walk away, allowing them to fall in disrepair, and be forgotten.

Wooden signs pointed to the many hiking options.

Some wound through Washington Park. Others disappeared into dense forest that in a few miles became Forest Park. Many of the trails dated back to the Nineteenth Century and had been refurbished or were in the queue for future attention. Kiki was on a portion of trail heading from the zoo back into Washington Park and to the city.

Her destination, where without Kiki's intervention, Teddie Biggs would die.

She'd been hiking for less than fifteen minutes.

Although the sun shone brightly and the day promised a hot afternoon, in the deep shade of the forest temperatures remained cool and comfortable. Here the trail didn't rise appreciably higher; this section ran along one of the park's highest elevations. Despite this, the rise and fall of the many switchbacks traversing a rather blunt mountain resulted in a more demanding hike than Kiki expected.

She was breathing hard, and felt small beads of sweat forming in her scalp, running down the back of her neck and back. Fortunately, she wasn't going much farther, and for that, ironically, Kiki had Morris Biggs Sr. to thank.

"The lazy bastard wanted a secluded place, but also one that wouldn't take long to reach because he wouldn't want to exert himself any more than was absolutely necessary."

She felt she knew the man. On an afternoon like this one in 2012, Kiki had secretly observed Morris Biggs Sr. He'd become a whale of a man, weighing, she guessed, closer to three hundred pounds than two. What she'd seen of him here, when she'd visited the business, was a man laying the foundation for the lifestyle that would take him there. There was always the possibility she was wrong, but pegged him as slothful, self-indulgent, selfish and mean. What she'd seen, here and now, confirmed that. As the boss of his own business, he reserved the real work, the hardest physical labor, for anyone but him.

In his mind, she was certain, that's why he had employees – and why he had a son.

She'd met a man who was well past his youth at thirty-one, and courtesy of his lifestyle, rapidly going to fat. He liked his beer way too much. Teddie had mentioned that, and was only just beginning to grow the gut that over the next thirty years would become a specimen to be reckoned with. Lazy and out of shape, his choice of where to lure his unsuspecting wife for a picnic, would be comparatively close-in and an easy hike.

Kiki remembered the staircase.

When she'd seen it in 2012 the staircase had been closed for many years.

It seemed to have appeared out of nowhere, and she'd almost missed it. A massive boulder had tumbled down from above virtually hiding it from view, but, ironically, for those that knew where to look, marked it clearly. The boulder was so large, twelve feet high and at least that wide, and wedged so tightly in place, that considerable equipment would have been required to move and risky to blow up. . There was no real reason to move it, and an easy call that it made the most sense to leave it alone and close off access.

In 1981, the boulder was already there, and Kiki navigated around it and looked down into the little valley and the picnic area.

The decision to close the now even more dangerous to reach spot, hadn't yet been made. From the trail the staircase descended approximately fifty feet, interrupted halfway down by a flat area, perhaps no more than a four-foot square, cut out of the rock and positioned like a natural landing that connected to its second section of staircase before continuing down.

At the foot of the staircase at a small meadow at the opening of a shallow bowl, a hidden valley tucked away where one couldn't be. Beyond the field of thick grasses beginning to yellow and dry from the arid heat of summer, was a surprisingly open view of the surrounding hills in the distance. Running though it was the trickle of a slowly moving creek that virtually dried-up during the summer. During the rainy season it would be much more impressive, fed by run-offs coming down the mountains.

Kiki could see two old picnic tables, just visible under ancient willow trees with thick, heavy branches draping over them. One was old and gray without benches, the other rather new looking. Behind the benches was what remained of an old cabin or storage shed that no longer had a roof. She could see through gaping holes in the walls.

For all of this, it was the staircase that intrigued her.

Thick blocks of stone, blanched by years of sun, gave it a look of antiquity.

There was no hand railing.

The steps were wide but its downward angle was severe enough to suggest caution in negotiating it if you were intent to even try. Kiki shuddered at the thought. The stones were bleached by the sun and worn smooth by weather and time, covered in shady places with thick moss.

Immediately to the right of the staircase, a portion of the hillside had given way and there was a steep, uninterrupted drop-off all the way down to the valley floor. The staircase itself was tricky and clearly dangerous to negotiate, but the area next to it was treacherous and unforgiving.

"You've chosen a perfect spot for what you have planned, Big Mo," Kiki said tightly.

Twenty minutes later she thought she knew how to use it to her advantage.

Chapter Twenty-Seven

ALLER ID WAS STILL YEARS AWAY, but Kiki played it safe, calling Teddie from a pay phone. This was a call she wanted to appear as innocent and low profile as possible. Taking no chances, she used a pay phone on the corner inside the parking lot of a Chevron station on her way to lunch.

"Hi, Teddie, it's Lainie. How are you doing?"

"Okay," she answered, but her voice was strained and Kiki doubted it.

"I wondered if you had time for a cup of coffee."

"I don't think I should come and see you ..."

"No, no, nothing like that, I thought we could meet somewhere, just two friends catching up, no more than that."

Teddie warmed to that idea. "Little Mo has a doctor's appointment later today, in one of the medical buildings by Good Sam. I've arranged to be out of the office this afternoon and could meet you. Would it be all right if I brought him along?"

"I'd love to see him," Kiki told her. "Is he sick? Nothing serious, I hope."

"Oh, no, he's fine, just his annual check-up," she said, rather unconvincingly.

"That's good. What time do you think you'll be finished at the doctor's? "

"I hope by three, it's always hard to know. Let's meet then, at the Quality Pie Shop, do you know where it is? Little Mo loves their chocolate cream pie. Always his treat after the doctor. The place has been there forever, it's a real Portland institution."

"Right across from the hospital, isn't it?" Kiki asked, remembering the 24 Hour landmark had closed in 1992, and how Portlanders mourned its passing and still talked about it. Twenty years later, it had a Facebook following with nearly five hundred members. Even the acclaimed Portland advertising agency, Wieden + Kennedy, got into the act, purchasing Quality Pie Shop's iconic sign, and incorporating *a slice* of Portland history into a wall of their offices.

Kiki had been a baby when it closed and had never been there, but her dad had talked about it with reverence. Her father claimed that without Quality Pie, he never would have made it those first years Good Samaritan. To go there, now, was an unexpected bonus, but caught up in the mystique and nostalgia, she'd made a mistake, needed to be more careful and realized it as soon as the words spilled out of her mouth

Kiki, of course, would know Quality Pie, but would *Lainie*?

Lainie was from Sacramento, but had visited Portland many times over the years, so it was possible, but not necessarily probable, to have dropped in at Quality Pie during one of the fictional visits to Portland she'd made with her mother.

Teddie, fortunately, wouldn't know any of this, so it wouldn't be a problem with her, but a slip like this one could pose a problem with others. Casual conversation was something she'd be better advised to take even more seriously, especially with people like Emma or Joyce at work. They were the kind of sharp-witted people who would pick right up on that sort carelessness. Kiki scolded herself, taking it as a reminder to exercise more caution and to think before speaking.

At three in the afternoon, with the lunch hour passed and the dinner rush hours away, Quality Pie Shop was nearly full. It was that kind of place, always busy. Kiki arrived early, worried about finding a place to park, but had no reason for concern. NW 23rd hadn't been discovered quite yet, and in mid-afternoon, parking was plentiful and free.

Incredibly, it still is, no longer plentiful but still free.

She ordered coffee, asked for cream, but it was good enough to drink black and decided to save the calories for some pie. Waiting for Teddie and Little Mo, she had time to study the other customers, and realized she was looking at an amazing demographic cross-section of Portland, Oregon, 1981. Quality Pie was a unique place in many ways; everyone was welcome and felt at home.

Kiki loved people watching and all types were well represented.

She saw men in suits and nattily dressed women that might be doctors or professionals with offices in the neighborhood, or had made the short trip from downtown. Other women had the look of shoppers from the suburbs, fond of the boutiques which were becoming increasingly popular and fashionable, a trend that would only accelerate. A few of the tables had nurses and medical technicians represented by men and women in hospital scrubs. Younger people, mostly in jeans and with long-hair, might have been students, urban hippies, or street people; there were more and more street people in Portland, especially during the summer when the weather was so accommodating. Two tables in back were home to young women dressed garishly and rather provocatively, hunched over coffee and talking in an almost conspiratorial manner. Kiki thought they might have been dancers from the strip clubs burgeoning farther down 23rd and throughout the city. She also noted men and women in UPS and Postal Service garb, and enjoying a snack of coffee and pie camped-out at the long counter running the length of the narrow restaurant.

Dottie, her waitress, energetic and smiling with black lacquered hair in a net, was just refilling her cup when Teddie and Little Mo Biggs walked in. Spotting Kiki, they waved and walking over sat down and joined her.

Little Mo smiled shyly, and blurted out, "Chocolate cream pie is my favorite!"

"So I hear," Kiki answered warmly, noting two fingers on his right hand were in a splint. "Did you hurt your hand?" She asked.

Before he could speak, his mother answered for him.

"An accident," she said, "he caught them in a door."

Kiki noticed a brief confused look cross the little boy's face and then vanish.

"I see, I'm so sorry you hurt it," Kiki clucked sympathetically, not questioning the story, but doubtful that it was the real one. "Does it hurt, Little Mo?"

"Not anymore. The doctor put it in a *squint*," he told her in a serious tone, "and gave me *Tybenol*."

Smiling at a young child mangling the language, Kiki asked, "When did you hurt it?"

"At dinner. I wasn't eating."

Teddie was looking down, pretending to be absorbed in the menu, obliviously evading Kiki's inquiring gaze. The scab on her split lip was still angry looking and Kiki realized it appeared to be fresh and recently reopened.

Dottie reappeared and asked if they were ready to order. Little Mo ordered a slice of chocolate cream pie to no one's surprise, lobbied for chocolate milk, but his mother vetoed that. Teddie said a glass of *regular* milk was part of the bargain if he was going to have this kind of late afternoon treat. Teddie went with hot apple pie and Kiki, torn between coconut cream and Marion berry, decided on the coconut cream. While they waited for their orders, Kiki made small talk. This changed once their orders arrived. With the little boy lost in chocolate cream heaven, in a soft voice she looked at Teddie and turned the conversation to more serious matters.

"So, how are things, really?" She asked softly.

"Like always, nothing has changed," she answered, a little defensively.

'I don't mean to pry, and you don't have to say anything you don't want to, but ..."

"But what, Lainie, what can I say? What do you want me to say?"

"Only what you want to say. You're safe with me, let's start there. You don't have to *hide* things from me. I know what I see with my eyes. When you tell me that *nothing has changed*, I know what that *means*. Don't forget I'm on your side. I'm your friend, and from what I see now, I think you need one. I'm right about that, aren't I?"

Teddie squirmed a little, and the aged vinyl of the bench in the booth made an odd sound.

Little Mo laughed, and covered his mouth with his hand, that came away with whipped cream on his fingers.

"How's your pie, honey?" His mother asked, grateful for the diversion.

"I LOVE IT! Can I have another piece, please?"

"Another piece, no, I don't think that's a good idea. One piece to a customer, mister, and it's plenty big, too!"

"Aw, Mom, I could eat a whole pie, wanna see?"

"I'll take your word for it."

"Am I right? Do you need a friend, Teddie?" Kiki repeated her question.

She nodded that she did.

Kiki tilted her head, indicating Little Mo's fingers. "His father?" She asked.

Teddie nodded again. "Sometimes he doesn't know his own strength."

Kiki had been holding her eyes, but Teddie looked away, saying nothing.

"He's trying, and he's promised me things will get better," she said finally.

"Do you believe him? Do you think things will get better?"

Teddie didn't answer, and Kiki pressed ahead gently.

"Little Mo's fingers and your lip; is that what he means by trying? Is that what you mean by things getting better?"

Teddie blushed and sat up straight. "Morris is sorry for that, he really is. And he's promised to make it up to me."

"And you believe him? Has he made promises like this before?"

"Well, yes, but ..."

"Has he kept those promises?"

"No, but he will this time."

"Has he told you how he's going to do that?" Kiki asked.

Teddie Biggs answered with the words rushing out excitedly, but Kiki knew she was clinging to a thread, an illusion, and wouldn't crush her spirits with the truth. She couldn't.

"We're going on a picnic, just the two of us. A week from Sunday, the thirtieth, I'm so excited. It'll be like old times, when we were in love and he was kind to me. Mo has everything planned; a sitter for Little Mo and we're going to have a whole day, a picnic, at this romantic, secluded spot he knows up in Washington Park. Doesn't that sound *wonderful*?"

Kiki didn't answer. She just smiled and looking down returned to her pie.

Chapter Twenty-Eight

THE REST OF KIKI'S WEEK was beyond busy. Nothing in her experience had prepared her for overnight immersion in a demanding real job. The rigors only began with the time commitment. She'd yet to work less than fifty hours a week and didn't think that would change. It was expected; this was a career gig. Take it seriously, work your ass off, and you survive and thrive.

If you don't, adios; this is the adult real world.

She'd had a part-time job during high school, when senior year was so academically boring that anything – even a crummy job – was more interesting than biding her time in the classroom until graduation. Clerking at one of last remaining video stores wasn't much, but she learned a little about movies, and it entitled her to early release during the first semester and most of the second semester until they went out of business. The summer after freshman year she worked full-time for her dad, subbing for one of the receptionists off on maternity leave.

Those jobs taught her two important lessons.

First, there was nothing worse than doing something unsatisfying that you hate.

Second, education is the chance to get passionate about something and do what you love.

The biggest lesson came with the job at CFSC.

She loved social work, really *loved* it.

After a long, hard but satisfying week, when the weekend came she knew she'd earned it. Late Saturday afternoon, she found herself thinking about work while she was getting ready to go out. Kiki was doing all she could to divert herself and avoid thinking about going out, that meant thinking about Clark. They were going to dinner and a movie.

It's not a date, she told herself. Insisting that was so, but not believing it, or wanting to.

In the weeks that had passed since their last *non-date*, she worked hard at drawing a strict line and telling herself that she was adhering to it. Facing the reality of what could be and what couldn't be, she'd set the rules and was prepared to live with them. What she'd come to think of as the rules of engagement, or more aptly, they were the rules of *non-engagement*. 1981 was one contradiction after another and none bigger and more confounding than her feelings for Clark.

For two months, she'd managed to ignore what she could and live with what she couldn't; almost believing she wasn't letting it get to her, that it couldn't get the better of her. Doubts were natural and she was only human. The key was accepting that she was complicating it by overthinking it. What made sense, and what didn't; what would work; and what wouldn't, couldn't have clearer. The line wasn't so hard to draw, and she'd drawn it. Now she had to live with it.

Of this she reminded herself constantly, and her brain listened.

The problem was that her heart didn't.

Clark would call for her soon, and her heart was racing.

She couldn't have been happier or more confused.

~~~~~

Clark's choice for dinner was *Café des Amis* on NW Kearney.

"It opened last year," he told her, "and everyone says it's great."

"You're saying you haven't eaten here? Wow, you're taking a risk," Kiki said, "I do like a man with an adventurous streak."

The restaurant was small, intimate and romantic without trying. Lace curtains, fresh cut flowers, impressive fine linen and a candle-lit ambience that was comfortable and unpretentious. She'd never eaten here, but remembered it as one of her parents' favorites, an anniversary and special occasion type place. Two rooms featured fine art displayed unobtrusively, accented by a few haunting Harold Altman photographs of Paris that recalled the city with an authenticity that seemed natural and appropriate. Her mom and dad had mourned the passing of *Café des Amis* a quarter of a century later, but there was no reason to share that with Clark tonight.

The mood was too perfect and the last thing she wanted to do was spoil it.

"What do you recommend?" Kiki asked.

"It's French with a Northwest flair," he began.

"The name hinted at that, but what have you heard?"

"Their signature dishes are a beef filet with a port garlic sauce, and duck terrine with pistachios. A friend who has been here many times raves about the wild mushroom ravioli. I'm really not a duck lover, so I'm torn between the filet and ravioli."

"Why don't we go with those two and split?" She suggested, and they did. Each ordering the beet salad with blue cheese and toasted Oregon filberts.

"Dilemma solved," he said, and added an Oregon Bordeaux from a new winery in the Hood River Valley the server promised would be a *bold red they'd remember at a great price.*

When the wine arrived, he raised his glass and offered a toast: "To the future!"

"Given the circumstances surrounding your dinner companion, that toast could be interpreted in different ways," she replied, and touched his glass with hers. "Delicious."

As was the food, which they enjoyed sharing and critiquing, both offering up rave reviews. After dinner, sipping her coffee, she looked up at him to find his eyes on her.

"Kiki, you really look wonderful tonight."

"Thank you," she said shyly. Grateful she'd made the last-minute mad dash in search of something along the lines of *a little black dress.* It had paid off. She'd struck gold at the same shop which had become her fashion lifeline.

It was a dress unlike anything she'd ever owned.

"I can't believe someone actually got rid of this," the clerk had gushed. "If it was my size, it never would have made it to the racks and would be hanging in my closet."

It was a beautiful dress, courtesy of some astounding shopping luck.

Sheer black silk that clung to her in just the right way in all the right places, its short length showed off her legs and the neckline plunged just enough to reveal cleavage that made its point effectively without crossing the line.

"I'll return the compliment, you look very handsome," she told Clark.

He smiled at that, "Shall we walk to the theater? I have to warn you that it's not a short walk, in the neighborhood of twenty blocks or so to the Guild. But they're city blocks, we have time, and it's a beautiful night."

Kiki agreed they should walk and they left the restaurant vowing to return soon.

Balmy summer nights in Oregon are warm, breezy and comfortable. Weather so good the rainy season is easily forgotten or at least forgiven. He took her hand when they crossed streets, swallowing up hers in his larger, stronger hand that felt warm and reassuring.

As they walked she realized how she was looking forward to those intersections, longing for his touch and losing herself in the closeness it offered.

The Guild Theater was built in 1927, the last single screen movie house in downtown Portland, and had a capacity of 425. Originally called the Taylor Street Theater, it was renamed *The Guild* in 1948. It closed in the summer of 2006.

"What are we seeing?" Kiki asked Clark.

"*Somewhere in Time* ... I hope you haven't seen it, I've been meaning to, and I love this old theater."

"I haven't, but always intended to."

"I've heard great things," Clark said.

"It's one of those movies I never got around to seeing. I have a vague idea of the story, but the title sure talks to me. It was one of Mom's favorites. She said the music always made her cry."

"Not to worry, I've got a handkerchief if we need it!"

Kiki needed it.

The score was beautiful but the movie moved her, and scared her.

The empathy she felt for the time-crossed lovers overwhelmed her with feelings that were beyond her ability to control. The story of their dilemma was too close to hers, making the fantasy too real, delivering pain too intimate and personal, with implications too immediate, too confusing and simply overwhelming.

At one point during the film Kiki realized she was sobbing uncontrollably, her face wet with tears that refused to stop. Clark reached for her hand, giving it a well-intended affectionate squeeze. It only made things worse. Her logic and common sense had been overrun by emotions. Every attempt she made to steel her heart and regain control failed miserably. Added to this, she felt she'd ruined a delightful evening

They made the walk back to Clark's car without speaking, each lost in their thoughts.

The touch of his hand crossing each street brought fresh tears.

Once seated in his car, she broke the silence, talking in a small voice.

"I'm sorry to be such a mess," she said. "I can't remember ever being affected so much by a movie. I've spoiled a wonderful evening, and I ..."

Clark stopped her, placing two fingers on her lips to quiet her. "No, Kiki, I need to take responsibility for this. The movie was my choice, and the truth is I chose it deliberately. It's a beautiful love story, and could there be two people it would mean as much to as you and me? You see, I was hoping ..."

"You were hoping what?"

"Nothing. Never mind," he said, and starting the car drove out of the parking garage.

~~~~~

"You don't have to walk me to the door, I'm a big girl."

"And I'm a gentleman," he said, and getting of the car and walking around to her side.

"Thank you for a wonderful evening," Kiki said, unlocking the door. As he followed her into the entry way, she added, "I'm a mess at times, but despite how it might appear, I had the best time and want to thank you. Can you forgive an emotional wreck who is unable to do much about it? I loved dinner, the movie, but most of all, being together. I want you to know that."

"You're welcome, I'm glad, but we need to talk," Clark said, "about more than tonight."

Kiki looked down, unwilling to meet his eyes. "What is there to say?"

"Everything, nothing, I'm not sure I know exactly. But I am sure of one thing. We can't end this night by walking away from each other pretending that's all there is and it's okay. As far as I'm concerned, it's not okay."

Without hesitating he pulled her to him and kissed her. Chastely, gently at first, but a kiss fed by mutual passion that grew long and deep. It was followed by more kisses that left them both breathless, and hungry for more.

"We can't do this. This isn't possible, we can't, we shouldn't," she said weakly.

"We'll sort out the future later, for now, let's live in the moment."

Clark led her by the hand down the hall to the bedroom.

Standing before him she slipped out of her dress and let it drop to floor.

She was lovely, and he gasped at the sight of her. Kiki reached for him, bringing him to her as she smothered him with kisses. Next, she began to undress him. His body was lean and strong, yet he couldn't have been more gentle and tender. As they fell to the bed as one, she was electrified by his touch, his scent, determined to get closer still.

Kiki was not a virgin, but her sexual experience was limited. Her perspective had been formed and colored by her relationship with Justin.

In bed, as in all things, Justin had been about Justin.

Clark was about her, about the two of them.

Kiki felt his heat and knew Clark felt hers. They seemed to fuel each other.

What wasn't her first sexual encounter was the first time she'd ever made love.

God help me, she thought. I love this man. I really, truly, love this man.

Her joy was mixed with fear, but she felt an indescribable need for him.

They fit so perfectly, as if made for each other, exploring each other's bodies with the unbridled desire of new lovers tempered by the patience of old lovers and familiarity of dear friends. Maybe it was the fact that she'd known him all her life, in a different way and at another time, that made what happened possible, and when it did, electric and life-changing.

Reaching heights she'd never imagined, when her heart seemed to be overflowing and incapable of more, a fresh wave of passion rose up taking them higher still, until she was nearly drowning in it.

The night was cooling comfortably into the fifties, but their bodies were wet with a passionate sheen. Breathless and spent they lay on their sides looking into each other's eyes.

Kiki's were wet with new tears, but this time they were tears of joy.

"What are we going to *do*?" She asked him weakly.

"Shh, not now, just let me look at you and hold you."

"But what are we going to do?" She pressed.

"I don't have the answer, and at the moment I'm not sure I care about finding it."

"Try, please."

He sighed, resigning himself to the fact that she wasn't going to let this go.

"As maddening as you can be, I love that you don't take 'No' well or at all, but there are times … oh well. Alright, let me take a stab at it. Here's what I do know. I wasn't looking for this when you walked into my office and turned my life upside down. I've spent the last two months trying to bury feelings that only grew stronger. I fully understand how impossible this is, and the reasons why we can't. But, I love you and I'm living in the moment, this moment. I'd like you to join me there. Before I go on, I've got a question for you."

"Go ahead."

"Do you love me?"

"After the last couple of hours, how can you ask? But I suppose you have to, I guess I would in your situation. Yes, I do love you and I'm terrified by it."

Clark nodded. "I knew when I met you that my life was changed forever. I guess I couldn't know then exactly what that meant. Now, we have some decisions to make, some hard ones, and important ones," he answered, gently wiping away her tears. "I've waited a long time for this, for you, Kiki. I've waited all my life for you," he said finally. "Don't think for a minute I'm willing to give you up if there's a way."

Kiki Kinsler, aka Lainie McCann, buried her face in his chest and cried.

Chapter Twenty-Nine

"YOU'VE GOT MAIL," **Clark said.**
"I always thought the title was the best thing about that movie," Jenna replied.

"Funny girl – actually, we've got mail, is more accurate. This morning when I looked in the box, I found a letter for each of us. Are you coming over?"

"Couldn't stop me, I'm already getting into my car."

"I'll make a fresh pot of coffee."

There were two letters on the now familiar dated letterhead, and they looked to have been cranked out on the same machine she'd used for her earlier communique. No doubt what served as state-of-the-art for most businesses of the day. Most likely, an IBM Selectric, typewriters tamed by secretaries that could make them sing at 90+ words a minute. More adventurous folks, hungry for the latest and greatest, would have stepped off the pier with antique word processors that demanded a lot but didn't deliver much in terms of output. They did allow files to be saved and edited. Software for these beasts was hard to use and usually temperamental when you did. Few had the intestinal fortitude, or wanted it badly enough, to put up with the pain.

But it wouldn't be long before all that changed.

1981 was the lull before the cyber-storm.

By the end of the decade, PCs would on their way to everywhere, changing everything.

Change, that once started, would never stop accelerating.

Dear Jenna –

I'm well. I'm writing separate letters because some things have changed.

After reading what follows, you'll understand this is my attempt to understand my feelings by sharing them with my dearest friend, despite the years that separate us.

With Clark's help, I have a job as a case worker for CFSC, the Community Family Services Consortium of Washington County. The people, especially Joyce Buckman, the Executive Director, are wonderful. I love the work, and can't tell you how fortunate I feel to have found a career path I intend to follow with passion and purpose.

I've met Teddie Biggs and, of course, Little Mo. We've become friends as I'd hoped. The circumstances of her life are tragic, I've seen it first-hand. She is a woman and mother with a small child in dire jeopardy.

I've also met Morris Biggs Sr. who is an abusive man and truly every bit as vile and horrible as I expected and feared. He beats Teddie, as well as his son to some lesser extent, and as we know is preparing to murder her.

I am taking steps to prevent it.

I believe I can. I know I can. I must.

Still, the things I'll be required to do scare me terribly, because they are in conflict with the laws of God and man. I tell myself that can be excused because it is all for the greater good, both for Teddie and Little Mo Biggs, and for my family. I remind myself that The Guardian has given me the capability to do so without reservations or limitations, and I can only hope and pray that I do what's right and afterwards can live in peace with those choices.

Oddly, this is comparatively the fairly easy-to-solve problem.

There are other issues complicating my life.

The Clark Bannion of 1981 is simply the most wonderful man I'll ever know.

He has been everything I could have hoped for in every way; his support and help, kindness and friendship, are humbling and invaluable.

From our first moments together, we felt an odd kinship and attraction.

To cut to the chase, as impossible as it clearly is, I have fallen madly in love with him. All of this happened after denying our feelings for months, for the obvious reasons. Amazingly, he loves me with an honesty and passion I've never known.

I may never recover from the heartbreak sure to follow when I return.

Despite this, our love is a gift that is worth even that steep a price.

Last Saturday night he took me to dinner at *Café des Amis* and a movie, Somewhere in Time, if you can believe the irony of that. Corny as it must sound, the story of time-crossed lovers couldn't have been more painfully real. While others in the theater were watching a beautiful, sad love story, we were living it. There is no way to put my feelings for him into words. *Words* are inadequate. I never dreamt my heart could be as full, or I could feel this way. When we made love it was a taste of heaven. Even if the memory must last a lifetime, I'll never regret it. I also know, for both our sakes, it can't happen again.

The Guardian, it seems, has given me more than one Gift.

I'll save Little Mo from his fate, and my family from theirs.

And I've learned how powerful and beautiful love can be and how fleeting it is.

In less than two weeks I'll return to my own time. I know I must, and for what I'm leaving behind, the happy thoughts of what I'll return to are comforting. I know The Gift is something I can't hoard, but have to share and this is as it should be.

There are so many things I don't know and can't know but must know. Things I won't know until I return.

All of which terrifies *and* thrills me.

I'll discover the consequences of re-engineering fate.

I'll learn how what I've changed, how it changes me, and those I care about.

Will my relationships and memories, precious before, remain so?

I'll soon learn the answers to these questions. If memories of the love I've found here are all I'm left with, then being deprived of them would be the cruelest irony. Loss, it seems, couldn't be more complicated, more difficult to live with or harder to understand.

Because of this, my letter to Clark was almost impossible to write.

What can I tell him? It may be that he *knows*, or will when I return.

Sometimes it seems too much. Is it destiny I'm altering?

As if the powers of the universe have handed me a celestial sword and all I have to do is wave it. At times I'm not convinced I have the right. Does anyone? Even me? I tell myself I'm not changing things as much as I'm restoring, correcting, what was meant to be.

Many of those questions I had before leaving are still questions. But I may have answered one of them.

Remember how we wondered why this wonderful and good man never married?

In some inexplicable, way, I can't help but wonder if it was *me*?

I'll see you soon, dear friend.

Love,

Kiki
August 16, 1981

When Jenna stopped reading, she realized Clark hadn't yet read his letter. He'd been watching her as she read, trying to decipher the expressions that crossed her face.

When she finished and looked up, he smiled and began to read.

Dear Clark –

Take no offense at the separate letters. I had some 'girl things' for Jenna.

I'm well, and in a few short weeks will return to you, Jenna, and my own time. It will be a bittersweet departure, because I've made friends here that I will miss terribly and always.

The Guardian gave me a wondrous gift.

For that I am truly and eternally grateful.

I accepted the gift, unaware of its unavoidable costs I'd have to pay, and that I now know are many.

Most precious to me in this time is my friendship with you.

That friendship, along with your support and counsel, has given me strength and confidence to do what I've come here to do. There are so many things I don't understand and probably never will. What is clear to me is that only by returning home will I understand the consequences of The Journey I've made.

Do you remember Joyce Buckman?

She's the Executive Director of CFSC of Washington County. You assisted her in the earliest days of your practice, and helped me to be hired as a counselor and caseworker. I can't tell you how much I respect her and admire the guiding mission of her organization. I love the work. Discovering that is a wonderful bonus. When I return I'll complete my undergraduate degree, go on to grad school and dedicate my professional life to helping mothers, children and families in need.

I've met the Biggs family; mother, father and son.

What I learned by meeting them confirms the righteousness of what in less than two weeks I'll do. This mother and innocent child are at risk. The father is as despicable a human being as I ever hope to meet.

What I must do, I'm prepared for, intellectually, at least.

The moral consequences, given the legal fine-line I may walk in doing it, are quite another matter altogether. I'd give anything for a moral compass, but after all this time I no longer bemoan the fact that there isn't one. The Guardian tried explaining that to me when I pressed him about it. At the time, I didn't understand. With time, I've come to understand and accept the simple wisdom of it.

The hardest part of leaving this time will be saying goodbye to you, here, now.

The loss of that friendship and affection will be very painful.

I know how funny that must sound since I'll be seeing you soon, but I guess you have to be here to know what I mean by it.

My greatest fear, what tears relentlessly at my soul, what I think about when I'm awake and what fills my dreams when I'm asleep, are the repercussions of what I'm doing. Regardless how noble and right my intentions may be, what I can't know is how the many relationships that are precious to me may have been altered as the consequences of my actions.

I'm terrified that my memories of my time here may be erased.

I pray it isn't so, but as with everything else, little is within my control. But I have to trust The Guardian's wisdom.

As it happens, time travel couldn't be more emotionally confusing and uncertain.

I prepared as much as I could, but how could anyone prepare for this?

You can't.

From the beginning of this whole crazy thing, I told myself I was willing to pay any price, but here's the problem. What that means looms more ominously the close I get to returning home.

I made that foolish promise in a vacuum, from the safe cocoon of the future, without any knowledge of the emotional costs I'd have to pay after living in the past.

At least it won't matter much longer.

Soon we'll toast past, present and future with your prized bottle of The Macallan.

Love,

Kiki
August 16, 1981

"Wow," Clark said with what looked like tears in his eyes, as he looked at Jenna. "She writes a helluva letter, doesn't she?

Chapter Thirty

KIKI HAD WRITTEN **the letters in Clark's office on Monday morning.**
What she would say and how she would say it didn't come easily.

Ever since that evening they had both agreed was as wonderful as it was perplexing and unnerving, the content had preoccupied her thoughts, making virtually impossible to think about anything else. At least one thing was certain: A dangerous threshold had been crossed. Having done so required coming to terms with its implications and that was easier said than done, and there were no simple answers. They both knew that. In the end, she decided it might help to unburden on Jenna, but there was no way to tell Clark, in 2012, the truth. How could she? And if she did, returning would be even more difficult.

On Sunday morning, waking up in bed had proven to be an amalgam of delight and confusion. She'd never been so happy, or so miserable, amazed she could feel both ways so deeply and completely. At first, neither of them had known what say. Weak smiles and an awkward kiss had to suffice. Thankfully, there was none of the clumsiness of a one-night tryst neither had wanted or expected.

Their feelings were genuine and real but couldn't have been more raw and confused.

"We'll think better with something in our stomachs," Clark said finally, breaking the silence. "I'll throw together a little breakfast, while you get the coffee on," he offered, avoiding making eye contact by peering into the refrigerator pulling out eggs, cheese, and an onion, and grabbing a tomato from a hanging wire basket Kiki had found at the Farmers Market.

"He cooks, too!" She chortled playfully, hoping to lighten the mood.

"I don't cook much, but when I do, I take it seriously. You're going to find that I've elevated scrambled eggs beyond the mundane."

"You're on," she said. "I'll handle the toast."

Soon the aroma of freshly brewed coffee filled the kitchen.

"It was sweet of you to think of me with your last order of Graffeo." UPS had left the box on her doorstep one day while she was at work. A note was inside the box.

A little something to perk-up your mornings from the Portland Coffee Fairy.

"Um, that wasn't me, it was the Coffee Fairy," he said, concentrating on eggs in a glass bowl that he was beating to a foamy frenzy with an old-fashioned egg-beater.

"The note made me laugh," she told him.

Admiring his handiwork, Clark lifted the egg-beater up and out of the bowl to assess his progress, and grunted with approval.

"These old things do a much better job than a whisk, and with a lot less effort. From the looks of it, I've got a feeling this egg-beater is older than both of us."

"It might be, except in my case, age isn't so easily calculated, is it?"

"Well, there's that," he admitted.

Seated across from each other at a small table in the kitchen, they dug in.

"Well, I have to admit, these are great eggs, and I'm impressed," she said, "I was hungry, and would have eaten anything, but these are amazing," she added, showing him her cleaned plate to prove her point.

"It was a rather energetic night. I can't think of a better way to work-up our appetites," he replied, providing an opening to broach the subject neither had yet been willing to touch. "And for me it was a wonderful night, a magical night. Does that sound weird coming from a man? Don't think for a minute it was just another one-night stand and you're just another notch on my belt. It was anything but."

Kiki looked down, eyes fixed on her plate, refusing to meet his.

"What's wrong? Don't you believe me?"

She looked up, eyes glistening with tears. "Of course I believe you. I really don't have much experience in this area and I've never been in situation like this one. If I hadn't known how you felt, last night wouldn't have happened, but …"

"But, what?"

"It was a big mistake," she blurted out. "Nothing good can come of it. We shouldn't have let it happen."

"No, something good has already come of it. It was no mistake, and there's nothing you can say that will convince me otherwise. Falling in love can't be a bad thing, even if its timing is inconvenient, or worse."

"Yes, but …"

"Let me finish, Kiki, okay?"

"Okay."

"I know the circumstances of us are more than a little unconventional, and at first blush impossible," he began.

"Now there's an understatement if ever I heard one," she replied, sounding as miserable as she felt.

Clark sighed, and ignoring that continued. "I'm not going to pretend I have answers. I don't. So, I'll move past that, and focus on what I do know. What I'll tell you is that I'm in love with you. You know that, you *feel* that, I know you do. Want to know something? I've been single so long, I thought I was immune, I really did. And I won't lie to you. Things would be a helluva lot simpler, and easier, if we didn't love each other."

"I know," she almost bristled, "that's what makes this so awful and impossible. I think I loved you from that first morning, when we met in your office, except I've known you since I was a baby. I denied my feelings, tried to bury them. I had no idea what to make of them, or how to deal with them. As hard as I tried, I couldn't make them go away. Every time we've been together, every day since I've been here, has been a combination of delirious happiness and miserable unhappiness. What a hopeless mess this is."

He nodded, and reached for her hand, bringing it to his lips and kissing it tenderly.

"Here's what I believe. Last night can't be wrong. What we have is imperfect, but that doesn't make it wrong or less real. For me, being with you last night was nothing less than the happiest and most wonderful night of my life. What we feel for each other is a gift, and what we have together is a miracle, and no one is ever going to persuade me differently. What we do about it is our choice."

"I wish it were that simple, I really do, but it isn't."

"It is that simple," Clark protested.

"No, it's not. Don't you see that? You're the most wonderful man I've ever known, but I've known you all my life as *another* man. You're my father's best friend, for most of his life and all of mine. You've been like a godfather or favorite uncle to me, I've always loved you. Now, I've fallen *in-love* with you, head over heels-style, completely, like in the movies. From the beginning, since the attack on my family and all that brought me here, I've been living in a world of non-stop contradictions. I doubt anyone could understand what it's like, or how it feels, and how insane it is. There is no firm footing, everything seems so unstable, and nothing makes sense. Everything is going to change because of me and then I go back to my time and my world like I was never here. I get to turn my back on the emotional wreckage I've caused and just disappear. It was okay when I first thought about it, there were no consequences. No longer; now there is you. Now I don't know what to do or what to think."

"I can help with that, if you'll let me try."

"I wish you could, Clark, but no one can. Let me try and explain what I'm feeling. Half of me can't help but wish that last night never happened, and the other half thanks God that it did. Could my feelings be any more confused? But I'm not here for me. I've come here for my family and for Teddie and Little Mo. Going back is the only way to find what else has changed because of my actions, and I have to know. Not doing that would be totally irresponsible and selfish. And there's more. I feel a duty because of the second chance I've been given. The Guardian told me I can do this again, and I feel obligated to repay The Gift by helping others."

"You could leave me so easily? You could disappear without a second thought, without regrets for what you've found here and turned your back on?" Clark asked.

"No! Of course I can't. Can you think for a minute that I could go back leaving the love of my life in the past without a broken heart? A big part of me would like to forget everything and spend the rest of my life with you, here, pretending I know nothing of the future."

"That's not what I meant," he said, sounding a little defensive and hurt.

"I know that, too, but it's where we are. I love you with all my heart, Clark. Now let me tell why last night was wrong. It's bad enough I have a broken heart, but because of last night, because I foolishly and selfishly allowed myself that wonderful night, all I can do is hurt you. What awaits me, when I return, is a living, breathing reminder of hurting you."

"Forget about hurting me. If that's the price, I'll pay it, gladly."

"It seems so unfair. Hurting you is the last thing I'd ever want to do."

"We don't have to decide today, we have time," he countered.

"But not a lot of time, only a week, and I have so much to do."

"I'll help you in any way I can."

"I'm grateful and need your help. We should focus on that, at least for now.

"I guess, you may be right," he answered, and fell silent. Frowning and marshaling his thoughts, seeking the right words that seemed to be beyond him. After a minute of silence, he spoke up. "When you're finished, you wouldn't have to return right away. You could stay for a while, give us some time. To figure things out and decide."

"Which would only make things worse, and harder," Kiki said softly. "We wouldn't be lovers. We'd be like inmates on death row waiting for the inevitable. Every day would be colored with the outcome we know is unavoidable."

Clark cursed under his breath. He stood and collected the dishes and took them to the sink. Without speaking he squeezed some dishwashing liquid onto a Dobie, and began to wash them.

Kiki rose from her chair. Walking over until standing behind him she put her arms around him and hugged him fiercely.

"He not only cooks, but does the dishes, too?" She asked in a whisper, and began to cry.

.He felt her body trembling against his, her hot tears on his shoulder, and turning around wrapped her in his arms. As they stood together, water running in the sink was the only sound.

"Oh, Clark, all this is my fault! I can't believe what I've done, what my stupidity and selfishness has allowed to happen. Can you ever forgive me?"

"Forgive you? That's crazy. Just what should I forgive, falling in love with me? Not on your life. We didn't get here because of you; we got here because of us. It was out of our control. I think it was meant to be."

"I do love you," she said, struggling to talk, her breathing was ragged from sobbing and tears that wouldn't stop.

"So that's it for us?" He asked.

"It's not what I want, but I don't know what else it can be."

~~~~~

That afternoon, hours after Clark had left to return home, the phone rang.

Kiki hoped it might be Clark, but it was Teddie Biggs.

"Hi, Lainie! It's Teddie. Have I disturbed you? I'm sorry to call you at home."

"Of course not, I gave you the number so you could call any time. Is everything okay?" Kiki asked.

Teddie hesitated, and then asked, "Could we meet tomorrow? Morris has a big job in Newberg. You could come here, any time after eight."

"I'll come see you between eight-thirty and nine," Kiki said, "No one will know."

Chapter Thirty-One

WHAT KIKI HAD SEEN **was an all too familiar retelling of the same sick story.**
Big Mo got drunk.

When he did, as was always the case, he got mean, and when he got mean increasingly physically threatening. And with time came the dual dangers of a man no longer able to control himself and a man no longer interested in trying.

"Morris was so sorry, he really was," Teddie insisted, repeating it, again and again.

Sure he was. Kiki saw Teddie working harder than ever to do whatever was necessary to persuade herself it was true. A woman so desperate she had channeled all of her terror into a single-minded purpose of maintaining the illusion. Convinced that whatever it took to keep the dream of a happy ending alive, in the end it would all be worth it. A happy ending she fervently believed to be within her grasp, almost here, only days away, on a romantic Sunday outing in Washington Park.

"Please don't take this the wrong way, Teddie, but let me see if I've got this right," Kiki said.

Teddie nodded, almost compulsively to show her pleasure, relieved Kiki was listening.

"The other day your husband comes to you contrite, sincerely sorry for his past mistakes. Eager to make it up to you, he's planned a romantic picnic on Sunday. Do I have it right so far?"

"Yes, that's right, exactly, right," Teddie said with a smile. When she smiled, the facial contractions revealed bruising her heavy make-up couldn't conceal. New bruising, Kiki could see, black and blue that hadn't yet yellowed as it healed.

Continuing on, she said, "Okay. Between inviting you on the outing and now, he has relapsed, and knocked you around some. How much I don't know, you didn't say, but I see it." Kiki waited for Teddie to dispute this, doubting she'd try, and when she didn't, took silence for her assent.

"You tell me he's sorry about everything, really sorry. You made a point, very clearly, just how sorry he is and that you're back on track for a lovely romantic y picnic in the park, just the two of you. Have I got it right? Is that how you see it, Teddie?"

"Yes, that's right."

"Good, I wanted to make sure *I'm* clear. I'm glad. I've got another question."

"Ask anything you like, I know you're my friend, Lainie," Teddie said genuinely, "and I trust you".

"Why did you call me, why did you want to meet?"

"Well, we're friends, and I thought we could get together. And talk."

"We are friends, but I'm not buying that's why you called. This isn't fun friends-stuff we're talking about, is it? This is real life and death stuff, your life, and your son's."

Teddie started to say something but Kiki raised a hand to stop her.

"Before you answer, Kiki said firmly, "I have another question. Through all this, have you seen the gun again? Has he threatened you like he did before?"

"Yes," Teddie replied, "but maybe I've made too much of it. Morris has always loved his guns," she said quickly, almost defensively. "He's owned a gun as long as I've known him, from the first days I worked for his father." She licked her lips nervously. Possibly without even being aware of it, her tongue paused briefly as it traced the scab on her perpetually split lip.

Kiki nodded, accepting that. "Yes, I understand that. Many men, and women, are gun enthusiasts and love their guns. My question is really isn't about the past, I'm interested in this time. How it might be different this time than it was before."

"Different *how*?" Teddie asked.

"How often have you seen a gun in his hand? When you called recently you told me he'd threatened you with a gun. Is that how it's always been, or is it a change in his behavior?"

"It's different. I never saw it as much and he never threatened me with it like he does now. And he seems ... to like it."

Teddie hung her head and then looked up.

"Are you telling me to refuse to go with him on Sunday?" She asked Kiki.

"No, I'm not telling you that. But I don't think you can be too careful, so maybe what I'm saying, more than anything, is *remember* that. I want to know what the plan is, without Mo knowing, all the details, the time and place. Let's hope you're right, but in case you're wrong, I'd like to know where you are and when you'll be there, so I can help you if you need it."

"Why?"

"Wouldn't you like to have that security? For you and Little Mo," she added, bringing home what meant what was most important to Teddie. "With a little peace of mind, you'll be able to enjoy your time together even more. And if plans change, I want to know that, too."

Teddie Biggs nodded enthusiastically and related the information Kiki wanted.

"If anything changes, I'll call you, Lainie," she promised.

Kiki thanked her with a smile, and at that moment had the strangest thought.

She now had something to do, something she never thought she'd ever do.

The time had come to buy something she never thought she'd ever buy.

She needed a gun and had to figure out how to get one.

And then learn how to use it and hope she never had to.

~~~~~

It was at times like these that Kiki really missed the Internet.

Research had been redefined by bringing the libraries of the world, albeit too often in an uncensored Wild West way, to our fingertips. With a few clicks she might have learned all she needed to know about private citizens purchasing handguns. With a few more clicks, a good idea of the right kind of gun for her and a comparison of models and prices. And with just a few last clicks, she'd know where to go to get it, when they were open and how to get there.

But, in 1981, Kiki was doing it the old-fashioned way: She was going to the library.

The Multnomah Library on SW 10th in downtown Portland would be expanded and remodeled in the late 20th Century, but had always been a more than respectable big city library. Kiki arrived, checked the map and found her way to Reference Room. Manning the desk was a smiling librarian. Her father used to talk with reverence about the selfless librarians during his college and medical school years.

"They are truly goodly folk, asking for nothing other than a chance to help, paid little for their efforts, and doing it out of a genuine respect for knowledge and the people who seek it. If that isn't noble, what am I'm missing?"

Dad would have loved this woman, Kiki thought.

Mrs. Bonnie Barton was about fifty, with a trim figure, graying hair pulled tight in a bun, plenty of smile lines around bright, lively eyes, and an attentive smile. She clearly loved her work and brought to the job the pure and simple goal of assisting whoever came to her desk accomplish whatever needs and objectives had brought them to her.

Her smile never dimmed listening patiently to Kiki explain what she needed to complete her research paper on handgun sales. When she was finished, the librarian deftly consulted the *Reader's Guide to Periodical Literature*, a staple, before the Internet, of reference librarians, both public and academic, throughout the United States. First published in 1901, the *Reader's Guide* is the go-to directory for recently published articles in periodical magazines and scholarly journals, and is organized by subject.

It took Mrs. Barton no time to locate a succinct update of gun laws, as she jotted a few lines about the entries on a well-used notepad by her right hand. Using the same resource, she discovered, to her genuine pleasure, a recent piece in a woman's magazine entitled *The Piece Mom Should Be Packin'.* The librarian jotted down the information for that article as well.

"These articles should get you well on your way, but let me know if you need more help," she said kindly, tearing off the page from her pad and handing it to Kiki.

"Thank you, I'm so grateful for your help, and glad I came in," Kiki said.

"My pleasure," Mrs. Barton beamed and as Kiki turned to find her materials, the woman stopped her. "Oh! I just had another thought before you go. With a project like this, are you planning on stopping by at the big Gun Show? I think you should, there is so much you could see and learn there."

Kiki stopped. "I didn't know anything about it," she confessed. "Would you happen to have information on the show?"

Mrs. Barton smiled, and neatly penned a few more lines on a page of her trusty note pad.

"It's at the Expo Center, this weekend. An annual event considered a real big deal with enthusiasts. There are hundreds, maybe thousands of people buying and selling guns, they come from all over. As I think about it, the show has grown so big it may even start on Thursdays, now. Here is the phone number for the Expo Center. You could give them a call or check for an ad in *The Oregonian.*"

"Thank you, again, you've really helped, Mrs. Barton," Kiki said, really meaning it.

"Any time, dear, it's what we're here for. Best of luck with your research," The librarian smiled, bringing the task to a conclusion as she prepared to meet, greet and tackle her next challenge, a scholarly looking senior that had just appeared in line behind Kiki.

~~~~

An hour later, Kiki had the information she needed. She could easily buy a gun.

Enforcement of gun laws for years had fallen under the auspices of BATF, The Bureau of Alcohol, Tobacco and Firearms. Ultimately renamed ATF, and handed off from federal agency to federal agency like a hot potato, going from The Treasury Department to the Department of Justice, and finally to the Department of Homeland Security when it was created in 2003.

No topic was more hotly debated than gun laws and it had always been that way.

The right to bear arms could be traced to Revolutionary War days, and was guaranteed by the Second Amendment, right after Free Speech. That said it all.

Change, even for the public good, came slowly when it came at all.

Even after the assassinations of John F. Kennedy, Martin Luther King, and Robert F. Kennedy, when The Gun Control Act of 1968 was passed, it required federal licensing of gun dealers, chiefly limiting sales to criminals and minors but little changed for private parties.

Like those attending gun shows.

Another assassination attempt, this one only months before Kiki's arrival in the summer of 1981, would trigger more substantive changes but those wouldn't arrive for more than a decade.

On March 30, 1981, James Brady had been shot and crippled during an assassination attempt on President Ronald Reagan, just sixty-nine days into his term. It would take Congress twelve years to pass the James Brady Violence Prevention Act in 1993, requiring a national system of federal background checks and a mandatory waiting period.

Even after so much tragedy, buying a gun will be no problem whatsoever.

She was glad for the convenience, but appalled that it was so.

Kiki knew a little about the Portland Metropolitan Exposition Center, site of the gun show, from attending Home and Garden shows with her parents a few times over the years. She read about it now, learning it had an interesting history. Much had changed since its construction in the 1920. Then, its primary purpose was for livestock expositions.

The Expo Center was renovated and expanded in 1959, where it was the site of the Oregon Centennial Expo. It was quite an event, half a million visitors passed through in its 100 Days. President Richard Nixon gave the keynote speech, and Raymond Burr, television's Perry Mason, was the master of ceremonies. The Expo featured appearances by such stars as Harry Belafonte, Merle Travis, Roy Rogers and Dale Evans – even Roy's horse, Trigger, and

Lawrence Welk. Network television also got into the act with CBS broadcasting Art Linkletter's House Party live.

Today the Expo Center is owned by Multnomah County, home to the County Fair, and a landmark feature of the Kenton neighborhood of North Portland, on the Oregon side of the Columbia River across from Vancouver, Washington. The Expo Center embodies a unique part of the city where Interstate 5, industrial, commercial and residential development are a stone's throw away from each other, and coexist almost comfortably.

Kiki had no experience with guns, but knew the appeal of firearms has no demographic limits. From her research, she'd zeroed-in on a .38 Special snub nose revolver. The gun was actually named for the cartridge that for decades was a favored load of the military and police departments. Nearly a century of demand yielded improvements and enhancements. One day in the future, these tried and true weapons would even come with laser sighting.

The shorter snub nose had been introduced in 1898 by Smith & Wesson as an alternative and improvement to the Long Colt, quickly becoming wildly popular. Easily explained because the .38 Special combines what might be the two most important qualities most people look for in handgun:

It's a serious weapon *and* is easily concealed.

There was no question, Kiki believed, that this gun was perfect for her purposes: Small enough for her purse, or to carry in the pocket of a jacket, with a load essentially identical to a .357 Magnum with a shorter cartridge length. '38' referring to the diameter of loaded brass case.

A .38 Special was a gun she could handle and promised *real stopping power*.

The gun show would be a perfect place to get one.

Despite everything, such a foreign thought made her shudder.

Chapter Thirty-Two

ON FRIDAY AFTERNOON, Kiki left work early.
No one questioned this. Over the past two months
she'd worked long and hard, and had earned Joyce's
respect and trust. Allowed, even encouraged, to work independently, Kiki could now come as go as she pleased without raising
eyebrows.

On her way to the highway, she stopped at the bank, withdrew five hundred dollars in cash, and began the slow crawl up I-5
joining the first wave of commuters returning home to Vancouver
from jobs in the Portland. Rush hour seemed almost tame compared to 2012. She exited the freeway just before the Interstate
Bridge and made her way to the Expo Center.

That morning Clark had called and asked about meeting for
a drink or a quick bite after work. She'd declined, with genuine
regret, knowing she'd hurt him, again. Since the weekend she'd kept
her distance, claiming she was too busy with preparations. It was
the truth, at least in part, but was more an act of protection and
self-preservation.

She simply couldn't trust herself.

Only from a distance could she steel her feelings, and even
then she knew it wasn't true. She reminded herself, continually,
that it was for the best, it was the right thing to do. She was doing it
for both of them. There was no choice.

In his presence she'd forget all that. All her good and wise
intentions would evaporate, her resolve would crack. Kiki's heart
ached to see him and her senses longed for his touch.

But she couldn't, not after breaking his heart, as well as her own.

Even from a distance, she could see the parking lot was already more than half-full and easing off to the right joined a line of cars slowly streaming in.

The Gun Show was being held in the largest hall filled with exhibiters' tables, with wide aisles separating the rows. The most serious dealers had professional displays with impressive back-drops creating booths, while others simply sat behind tables showcasing their wares. She waded through hundreds of people that were milling about, inspecting an array of handguns, rifles, shotguns, swords, knives and memorabilia from wars that men and women had lived and died fighting in.

The people in attendance, both the exhibiters and visitors, couldn't have been more diverse. There were men and women, young and old, white, black, and brown, long-haired hippies and short-haired conservative preppy types. Many of them were hard-looking, serious about the business of buying and selling weapons that appeared for them far more than collector's items or curiosi-ties. Others seemed to be rather out of place, more like cultural outliers with no business being there, who really didn't belong. Like Kiki.

The old Kiki – the new Kiki should feel right at home.

The single-minded purpose bringing her here would stand-up to anyone's.

She spent an hour or so meandering up and down the aisles, casually taking-in the wide variety of items from a safe distance, until she believed she had a fair idea of all that was on display and could begin to thin down her vendor choices. Having done that, she decided to make a second pass, before taking the next step of choosing one of the exhibits and actually talking to someone about buying a gun.

Ten minutes later, she stood in front of Honest Dave's Guns out of Oakland, California.

A vinyl sheet hanging behind Honest Dave shouted his name in silver and black.

Kiki noted that these colors were consistent with the Oakland Raiders tee-shirt he was wearing, barely able to contain thickly muscled biceps and forearms. Honest Dave looked to be in his later forties, or possibly his fifties, well over six feet, at least two hundred pounds, and with a graying pony tail that was braided and hung to his waist. His black jeans were clean but not new. They were faded and looked comfortable. A large diamond stud was in his left ear. His wrists sported wide, black leather bands with heavy silver studs. Both of his arms were covered with tattoos, almost commonplace in 2012, but much less so in 1981.

He might have once been a soldier, or a mercenary, or a member of Hells Angels, or spent some time in a carnival, or in prison, or even all of the above. None of those possibilities seemed a stretch or would have surprised her. Kiki knew, or thought she did, that this was a man who really knew his guns, and walked up to talk to him

"Can I help ya, pretty lady?" He asked amiably, and coolly appraised her. "Ya look a little outa place, no offense."

"None taken … you're right. I've never bought a gun before," she said hesitantly.

"Figured," he said simply. "Got anything in mind, know what you're lookin' for?"

"I think so. I need a .38 Special for self-defense."

"Always a good choice, and something a woman your size can handle," he replied and pointed to half a dozen on the right side of the table. "Somebody troublin' ya?"

"I live and work in a rough part of town," she lied, "so I'll sleep better having a gun," she said. At least that much was true.

"Mind if I ask ya another question?" When she shook her head no, he asked, "Ever shot a gun before?"

"No, I haven't," she blushed. "I was hoping you'd show me what I need to know."

"I can do that, not a problem. Let's get started. Why doncha choose one, pick it up and see how she feels."

"Okay," she said, liking this strange man who, passing him on the street, encountering him in a bar, or in most any other situation, would have scared her off. But he had a calm way of going about his business, speaking simply, and dealing patiently with an admitted novice. All this put her more at ease than she expected. She'd made a good choice, or a lucky one, and as her father had always said, *it's better to be lucky than smart.*

Kiki was feeling surprisingly good, until reaching for one of the guns on the table.

Her hand trembled slightly. No doubt Honest Dave had seen it, and she willed her nerves to settle down. The gun she selected was the smallest one, with black rubber grips. She wasn't looking to impress anyone and it seemed suitable and less ostentatious. And if her hands were sweaty, from the heat, or her nerves, or her fear, she hoped it was a wise choice because she could control it more easily. Kiki made a mental note to ask him about that.

The gun itself was heavier than she expected, of a cold, blue-black metal she guessed was steel. As she thought about it, she didn't think she'd ever seen that particular color before. Or perhaps it was the context of holding something in her hand that, until recently, she would have sworn was, more than just improbable, but simply impossible.

C'mon, a gun? Me? Get serious!

But here she was at a gun show, holding a .38 Special in her hand, ready to buy it and use it, if she had to. What shocked her more than anything was that this inanimate object felt alive in her hand. The gun seemed to possess some sort of energy, for lack of a better way to describe it, unlike anything she'd ever experienced.

Crazy as it seemed, she believed she felt it.

She wondered if every weapon has a spirit and an unarticulated history.

Had some other woman at some point in the past felt it and held it as she did now?

Would still another unknown woman feel that way at some point in the future?

Kiki had to admit, there was something about the oily smoothness of the steel that, while it frightened her, also instilled confidence. Maybe the power of weapons was at the heart of their allure for so many. Or the fact that being alone was different with a gun in your hand, and vulnerability didn't feel as helpless and overwhelming.

"Differences between these .38s are mostly cosmetic. They're all pretty much the same weapon and use the same cartridges, although they ain't all on the same frame. You're holdin' the M frame', smaller and lighter, Smith and Wesson used it for what they called *The Lady Smith*, but don't let that fool you. Its size makes it an attractive option for women, but the FBI loves 'em. So do bad guys. Anyway, once a gun is introduced, lotsa companies end up making 'em. Two main things to keep in mind, though. Ya pay more for fancier stocks. Choices are things like in-laid pearl, wood, black rubber – like *The Lady Smith*," he said. "The other thing is some are five-shooters and others are six-shooters. Industry talk is they'll be makin' these to handle 9mm loads, and up to eight rounds, but that ain't the case with these."

"You're very helpful," Kiki told him sincerely, "I appreciate that … could you show me how it … works."

Deftly, surprising her with his gentle touch, he adjusted the way she was holding the weapon, guiding her left hand until she was bracing it with her right. "It's a point 'n shoot, ya look down the sight and squeeze the trigger without jerkin' it, holdin' steady as ya can and stayin' true, if that makes sense."

"It does, like I see on TV and in the movies. How do I load it?"

He spun the barrel, flipping it open to reveal where the cartridges slipped in snugly. Then he spilled them out into his hand.

"These are blanks, nothin' to worry about. Try it, she practically loads herself."

Kiki tried, and he hadn't exaggerated about how easy it was.

"Do you sell bullets?"

"By the box or case," he said, and pulled out a box from beneath the table. "Whatever you need … I could show ya how to fire it, not here, of course, it would hafta be when the show's done."

Giving him an odd look, she said, "Thank you, but I'll manage."

Honest Dave put up his hands, "Didn't mean that like it musta sounded, not hittin' on ya, though I'm guessin' a fair share does. Don't mean any disrespect. What you might do is go to a shootin' range, and try 'er out. If you ain't satisfied for any reason, just bring 'er back and we'll get you inta somethin' else. I'm here 'til Sunday when the show ends, and then headin' up to Tacoma for a show next week."

"I'll take it," Kiki said firmly. "How much?"

Honest Dave scratched his stubble thoughtfully. "Well, I think two and a quarter, but let's call it two hunerd and I'll toss in a box of shells. Ya want a shoulder rig? If you're plannin' on carryin' ya need one … although I'm supposed to tell ya that it's illegal to conceal it that way."

"No, just the gun, no holster, thank you," she said and handed him the money. Dave put the gun in a small bag that looked to be of crushed black felt with silver draw strings, and handed it to her.

"Even the bag is Raiders colors," she noted with a smile.

"Impressed you noticed, but I guess I'm pretty obvious about it, huh? Love them boys, since I was kid; they play the game the right way, if ya ask me." Changing the subject, he asked, "Mind a little friendly advice?" He waited for her to answer.

"Not at all," Kiki said, "you're the expert."

"You've made a good choice, it's a fine weapon. Don't know what the deal is, and I hope ya never hafta use it, but if ya do, remember this: Ya find yourself in a situation when you're pointin' her at someone, be ready to pull. Usually, times like that, if yer facin' a dude with a gun, the guy holdin' will. He who hesitates dies, get me?"

"I understand," Kiki nodded. Then said, "I hope it doesn't come to that, but if it does, I plan to be ready."

Chapter Thirty-Three

SATURDAY MORNING **Kiki called Clark.**

"You've been avoiding me," he said flatly.

"Not the word I'd choose, I've been busy," she said, tempted to say more but knowing sometimes the less said the better.

"Tomorrow's August 30th. You've been getting ready."

"Yes, I have."

"Are you, ready?"

"Yes, I am."

"Anything else you want to tell me?" Clark asked.

"I was hoping we could have dinner. I'll fill you in. And it will give us a chance to talk about … everything."

Clark didn't answer right away, was oddly silent, totally out of character.

Kiki was afraid that meant he didn't want to see her, or couldn't bear to, that she'd hurt him too deeply. All of those possibilities were deflating and demoralizing.

"I'd love to," he said at last. "Have you got anything in mind?"

"Chinese?"

"That always sounds good. Portland has so many to choose from. Have you ever been to Canyon Pearl?"

She loved Canyon Pearl. It had great Szechuan and was another family favorite. Her parents had frequented it for years … until it closed, and reopened with a new name in Lake Oswego. The new location was in a strip mall, close to where I-5 met Hwy

217. The Kinslers thought the food was still excellent, but missed the old place on Canyon Road. It just wasn't the same.

But what was still the same?

Especially lately, when it seemed everything and every place in 1981 no longer existed, or had fundamentally changed, by 2012. Kiki felt clubbed by the impermanence and the frailty of so many things, large and small, all weighing more heavily than ever, discouraging her, as if they were portents of a future she couldn't escape. A future waiting for her that she'd soon have to face.

"I love Canyon Pearl. Home of the best General Tso's I've ever eaten."

"I'll pick you up," Clark said. "How's seven work?"

"Perfect. And Clark?"

"Yeah?"

"I can't wait to see you," Kiki said in a tiny voice.

"Then I'll see you at six. No one is more easily motivated by a beautiful woman," he said, "especially one about to disappear from my life."

~~~~~

They sat across from each other at a table in the smaller of two dining rooms.

"Busy tonight," Clark remarked absently.

"They've always done a great business. Dad used to say to eat Chinese where the Asians go, and I'd say this is the place," she said. "Looking around, he would have approved."

They complemented the General Tso's with Beef and Broccoli, vegetable fried rice, an order of spring rolls, and pot stickers Clark claimed he couldn't live without.

"Everything is delicious," Kiki said, "but we ordered waaay too much. We'll never finish it."

"Don't worry about that, you're having dinner with a guy who thrives on left-overs, so it was part of my plan," Clark countered. "Of course, only one of us will be around to enjoy them, so they come home with me!"

"With that artful segue is it time to talk?"

Clark tilted his head signaling that was fine and for her to take the lead.

Kiki's eyes filled. "This is so hard for me. Are you going to make this even harder than it already is?" She asked him, her face showing the pain she felt.

"I wouldn't try and don't think I could," he snapped, and then quickly apologized for his sharp tone. "Damn, I didn't mean it to sound like that. Sometimes the words spew out, and there's no tone in my head but there is coming out of my mouth." He sighed, lowered his head, and then looked up. "I'm trying to play the tough, steel-hearted guy, getting myself ready for the fact that in a matter of days you'll be gone. When I see you again, if I see you again, I'll be old enough to be your father. So you'll have to forgive me if I'm not at my best tonight. I'm trying my best; it just isn't good enough – or sensitive enough." With that he reached across the table and took her hand in his. "When do you leave?"

Finding herself emotionally overwhelmed in a restaurant was inconvenient, but she didn't care, and couldn't deny her tears any longer. Kiki was crying softly and silently, shoulders shaking, heaving convulsively with hot tears streaming down her face when she looked up.

"Oh, God, what have I done to you?"

Clark looked at her and was about to say something when she corrected herself.

"To us – what have I done to us?"

"We fell in love, but let's not apologize for that, okay?"

"I'd never do that. That's not what I mean."

"Yeah, maybe that was unfair. Sorry."

Kiki smiled tightly. "What's the old movie cliché? Love means never having to say you're sorry? Has *Love Story* come out yet?"

"Yeah, at least ten years ago … dumb line, I always thought. The movie was kinda dumb, too. When it comes to love, there is no shortage of quotes on the subject."

"Try me," Kiki said.

"Maybe later. So, when are you going back?"

"If all goes well, no, that's not what I mean. If things go as I plan, in a couple of days, maybe three."

"Is there any rush? The future is waiting and isn't going anywhere, right?"

"I guess so."

"Do you need my help? Anything I can do?"

"Isn't it best that I keep you out of it?" Kiki asked. "I don't want to implicate you, if things get out of hand. I'd be leaving you to clean up my mess ... I have to tell you something."

"What?"

"After work yesterday I went to the Rose City Gun Show."

"Up at Expo Center in Delta Park? Ahh, geez, things just get better. Okay, so tell me, were you window shopping, or are you packing a piece?"

"Well, you could say I'm packing but not *carrying* at the moment."

"That's a relief. I'm safe ... for now," Clark said, offering a small smile that failed to reach his eyes.

"As long as you behave yourself," Kiki said.

"I've never owned a gun," Clark admitted. "But then I never had any reason to own one. What kind did you buy?"

"I'm now the proud owner of a .38 Special, actually, mine is a Lady Smith, by Smith & Wesson."

"No kidding, how did you settle on that one?" Clark asked.

"Honest Dave from Oakland educated me. He was really a nice guy in his way, and a major Raiders fan. I liked him."

"Tell me you aren't really planning on using it ... or are you?"

"Only if I have no choice and have to protect Teddie Biggs or myself."

"And that's tomorrow?"

Kiki nodded, and closed her eyes for a moment. When she opened them, Clark was staring at her and smiled. She smiled back.

"Can I tell you something?"

"You can tell me anything," he replied.

"You are the most wonderful man."

"You aren't going to embarrass me with what sounds like awarding me a romantic consolation prize, are you?"

"Funny, Clark. Here I am speaking from the heart, and you make fun of me as I'm baring my soul."

"I'm sorry. I shouldn't have interrupted ... a bad habit of mine, especially when I'm stressed."

"Don't think for a minute you've been a diversion for me. You aren't something I could play at until I safely escaped into the future unscathed. If we're star-crossed lovers, we're also time-crossed."

"I don't know if that dooms us or gives us a chance. Do you?" He asked.

"I'd like to think there is some chance for us. I refuse to believe there isn't, even if we can't see it now. The last few months have changed not only what I believe but what I believe is possible."

"You'll get no argument from me on that," he said with a snort.

"I couldn't have known any of this before, but when I think of what I've found, we've found, had I known what would happen I wouldn't have changed anything. If I'll never know love again, I wouldn't trade it. I'd consider it a fair price and pay it without regret. Do you believe me when I say this?"

"Since we're baring our souls for dessert, it's my turn. I feel the same way. I refuse to look back with sadness, and won't. Instead, I'll look forward with hope. Anything else would be a self-imposed death sentence."

"Before I go, after tomorrow, I'd like us to have a last night together," Kiki said in a voice so soft he had to lean forward to hear her. "I don't care what we do, I just want us to be together, if you're willing."

"Of course I am. There is nothing I want more."

"Thank you. I was afraid …"

"That I'd let go without seizing every minute I can? I couldn't. In some bizarre fashion, I'm coming to terms with this. Have you ever read Emily Dickinson, Kiki?" Clark asked, and when she shook her head he continued. "I'm not an avid reader of poetry, but as an English Major I was grateful for the exposure I had in college to the great poets. I know poetry isn't considered a manly pursuit. It makes many people uncomfortable, and I understand that. It's hard to read, can be even harder to understand, and even when you do, too often it seems corny and contrived, sometimes academic. Anyway, Emily Dickinson was a reclusive eccentric, and most of her work, nearly two thousand poems, weren't published until after her death. She was an odd duck, and led an odd life, but in a way her life and her work explain what makes poetry magical. How a few words, artfully constructed, capture the most complex and mysterious of human emotions and give them meaning that comforts and soothes the soul. I've always thought language is a miracle that way."

"Can I hear some of it?"

"Sure. The poem is entitled Parting and it's very short, not even a dozen lines as I remember, but the last line says it all."

"*'Parting is all we know of heaven, and all we need to know of hell.'*"

"That's beautiful. And says it all, doesn't it?" Kiki reached for his hand.

He leaned forward and kissed her softly, lingering only briefly on her lips.

"Spring term I had a course that was an overview of the Classic Greek Philosophers. It seemed a good idea, part of becoming an educated woman, or so I thought when I registered for it. Truthfully, much of it was painfully dry, maybe most of it, but every so often there was gem. There would be a few words that were so profound I found them coming to mind for days, at the oddest times. A few of them stayed with me."

"And you're thinking of one now?" He asked.

"Yes, something Plato said: '*At the touch of love, everyone becomes a poet.*'"

"If nothing else, I suppose coming to terms with our ill-fated relationship attests to the value of higher education in some strange way. We'll have our night, my love, even if we have to make it last a lifetime."

Chapter Thirty-Four

ON THE DAY SHE HOPED would change everything, Kiki awoke with optimism and dread. None of what she planned was *her*, and as she contemplated all that lay ahead, barely recognized herself, but didn't dwell even a little on its meaning. Some things are better ignored and left alone. The time had come to banish distractions, second thoughts, regrets and moral dilemmas for another time and move on.

That innocence and youth were no longer her companions made her sad.

So often, as a child, and then as a teenager, more than anything she'd wanted to be grown up, to be treated as an adult, and not a child. To be allowed to do the things that adults do. Be careful what you ask for, Mom used to say, you may not like what you get.

And what a fantastic understatement that had proven to be.

Today Kiki Kinsler felt like the oldest twenty-one year-old woman on the planet.

Sunday, August 30th, it was late summer. Labor Day was a little more than a week away.

The gorgeous weather wasn't over, but the signs of seasonal change were everywhere. Oregonians, in good years, are treated to Indian Summers that can stretch almost to Halloween, as if handed meteorological recompense for enduring months of relentless rain.

In late summer, the ebullient greens of grasses, shrubs and leaves battle to remain so.

It's a losing battle.

Long awaited dry stretches and fierce heat have their way, turning verdant vistas a wilted parched brown. During the winter rainy season, that the Northwest could don such an opposite burned-to-a-crisp face seems implausible, if not impossible. Winters of indeterminate length dim memories of summer sunshine, forgotten under the soggy weight of unending of overcast and rain. There is no normal or predictable here. Northwest weather is two-faced, schizophrenic and enigmatic. Each year is a uniquely and unlikely composite of storm systems incubating in the Pacific and Gulf of Alaska, churned onshore by a whimsical jet stream that is cruelly indifferent.

It's weather with a sense of humor.

When you stop worrying about flooding you begin fretting over drought and wildfires.

Teddie Biggs had called as she'd promised, and Kiki knew the Biggs' plans for the day.

A sitter was coming late morning to watch Morris Jr. Teddie and Big Mo would drive to Washington Park for a picnic, having a special day for just the two of them. They wouldn't be returning home until late afternoon, possibly six p.m. or even later. The woman's excited, hopeful chatter was hard to listen to.

Kiki knew too much of what lay ahead for Teddie Biggs.

She hoped she was ready, but ready or not, the time had come and there was work to do.

How will I know to do what's right ... and do I have the right? Does anyone?

For months she'd asked these questions, not once comfortable with the answers.

This time, inexplicably, she was.

The Guardian gave me this chance.

I wouldn't be here, now, if they didn't have confidence I'd know.

Running through the scenarios one last time, reviewing what she knew, what she believed was reasonable to expect might occur, and framing those possibilities in the context of the trail. The challenge was to know exactly what she hoped to do, but be prepared for all she might have to do. Her plan could work, at times she was confident that it would, but with so many variables beyond her control, it also seemed flimsy and thin, vulnerable like a house of cards ready to tumble down at any time.

Not long ago, that realization would have rocked her, but it didn't now. She was past that. After doing all she could, Kiki felt prepared, but suspected there was no way she really could be.

Altering the destinies of intersecting, quixotic, human lives isn't easily prepared for.

The official cause of death for Teddie Biggs was a tragic fall from the top of the stone staircase to the valley floor more than fifty feet below the trail. Time of death was estimated to be late afternoon, before sunset. This would be after the outing, when the Biggs reached the top of the staircase to hike the trail back to the zoo.

Big Mo was a heartless monster and a killer, but no fool and had planned carefully.

Kiki expected he'd have the gun with him, using it if necessary to intimidate but not kill; he was staging an *accident*. As a man with experience in the justice system, Big Mo knew better than leaving forensic evidence suggesting it was anything other than an accident. Using a gun would provide a ton of it. What the gun did give him was the perfect tool to terrorize his wife into submission and effectively manipulate her as he needed. After that, he'd have no reason to dispose of it. The authorities would have no interest in a gun legitimately owned by a private citizen that lost his wife in a tragic accident where no shooting was involved.

Kiki's gun posed two challenges.

She was better off having it, but needed to avoid using it.

What had to happen was rather simple.

The how-to part was where things got complicated.

Kiki had to intervene and change the events of the day, before Big Mo sent his wife down the staircase and off the cliff. Big Mo Biggs had to trade places with his wife, and become the victim, falling to his death instead of Teddie. Nice and neat, but how would she make it happen without using her gun? There was no way to know and when it happened, it would happen fast.

What she needed was a little soldier or Rambo in her, but without any experience with anything like this knew of no way to get it. Unexpected counsel came remembering a movie she'd watched with her father during Spring Break. John Travolta in

Broken Arrow, a film her dad called a mediocre movie with one of his all-time favorite lines about soldiers in battle. Truth from the mouth of a deranged professional warrior:

Battle is a highly fluid situation.

That talked to her.

She realized that for her, frame of mind was more important than experience.

Keep it simple, stay disciplined and focused, and look for every opportunity to gain and leverage surprise. Seize the moment and act decisively, be ready to adjust and expect fluidity, stay calm and strong and succeed. But what about the gun?

Using a gun was the last thing she wanted to do, and shooting anyone, even Big Mo Biggs, was an appalling thought. And if it came to that, could she? She guessed yes, but if she did, forensic evidence would be a bigger problem and trigger an entirely different investigation. She'd be long gone, but it risked what she'd leave behind backing up on Teddie and Clark, even Joyce and CFSC. Whatever happened, vanishing and dumping it on their doorsteps was simply unacceptable.

Kiki hoped by altering an accident, one that was already destined, she'd leave no such mess behind. Her disappearance would be unconnected to it. In the end, nothing more than a below the fold news curiosity that would quickly fade, and an open missing persons case that, after dead-ending and going nowhere, went cold, was dropped and soon forgotten.

But for Kiki, another critical consideration was the quality of Teddie's life, afterwards.

This was a woman that deserved a chance to raise a whole and healthy child, and Kiki was determined for her to have it. The objective was a positive outcome to a family tragedy. For that to happen, Teddie would need to move on from her husband's death without having been emotionally scarred or crippled by horror or guilt. They could not become collateral damage.

Kiki knew where she'd position herself to discretely observe them while awaiting their return to the top of the staircase. Poised and ready to act before Morris Biggs could, she had a sense of how things would happen, and hoped some of it might even be true. She believed her adaptability in a fluid battle situation was the key to success, and hoped the experiences of her recent past endowed her with the capacity to prevail.

For nearly three months Kiki Kinsler had lived a life that was equal parts nightmare and fantasy. The Guardian had graced her with The Gift to restore her world as it had been. Now, nearing the end of The Journey, she stood on the brink of redemption and healing, wondering why such ultimate victory felt so hollow and lonely. The answer, of course, was the second gift, the gift of love coming at the steepest price of all, a broken heart.

What a time to find love, she thought miserably. How could I let this happen?

This wasn't her time, or her home, and couldn't work.

Kiki wasn't guilty of looking for love in all the wrong places.

She hadn't been looking at all. Her time here had been defined from the beginning.

Only as long as required to do the work. To have found love here couldn't have been more painfully cruel and unfair. The joy she should have felt to soon be seeing her mother, father and sister had been bested by the dismal prospect of saying goodbye to Clark Bannion, this Clark Bannion. Forever.

~~~~~

Teddie had a few final instructions for the sitter while her husband waited in his truck.

"We should be home before dinnertime, so enjoy the day and make sure that you mind Clarice, Little Mo," his mother told him, wiping his face and hands with a wet wash cloth and kissing him on both cheeks. Turning to her son's favorite babysitter, Teddie added, "He's had lunch and really ate a lot, but I'm sure he'll be hungry long before we're home, so you'll find all kinds of things in the fridge. And the freezer is full, so help yourself to whatever you like, honey."

"Thanks, Mrs. Biggs, I'm sure we'll manage just fine. Don't worry about us, just have a great time. You've really lucked out with the weather, what a day you have for it!" Clarice was fifteen, a terrific young woman, and Little Mo loved when she sat for him.

Teddie was about to say more when a blaring horn stopped her.

Big Mo was ready to go, had lost patience and letting her know it.

"I'm sorry, Morris," Teddie said, joining him in the truck minutes later. "There were a few last minute things I wanted to go over with Clarice."

"You know I hate it when you keep me waiting," he said. "The girl knows what to do, and nothin' you had to tell her she hasn't heard before."

Teddie eyed her husband, recognizing the troubling signs of the little things that could so easily set him off, wanting to make peace and defuse them before they did.

"I said I was sorry, and here we are, ready to go and on our way. Please. Let's not let anything spoil our day!"

He grunted his agreement but didn't say anything else.

As they made the drive to Washington Park without speaking, Teddie took his silence as a victory. He seemed to be in a funny mood, she thought. There was nothing funny about Big Mo's funny moods but she'd grown used to them over the long difficult years of their troubled marriage. This outing had been his idea, and that surprising turn made her happy, even a little hopeful. He could make an effort, just a small one. To her that seemed the least he could do.

But, no, not Morris Biggs Sr., that would be so unlike him

Remaining silent had become her custom, whatever it took not to upset him.

The hiking trails were easily accessed from just past the zoo's parking lot, but when they arrived found that it was already crowded and rapidly filling up.

"Fuck! Look at this shit!" Big Mo spat, clearly pissed off at the inconvenience.

"I'm not at all surprised," Teddie said. "It is Sunday, and a lovely warm, dry day, perfect to bring the family to the zoo ... or to picnic in the park. I'm sure we'll find a spot. Why don't you try looking up past the main entrance? I'm sure we'll find something up there, and those spaces are closer to the trail heads. We'll appreciate that coming home."

"Thanks for the advice I didn't ask for," he said sarcastically.

Teddie patted him on the shoulder and he flinched, startling her.

"You're really on edge. What's the matter?" She asked her husband.

"Just wanna find somewhere to park … there's one, finally," he grumbled, and guided his truck into the space.

"Well, look at this," Teddie said. "It's shaded, too. The cab won't be an oven when we get back, *and* it's less of a walk to where we're going. I knew things would work out!"

"Yeah, you're right again, huh?"

Teddie gave him a look but kept her mouth shut, climbing down out of the cab and lifting out the picnic basket she'd packed, crammed full of his favorites. Fried chicken, potato salad, Cole slaw, an antipasto tray with olives, peppers, pickles, salami and cheeses, and a six-pack of beer in a soft-sided cooler which had been part of a giveaway at a Mariners game last summer.

"If you drink all that beer, I'm driving home, Morris," she warned.

"We'll see about that," he replied, pulling a blanket out from behind the seat, throwing it over his shoulder. "I'll carry the picnic basket, you can bring the cooler. Not a long hike to where we're going, but easier for me to haul it than you."

"Thank you, Mo, that's sweet," she said, taking the lead. Breathing in the fresh air, she headed towards the trail head.

From behind and under his seat, he pulled out a 9mm pistol, slipping it into his jacket.

Chapter Thirty-Five

KIKI HAD ARRIVED AT THE STAIRCASE **two hours earlier, just after ten that morning.** Hours before Teddie and Mo Biggs would arrive, but she wanted to scout the area again. She was looking for the best place to observe them from a safe distance as they came up the trail. After they descended to the little valley below, she would move to her next position. On her earlier visit she'd found a good-sized notch under the backside of the enormous boulder. A large chunk had broken away upon impact, creating a small cave where she could watch unseen from the shadows.

To have found a feature like this was fortuitous but she didn't let it go to her head. It was also dangerous and it left her feeling a little nervous. That a piece of rock so large had broken away made her wonder if it signaled dangerous instability. She shuddered at the thought of finding herself in the wrong place at the worst time, trapped underneath, helpless and buried alive.

Still another concern made her even more uneasy.

The massive boulder was wedged firmly in place. In many places it was embedded deep in the earth, as much as a foot below the surface, but perched precariously close to the edge. She saw where at some point in the recent past a large part of the unstable cliff face had collapsed.

The place beneath the boulder was safe, hidden, an ideal location to observe.

Unless the promontory picked an inopportune time to crumble away.

~~~~

The sun was bright and the day warming rapidly. The low nineties had been predicted, unusually hot for Portland this late in the season. Teddie and Big Mo found a shady spot under the willows near the creek. Birds were singing. A steady breeze kept things comfortable and the air fresh. She spread the blanket on the ground, and placed the picnic basket on top of it.

"Are you hungry, Mo?" Teddie asked.

"Could always eat," he said.

"Help yourself, anytime, honey," as Teddie lifted paper plates and some Tupperware containers out for him.

"Guess I'll start with a beer or two," he replied, unzipping the soft-sided cooler and popping the top of a Bud Light. His father was a lifelong Budweiser man, hard not to be when you lived in St. Louis and worked for Anheuser-Busch all those years, but his son drank Bud Light. A modest concession he made to the battle of the bulge he was losing and his wife's attempt to help him moderate calories and stave off the extra pounds.

He downed the first one quickly, and didn't dawdle much with the second.

Teddie was a little disappointed that, uncharacteristically, Mo picked at the food, not devouring it with his usual gusto.

"Don't you like the fried chicken?"

"Huh? Oh, no, it's fine. Not really hungry yet, we got time."

Teddie nodded, accepting that whether he ate now, later, or not at all was his business. She'd stay out of it and leave it alone. After all their rocky years, his manic mood swings and violent outbursts, she knew better than to get into a discussion about, well, anything. Better for her to enjoy the day and not worry about him.

Still, he seemed distracted and distant, even more preoccupied than usual.

She wouldn't ask about that, either.

She stretched out on the blanket and closed her eyes, enjoying the breeze rustling through the willows overhead, playing lightly on her skin. It was such a lovely spot and a perfect day. She'd make the best without any effort from her husband, as she always had. Then it hit her.

I'm such a fool. What was I thinking?

She knew the answer. This would be no romantic outing today. Teddie and her husband wouldn't recapture the lost magic in their fatally strained relationship. There would be none of that because her husband didn't love her. Had he ever? Marrying him was the biggest mistake of her life. The truth of it was clearer every day, if she was honest about it, as it had been for as long as they'd been married. Teddie had denied it almost from the beginning.

Why did I marry him?

I was pregnant, of course, and he is the father of my child.

A wonderful and precious little boy he has no time or patience for, or love to give.

Little Mo and I would be better off without him.

And there it was. She'd finally admitted that to herself. There was a freedom of sorts that came with such a realization.

Teddie kept her eyes closed. If she opened them the tears would come.

She heard the sound of another can of beer pop open. His third, and knowing where this was heading, dozed off to escape her husband, if only for a little while.

~~~~~

Kiki checked her watch. It was two-thirty as she left the cover of the forest.

She was careful moving around the boulder and slipping under the notch to the little cave without being seen. Other than Teddie and Morris Biggs, no one had appeared on the trail, from either direction, for hours. Her position allowed her a clear line of sight, but the Biggs were too far away to see much detail.

"I should have brought binoculars," she said aloud, at first, angry at herself for the oversight, but stopped.

"What difference does it make? I'll see them when I need to."

~~~~~

Two hours later, shadows were encroaching on the meadow and valley below.

The weather was changing unexpectedly.

Oregon weather doesn't like to be taken for granted, and the sudden about-face was the latest reason why it can't be. Hot east winds had been replaced by cooler winds off the Pacific and the warm-to-hot summer day had taken on a feel of early fall.

Kiki was sipping water from an army surplus canteen she'd found in the garage. It would be years before everyone toted around a personal water supply, and cases of water in plastic bottles were unknown. Few, if they knew what was ahead, would believe it.

Why on earth would anyone buy – or sell – water like that? C'mon, in Oregon?

She saw movement below, and tried squinting to bring it into sharper focus. The attempt wasn't particularly successful, but she could see enough to know the Biggs were packing up and would soon be climbing the staircase.

The signal it was time for her to leave the cover of the cave.

She'd wait on the other side for them to reach the top, and be ready when they did.

She looked around to make sure she didn't leave anything behind.

It was unlikely anyone would look in this spot. It was well concealed and had taken her a long time to find. She'd been looking for something just like it and had still almost missed it. On the ground was a small baggie of trail mix she'd brought with her. Picking it up, she put it into her backpack, along with the canteen, a windbreaker, a pair of aviator-style sunglasses and The Lady Smith .38 Special.

Better safe than sorry.

~~~~~

She heard voices. They were faint, but she recognized them and they were getting louder as the Biggs made their way up the stone staircase and drew closer.

"Christ, Teddie, get a move on, willya?" Big Mo complained, after reaching the top.

"I'm coming, I'm coming," she said, short of breath. "It's so steep going up, but we've got plenty of time. Clarice isn't expecting us until six at the earliest, and it's only just five."

"Yeah, well I'm ready to go," he said, slurring his words, sounding a little drunk and more than a little angry.

Big Mo Biggs was waiting for his wife at the top of the staircase, barely moving when she reached it. Teddie placed the picnic basket on the ground, and turned to rearrange one of the items inside it. As she did this, her husband made his move.

From his jacket pocket he pulled out his pistol and raised it above his head.

At that moment Teddie turned back to him, "Morris, what? Why …?' she asked, with just enough time to glimpse what was coming. She had no time to deflect the blow or process what was happening. He clubbed her hard on the side of her head above her right ear.

Teddie crumpled to the ground unconscious and unmoving.

Morris Biggs Sr. stood over her, looking down scornfully with no emotion.

"Won't miss you," he said coldly. "If only I could figure a way to send the kid to the Promised Land with you." He paused and looked around. A pair of hikers was approaching and moving to block any view of Teddie with his body, he waited until they had passed by.

So that's how he did it, Kiki realized. He's going to push her over now.

Gun in hand she edged slowly and silently around the boulder.

Big Mo had his back to the staircase, preparing to drag Teddie by her feet to the edge where the drop-off to the rocky floor below was unimpeded. How easy it would be for him to knock his wife unconscious, send her to her death and hide the truth. After such a horrific fall, the blow to her head wouldn't be viewed as anything other than the predictable product of landing forcefully on the ground after a fall from such a great height.

When Kiki came around the boulder, she was no more than eight feet from him. He was unaware of her, absorbed in dragging his wife to the edge. With a foot in each hand, he paused, adjusting for a better grip before finishing the deed.

"Stop right there, Mr. Biggs," Kiki said in the strongest, most confident voice she could muster. "Let go of her now and move away."

"Huh?" He said, angered at the intrusion and about to object when he saw the gun.

Kiki saw his pistol on the ground next to his foot.

"Slowly kick the gun towards me with your *left* foot," she ordered, thankful for having watched so many cop shows on television. "Your left foot, *slowly*," she repeated for emphasis.

"I remember you," he said, squinting at her. "You came by our office looking for a bid for that lawyer. What do you expect to do? A bitch like you isn't takin' me down, no way."

The man wasn't short on bluster, she thought, but it seemed hollow and unsure.

The gun in her hand felt strangely … right, giving her confidence.

"Do as I say or you'll find out soon enough."

"You don't look like you know how to use that thing," he sneered defiantly, expecting it to rattle her, and clearly surprised when it didn't.

" Believe what you want, but do you want to take that chance?" Kiki asked, cocking the pistol and taking pleasure watching him flinch at the metallic sound of a cartridge moving into firing position in the cylinder.

He didn't answer.

"Here's what you need to know. I'll use this gun if I have to, and the truth is a big part of me wants to," Kiki said, shocked by her own words. "God know you deserve it, so try me and find out," she challenged.

He still didn't answer.

"One more time, kick the gun over with your *left* foot," Kiki repeated. "Last warning, I'm losing patience, Morris."

His eyes narrowed, she could see him considering his options, contemplating making a move, but thinking better of it, didn't. She saw him clearly for what he truly was. Tough with women and children, but cowardly in a fair fight, and the gun she was holding on him more than evened the odds.

Big Mo Biggs grudgingly nudged the gun towards her as she'd asked.

He'd complied, for now, but she knew better than to think it was over.

Kiki felt such a seething hatred for this man, for all the wrongs he'd committed and the lives he'd so callously destroyed. And then there was all the sorrow and heartache that would come from his deeds in the future if he wasn't stopped.

It was all up to her.

"Smart move," she told him, when his gun was well beyond his reach.

"Okay. What do you want with me?" He asked, clearly hoping to buy some time.

"I'm preventing your wife's murder, and saving your son."

"You're what? No, I wasn't ..." he protested.

"Of course you were. I know exactly what you are doing," Kiki said, and a little voice warned her that this wasn't time to get seduced into conversation with him; he wanted that, he needed that to buy time.

The gun was in her right hand, and she transferred it to her left, keeping it trained on him. At point blank range she wouldn't miss, but wasn't planning on shooting him. She had something else in mind, and was now holding a rock the size of a baseball in her right hand.

Morris Biggs stood up, eyes darting from side to side, looking everywhere for an escape, but seeing none, calculating his limited options. As if she could read his mind, Kiki knew what he was considering and anticipated his next move.

"Don't try it," she warned him. "I'm not afraid to use this."

The expression on his face told her that while he now believed the threat, he wasn't going down without a fight. He was in trouble, and with nothing to lose was willing to gamble. Big Mo faked, as if stepping to his left, preparing to lunge right, hoping he could catch her off guard, tackle her and bring her to the ground.

Kiki saw it coming, and before he could try reached back and threw the rock at him with all her strength. She'd find out if all those years of softball practice and catch with her dad in the back-yard would finally pay off. They almost did.

Big Mo ducked and stepped away.

The rock hit him, but not as squarely as she'd wanted, delivering only a glancing blow, grazing his head and deflecting off him before disappearing and dropping harmlessly over the edge. He was stunned but quickly regrouped, rushing blindly at her.

Overconfident in his ability to overpower her, he'd committed to a course he couldn't alter. Halfway to her, hopping neatly to her right, she pivoted and hit him on the side of the head with the pistol. Big Mo Biggs howled in pain, shaking his head, trying to clear it. Furious to have fallen for such an obvious ploy, his only thought was to get as far away from this woman as he could. He jumped back, three quick steps, paying the ultimate price for that decision.

The ground was covered with a loose layer of rock, and was slick like gravel. He lost his footing, and, as if in slow motion, Kiki watched his feet slipping out from under him as he began sliding back. He'd landed face down, and his momentum was carrying him towards the edge feet first. Arms flailing wildly, desperately searching for anything to grab on to, but there was nothing for him to grab on to and slow his progress. Sliding, unable to stop, he would soon be tumbling over and drop down to his death on the valley floor.

His feet led his lower body over the edge as his weight carried him the rest of the way. Strangely, when he was almost over, for a brief moment he stopped. With only his head and shoulders visible, the rest of his body was suspended over the edge, hanging in space. Clinging pathetically, digging his fingernails into the rocky earth, with no way to raise himself back up to safety, his eyes pleaded with her to help.

Big Mo was no longer a threat.

"Help me, you fucking bitch," he demanded. "You can't just let me die like this."

"Is that your final appeal for mercy?" She almost laughed.

His fingers were clawing at the ground, but it was a losing battle, as he kept slipping back. Kiki knew it wouldn't be long now. There was no way she would save him, but she actually felt compared to hasten him along to his fate. She kicked some rocks in his face, and as his hands flew up reflexively to defend himself, he disappeared over the edge.

Kiki was surprised that he made no sound on his way down.

A brief *thump* startled birds into flight, but even that was short-lived.

Distrusting the ground, she took slow, careful steps until she could look down.

Morris Biggs lay face down, with his head at an impossible angle, unmoving.

Kiki had no doubt he was dead.

In a matter of minutes, after all she'd been through, it was over. After the horror, fears and doubts she'd overcome, the questioning of her core beliefs until finding it in herself to do unthinkable acts, it really was all over. She'd done it, but didn't celebrate.

She couldn't, it wasn't that kind of victory. The happy future she'd restored had come courtesy of a seismic shift changing her values forever. From this day forward, and for the rest of her life, she'd know she'd taken a life.

But although Big Mo's death had come at her hands, she had no regrets.

Was she a murderer?

Kiki didn't think so, although legally, she supposed, in some way that's what she was. The man had attacked his wife and had been about to attack and kill her. After killing her, he would have finished Teddie. And with his wife dead, she knew what the years that followed would bring.

At worst, clearly self-defense, and totally justified, if in a convoluted context.

Either way, it didn't matter. All that did matter was that it was over and he was dead.

She turned and walked over to Teddie Biggs, still unconscious on the ground.

Chapter Thirty-Six

KIKI SAT ON THE GROUND with Teddie Biggs' head cradled in her lap.

Dabbing her face with a damp handkerchief, the woman had regained consciousness. She didn't appear to be seriously injured, although Kiki expected a slight concussion might be possible and a nasty headache was likely.

Her emotional and mental state careened wildly.

Teddie moved from shocked and confused to panicked and terrified, from grief-stricken to almost giddy. Kiki listened to her manic soliloquy, stroking her head reassuringly.

"Hide me! He'll be coming back for me!"

"He can't be gone. Where is he?"

"He's my husband, how can he be dead?

"Do we call the police? What will we tell them?

"What do I tell Little Mo?"

"Little Mo, I have to get home to him!"

"He hit me on the head, Lainie," she told Kiki, "with his gun. I think he was planning to kill me," she said dully, accepting it, understanding the truth of it, and again began to cry.

"He was. I'm sorry, there's no doubt about that, but what matters is you're alive. When I came by, he was dragging you by the feet towards the edge of the cliff. He was going to dump you over. Look, I know this is beyond crazy, but that's what *I saw*. Do you understand that?"

Teddie nodded. "What happened to him? Where is he?" Her eyes darting around, her face showed more fear that he'd reappear than concern for him.

"This may be hard to hear. What he planned for you, well, that became his fate. He slipped and fell, and dropped over. That saved *your* life. Do you want to look?"

Teddie shook her head vigorously.

"I can't … is he dead?" Her voice was escalating in pitch as she asked.

"I think so," Kiki answered. "What about you? How's your head?"

"It hurts a little, but I'll be alright. I was turning when he hit me, I saw it coming. God, it was horrible, but it might have been much worse if I hadn't turned. I'd be …"

"Here, drink some water now," Kiki told her, and tipped the canteen to her lips.

After Teddie drank, she asked, "What am I going to do, Lainie?"

"We need to talk about that. There isn't much time and you have important decisions to make, starting with how we handle this. How you deal with is going to have a big impact on your life and future, yours and Little Mo's. I've got some ideas, things you should consider, but the choices you'll make are yours, only you can make them. We can discuss them if you if you like. Do you want to?"

Teddie was strangely calm and composed. Her eyes red but she was no longer crying.

"I trust you, Lainie. What do you think?"

"Okay, here's how I see it, Teddie," Kiki began. "This comes from a friend, not a caseworker. They say the truth will set you free, but when it comes to the law and the judicial system, sometimes it works just the opposite way. So we'll tell the truth, but do it in a way that leads them to the right conclusion."

"How do you mean?"

"It means we need to be selective with the story we tell the police. Most important is that Mo's death is viewed as an accident, so that the information we give them is what they need and helps steer them that way.

"Keep the story simple, and truthful. With no history of domestic complaints, hopefully they won't go there. He attacked you but didn't die at your hands in self-defense. You were knocked out, and I can confirm that. They should see it as an accident, and that's what we want. If they don't, it raises a different set of questions and quite possibly becomes a criminal investigation and in that case you'll be interrogated differently. We want to avoid that."

"Why?" Teddie asked.

"In a criminal investigation they'll look at you skeptically, because the spouse is always the first suspect. If that happens, then you've got legal defense and estate issues. The assets, the business, can get tied-up. And that's not the end of it, things could get even worse," Kiki said, pausing to emphasize her point.

"How could they get any worse?"

"Easily," Kiki answered ruefully. "They'll start digging hard into your background with suspicious minds, it's how they operate. You're guilty until proven innocent. Little Mo could be taken from you and placed into protective custody while things are sorted out, and nobody ever accused the justice system of moving quickly. You would have to deal with all kinds of things, when you should be focused on one thing, and that's you and your son's lives."

"How can I avoid that?" Teddie asked.

"Let me run this story by you and see what you think."

"Okay."

"I was hiking in the area. When I came by I saw you lying on the ground, unconscious. I didn't see your husband strike you, but you'll tell them about that. He hit you with the gun and knocked you out, which is here. I'm sure they'll quickly confirm the gun is what he used to do it. His fingerprints will be on it, and they'll probably be able to match it to your wound.

"I'll tell them just what I saw. As I came over, he was dragging you by the feet to the edge. While doing it he was closer to the edge. The only reason he could have to do that is he intended to throw you over. That's when I rushed up and screamed to try and stop him before it was too late. He was startled, slipped and fell, and I grabbed your arms to keep you from falling over. From what I could see, I assumed he was dead. I didn't worry about him, because I was concerned about you.

"The best thing about this is that it's the truth and I can corroborate your story with what I saw. You were unconscious, I did see him fall, and they'll probably be able to see where he slipped. The ideal scenario is for the police to call it an accident, allow you grieve and get on with your life with minimal legal complications. How does that sound?"

"That's what I want, to get on with my life, with my son."

"Speaking of getting on with your life … you seem fairly calm now," Kiki said.

"Everything happened so fast, I'm numb. Maybe it will hit me later, but I guess none of it really surprises or shocks me. You know, while I was lying on the blanket while Morris was getting drunk enough to try and kill me, I guess I came to terms with how little we had. How wrong and hopeless or marriage was. I may have prayed for this, for a way out, from my mistake in marrying him. Does that sound crazy?"

"Not to me, but even battered wives may want to show the cops a little more emotion."

"I'll keep that in mind, but he did attack me. I'll balance the two. What do we do next?"

"You stay here. I'll hike down for help, call the police, and be back as soon as I can."

~~~~~

Kiki made the short hike back to the zoo parking lot, grabbed a jacket from her car and put the backpack with the gun in her trunk. Preparing herself to appear more panic stricken than she felt, at the main entrance of the zoo she explained to a woman working in the ticket office of a horrible accident on the trail to Forest Park. She was immediately ushered inside. Kiki made sure her tone was the right blend of hysteria and shock at what she'd seen

A balding middle-aged man in a short-sleeved dress shirt and a tie soon appeared. He approached and seeing her agitated state, in a steady, calm voice asked how he could help.

"Oh, God, please help me! There's been a terrible accident on the trail to Forest Park," Kiki said with her voice rising, sounding upset and disconcerted. "A man fell over the cliff and a woman needs attention desperately. I was on my way back from a hike in Forest Park, and had just come up to that old stone staircase. Do you know the one that I mean?"

"Yes," he said, frowning, "I do. That's a dangerous spot to get to, all right. What did you find there?"

"I'm not exactly sure what happened, but the woman may have been attacked. What I do know is that *he* slipped and fell off the ledge. He may be dead, but from a distance I couldn't be sure. Can you call the police? I stayed with the woman and tried to help her, but didn't go down to check on the man."

The police were called. Before leaving, Kiki thanked him and said she was going back to remain with the woman until they reached her.

"She had just regained consciousness when I left her to come down for help, but she shouldn't be alone any longer than necessary," Kiki said, rising to leave.

"That's kind of you," he said. "The police are on their way."

She hiked back to Teddie.

Less than thirty minutes later, a detective and two uniform officers arrived.

Detective Charley Moore was a Portland Police Bureau veteran in his late fifties. Tanned and lean, with clear blue eyes, and slightly rounded shoulders. He was deceptively strong and fit for a man of his age. After introducing himself, he asked for Teddie's driver's license and listened attentively as she told him the story of the picnic, the attack, and waking up with her head in Kiki's lap not knowing what had happened.

"Mrs. Biggs, had your husband hit you before?" Detective Moore asked.

She hesitated, despite the circumstances not anxious to answer that question.

"Mrs. Biggs? Has your husband hit you before?" Detective Moore repeated with an expression on his face indicating he'd already guessed the answer.

"Mo has always had a temper."

He looked closely at her, noting the bruises and scabbed lip, recognizing the signs. "Have you ever filed a formal complaint, with us?"

"No, I always hoped it would get better. I thought that's what this picnic was about."

"Uh, huh." Detective Moore said, and turned to Kiki. "And you are?"

"My name is Lainie McCann. I was hiking by and saw Mrs. Biggs on the ground. I didn't see what happened before, but she was unconscious, and I guessed she didn't knock herself out."

"Right. She's got quite a lump and a fair amount of bruises. What was happening when you came up on them, Ms. McCann?"

"Oh, God, it was horrible! He was pulling her by the feet towards the ledge, I was afraid he was going to push her over."

"Looks that way from what I see … clear where he dragged her … you can see the trail of her shoes in the dust. We'll have techs get some pictures, and maybe cast some of the tracks. Okay, what happened next?"

"I didn't know what to do, so I ran up and screamed at him hoping I could get him to stop. He was startled, popped up, stepped back, and then he slipped and toppled over."

Detective Moore was nodding his head. "Yeah, there's evidence of that, too."

"I used my handkerchief and water from my canteen to wipe Mrs. Biggs' face, made sure she was okay, and hiked down to the zoo office to call the police for help. Then I hiked back here to wait with her until you arrived. That's about it, Detective, that's all I know," Kiki said.

"What is it you do, Ms. McCann?"

"I'm a counselor with Community Family Services of Washington County."

"I know of them. Is Mrs. Biggs a client?"

"No, but after talking with her it was clear that she needed help," Kiki said, lowering her voice. "I see clear signs of abuse."

He nodded. "I'm thinking that, too. Will you be available if we have further questions? Might not be necessary, from what I see so far, doesn't seem to be much mystery with this one."

"I was planning on returning home to California for a visit later in the week. If you need me, I can delay my trip. If not, while I'm away, you could reach me through my attorney." At that the detective's eyes narrowed and he gave her a quizzical look.

Kiki laughed softly. "It's not what you think, Detective Moore. It's not a criminal matter. Clark Bannion helped me with my mother's estate. She passed away a few months ago,"

"Condolences. I've met Bannion. If you're in town for the next day or two I think that should enough. Just in case, I'd like you to come down to the station and give a statement."

"Of course, I can do that," Kiki said. She gave him her number and offered to call the next day and come down to make it."

"I appreciate that, but it would save us all time if you could give it tonight. Then you wouldn't have to worry about anything else, leave on your trip as you'd planned."

"That would be best for me," Kiki said, "and I'd rather give my statement as soon as possible. Anything I can to help Mrs. Biggs get her life back to normal as soon as she can."

"Detective Moore, is there any way to contact my babysitter?" Teddie spoke up. "My son is only five and they were expecting us home by now. I don't want them to worry. If I'm going to be longer …"

"We can patch you through, to let her know you'll be awhile. We'll get you checked-out at the hospital, you should be able to go home after that," he said, slipping Big Mo's pistol into a clear plastic evidence bag.

"Would you like me to help Mrs. Biggs back down the trail Detective?" Kiki asked.

Before he could answer, EMTs appeared pushing a wheel chair along the trail.

"No, I'd say Mrs. Biggs has earned a ride back down, wouldn't you?"

"Do we need to send someone down to get the car keys from your husband, Ma'am?"

"No, the truth is my husband was shit-faced drunk. I took his keys when he started on his sixth beer. He wasn't happy about it."

"Looks to me like he was more than a little unhappy, Ma'am," Detective Moore said.

Chapter Thirty-Seven

TEDDIE BIGGS WAS RELEASED **Sunday evening from the hospital.**
Crime Scene Investigators, taking a special interest in what the ER physicians told them about the blow to the head, collected a DNA sample to compare to trace found on the gun they believed her late husband had used to hit her, and took pictures of the wound they would use to further confirm it. Happily, there was no sign of a concussion, which the doctors remarked was lucky break given the nature of the blow she'd taken.

Teddie alternated between tears and outrage at the death and evil of her late husband.

Privately, she didn't grieve, and neither did her five year-old son when he was told.

Detective Moore sat with Kiki as she made her statement that night at PPB Headquarters in downtown Portland. As a courtesy, he'd telephoned Clark Bannion the next day, informing him that conclusive evidence would enable them to close the case quickly, expecting it to be ruled an accidental death, in the next day or two. Adding that his client, Ms. McCann, had been extremely helpful, and he didn't expect that she would be needed for anything further.

Privately, he also told him that a gal like her might be just what Clark needed.

Clark thanked him for his advice, and told him he'd think about it.

Local television picked up on the story.

Sunday is a slow news day, but even so, local stations gave it less than a minute on the late news, while *The Oregonian* deemed it worthy of less than two inches in the Metro News round-up of their Monday morning editions.

Kiki had previously arranged for some time off from CFSC.

How much time would ultimately shock her co-workers and Clark told her not worry about that. He'd handle Joyce when the time came.

"I'm sorry to leave you to clean-up," Kiki said and kissed him, adding, "I wish it wasn't necessary."

"I wish lots of things weren't necessary."

It was Wednesday night when Kiki and Clark lay in bed, knowing it was the last night.

She would soon input September 4, 2012 on the band around her wrist and go to sleep.

When she awoke, she'd be in this same bed, or at least this same place.

But it would be in her time.

What had brought them to this point would have surprised both of them even days ago. They had spent the past three days like honeymooners, new lovers who couldn't get enough of each other. Knowing their time was limited; they were determined to make every day, every hour, and every minute count.

For Kiki and Clark it was no corny cliché.

For them it was the absolute truth.

After giving her statement at PPB headquarters on Sunday evening, Kiki had driven directly to Clark's house. He opened the door and she'd flown into his arms. Alternating between showering him with kisses and tears that came, disappeared, and returned, over and over, she related the events of the day.

"I guess that's it, then," he said simply, "and that's a good thing. I know Charley Moore; he's a respected, straight-up cop and a good guy. I'll hear from him tomorrow, and from what you've said, I'm betting he'll tell me they're satisfied and are closing the case as an accident."

"I think so, I sure hope so," Kiki said.

"So why are you here?" Clark asked. "Have you come by because this is our goodbye?"

"I'm here because there's nowhere I'd rather be. I'd like to think that until I leave, it's where I belong. Unless it's easier for you if I leave now."

"Try it and I'll tackle you at the door, if I have to. You know I want you to stay as long as possible. I'm a little surprised you're okay with this, knowing the sands of our love affair's hourglass are about spent."

"I love a lawyer who talks like a novelist, it's so romantic."

"I got carried away, but seriously, what changed with you?"

"Last night I told you that I wanted us to have one more night together, but if it's okay with you, I want more than that. I'm planning on staying for a few days to make sure Teddie and Little Mo are well, and in case Detective Moore has a change of heart and comes looking for me with a question he forgot."

"Probably a good idea … is there anything else?" He asked knowingly.

"Yes, a selfish one. *You. Us.* As much time together as we can wring out of it. If you agree and can stand it."

"You still haven't answered the question: Why?" Clark asked, taking her hand in his.

"I guess it came down to a pretty simple choice," Kiki said.

"And that choice is …?"

"We can punish ourselves and not be together because we know it has to end when I go, or, we enjoy every moment of the time we have left. I made my decision, that's why I came straight here from PPB, dirty, sweaty and recently interrogated."

"You made the right choice," Clark agreed.

"After a day like today, I desperately need a shower," Kiki told him.

"I'll wash your back," he said.

~~~~~

Clark called Traci to tell her he'd be out of the office for a few days.

"You can reach me at home if there is an emergency," he said not meaning it.

"There won't be one," Tracie told him flatly and meant every word.

256

Tracie made good on her pledge.

Other than being interrupted twice by brief phone chats with Detective Charley Moore who was wrapping up the Biggs case, Kiki and Clark had the time to themselves. They filled their days with walks, exploring the city like first-time visitors, marveling delightedly at nearly everything, genuinely happy just being together.

Both knew the fantasy was rapidly coming to its end.

Neither talked about it or allowed it to diminish their happiness.

Living in the moment had become far more than a casually bantered about philosophical catch-phrase; they were living it, understanding its meaning as few ever can.

The last night dinner was at the Kinsler house.

Kiki grilled steaks, adding twice-baked potatoes that she'd learned were Clark's favorite, and tossed a Caesar. They ate on the patio and stayed outside until long after dark. Both had been pensive, but remained relaxed, wishing there was some way to slow the clock and bend time to their will, but accepting that they couldn't. Kiki cleared the dishes. They stood at the sink together, rinsing and loading them into the dishwasher. Even such a small and mundane task was something to do together that night.

"Time is so uncooperative," she said softly.

"Let's go to bed, my love," Clark said simply and led her by the hand.

Gentle kisses quickly turned to an urgent and passionate need for each other.

Their intense physical union was transcended by an emotional and spiritual coming together; humbling and satisfying in ways both suspected they would never know again. Each found a closeness and intimacy that exceeded anything they'd yet experienced.

The miracle, they agreed, under the circumstances, was achieving it.

They knew that there was no certainty of a next time.

Unspoken was the knowledge that this time, this night, might have to last them forever.

When they had finished, they lay beside each other, breathless and with pounding hearts. Neither could speak, but that was its own blessing, because neither knew what to say.

They made love a second time.

Unhurried, slower and more deliberate, as if by doing so they might endow touch with memories so deeply engrained they would never dim or be forgotten.

"I never knew I could be so happy," Kiki said to Clark, "or so sad."

"I suppose we've learned that love has a lot of each," he answered, and ran a finger over the band around her wrist.

She sighed and was about to say something when Clark got out of bed, gathered his clothes trailing across the floor, and began to get dressed.

"What are you doing?"

"It's time for me to go," he said in a voice that was low and thick.

"I can't believe I never thought about this, this moment, I mean. I guess I assumed you'd stay the night. And that we'd be together until the end, until I was gone. I never thought … I really never did, that you'd leave." Kiki's voice, choked and hoarse, trailed off to nothingness.

"If I stay, I doubt I'd sleep. No, I *know* I couldn't. And with me lying beside you, it would be harder for you."

'But …"

"Listen to me now, my sweet girl. I have to say this, and you need to hear it. In some way I hope it helps you. It helps me," he sighed, "and I thought I was beyond help."

"I'm listening."

"All the days, no the weeks we've had, I wouldn't trade them for anything. You know, I think I fell in love with you that first day, or maybe it was the second. Anyway, I just *knew*."

"I think I knew, too, Clark," she breathed.

"Every day the clock was ticking and the calendar pages were turning. Each day I was dreading the ending that was a day closer. All I could see was the loss, the finality of goodbye, and losing you forever. Could it have been more hopeless? Then I realized I was ignoring how lucky we are, if in the most bizarre and inconvenient way. What we had was short, yeah, too short, but it couldn't have been better or sweeter or more amazing. Some people never, ever, feel what we feel. I'll treasure you, Kiki, not regret you. I'd rather have had you to love and been loved by you, even for such a short time, than to never have known you. I'd be a lesser man and poorer for it.

"Now it's time for me to go just as it's time for you to return to your life. You know how desperately, and totally, I love you, Kiki. God, I always will. I wouldn't want it any other way. If only I could find the words to tell you what's in my heart, but there aren't any powerful enough. I have to trust that you know what I *feel*, that you *feel* what I feel."

Kiki was crying softly, but couldn't answer. Finally, she gathered herself and placed her lips to his ear. "You know I do. And know I'm taking your love with me. I'll cherish it and love you every day of my life."

"I want you to stay with me, Kiki. Here, now. I know you can't. Please God let me see you again. Sometime," he sighed. "But I have to go now. It's best for both of us that I do."

"Clark."

Leaning down, he kissed her, long and tenderly, lips lingering on hers until pulling away.

"Clark," she said again. "I don't know when, or how, but I'll find a way back to you."

Clark leaned down and kissed her again.

Wrapping her in his arms, she sensed him breathing in her scent, hoping somehow to memorize it, capture it, as if refusing to let it go. Knowing he would have to let go and when he did, it would all be lost to him and she would be gone forever.

He smiled, and caressed her cheek with the back of his hand.

Rising up, Clark Bannion turned from her and walked out of her life and out of her time.

Kiki Kinsler ran a finger across the bracelet as a tear dropped down upon it.

The control panel appeared, awaiting her commands.

As if frozen in time, she couldn't yet bring herself to enter them.

Chapter Thirty-Eight

ISHOULD HAVE KNOWN I'd have these feelings! Kiki wept, knowing that it wasn't possible.

Expectations are like empty promises, broken when we make them, and impossible to keep. Even with knowledge of the future we're blind to the aggregate experiences shaping it.

Experiences are forged by the living of life, they aren't preprogrammed. We're not allowed to impose our will, and can only hope we're strong enough for what comes. No one forces life to conform. We're along for the ride without promises, and counting on what we can't possibly know is a losing game sure to disappoint.

Clark's words would stay with her, she hoped forever.

She'd felt the emotion of them, and heard the truth and the lesson in them. He'd made an eleventh-hour life change. It was less about understanding, and more about the living.

Our lives, it seems, are forged by perpetual change.

We can't fight it.

We can only go with it, hope for the best and make the best.

Change is inevitable and all we can do is accept its relentless constancy. Such acceptance is made without much thought or argument, because we have no choice but to live it day by day.

There is no *normal*.

Unless normal is change.

The world of 2012 through a 1981 lens is unimaginable.

In 2012 it's nothing more than what we're used to.

Over time we get used to almost anything, barely noticing even the most profound and shocking changes. Ultimately, as with everything, even that becomes the new normal, and all those changes that made it that way, who noticed?

We remember what *is*.

What *was* is harder to keep from fading from memory.

The portrait of any place at any time was commenced long ago, rendered on an ancient canvas. All the progress and technology, the booming development and economic expansion, all are merely the most recent brushstrokes of a work in progress never to be completed.

The time had come for Kiki to return home, knowing she had been changed forever by her many unexpected lessons, some profoundly painful, others precious and sweet.

Home is not merely a place, but also *a time*, and *love* calls neither *master*.

Kiki stared at the settings displayed for her.

5:30 a.m.   Wednesday   September 5   2012

She confirmed them, and closing her eyes reverently murmured a last thought.

I'll always love you.

There was a sense of primal motion, flying, soaring but without any movement at all.

A Journey made through dimensions of light and darkness, warmth and chill, water and air, free but tethered. Every component of sensation and perception seemed well represented, but randomly presented. If their lack of form seemed incongruous, it wasn't troubling, it seemed natural. Kiki sought no explanation for any of it. At peace, she accepted what was.

Sleep came, it might have been sleep, this time she dreamed.

Images, some distant, others close, clearer and sharper.

Many seemed close enough to touch but remained just out of reach.

Most were known to her, bringing a feeling of happiness and contentment.

The earth and sky of city streets and high mountain vistas appeared and vanished.

There was Clark, smiling and looking up at her, arching an eyebrow.

Did he see her?

Her father, God how long since she'd dreamt of him.

Was that their yard?

Janie and Mom and Jenna in her house, did Jenna wave?

She saw a family, a man, woman and their children.

Did she know them?

The images began to fade, all slipping farther away from her.

Wherever she was, it suddenly had become darker, or perhaps she had closed her eyes more tightly, or given herself up to sleep more deeply and completely. Or maybe finally letting go without a care or thought as to what she was letting go of.

Or why she was letting go at all.

What mattered is she was secure and safe and trusting in it.

Letting go of the past, Kiki had returned home.

Something was blooming outside her window, a laurel so fragrant it perfumed the room.

Birds chattered happily, and in the minutes remaining before dawn, the sky brightened.

Kiki opened her eyes and looked around her room.

She saw items familiar to her. Her things, her posters and pictures, the bulletin board and bookshelves filled with the mementos of childhood and school. A few of her college textbooks were stacked neatly on a corner of her desk.

She became conscious of another smell, this one strong and pleasant.

Fresh coffee just being brewed, wafting through the house, had reached her room.

Jumping out of bed, she streaked down the hallway to the kitchen.

Reaching it, she stood outside the doorway, peering in.

A woman was at the sink, standing with her back to her. She was rinsing a frying pan. Getting ready to prepare the eggs Dr. Kinsler started each day with and refused to give up.

Tears, joyous tears, streamed down her face as Kiki went into the kitchen.

"Hi Mom," she said.

Epilogue

CLARK BANNION – 1981

It was sometime before Clark was no longer fielding questions about Lainie McCann and her mysterious disappearance. Stinging at first, bringing it all back in painful ways he surely didn't need. But over time he came to almost enjoy it, deftly tailoring his account of the story to suit the needs of each audience. The task became a game of sorts, bringing Kiki closer in an odd way, reliving it, and remembering a secret only the two of them shared.

He helped Teddie Biggs with her estate, pleased to watch as their family prospered. Kiki had given them a chance. Teddie accepted his explanation that Lainie, had gone abroad to find herself. She wished all of them well, but had no specific plans to return or not. Time would tell.

Joyce Buckman was somewhat more challenging.

"My antenna, from Day 1, was screaming, Clark," she told him, "and I don't care what you say, there's *a lot* you aren't telling me. Are you denying that?"

"You overestimate me, Joyce, and give me more credit than I deserve," he said, lying glibly, blending just the right amount of light-hearted self-deprecation. "Lainie was a special girl, I hope she comes back, but I have no idea if she ever will. She learned a lot here. Nothing more than, on her own now, it was time for her to see the world and figure out her place in it."

Joyce pretended to accept that. He knew better, but played along.

He visited the Kinsler house once, to remove all traces of a young woman living in it for almost three months. He laughed, *sanitizing* it like an intelligence agent. Kiki had left a nightshirt on the back of the bathroom door, still smelling of her perfume. Clark breathed it in and cried.

He took it home, and hung it in his bathroom, hoping she'd need it someday.

263

Kiki Kinsler - 2012

In late September, Kiki and Jenna returned to their apartment in Eugene for their junior years at the U of O. Her sister, Janie, a freshman this fall, was living in Carson, complaining about dorm food, but loving college, and possibly having *too much fun*. Kiki and Jenna were already talking about a larger apartment, or maybe a house, next year, so Janie could move in.

Kiki loved her classes, and with the help of a supportive professor secured an internship with a local Family Services agency in Eugene. She was making plans for grad school.

She and Jenna were discussing how to next use The Gift.

There was good work to do and Kiki felt it was both her duty and a privilege.

Her father had started grumbling about retiring, something her mom said he'd never do, but humored him by listening seriously to all he planned when he stopped practicing medicine.

"I shudder at the thought of him home all day," she confessed to her older daughter.

Teddie Biggs and her son, Morris Jr., had had a good and happy life.

Kiki learned that Teddie had died in 2007. Little Mo had been running the business since 1999, and by providing quality work and superior service had built it into a resounding success. He'd been happily married to his high school sweetheart since 2002.

Teddie's last years had been spent doting on her three energetic young granddaughters.

Kiki had a world of friends, but wasn't dating, had no interest in it, and was fine with it.

"Perhaps, one day," she told herself from time to time, but never believed it.

She couldn't avoid Clark forever, but the thought of seeing him thrilled and terrified her.

Changing the past changed her future, but at what cost? Did he remember?

I remember everything ... but that may not be the case for others, for anyone else.

A few weeks after her return, summoning her courage, Kiki went to see Clark.

"Nice to see you, Kiki," Tracie said, waving her in, "You look terrific."

Kiki smiled her thanks and went into Clark's office, closing the door behind her. He was seated in the familiar high-backed leather chair, thirty-one years older than the last time she'd seen it. As was he, but he looked wonderful, she thought. His hair had gone to gray, but he still had almost all of it. He'd gained weight, but not so much that he couldn't carry it well.

Unchanged were his soulful eyes, and how they lit up at the sight of her.

"You haven't aged a bit," he said. "As you can see, I haven't been so fortunate."

He rose and walked around his massive desk, and embraced her. They stood that way for a long time without speaking. Kiki stepped back, and wiping her eyes, tried to catch her breath.

"You remember ...?"

"*Everything,*" he interrupted, "with the greatest pleasure and without regret."

"I'm so sorry, but so glad," Kiki answered.

"Don't be sorry. I've had ample time to come to terms with it. Truthfully, I cherish it."

"My father?" Kiki asked.

"A secret I've kept from my best friend all these years and will take to the grave."

Leaving was hard, neither knew what to say, but they promised to meet again soon.

"We'll need time to get used to this. You have more of it left than I do," Clark laughed.

On December 3rd, her birthday, she returned to retrieve the Polaroid photo of them taken in Clark's office in 1981. She wanted to have that memory.

Clark greeted her warmly. "The picture is yours, of course. When I opened the safe to get it for you I found something else. It's a birthday gift. And a letter from … well, you know." A message and the date, todays date, only thirty-one years ago, was written on the envelope:

Happiest of birthdays, my sweet girl – I thought it was time to drop you a line …

If you enjoyed *The Do-Over,*
please sample *Imperfect Resolution,*
a Cups Drayton crime thriller

Visit Andrew's website:
www.PleaseReadMyBookBeforeIDie.com

Tell him what you think:
andrew@PleaseReadMyBookBeforeIDie.com

Imperfect Resolution

Chapter 1

Grant Appier glanced at his watch. He'd been walking for nearly an hour. Today, in modest defiance of the stress and emotional turmoil leading to his decision, the lanky middle-aged man was unhurried. Beaten down and defeated, he meandered along. It seemed only fair to glean any enjoyment he could from a life that had disintegrated into an inescapable hell. He'd wring one last shred of pleasure from his favorite San Francisco hike. A four-mile shoreline walk along the bay from the Aquatic Park to the Golden Gate Bridge: The Golden Gate Promenade.

On the way he passed Crissy Field. Its rich history began as a gathering place for the Ohlone, the Native Americans who in the late 18th Century greeted the Spaniards when they'd first arrived in Northern California. The Ohlone had made this part of the world their home for over 10,000 years. It didn't take long to become a common landing place, not only for the rush of Spanish explorers, but also the Russian, English and Boston traders who soon followed. In 1915 it was the site of the Panama-Pacific International Exposition, and for years after that, one of America's most important military airfields until shuttered for good in 1974.

In 1962 Crissy Field was designated a National Historic Monument and became part of the Golden Gate National Recreation Area. The old military buildings remain, still hinting at the glory days of the 1920s. The area has since been restored to its original state, essentially tidal salt marsh, and simultaneously developed as another highpoint of San Francisco's bay front. Today, a favorite destination for locals and tourists, near the Marina and Fisherman's Wharf, boasting museums, cafes and shops, pedestrian and bicycle paths and world-class wind and kite surfing.

At the base of the bridge, actually *under* it, stands Fort Point, another unique historical attraction linking modern San Francisco to its storied past. Fort Point is one of only three brick and granite forts ever built west of the Mississippi, completed just before the Civil War. At the time its stated purpose was to defend San Francisco Bay against the perceived threat of hostilities,chiefly Confederate Navy warships feared to be arriving by sea.

That never happened, but during the war impressive batteries of cannon were manned by Union artillerymen, vigilantly remaining on duty, ever watchful for an enemy they would never see. In the 1930's, Fort Point was threatened by the construction of the Golden Gate Bridge, but in the end was rescued. A most unlikely supporter came to its aid with a solution to save it.

Chief Engineer Joseph Strauss revised the design of the bridge to make Fort Point's demolition unnecessary. Strauss said, "While the old fort has no military value now, it remains nevertheless a fine example of the mason's art ..." In 1970, the Fort Point National Historic Site was created. The old fort's historical importance, generous brick arches, spiral staircases and hailed panoramic views from a variety of settings, has surprised and delighted visitors ever since.

The walk to the Golden Gate, the arduous walkway that begins at Fort Point, saves its most rigorous portion for the very end. Just across from the U.S. Park Service Fort Point administrative office is a formidable stairway that leads to a series of paths and ultimately up to the bridge. The newest path is wider, more accessible, easier and shorter. The older footpath to the Golden Gate is more ambitious and mysterious; it is less used and for most, forgotten.

It was this path that Grant Appier selected, the covered path through Battery East.

As the dirt path slopes uphill it is lined with flowers and shrubbery along the stairway, with high earth berms and brick arches. Cars heading up ramps to the bridge are at times just along side, roaring by and, in places, seem almost close enough to touch. For hikers, the thunder of cars rushing past is a constant companion on their way to the bridge, even when unseen they are sensed, and felt. The path winds up and down and around like an urban switchback, passing under the ramps before again climbing higher.

On the right are some arched openings in the chest-high brick walls built into the earth. Part of 1870's fortification named the Battery East, its arches are the old gunpowder magazines, the brick walls the parapets protecting cannons and the soldiers minding them. Unexpected and often curious detours took Grant through the old path's nooks and crannies, now disturbingly populated with fast food wrappers, discarded newspapers, empty bottles and cans. He frowned at the irresponsible refuse left behind in such a magical place. By unseen teenagers,

he guessed, visiting late at night, or the homeless, seeking shelter from the elements and a place to sleep.

By the time he reached the bridge, he'd worked up a sweat, and ducked into the MENS restroom. He wiped a paper hand towel around the base of neck, and splashed cold water on his face. Grant Appier didn't like the face in the mirror staring back, and hadn't for some time now.

He looked older, sadder, crushed and deflated, he thought, knowing he was all of that.

Once thick, black hair was thinning and going to gray. You just deal with it in your late forties, Grant thought, nothing you can do but accept reality. Far worse were the ghastly dark circles under the dull, bloodshot eyes, the sunken, sallow cheeks and his almost sickly pallor. The sad truth was that he looked a helluva lot older than his forty-eight years. Indisputable physical confirmation he scarcely needed of a life embroiled in crisis, calling him to the bridge today. Grant couldn't remember the last time he'd smiled and wondered if he still could. He'd been going downhill for as long as he could remember and was still gaining momentum.

The Golden Gate Bridge is not quite two miles in length, and connects the city of San Francisco, on the northern tip of the San Francisco Peninsula, to Marin County. When completed in 1937, it was the world's largest suspension bridge. Since surpassed by seven newer bridges around the world, the Golden Gate remains the second longest of its kind in the United States.

Grant walked the almost mile to the middle of the bridge, passing couples ambling hand in hand, mothers pushing children in strollers, speed-walkers, runners, and cyclists. A teenager on rollerblades whizzed by, nearly running him over, without a word of warning or apology.

"Beautiful day," one of a pair of senior walkers said, with a smile.

"Always windy and cool up here," he replied, without one.

Gazing down at the blue waters of San Francisco Bay, he considered it all one last time.

Grant missed his family. His wife Kristin and their two teenagers, Brooke and Ryan, had been gone almost a year. A tractor-trailer long-hauler, almost home, transporting roofing material from Ohio, had pushed too hard for too long, and taken them out on I-80. The pain was as fresh today as when he got the call from CHP. A once idyllic life had already been imploding, unraveling in the ugliest of ways. His problems had begun long before that crippling, numbing loss. His family's deaths were a tragic complement, and in the weeks that followed, things worsened.

Grant had grown up in Portland, graduated from the U of P, and moved the Appier family down to the Bay Area five years ago. Following his successful run at Intel, he'd boldly stepped out on his own to chase his dream. Pooling everything he could sell, beg, borrow, or steal, and launching, with confidence and high hopes, his own software company.

For three years the fledgling start-up prospered beyond his grandest notions. Rocketing overnight from humble, not quite rags, to showy, not quite riches. Seizing the brass ring, the Appiers were living *La Vida Loca*. There was no reason to think the good days and boom times wouldn't last forever. They didn't. To roll out his products worldwide, Grant had leveraged the business to the max, and in order to pull it off, he'd leveraged all of his personal assets, too.

Despite all of that, things still might have worked out, but he awakened one morning to the grim news that technology's fickle finger had deemed his applications redundant and passé. His niche had disappeared overnight, and with that, his customer base vanished. Without new products to replace obsolete ones, his company had gone from feast to famine in a nanosecond.

Then the financial meltdown turned the credit well dryer than Death Valley. The last resort, prohibitively costly venture capital he'd happily have paid any price for, wasn't an option. That, too, was no longer available. The end wasn't near; it had come. It was all over.

Nothing dies harder than dreams.

Unless he could rebuild from what few assets were left, and do it quickly, there was no hope. In a crippling self-indictment, Grant accepted that he had no one to blame but himself. He needed a miracle and a miracle worker.

Without one, he was done; the family was done.

That night a chance call offering a glimmer of hope came from Bryce Hamilton, another wounded entrepreneur, a friend and kindred spirit. Although his friend's circumstances weren't nearly as dire, the call hinted at a possible way back for Grant.

Bryce had made a lot of money, before losing much of it. Anxious to recoup his losses, Bryce was aggressively going after it, and claimed to be making some headway, thanks to a private equity firm he hoped might also be able to help him. With the best of intentions, Bryce introduced Grant to Mirror Mar Global Partners.

Mirror Mar didn't solicit new clients, and Grant learned that they accepted new ones only by referral from current clients. Like a club, you had to be invited. With elegant offices in a prestigious building in the financial district of the city, it appeared they could well afford to be highly selective.

Bryce cautioned that private meant not only discrete but unconventional.

His own rapid appreciation came with serious fees and the voluntary sacrifice of control. Mirror Mar took over and called every shot.

"The Investor – Client Agreement is airtight and slanted in their favor," he told Grant.

After letting that sink in, he continued.

"This is the question you need to ask yourself: How badly do you want the money? I was lucky. I still had the luxury of walking away if I wanted to. If I'm hearing right, you don't, you're out of options. I guess that makes your decision pretty clear-cut. For you, all it comes down to is how badly you need the money, Grant. That's it, nothing more."

Bryce also added that, many, if not most, of the investments were offshore, and that even his accounts were in foreign banks ... in other words, unconventional, maybe marginally legal.

"Mirror Mar has been great for me, I've done very well," Bryce assured him.

"Enough for me, all I have to hear. I'm fucked and couldn't be more desperate," Grant said tersely. "To raise the cash I need I'll accept any terms I have to, what choice do I have? If you're okay with it, I need you to refer me."

Looking back at it now, Grant saw that Christine de Lane, Mirror Mar's co-founder, had sure seen him coming. Probably licking her chops, Grant ruefully admitted to himself later. He'd bit after a spellbinding presentation from a stunning, thirtyish spiky-haired blonde; a woman so charismatic she was mesmerizing. Grant bought it all, the whole package, and went all-in in the worst way. The woman had sold the holy shit out of him, and he'd ignored red flag after red flag.

After having made big money faster and easier than he had any right to, he was on the verge of losing it even faster. Cobbling together as much capital as possible, his eyes wide open but refusing to acknowledge what they saw. He signed the Power of Attorney, and even assigned the Appier's personal life insurance benefits. He wasn't totally broke –at least not quite yet – but he was getting there. Without making a final stand to raise cash, he would be. Soon.

The company desperately needed cash, and not tomorrow; six months ago.

For his company to survive, he had to work all the cash he could, and grow it in a hurry.

At first things actually appeared to go well. Mirror Mar showed impressive early results and encouraging returns on their investments, and even secured a little VC funding for him; an eleventh hour spike in cash flow that briefly resuscitated the business, giving him brief hope.

On paper at least, he was still afloat.

Two months later, it all changed. First, Bryce called in a panic, distraught and confiding he'd suffered staggering setbacks. Fearing the worst, as he listened, Grant had a sick, sinking feeling, and then a financial epiphany of the worst kind. Time to find out just how bad things were, or might get, and how quickly, so reaching for his phone, he made the call.

The news was not good

It was much worse than that, a flat, fucking four-alarm disaster. Well past dinner, the drive home to his family that night had never been harder.

After weeks of ever more punishing days that had become months now going on a year, the truly sobering realization hit him with cold clarity and a harsh finality. Just when he'd thought things couldn't possibly get worse, they had, and breaking it to Kristin wouldn't be easy. Pulling into the two-car garage he was puzzled to find it empty.

That's odd, he thought. Where is everyone? There was no sign of Kristin's SUV.

On what had been the worst day of his life, Grant Appier had walked into a completely deserted house. Dark and quiet at 9 p.m. on a school night, it made no sense. Even the dog was gone, probably along for the ride. He made calls to family and friends but no one had seen or heard from his wife and children.

The next two hours passed in slow motion, every second seemed an eternity. To this day he barely remembered any of it.

Then the phone rang.

The call he'd never forget. The call he'd never recover from. "Hello," he answered, certain it would be his wife and shocked that it wasn't.

"Mr. Appier?" The caller mispronounced his name; almost everyone did at first.

"Yes?" Grant answered, surprised it wasn't Kristin. "Who's calling?"

"Mr. Appier, this is Sergeant Earl Stevens of the California Highway Patrol. There's been an accident."

The trooper paused and Grant fearing what was coming, trembled slightly.

"I'm afraid I have some terrible news," he told him, and paused

"My ... family?" Grant asked weakly. His voice didn't sound like his own.

"Your wife and children didn't survive, Sir. I'm so sorry."

Stunned, Grant dropped the phone, oblivious as it bounced off the kitchen tiles, skittering away and ending up under the table. In a near catatonic state, overwhelmed by shock, overcome by helplessness and drowning in utter despair, he could faintly hear Sergeant Stevens' distant, tinny voice calling to him from the handset on the floor, but in a daze, couldn't respond.

"Mr. Appier? Are you there, Sir? Mr. Appier?"

Numb, he stared at it blankly, didn't move, and said nothing.

Words wouldn't come.

Grant Appier was on the brink of losing his company. What little he had left was in utter jeopardy. And now the family he loved so dearly had been taken from him. All of it, all of them, gone, everything, there wasn't even the life insurance. In every way, his life was over.

On the Golden Gate Bridge it's always colder and windier than in the city and the city has a reputation that belies the allegedly temperate Northern California climate.

Like Mark Twain said: *The coldest winter I ever spent, was summer in San Francisco.*

As touristy as it sounds, and is, travel books counsel that, whatever you do, an essential part of any visit to San Francisco is a walk across the Golden Gate Bridge. Don't miss what is nothing short of an architectural marvel and engineering masterpiece, they insist. Your reward is that from the bridge, the views of the city, the Bay and the Marin Headlands are incomparable.

Having once been a tourist, long ago, Grant had a vague memory of it. He recalled it as the one time the real thing actually lived up to the hype: Just remember to *dress appropriately.*

Today, Grant hadn't bothered.

Since the day that stripped him of any reason to live, he hadn't bothered with much of anything. Ghastly luck dealt him a royal screwing; his poor judgment made sure it was fatal. He briefly considered calling his old friend, Cups Drayton, a big time FBI agent in Portland, but embarrassed and forlorn, dismissed the idea. He didn't want sympathy, and asking for help now seemed absurd ... *Forgive me, for repeating my mistakes and not learning my lessons ... help me because I'm a fucking idiot and a fool on top of everything else.*

No, it was way too late for any of that. Grant decided to write Cups a letter. It was too late for him but maybe by telling Cups the story he might help others avoid his fate. Grant Appier had reached the point where nothing mattered, or ever would again.

Staring down into the bay, he knew it was a mean distance of 220 feet at high water.

There was no suicide barrier to overcome. Grant Appier was standing in the center of the most popular suicide venue in the world. The confirmed count, he'd read recently, understated and incomplete because so many weren't witnessed and went unreported, had exceeded 1200 by 2005. Since that time suicides had averaged an unofficial one every two weeks.

Number Two on the Suicide Venue Top Ten is the Aokigahara Forest in Japan. *The Sea of Trees* at the base of Mount Fuji, a very distant second on that saddest of lists.

From the bridge, in four seconds he'd hit the water at just under 80 miles per hour.

Impact would be much the same as a nosedive into concrete.

Made in the USA
Charleston, SC
13 April 2012